A Bad Case of Dead

A Bad Case of Dead

by

Jim Breyfogle

First printing: 2024

ISBN:
Trade: 978-1-960381-20-0
Hardcover: 978-1-960381-21-7
eBook: 978-1-960381-22-4

Cover: Wistmoor Studios

Also from Cirsova Publishing

Jim Breyfogle:
Tales of the Mongoose and Meerkat:
Pursuit Without Asking (2020)
The Heat of the Chase (2022)
The Redemption of Alness (2023)

The Paths of Cormanor (2021)

Misha Burnett:
Endless Summer (2020)
Bad Dreams and Broken Hearts: The Casefiles of Erik Ruger (2021)
An Atlas of Bad Roads (2022)
Small Worlds (2023)

Michael Tierney:
Wild Stars:
The Book of Circles [Anniversary Edition] (2019)
Force Majeure [Anniversary Edition] (2019)
Time Warmageddon [Anniversary Edition] (2019)
Wild Star Rising [Anniversary Edition] (2019)
The Artomique Paradigm (2022)
Orphan of the Shadowy Moon (2023)

Sky Dance of Winter Fire (2023)

JD Cowan:
Star Wanderers (Coming 2024)

Leigh Brackett:
The Illustrated Stark:
Queen of the Martian Catacombs (2019)
Enchantress of Venus (2019)
Black Amazon of Mars (2019)

Julian Hawthorne:
The Cosmic Courtship (Cirsova Classics Edition) (2021)
The Strange Recollections of Martha Klemm Vol 1: Absolute Evil & A Goth From Boston (2022)
The Strange Recollections of Martha Klemm Vol 2: Sara was Judith (2022)
Doris Dances & Fires Rekindled (2022)

Various
The Mighty Sons of Hercules, Volume 1 (2023)

For more information, visit Cirsova.wordpress.com!

A Bad Case of Dead

Chapter One

LONDON – AD 1846

Edward paced along the walk, looking through the ornate iron fence at the mansion's garden inside. Becca must bring them out. She just must. Her day off wasn't for two weeks, which might as well be eternity, and spring made the weather chancy. He couldn't guess when there would be another day like this.

He pulled his watch from his pocket and checked the time. He only dared linger a few minutes longer; lunch would soon be over. Mr. Webley wasn't understanding of tardy workers and had no compunction about turning somebody out for the slightest cause, even if his partner, Mr. Turner, was of a different mind.

Ah, but it *was* a glorious day. Yesterday's rain had scrubbed the soot from the air and today's warmth made people open their windows rather than light the fires. The sun shone brightly in the blue sky. For just for an instant he could forget the soot and noise and stench of London and pretend he was back in Cornwall.

Surely Becca—Rebecca, he reminded himself, a name more befitting her employment—surely she would bring the children outside. What could be more perfect than this bird-filled Eden with statuary gods and goddesses posing in the sun? He had brought horehound candies, not their favorite, but easily explained as cough relief should any raise objections. They would buy a few minutes of conversation.

He glanced once more at his watch, sighed, and slipped it back into his pocket. He must be leaving.

The door burst open as if it couldn't get out of the way fast enough. Two children, a boy and a girl, tramped down the steps, sending the birds fleeing into the sky.

A young woman followed them, catching the door before it could slam shut. She dried her hands with a small towel that she then tucked into the bulging pocket of her apron where it draped over a pinwheel and obscured the magpie on the cover of a nursery book.

Edward lifted his hand, waited for her to see him, and waved once.

"Rebecca!"

Rebecca looked at the house before coming down the steps to him.

"Edward." She smiled, quickly, as if lacking the energy for more. "Today isn't a good day."

"Oh," Edward said, feeling his heart sink. "Well, I don't really have time anyway." He smiled for her benefit and held out the bag of candies. "Here, I brought the children some candy."

"They certainly don't require any. Nor," she added, "do they deserve any." She brushed back a curl of hair that had escaped the bun at the nape of her neck. With a glance over her shoulder she added, "Letitia is on the war path, too."

Letitia was the Barings' cook. Bad enough she was so old and ugly that she scared the children, but she seemed to have something against Rebecca and would gleefully report any transgressions to Lady Baring.

"Yes," Edward said. "Best I return to work. Here," he held out the candies again. "If not for the children, they're for you."

Rebecca hesitated before taking the bag and thrusting it into her apron pocket. The children shrieked, and she turned. "Oh, Saints help me." The boy stood precariously on the shoulders of Zeus, threatening his sister with imaginary lightning bolts. "William!" She hurried to catch him as he fell. Far from being grateful, William abandoned his lightning bolts to strike at her with his fists.

Edward watched for a moment, but Rebecca didn't look his way. He thrust his hands into his coat pockets and walked away.

Would that he had never come to London, but a fellow must rise in the world. It had been hard enough to leave Rebecca in Cornwall. He planned to take a ship to South Africa or the Indies, and the thought of returning home to green fields and her beauty lent such a voyage a romantic allure.

Rebecca followed him to London, and he found he could not so easily leave. The Barings' garden aside, London lacked green fields. He hated the dirt and the crowds and didn't want to leave Rebecca in such a place. If he were honest, he trusted Rebecca, but he didn't trust any of the young men who guested with the Barings. They might be of the "better sort," but "gentleman" was merely a disguise they wore.

He glared down the street at the mansion before turning the corner.

He did well enough clerking at Webley & Turner, was able to lay a little money aside, and could stay close to Rebecca, but he dreamed of finding his fortune in foreign lands and returning in triumph. He sighed. Fantasy aside, he didn't want to be forced into fortune-hunting by being sacked. He quickened his pace.

He didn't have time to return along Grosvenor Canal. He could save time by taking alleys and coming out on the canal by the Elizabeth Street Bridge.

This was an odd part of London, home to strange folk from all of the isle, and indeed of the world. All manner of things went on here, some mysterious and occult, some just criminal. The gentry came here looking for the unique and bizarre, for strange herbs and potions, artifacts looted from ancient tombs, and for pleasures the police and the church could not drive completely out of England.

The first alley, dark and twisty, and from which cold air flowed like water, seemed as far from London as the river Acheron. Edward faltered, his foot slipping over the cobbles. It did no good to hesitate; it was lack of time that pushed him here. Nothing in the alley could be worse than being sacked for tardiness.

The buildings hedged the narrow way, casting it deep into shadow. He stumbled through cast-off clothing and ended up hopping down the alley on one foot, trying to free the other from sodden, rotting trousers.

Cursing, he finally kicked his foot free only to stomp into a puddle, filling his shoe and splashing foul water over his legs. He pressed on, hoping the stench in his nostrils was the rubbish around him, not the water soaking his leg.

Suddenly a door above him crashed open. Edward shied away as a man stepped onto the landing, outlined by the light from within the shop. He wore a billycock hat and long frock coat. "What are you doing here?" he demanded.

"Trying to return to work," Edward retorted, overcoming his surprise.

The man glared. "Have you seen—a creature? Small, like a cat, but with wings?"

"I haven't." He gestured at the filthy alley. "It wouldn't surprise me if the rats have gotten it."

The man snorted. "Pity the rat that tries. If you see it, you'd do well to stay away." He surveyed the alley then drew back into the shop. "No, it's not out back, curse the—" The door closed and cut off his words.

Edward took a deep breath and tried to calm his racing heart. "God help me," he muttered. He would surely be late.

A soft, angry hiss made him lift his head. At first, he couldn't see anything, but then movement in the darkest shadows under the eaves caught his attention. Something shifted again, crawling headfirst down the wall, its head lifted up and hissing at him, coming into the half-light where he could see it better.

Bat-like wings trailed behind it. Its mouth was open, revealing sharp teeth set in front of very red gums and a tongue almost like andirons before a fire.

"What in Heaven?"

At his words, the thing snarled and launched itself at him. He threw up his arms and cried out. It struck him, and he staggered. A whirlwind of wings, teeth, and claws batted at him, tearing at his sleeves as it tried to reach his face.

He flailed at it with one arm, still trying to protect his face with the other. He struck it; it was furry and light. Using what little room he gained, he struck it again. It tumbled away and hit the cobbles with a hollow thud. It crouched, poised to spring again.

"The Devil take you!" Edward swore. The creature flinched and cowered, and shrank back, though still growling and hissing. Edward stepped toward it and drew back his leg.

It scampered back to sulk in the shadows before disappearing completely.

Edward thought of calling to the man in the shop—surely this was the creature he sought. But he did not have time; in fact, he would have to run.

He ran, afraid his shortcut had cost him more than he could afford. He would cut through Trinity churchyard— the priest didn't look kindly on that, but there was nothing for it now.

He exploded out of the alley, running full tilt, ducking between people and ignoring their angry shouts.

The church carillon began to play.

His heart raced faster than the notes of the bells, infinitely faster as his feet pounded the paving stones and his breath rattled in his lungs. There was the church up ahead.

He dashed through the iron-gate into the yard. His wrist burned, and he spared a glance at the small cut he hadn't even known he had. He wove his way through the gravestones as the bell kept tolling.

He ignored a startled friar, leapt a stone bench, and grabbed a gatepost to help him turn onto the street as he exited. The priest shouted after him, but he couldn't make out the words.

The front of Webley & Turner was just half a block away.

The chimes finished their tune, and began to chime the hour. There was only one hour to toll.

The hour struck.

Edward burst into the building, panting heavily, drawing the attention of Mr. Turner who stood behind the counter. There was no sign of Mr. Webley.

"You look like you're being chased by demons, Edward," Mr. Turner said pleasantly.

Edward straightened up, and straightened his coat. "No, Sir, I just didn't want to be late."

"Commendable indeed, but I think we can spare you a few seconds for the sake of decorum. You're not the sort of lad to abuse the privilege."

Edward let out a long, slow breath, willing his muscles to relax. "Thank you, Sir. I appreciate that." If only Mr. Webley would be so understanding.

He took off his coat, folding it over to hide the tears, and paused to look at his scratched hand. Only the barest scrape, a faint red line, and it merely itched. He rubbed it once and put it out of his mind.

Mr. Webley strode from the back of the shop. He didn't acknowledge either of them, walking to a ledger on the counter and began to examine the accounts. He sniffed and looked up. "Good God, is that you?"

It took Edward a moment to realize what Mr. Webley meant. "Yes, Sir, I'm afraid so." He looked down at his wet and mucky trousers. "I stepped in a puddle returning."

Mr. Webley wrinkled his nose. "You can't work like that. You'll drive away the customers. Go home and change. When you return, you'll work the rest of the day without pay, and consider it a lesson learned."

Mr. Turner shrugged. No help there.

"Yes, Sir. Sorry, Sir," Edward said. At least he hadn't been fired. "I shan't take long."

Edward spent the early evening washing his trousers and socks. The water had been so foul it not only left a lingering odor but stained his trousers as well. Once finished, he polished his shoes. He started to mend his jacket, but threw it down in frustration.

He must get out. He thought about returning to the Barings' mansion but decided against it. The air cooled rapidly once the sun set, and Rebecca would keep the children inside. Well, next best was a pint or two at the pub.

His room was on the second floor, one of four in the somewhat shabby boarding house. He was not the only one in the common hall.

"Going out?" asked the foreign chap who lived in the room next to his. He was a swarthy fellow, invariably nicely attired, who nonetheless always seemed to have something peculiar about him. His speech seemed to have wandered all over the world, picking up strange accents in odd corners and melding them into something uniquely his own. He made his livelihood as an apothecary.

Edward had happened into his shop once, by chance, and spent an hour gazing at rows of patent medicines; tobaccos from America, Anatolia, and Russia; teas from the Far East, and cures for diseases both known and unknown to man. All the while the little man gave out a steady stream of advice to a parade of old women and one soldier returned from Jamaica who claimed to be cursed by a "voodoo witch."

Edward couldn't remember his name; it was something odd and was printed on a small placard affixed to the door if he cared enough to read it.

"Yes," Edward said shortly, wiping his face with the back of his hand. He felt warm. "I feel the need of some air."

The man smiled. "Your lady friend, no doubt. It is good to be young and in love."

"No such luck," Edward said, jiggling his key in the lock, trying to engage the tumblers. "I'll just grab a pint or two with the lads."

The apothecary opened his own door. "Then the best of the evening to you."

"And to you, Sir." The key turned, the bolt slid home, and Edward was away.

The cool air felt good. He stayed on the streets, eschewing the alleys, and laughed at himself for it. Rubbing the scratch on his hand, he thought of the adventure that brought it and wondered at the creature. He could not recall hearing of anything similar. Likely it was an escaped pet brought back from the Far East.

He shouldered his way through the swinging doors in the *Cariad Gadael.* The sound of voices and laughter slapped him while the smell of beer and beef pie assaulted his nose. The old Welshman behind the bar saw him enter and drew a pint of old ale. He slid it down the bar, the dark beer motionless in the glass even as it traveled ten feet to rest before Edward.

The men at the far end of the bar were playing fives, holding their darts in one hand, their pints in the other. Several men leaned against the bar, and a couple dozen more clustered in groups of three or more around the tables.

Edward automatically took his ale and made his way through the tables. He would be welcome at several, but chose the one where other clerks sat. Nate, John, Andrew and Bill; they were much his age except old Bill. Bill claimed to have clerked in the army, an idea much disparaged by the others. It might be true, it might not, but Edward always treated Old Bill with respect.

The others nodded to him as he slid into a chair. Andrew was just recounting the day's news.

"Bostock, the brass finisher, was killed today."

"That's a shame. I'd thought young Wicks wanted to do him in," Nate said. Nate worked at a colliery on Eccleston wharf.

"It's young Wicks that did it," Andrew answered.

The men at the table laughed. Old Bill lifted his tankard and said, "To young Thomas Wicks, who raised the quality of men on Drury Lane and will himself be raised because of it."

The laughter washed over Edward again, though he could only muster a faint smile. The ale felt like a boiling ball of lead in his stomach.

"That's just an everyday sort of murder," John said. "But h've you heard of the Painted Man's death?"

"That old Scotch fraud?" scoffed Andrew.

"'e's not a Scot, and he's not a fraud," John said.

"Dead now," Andrew said, lifting his mug and talking into it before taking a long drink.

"Aye, his head bashed in and his shop turned out."

"He had some queer stock, he did," Bill said. "Things that would make John Hunter think twice about collecting."

"He once tried to sell me a kilt pin, claiming it came from Lyonesse," Andrew said. "Not like any kilt pin I ever seen before, but damn me if I'll pay fifteen shillings for a pin and a faery tale."

"You ever see those creatures he kept?"

Edward pushed his pint away, sloshing a little ale on the table. The mention of creatures caught his attention.

"Looked like he had bred them to the devil."

Edward was losing track of who spoke. The voices swirled around him like smoke.

"Well good riddance to him. Those tattoos always made me shiver, not proper tattoos at all, the way they crawled around his skin."

"You're daft! They never moved at all."

"So says you, but I says different, and I saw them."

Edward tugged at his collar and took a deep breath. He couldn't get a proper picture of the Painted Man; he knew he had seen him standing in front of his shop by the canal as he returned from the Barings'.

"Are you feeling well?"

Edward blinked; Bill looked overlarge, eyes bulging, face looking like it had been stretched back. The bar was a mélange of color behind him.

"No," Edward said. "I'm not."

"You either need to sleep or drink, lad."

The ale in Edward's stomach roiled, and he bit back the urge to vomit. "Not drink," he said. He stood up and wiped his face. "It'll pass." He needed to get through the morrow, then he had a day off.

☠

When he woke the next morning, his mouth felt as dry and cracked as the paper peeling from his walls. His hands and feet were numb, and everything looked a little fuzzy around the edges.

He staggered to his feet and fumbled his way through his morning toiletries. His limbs felt heavy as he shaved, but he dreaded Mr. Webley's acid tongue if he couldn't put on a better showing.

He wouldn't normally trouble people, but perhaps his neighbor, the apothecary, had something that would help.

He read the placard on the door: "Undulark Malfousa." Small

wonder he hadn't remembered the name earlier. He knocked.

Undulark opened the door, smiled, and said, "Good morning. What can I do for you?"

"I apologize for troubling you," Edward said. "But I haven't time to visit your shop before I must be at work. You wouldn't have something—invigorating? You see I'm feeling rather poorly."

Undulark bobbed his head. "I have a few things. If I don't have anything suitable here I can have a boy run it to your employment."

"That would be most welcome."

Undulark regarded him closely, his brow creased. "What is the problem?"

"Just general malaise," Edward hedged.

"You don't look good."

Edward smiled at the understatement, feeling his skin draw tight across his face. "I've felt better."

Undulark peered at him, drawing closer, sniffing. He rotated his head as if trying to both loosen his muscles and figure out where an odor came from. "I've not smelled that in London before. What fool brought it here? Not you, surely?"

"What are you talking about?" Edward asked, backing up a step.

Undulark followed, still sniffing. "Maybe, maybe I'm mistaken. Come inside. Let me look at you." He turned abruptly and returned to his room, stopping in the doorway to beckon to Edward.

Edward hesitated. Undulark was a strange one; he wasn't sure what to expect in his room. But he *had* seemed to recognize the sickness.

The room looked—ordinary. Dingy wallpaper with vertical rows of flowers and ribbons. A small collection of chairs and occasional tables clustered around an oval braided rug. A copy of *Lloyd's Illustrated Weekly* sat neatly folded on one of the tables. The odor of sausage still lingered; a glance through the doorway to the next room afforded him a look at the pans and dishes of breakfast drying in the rack.

"Over here, please." Undulark stood next to the only window in the room. He tilted Edward's head up and peered into his eyes. He shook his head, took Edward's hand and pressed his fingers to Edward's wrist. He looked up sharply. "Cold."

"I don't feel cold," Edward said.

Undulark didn't answer, just laid his hand on Edward's chest, fingers splayed. After a moment he let his hand drop. "I know what's wrong."

Edward waited for him to continue.

"You're Dead."

"Dead?" Edward scoffed. "Don't be ridiculous." He didn't like being mocked. "I came in because I thought you could help."

"You're a young man, normally healthy, currently walking about even if you look a little peaked. You should be breathing, yes?"

"Of course."

"You seem to have forgotten."

"What?" The statement made no sense. How could you forget to breathe? He drew in a great lungful of air. "I'm breathing."

"Because you are thinking about it." Undulark held up a finger. The nail was clean and cut short, and a small silver band encircled the base. Curious, both for its fashioning—entwined gold leaves with enameled violets—and the fact he wore it on his first finger.

"But, distracted, and you forget to breathe—like now," Undulark said. He snapped his fingers, making Edward blink and shake his head. He must have seen the disbelief Edward felt. He rummaged through the sideboard. He found what he wanted, but kept it hidden. "Give me your hand."

"What?"

"Your hand. I will demonstrate." He did not wait, but grabbed Edward's hand and, before Edward could prevent him, jabbed a thick silver pin into Edward's palm.

"Ow!" Edward snatched his hand back, pulling the pin out of Undulark's grip. "Why did you do that?"

"No blood," Undulark said simply.

Edward stared at him, then down at his hand. He plucked the pin from his palm. A small, dark, red dot marked the wound. No blood flowed, or even welled up. "What?" He pressed in on the wound and a small amount of blood pooled around it, but when he stopped, so did the blood.

"No heartbeat to push the blood out," Undulark said softly, almost with a note of regret. "You're Dead."

Edward checked his wrist, then his throat. No pulse. He checked again. And again. "There must be some mistake."

"Yes," Undulark agreed. "A mistake that brought Dead to London, but misfortune that you caught it."

Edward stopped checking for a pulse. It seemed all the energy drained from his body. He shuffled over to one of the straight-backed chairs and sank into it.

"But I can't be dead. I'm walking, talking, breathing, well, not breathing, but walking and talking! I'm hardly a corpse."

"You have Dead, but you are Not-Dead."

"Talk sense, if you please."

"You are one of the Not-Dead, the walking corpses. A *zumbi*, a revenant."

Edward flinched. He had heard of the West African *zumbis*. "No, they are horrors, while I, I think I am feeling better."

Undulark smiled, just briefly. "You are not a horror yet. But you are not alive; your body will begin to decay. It will happen, and you will change."

"NO!" Edward clenched his fist, hiding the offending drop of blood. "I'm not DEAD!"

"Have you been bitten by a strange creature lately?"

The question was like cold water, and it calmed Edward. He rubbed his wrist. "Bit or scratched, I don't know which." He looked at Undulark warily. "Why?"

"What kind of creature?"

"I don't know. It was in the alley behind the Painted Man's shop."

Undulark hissed, a surprising sound of anger. "Yes, that would be the one. A dark man who deals in dark things."

Dark things indeed. Edward recalled the creature and shuddered. "Say, for a moment, you are right. What can I do about this?"

Undulark rose and walked into the next room. Glass clinked and he returned with a dark bottle. He held it up to the window and swirled it, and shook his head. "Wrong bottle," he muttered and left the room again. He did this twice more before handing the bottle to Edward. "If you drink this, it will slow the process."

The bottle nestled Edward's palm. It was an odd size, more than half a pint, less than a full one. It felt solid; either it contained a heavy liquid, or the black glass was thick. "How long?"

"You don't need much, so quite long. Six months, perhaps, before you start to see any real effects of Dead. Then Dead starts to take over."

Edward looked at the black bottle dubiously. "This will last me?"

"If you take care, yes."

Edward worked out the stopper and sniffed; it smelled of bitter licorice and spice. "What is it?"

"*Aqua vitae, Eau de Vie*, those take their names from this. This is the true Water of Life."

"But what is it?" Edward persisted.

"Palm wine and myrrh, mostly. A touch of natron, some anise, a few other things." Undulark shrugged, "It's an acquired taste, but it goes well with shellfish. Not that I'm Dead," he hastened to add. "I just like it with shellfish."

Edward snorted. "But what then? After six months? Surely there must be a cure."

Undulark sat down, his expression thoughtful. He tapped his front teeth before coming to a decision. "Let me tell you a little of such things as are magic and faerie. Your church has burned and purified the land for centuries. Your people have hunted pixies as you hunted wolves, for pixies *are* troublesome creatures. As for giants, there were never many. The heroes killed them for glory's sake. Not the giant's glory, of course, for giants were slow, and stupid, and no danger to anyone.

"None of this really matters," he went on, "for it is just another changing of the world, but it means there have been no necromancers in England for five hundred years. Normally this is a good thing, but it causes you problems."

Undulark drew a deep breath and Edward started, realizing he was not breathing. He forced the air from his lungs and drew in another breath.

Undulark continued. "And, I think, a necromancer is the only thing that might help, if one would." He glanced at Edward, his expression sheepish. "They act for their own reasons, considerations beyond our understanding. They would not help from any charitable impulse."

Edward rose and paced around the room, stopping to look out the window at the dirty brick wall of the next building. "Where can I find a necromancer? If not England, then France? Africa? Siam? Where in the wide world can I find one?"

With a shake of his head, Undulark said, "Not in the Wide World at all. You can find one in the Narrow World. The world where fey and mortals mix, where magic is not a child's tale or the church's imaginary monster."

Edward turned to look at Undulark, not sure what to think. After a few seconds, the apothecary shuddered.

"That look," Undulark said, "is very unsettling. You must remember to blink, to breathe. People can sense when something is wrong, and, forgive me, there is something very wrong with you."

"Yes, I'm Dead," Edward muttered. He thought about tales of dark portals and magical gates. "Where do I cross over into this Narrow World?"

Undulark shook his head. "There is no doorway. You must sail. But," his face lit with a tremendous smile, "in all your misfortune there is one good thing." He leaned forward. "There are those who travel between the Narrow and the Wide Worlds, and one such person sails today." He reached into his pocket and drew out a watch. "But you must hurry! He sails in an hour! Ah, curse me for talking so long!"

"An hour? But—"

"I know of no other. The *Twilight Rose* is berthed at the St. Katharine docks. Captain Davies is very fond of money, but honest nonetheless. But I repeat, you must hurry."

Edward looked at him in astonishment. Could he really be expected to be ready to sail in an hour? He needed to make arrangements with Mr. Webley and Mr. Turner. He most definitely needed to talk with Rebecca.

Undulark saw his indecision and rose, and placed his hands on Edward's shoulders. "I am sorry, I truly am, but you may not get another chance. Other ships sail, but rarely, and even then they may not give you a berth. You must sail with the *Twilight Rose* if you wish to live again."

Edward nodded. "I'd best gather a few things." He went to the door, stopped, and looked back. "Thank you."

What to pack? He didn't know, and feared he was losing the ability to think. A change of clothes, of course, and some sturdy boots. Some money. He should take some stationery, for he might be able to send back a letter, maybe, if they ported before reaching the Narrow World. With an impatient motion he swept a bunch of random objects off his nightstand and into a bag.

He mustn't forget the small black bottle containing the Water of Life, or, as he thought with no small touch of bitterness, the health of a dead man.

He paused by the mirror, checked his reflection, and leaned forward to breathe on the surface. Nothing. "Too cold," he muttered, disappointed. One could hope.

There came a knock on the door. He looked up.

Undulark stood in the open doorway. "These—may—help." He held out a palmful of small coins. They were much the size of a farthing, but bronze, not copper. Edward picked one up. On one side was the portrait of a man, on the other a clutch of violets inlaid with mother-of-pearl, though more purple than Edward had ever seen it.

"What are they?"

"Coins, tokens." Undulark shrugged. "Favors. An old idea that didn't work, but binding nonetheless. I can't use them." He poured the rest of the coins into Edward's hand. "Good luck. This is no small task before you."

"What choice do I have?" Edward stared at the coins before slipping them into his pocket.

"Go and try to live, or stay and rot. As you say, not much choice. Take care of your tonic, and remember to breathe. And blink. But hurry. Find a necromancer and convince him to aid you."

Edward clapped the man on the shoulder. "My thanks." A thought struck him. "If I could ask one more favor, could you get word to Rebecca Teague? Tell her I shall return. For God's sake, don't tell her I'm Dead."

"Certainly."

"She works for Lady Baring."

"I will do as you ask, but you must hurry."

"Yes, yes." Edward dashed down the hall. "Thank you," he called back over his shoulder.

Within minutes he was running down the streets. He hadn't lied earlier; he did feel better. Maybe he was getting accustomed to being Dead. He felt almost normal as he ran toward the St. Katharine dock.

Chapter Two

His bag bounced against his back, that hurriedly stuffed bag of—stuff: the few things he knew he needed and the other things that just happened to get swept along in his haste. He ran because he didn't know where in the St. Katherine docks the *Twilight Rose* berthed; it could be in either the east or west basin, and he feared for time.

Soon he was ducking around stacks of boxes, threading his way amongst coils of rope, checking the names of ships as he hurried along the quay. He heaved a sigh of relief when he spied her name painted across her stern.

The *Twilight Rose* was just short of a hundred twenty feet long, black hulled, with two masts. She had a low deck cabin aft of the main mast.

A tight ship, Edward thought. He had picked up bits and pieces of nautical information since coming to London, and he recognized her as an American-built schooner. She had two gaff-rigged masts that climbed into the sky only to be lost among the welter of rigging of the larger ships around her. From where he stood, she looked to have a narrow beam to complement her clipper bow and raked stern.

Even as Edward hurried to her side, a sailor appeared at the rail and started to haul in the gangplank.

"Wait!" Edward called. "I need to arrange passage!"

The sailor paused long enough to audibly clear his nasal passages and hock the result into the river. "We don't take passengers." He resumed pulling in the gangplank.

"You must take me," Edward pleaded.

The sailor paused again. Edward thought about jumping onto the half-retracted plank, but didn't trust the sailor to hold his grip. "I need to travel to the Narrow World."

The sailor looked up and down the quay. "There's not many who know where we're going," he said. "But that doesn't change the fact we don't take passengers."

"Let me talk to your captain." Edward tried not to beg, but he knew he failed.

"My word's good enough for you." And with that, he finished pulling the gangplank aboard.

Panic crashed over Edward. He took a step back and, reclaiming the step with a rush, threw himself across to the ship. As his feet hit the deck, he grabbed the rail and pulled himself forward.

"The decision isn't yours to make," he said, trying to sound calm and confident.

"Damn you, Trog!" came a shout from behind Edward. "What is that man doing aboard?"

The sailor—Trog—blinked his surprise. "He's leaving." He dropped the gangplank and reached for Edward.

"I'm here to negotiate passage," Edward shouted as he moved away from the still-open gate in the rail. He kept his eyes on Trog, for the first time noting the sailor's thick neck, flat face, and long, wispy black hair.

"We don't take passengers," Trog said, lunging.

Edward batted his hands aside.

"Hold!" shouted another voice in a tone that expected obedience. "Lay out the gangplank, Mr. Trog. He'll leave like a gentleman."

A man emerged from the aft cabin. He came forward, his hands clasped behind his back, his pace perfectly measured. He wore a blue wool jacket, the type with a broad collar and lapel that could be turned up against the weather.

His forehead was white, where the bill of his cap protected it from the sun, and his cheeks were red. His nose was also red, though more from wind than from drink. The rest of his face hid behind a full, but neatly trimmed, black beard.

"And what, young man, makes you invade my ship like this?"

"I need passage to the Narrow World," Edward said.

"We don't normally take passengers," the Captain replied. "Although, we have before." He turned to Trog. "There was the biologist, if you recall? The Frenchman? Leveque?"

Trog straightened up from laying out the gangplank and grunted. He scratched his face. "Bad. Bad, bad."

"No doubt, but we have had passengers before." He fixed an eye on Edward. "Can you sleep in a hammock?"

Edward nodded. It occurred to him that had he remembered to breathe, he would likely be holding his breath right now.

"And stay out of the crew's way?"

Edward nodded again.

"Then there's just the matter of cost." He drummed his fingers on the rail. "Shall we say twenty-five pounds?"

"What? That's almost the price of a first-rate cabin to Philadelphia!" Undulark had mentioned the Captain was very fond of money, but asking twenty-five pounds skirted insane. Worse, Edward didn't have twenty-five pounds.

"We're not sailing to Philadelphia," said the Captain.

"I'm not getting a first-rate cabin, either! Eight pounds is more than fair."

The Captain shrugged indifferently.

"Maybe you can get another ship to take you to the Narrow World for eight pounds."

Of course, no other ship was going. Edward had no leverage and the Captain knew it. But some profit was always preferable to none. "Maybe." Edward shrugged, affecting nonchalance. "Pity. We're close to what we each want. I want passage, you want money." He forced himself to smile. "I'll find passage somehow. Good luck finding your money." He nodded politely and turned. He expected the Captain to stop him.

He faltered a little, but forced himself onward, when he reached the top of the gangplank. Nobody said anything. His footsteps sounded muted, and the gangplank bounced as he descended. The scummy water of the East Basin lay flat below; and he feared he had badly misjudged the situation.

His foot hit the quay with a jolt that lurched his stomach. Should he return and beg? But he didn't have twenty-five pounds.

"Lad."

He turned and looked up. The captain had a bemused smile on his face. "You've spine, I'll grant you that. It's clear you're desperate to reach the Narrow World, but not many can walk away like that and make it stick." He took a deep breath. "I'll tell you what. You can have passage for twelve pounds."

Edward didn't trust himself to speak; he merely nodded. Twelve pounds was still too much and wouldn't leave him much extra, but he knew better than to push his luck too far. He retraced his steps up the gangplank.

"I am Bartholomew Davies, Captain of this vessel." Davies held out a hand.

"Edward Truscott, at your service." Edward shook Davies's offered hand.

"Your hands are cold, lad, best you warm them." He turned his head. "Pull in the gangplank, Mr. Trog. Mr. Truscott will be staying aboard.

"We'll be sailing once the last of the cargo is stowed," Davies told Edward. "Stay out of the crew's way, and I'll send a man to show you the ship."

"Thank you, Sir."

The Captain returned to the cabin, and Edward hurried forward, wanting to find a quiet spot so as not to draw attention. He walked along the aft cabin, head turning and turning back, looking around so that he nearly ran into a sailor. He twisted, stumbling to a stop too near the man, but couldn't go forward because the deck was blocked.

"Stay out of the way!" The sailor punctuated his words with a shove, pushing Edward away from the open hold and the crates and barrels stacked beside it. He started to turn away but looked back. "Who the Hell are you?" he demanded.

The words, "He's a paying passenger, Mister Grimms," floated from the stern.

Mr. Grimms looked disgusted. "Make sure you stay out of the way."

Edward nodded, retreated to circle the aft cabin, and hurried to the bow where he could be sure to be out of the way and watch the men in a towboat fixing lines to the *Rose*.

☠

H e stood in the bow, alone, when the ship began to slide away from the quay, so slowly as to be imperceptible. Men in the small boat pulled in unison, and slowly the *Twilight Rose* gathered speed—slower than a man could walk, but definitely noticeable.

Wait for me, Becca. Don't let any gentlemen turn your head while I'm away. Of course, she didn't even know he was gone yet.

He turned his attention from London, the city he was leaving, to the ship, his method of leaving the city.

Runes were carved into the rails, arcane symbols that now caught his eye. They had been carved deep and the bottoms of the shapes painted in vibrant shades. It appeared to be some ancient or mystic language, but interspersed among the runes were serpents and mermaids and other creatures.

Further forward, the figurehead rode over the Thames. A gilded serpent seemed to grow out of the hull. It held its head high, looking forward, unmindful of the ship that trailed behind or the grasping roses that entwined it and held it fast to the hull.

Edward felt a pang of pity for the beast, and reminded himself it wasn't real.

Madness, he thought. *To be here is madness. To be Dead is madness. Even now I must still be abed: dreaming.* But there was a cold certainty inside him that said otherwise, as did the edges of runes carved into the rail beneath his fingers.

As the ship slid down the Thames, Edward realized he couldn't turn back. He might still swim ashore, but twelve pounds poorer and still Dead. And he hadn't shown up for work or sent notice of his illness. As certain as the sun rose in the east, he no longer had a job.

"I hope this is worth it," he muttered, laying his fingers on his wrist and searching for a pulse. Nothing. He repositioned them to try again, then switched wrists. Finally, he poked at the wound in his palm, now a black clot of blood that felt like a pellet embedded in his skin.

He wanted to disbelieve in spite of the cold certainty, so he took a deep breath and held it. Soon, he expected, his lungs would start to burn; but as the seconds ticked by, he didn't feel anything. He looked around, looking for a way to gauge time, and started counting in his head. At sixty, he slowed down, at ninety, he added "and" between each number. *Ninety, and ninety-one, and ninety-two.* At two hundred fifty, he thought he was being stubborn, and at eight hundred, he gave up. He didn't need to breathe.

Truly, no turning back.

Instead, he turned from the rail to see what kind of crew he had landed amongst. Trog, he knew. The sailor stood near the bow with another man securing the capstan that raised and lowered the anchor. Trog said something, and the other man turned to look at Edward. He shrugged and returned to work. Trog spat over the side and glared first at the other man, then Edward.

"And why're you so desperate to get to the Narrow World?"

The voice came from beside him. A small, broad-shouldered man had come up without his hearing. His black hair moved in the breeze, but he seemed solidly part of the ship, not the least bothered by the slight movement of the deck.

"Pardon?" Edward asked.

"I's wondering why you're so keen to get to the Narrow lands. Most lets the captain do their trading for them. Some wants to see for themselves. But nobody shows up half an hour before sailing in a panic to join us."

Edward shrugged. "I only learned of your sailing this morning."

"Aye," the little man nodded. "That would light a fire under you, but why sail in the first place?" He cocked a bushy eyebrow at Edward.

"What other chance will I have?" Having kept his secret thus far, Edward wasn't about to blurt it out now. Recalling Undulark's mentioning pixies and giants, he noted the little man's thick chest, his dark eyes, and the way his muscles stood out on his arms. "Are you...a...dwarf?"

The little man laughed. "A dwarf?" He chuckled some more. "Me? No, lad, I'm just short."

"Oh. Sorry. I didn't mean—"

The little man waved him off. "There's dwarfs and there's dwarfs, if you take my meaning; but I'm neither. Samuel Fairweather, at your service."

"Edward Truscott. The pleasure is mine."

Samuel laughed. "I asked for that right proper, didn't I? I'm Sam, and you're Ed. No London formality shipboard. You'll not find it in the Narrow World, either."

"How long to reach the Narrow World?" Edward asked.

"Well, now, that's a good question. I can't say it's taken us less than two months, a few times it's taken as much as five, but generally we should get there in about three and a half months."

"Five months," Edward said, and his voice sounded dead even in his own ears.

"Cheer up, Ed," Sam laughed. "We've a good witch. At least we've never gotten lost yet." He leaned forward, a twinkle in his eye, as he said, "Sometimes a witch steers wrong—to the wrong spot of magic. I've heard tell of ships aground at Cardiff with their prows pointed toward Stonehenge."

Panic surged through Edward and just as quickly subsided. "But that's never happened to this ship, has it?"

"No, no. Not likely, but navigating to the Narrow World is a tricky business. Come," Sam slapped his open palm on the rail. "I'm to show you the ship."

They paused amidships where the work crew still stowed the cargo. Edward wondered why it wasn't done before sailing but didn't feel it was his place to ask.

"Raise 'er!" ordered the sailor who had pushed Edward earlier.

"Mr. Grimms is the First Mate," Sam said, and paused to watch the men work.

A sailor on the far side of the hold hauled a rope, drawing up the corners of the net, pausing while one of the haulers snagged the net with a hook on a long pole, then lifted while the man with the hook guided the crate over the open hatch.

"Send 'er home," called Mr. Grimms, and the crate slowly dropped into the hold, the man feeding rope through the block and tackle to allow its descent.

"That's Lincolnshire corn, that is," one of the men said, pointing at a pile of sacks now visible with the crate removed. "You can see the markings."

"And I'm telling you," replied the other, "me Da has a farm in Lincolnshire, and there weren't no harvest last year on account of the late rains."

"Then how do you account for the markings?" demanded the first.

"Holden's a fool. Common fact is the best corn comes from Lincolnshire. Somebody packed another's corn in Lincolnshire bags and asked a higher price. Holden fell for it."

"Holden," Samuel told Edward, "is the cook. You'll come to know and curse him before the voyage is out."

"Mr. Briggs, attend your job!" The Mate put an end to the men's conversation. Briggs, the man with the hook, snagged the empty net and drew it away from the hatch so it could be lowered to the deck and reloaded.

"So, Ed," Sam said, still watching the men work, "you haven't really told me about yourself."

"Until this morning I clerked for the Turner & Webley Colliery."

Sam shook his head. "I don't doubt you, lad, but you haven't the accent for London."

"Why such interest?" Edward wanted to keep his secret.

Sam grinned. "You're new aboard, and I haven't had the same conversation with you twenty times already." He seemed to be staring at Edward.

Edward deliberately blinked, and Sam shuddered, as if waking from sleep.

"I'm from Cornwall," Edward said. He feared refusing would just make Sam delve harder.

"Ah," said Sam, as if he had discovered an unexpected pleasure. "Cornwall. We're carrying a part of Cornwall as our cargo."

Edward felt polite curiosity and examined the bales, crates, and sacks still on deck. "That's China Clay!" he exclaimed. "Those are from Lord Camelford's mine."

"You recognize it?" Sam asked with surprise in his voice.

"Well, it's not Camelford's anymore," Edward said. "He's been dead for years. But I should say I recognize it. I used to work for Lord Barstone, who owned the land next to Camelford."

Sam pulled on an ear. "You're a lad full of surprises. How did you go from mining to bookkeeping?"

Edward chuckled. "I wasn't a miner. I kept the books there, too. Although," he added, "I can mix whatever porcelain you want. Hard paste? Soft paste? Bone china? I can make it all."

"There must have been a future in that."

"Oh, we didn't make anything. Lord Barstone wanted to be able to demonstrate the quality of his clay, so we would mix batches of various porcelains for the china makers." Edward shook his head. "It was just another chore added to my work. Nobody made money there except Lord Barstone."

"You could have a go at it in the Narrow World. Right love the stuff, they do. That's enough of this," Sam said. "We stand here too long, and they'll make us work." He stumped past the men, beckoning Edward to follow.

The sailors were still arguing as Edward hurried after Sam.

"Yer daft, nobody cares enough to lie about corn." The man lifted one of the bags in question and dropped it on the net.

"They mowt," said the Lincolnshire-raised sailor as he dropped a second bag on top of the first. He glared at Edward. "Get along, for I get mardy."

Edward didn't know what "mardy" meant, but it didn't seem a good idea to find out. He quickened his pace.

Hammocks were slung in a dark, close space beneath the decks. Sam didn't have to duck, but Edward hunched over to avoid striking the deckhead. The space stank of tobacco, sweat, and the jumbled mess of food and drink long past but still lingering in the corners and cracks of the deck. A lamp hung from a hook in the deckhead; it was cold and dark, and Edward wondered if it could illuminate the space even when lit.

The galley was small. The cook had a small kitchen adjacent to an only slightly larger eating area. A dozen men could crowd onto the hard benches. The crew had assigned mealtimes, but Edward could eat at any of them.

Forty-three men, and one woman, crewed the *Twilight Rose*. Sam sought out the woman at the stern, where she stood puffing a golden-brown meerschaum pipe.

"Jenna is our Seawitch," Sam said. "She makes sure we get to the Narrow World. Without her, it would take a miracle to reach there. That isn't just a turn of phrase."

Edward bowed to the woman. She nodded in reply. Edward didn't know what he thought a Seawitch should look like, but Jenna wasn't it. The first word that came to mind was "sturdy." The second, "robust." Though not exactly fat, Jenna stood as tall as he did, and likely weighed three stone more. Her hair was either short or coiled beneath the wool cap she wore. What he could see of it was black, well on its way to grey. Her face was weathered, browned by the sun and lined by the wind.

The lines of red in her eyes matched the wrinkles around them. Edward thought those in her eyes would disappear when the smell of whiskey left her breath.

"A pleasure," Edward said. "I've never met a Seawitch before."

Jenna snorted and took the pipe from her mouth. "'Course you haven't. Likely only a half-dozen o' us worth anything." She eyed him, making no effort to hide her roving eye, taking him in from head to toe. "And what is it you do, Mr. Truscott?"

"I keep accounts."

"Saints above! A man of letters, or numbers at least, and they're the things that drive the world. You can help with the ship's accounts. The Captain thinks the sum of two and two is three—but only when calculating our pay."

Edward chuckled politely. "How does a Seawitch find the Narrow World? Isn't the second mate in charge of navigation?"

"He can only travel to the points of the compass. Up and down, if you count the curve of the earth. But magic is a dimension, just like space, and he's worthless trying to sail through *that*."

Sail through magic? Edward didn't understand, and didn't want to ask, but Jenna laughed.

"Don't expect a scientific answer," she said, knocking her pipe upside down on the rail so the tobacco fell into the river. "It's *magic*. But it is denser some places than others. Naturally, it is densest in the Narrow World. By grabbing onto the magic current and tracing it back, you pull yourself to that reality." She reached out and patted Edward on the cheek. "Don't worry yourself. I'll take care of it." Laughing again, she strode past him and into the cabin.

"And that's the *Rose*," Sam said, summing up the tour. "She's a good lass."

Edward didn't answer, caught by the view astern. The trees, hills, and twists of the river Thames obscured London. He didn't mind not seeing the city but wished for a glimpse of Rebecca, and having left without speaking with her gave him the feeling not that she was lost inside London, but that he was lost without her.

He sighed; so different than he had pictured adventuring. He had always thought he would be off to the Gold Coast or trying to make his fortune in India or China.

He had pictured a long and tearful goodbye from Rebecca, as he promised to return with a fortune, and she promised to remain faithful until that day. It would not be a frantic dash for the docks and his life, leaving behind a few hurried words passed through a neighbor.

Yet a frantic dash it was, being chased by the monster he would become if he didn't find a cure.

"Have you sailed to the Narrow World before?" he asked Sam.

"To be sure. This'll be my fifth voyage."

"What's it like?"

"Port Astarte is light and dark all mixed together. Life is different there, slower. There is no fascination with industry and capital. A strange people, used to the unusual."

"Magic," Edward said.

"Aye, magic."

"There's dark magic there?" Edward asked, trying to sound astonished, amazed he could ask the question so easily.

Sam frowned. "That's not what I meant, exactly. There's darkness there, to be sure. But not darkness, if you take my meaning." He blew out a great gust of air. "I'm not telling it well."

Edward waited for him explain.

"There's nothing to fear in a shadow," Sam said. "But nobody, in the Wide World or Narrow, wants something that hides in shadows so it can do evil. Here we're as like to fear the shadow, in the Narrow World they're not."

"Not everything that walks at night is evil," Edward said.

"Exactly! Ex-actly! So, you're likely to find an old crone who can weave you a cloak of darkness, but not a Ghoul devouring small children."

"Can you find," Edward hesitated, decided to take a chance, and plunged forward with his question, "Can one find a necromancer there?"

Right away he knew he made a mistake. Sam's eyes widened and he leaned away a bit, frowning.

"A woman," Edward croaked, pushing the words through his dry throat. "I need something for a woman." *Forgive me, Becca, it's not your fault.*

"Any woman who wants something from a necromancer is not a woman for you," Sam said. He took a very small step back. "How long have you been mixed up with this woman?"

"I've known her for some time," Edward said, forcing himself to smile in a way, he hoped, was rueful and disarming. "She'd never—" He pretended Sam's reaction just became clear. "Are you saying necromancers are… what are you saying?"

"She's cast a spell on you," muttered Sam. He scowled. "Necromancers deal in death magic. Evil they are, and shunned for a reason. Only dark magicians traffic with necromancers."

"I didn't know," Edward said. As long as Sam thought him ensnared in another's designs, he wouldn't suspect the truth. He made a show of blowing out a great lungful of air. "I'm in over my head. That's certain, and I'll admit it."

"I don't know anything of necromancers," Sam said, a bit of heat in his voice, as if offended that he might. He wagged a finger at Edward, though it only reached chest high. "If you're wise, you won't learn!"

"You're right, I'm sure. But I've come this far." He nodded toward the shore. "What am I to do? Maybe," he tried to sound uncertain, "there is something—better—I could find for her?" He needed to play out this charade, allay Sam's suspicions, and avoid the subject in the future.

Sam scowled, but then smiled. "You're not the first lad to make himself into a fool for a girl. Take my advice. There's sights to see in the Narrow World—things you won't forget until the day you die. See them, but stay away from necromancers. Find something else special for your girl, and if she won't have you without a necromancer's gift, well, then she's not the girl for you."

Edward nodded. "I hope you don't think poorly of me?"

Sam chuckled. "No, lad. I should have guessed, your boarding us like you did. A man only makes himself such a damned fool over a woman."

☠

Sam had duties, so he left Edward alone at the bow watching England slide by. They would, Edward learned before Sam left, turn west and sail through the Channel. Once in the Atlantic, Jenna would set their course for the Narrow World.

Gravesend lay behind them. With little to see, Edward began to prowl around the ship. He remembered the Captain's orders, so took care to stay out of the sailors' way. It seemed, to his eye, they did little. Men would go aloft or change the sails if there were a change in course or wind, but mostly they did mundane tasks at a leisurely pace.

Some of the crew scrubbed the decks with holystones. One man rested in the rigging, ostensibly on lookout, but in deep channel and with no ships near, he didn't have much to do.

"Too good to work, are you?" muttered Trog, just loud enough for Edward to hear as he walked past.

Edward faltered. It took a moment for his foot to find the deck, but he carried on, returning to the bow that he was starting to think of as a refuge.

He took out the black bottle of elixir. He unscrewed the top and smelled it. He took just enough to cover his tongue. It wasn't candy, but he'd had worse. Now he took a full sip. Heat coursed down his throat and radiated outwards from his stomach. He felt his spirits lift.

To Hell with Trog. Perhaps the sailor resented Edward's leaping aboard, perhaps he hated everything; but Edward wasn't going to listen to him. What, he thought a little bitterly, could the sailor do that was worse than had already happened?

☠

Edward couldn't sleep. It might have been because of the cramped quarters and movement of the ship; it might have been because he was Dead and didn't need sleep. He lay staring at the deckhead, trying to sort through his thoughts, trying to make sense of the last two days.

Did he need to sleep? Did he need to eat? He had eaten with the rest of the crew, but he had little appetite and the food sat heavy in his stomach.

What did he know of *zumbis*? Little, he realized. He had never heard of one speaking. In every tale, they were clumsy creatures that attacked for reasons of their own, or no reason at all—mindless horrors of rotting flesh, all the more terrible because they had once been human.

That was what he would become if he couldn't find a way to cure his Dead.

And, apart from that, where could he find a necromancer to cure him? What did he know of the Narrow World? Even less than he knew of *zumbis*. It was a place of magic, which he hadn't believed in two days ago and wouldn't believe in now if he weren't Dead.

He rolled over, his feet hitting the deck with a soft thud, and groped his way to the ladder. Once out in the sea air, he crossed the empty, silent deck, and went to the bow. "At least you know where you're going," he told the figurehead as he leaned on the rail.

The young crescent moon cast dim light on the ship and sea. The English coast was little more than shadows. The Channel ahead was clear, while behind…

A ship closed on them from behind.

Edward straightened. If he suspected danger so close to home, it would have been from Cornish wreckers luring unwary ships to the rocks, but people spoke of ships disappearing near the Channel Islands—if the night were dark and the ship unwary.

He looked around; had the sailor on watch spotted the ship? Did they know it was friendly? Two people stood by the stern, watching the approaching ship. Edward hurried back.

They faced away, but the light breeze carried their conversation back to him.

"They're going to steal our wind, the bastards."

"And why do they run so close, I wonder?" said Jenna the Seawitch, by the sound of her voice.

Edward cleared his throat, and Captain Davies and Jenna turned at his approach.

"Having a hard time sleeping, Mr. Truscott?" the Captain asked.

"It looks like they want a word," said Jenna. The Captain didn't wait for Edward's answer but returned his gaze to the approaching ship.

It looked much like the *Twilight Rose* with a clipper bow, narrow beam, and raked stern. This ship was fully rigged, giving her greater speed in the following wind. Her dark hull sent up spray as she sliced through the seas.

The moon illuminated her sails, giving them a silver glow, as if the ship sailed with the wings of Heaven. Shadows stripped the deck, and a group of men stood near the rail, within the shadows of the sails. Stolid, unmoving outlines of men in frock coats and billycock hats waited patiently for the ships to draw near.

Shock coursed through Edward. It could not be a coincidence that these men and the man behind the Painted Man's shop dressed alike. After the shock, fear crept up his spine.

"Who is that?" he asked. *Go cautiously, remember Sam's reaction to necromancers.* Still, he withdrew a pace, and wanted to back further but dared not draw attention to himself.

"The *Reach of God,*" the Captain said, without taking his eyes from the black-hulled ship.

"They'll be in the Narrow World before us," Jenna said before Edward could ask another question.

"Undoubtedly," the Captain said. "Though it's no slight on your talents."

Jenna snorted. "Prester Ellis is a rigid, grasping man, but when he seizes a thread, there's no shaking him loose."

"I was referring to their rigging," the Captain said mildly. "They make better headway."

"They always drive hard," Jenna said, and Edward sensed she meant more than just sailing.

"They're headed to the Narrow World?" Edward asked.

"They'd not take you aboard," the Captain said, "if that's what you're thinking. They've a very different business."

"Who are they?"

"The fine and ancient order known as the Custodians of the Light," Jenna said. "Their Latin name escapes me. *Custo*-something."

"I've never heard of them," Edward said.

"You wouldn't, unless you were in this business. They act as watchdog over…" she paused, as if looking for the proper word, "over things of a dark nature."

"Magic?"

"Dark," she repeated, taking her pipe out of her pocket and putting the amber stem in her mouth and sucking a few times to test the draw. "Things touched by Hell, they say, things that do harm to the folk of England."

She drew a pouch of tobacco from her jacket and filled the bowl of her pipe. "Mind you, I might argue with some of the things they call dark."

They'd surely find harm in a *zumbi*. "What are they after?" *Not me, surely. They can't possibly know.* He desperately hoped that was true.

"That," said Captain Davies firmly, "is their business, and best left to them." He raised his hand and hailed the *Reach of Goa*. "Ho, there!"

"A word of warning to you, Captain Davies," came a voice across the waves.

"The Prester himself," Jenna said.

"There are things in England that don't belong; implements of mischief and grimoires to revive magic best forgotten. We have stamped them out of London, and now we go back to their source."

"I have always been most careful in my trading with the Narrow World," Captain Davies shouted.

"Then this warning should suffice. See that it does."

Edward felt a prickling sensation. His own fear, nothing more, he thought as he tried to make out the shadowy men, as, he feared, they were trying to do to him. *Unaulark could smell Dead, but he stood next to me. This Prester Ellis can't possibly know with a stretch of ocean between us.*

Jenna took a deep breath, but the Captain said, "Peace. It does no good to argue with the Prester." He lifted his voice again, "My thanks! And good fortune on your hunt."

Nobody called back. The *Reach of God* forged on, inching ahead of the *Twilight Rose* until the *Reach* was far enough ahead that the *Rose* got the wind back.

The three watched silently until Jenna struck a Lucifer to light her pipe. She threw the match overboard. "It's a bad thing for us to arrive soon after the *Reach*. The Narrow World will be on edge."

Edward blew out a lungful of air and marveled that the action had nothing to do with breathing. He would have to stay away from this Prester Ellis. He wondered if it would be possible.

Jenna seemed to sense Edward's questions, and answered what she must have thought he wondered. "Mostly the Wide and Narrow Worlds leave each other alone. Only a few folk traffic between them, and those that try to stamp out the darker aspects are content to do it in the Wide World. But Prester Ellis is taking his fight to the Narrow World."

"Surely they have done this before," Edward said. "They have a ship, after all."

Captain Davies answered. "They have commerce of their own, yes. But this voyage doesn't appear to be for commerce."

"And do not think they are against magic," Jenna said. "They embrace light magic, for it can be hard to distinguish between magic and a miracle. But they are the ones who determine what is light and what is dark. They drove out the pixies."

"Were pixies evil?"

"No, pixies were heathen." Jenna blew out a lungful of smoke, which drifted away on the wind. "As were the other fairie. The Custodians were part of the Medieval Inquisition, the only part of the Church taken over by Cromwell. After the Restoration, they went off on their own, but they still harken to their Church roots."

"They are zealous defenders of England's virtue," said Captain Davies. Edward could not tell if he were being sarcastic or not. "Did you fear them pirates?" He chuckled.

"I did not know," Edward said. The *Reach*'s wake glistened in the moonlight, slightly brighter than the rest of the sea. They carried their fight to the Narrow World, having already fought it in England. "It seems strange," he said, "that there should be a war in England and nobody even know about it."

Captain Davies snorted. "There are more things in heaven and earth than ever you dreamt."

How true that was.

He did not dream, this morning when he woke, that before midnight he would be shipboard in the Channel, bound for a world where people worked magic and trying to find a way to be restored to life. How very far away, and very long ago, it seemed.

Sam found him, and they leaned on the rail together. "You've heard of the undead?" Sam asked. "The revenants, the vampires, and the draugr?"

"Yes." Why had he mentioned the undead?

"There's more folk all the time that don't believe in them, but they're real. Life and death, all mixed together. The Narrow World is like that, a mix of magic and not. Makes some folk a little different." Sam shrugged, seemingly at a loss of how to explain the difference.

"Are the Not-Dead common?" Edward asked, keeping his voice steady, trying to sound casual.

"Nah. O' course not." Sam rubbed the back of his neck. "Not sure why I said that. It's just that things you might think cracked are taken for granted. Nobody questions the existence of vampires. It's a place of people who believe in magic, and a fair number of them can do it, and magic marbles their lives like fat in bacon."

"Ah."

Sam watched him from the corners of his eyes, clearly wondering something. It made Edward uncomfortable, but he didn't want to ask what, because then he would have to answer.

"I like you, Ed," Sam said finally. "But there's something odd about you."

Edward shook his head, denying it. "I'm just trying…" he wasn't sure what he was trying to do. "So, Port Astarte is the main city?"

"Aye. The Narrow World's an archipelago, so there's other towns, but Port Astarte is the largest."

Chapter Three

A lassitude came over Edward. His limbs felt heavy as he shuffled over to the deckhouse and settled onto a large coil of rope. Above, the stars grew brighter as the moon waned, but gradually the moon, the stars, and the sails all faded from his consciousness. He still saw them, but they became less clear, less real. He grew still, his only movement caused by the gentle rocking of the ship. The sounds of the ship and sea receded.

Is this what sleep has become?

He knew time passed, but it meant nothing.

If he concentrated, he realized the stars were moving across the sky, and they, in turn, started to fade as dawn approached.

"Ed? Lad?" The voice came from far away. A fuzzy shape blocked his view of the sky. "Ed?"

With tremendous effort Edward blinked, his lids scraping on dry eyes.

"Ah, good lad. You gave me a start there, you did."

A few more blinks and the fuzzy shape resolved into Sam, a relieved look on his face.

Edward lifted his hand—the movement felt foreign, stiff, and awkward—and rubbed his face. "What?" The word scratched its way out of his mouth.

"You right scared me," Sam said. "Thought you were dead."

Pushing himself up, Edward stood. He rotated his arms, working his shoulders, then his elbows, feeling his body loosen and his movement become more natural.

"Dead?" he asked, trying not to sound alarmed. "Why?"

"Eyes staring, skin pale, didn't look like you were breathing…" Sam shuddered.

Edward made a point of drawing a deep breath; it helped loosen the muscles in his chest. "I couldn't sleep last night so came out on deck," he said. "I settled onto the rope and must have finally fallen asleep. My eyes were open, you say?"

"Aye."

"Last time I'll do that," Edward said, feeling more normal. "Don't you sleep on a pile of rope, Sam. I'm sore all over. My eyes were open?

I've heard of folks doing that, but never me. That I know, of course."
He chuckled.

Take care, he told himself. *You'd be a fool to press it.* And he thought, *Maybe I should tell him.* Then he thought of Sam's reaction when asked about necromancers, and discarded the idea.

"Aye," Sam said, rubbing the back of his neck. "I've heard of it too. Breakfast is laid out at seven bells of the morning watch, and Holden swears he won't serve a soul past the second bell of the forenoon watch." He pointed to starboard. "Make your good-byes, Ed. We're passing Cornwall now."

"Selevan?" Edward felt a pang at the sight of the grey cliffs and green hills. Cornwall, more than London, was home.

"No, St. Levan."

Edward snorted. "It's the same place. St. Levan is what the English call it. Selevan is the Cornish name."

"Huh, damn me if I know why a place needs two names. I'll be heading aloft now." Sam shook his head. "Sleep with your eyes closed from now on. The other way gives me the willies."

The *Reach of God* was a white speck on the western horizon. Edward stood alone on the deck, absently patting his clothing as he tried to gather his thoughts. The black bottle of tonic was in his jacket, Undulark's coins in his trousers.

Now would be the time to take inventory of his things and start the day, so he quickly fetched his bag from the under-deck space and began to search through it.

First out of the bag was a book. He turned it over to read the title: *The Black Tulip,* by Alexander Dumas. He hadn't read it, so good fortune that he happened to grab it in his haste. He pulled out several pairs of underclothes, which, he thought wryly, showed his wisdom.

Next out of his bag came his money purse. A quick count tallied six pounds, eight shillings, and eleven pence.

He found a ball of twine, a few crumpled sheets of paper, a pocketknife, a short pencil, and a small packet of Lucifer matches. Finally, he found his comb, razor, toothpowder, and pig's bristle toothbrush all jumbled together at the bottom of the bag.

Satisfied with his discovery, he could now start his day. He went through his daily routine, brushing his teeth. His chin, however, was as smooth as when he shaved the previous day.

I'm Deaa; I guess I don't need to shave. But what if the other men saw that? He lathered his face and carefully, very carefully, began to go through the motions of shaving. He wouldn't heal if he cut himself.

The smells of breakfast wafted from the galley—fresh food being used before it went bad. He could smell black pudding and toast, and even fancied he could make out the odor of frying eggs.

The black pudding, blood sausage, smelled good. The rest he didn't care about, but that sausage… He dried and folded his razor and went to the galley.

A half-dozen men sat at the tables. Quick recollection put that at less than half the crew, and Edward only recognized Trog. Light came from three portholes. Two glowed as the sun illuminated salt-crusted glass; the third was open to let out smoke that escaped the galley stove.

He picked up a pewter plate and held it out to the cook. "Black pudding, please."

The cook stabbed a couple links and, using his greasy fingers, pushed them off the fork onto Edward's plate. He then reached for a piece of toast.

"Just the pudding, thanks," Edward said. The cook shrugged and pushed a mug toward him. "Just the pudding," Edward repeated.

"Got some rhubarb," rumbled the cook. "And the eggs are fresh."

"Just the pudding." Edward remembered the cook's name: Holden.

"Best eat the rhubarb now. Shan't have it long."

"Just," Edward said, pulling his plate away, "the pudding."

"Shouldn't take passengers," Trog said. "They get in the way."

Edward chose the seat farthest from the sailor, though in the cramped space that was still only a few feet away.

"True," agreed another. "'E got in the way of loading yesterday."

It must be one of the men loading supplies. Mr. Briggs or not, Edward didn't recognize him.

"Leapt aboard, he did, like he owned the ship," Trog said.

"An' if we make more money on the voyage, I don't see why it should trouble you," said another sailor. He lifted his mug to Edward before taking a long pull.

"It was the Frenchman who let the ship burn," Trog said. "Started the fire, he did."

Does this man not like me because he thinks I'll burn the ship? Perhaps Trog didn't like anybody.

The black pudding tasted better than Edward ever recalled. He took the black bottle from his jacket pocket and sipped the *aqua vitae*. It had a bitter taste but warmed him through, almost feeling like it cleansed him.

Trog turned his complaints to the food, the tartness of the rhubarb, the lard dripping from his egg.

"You'll be remembering this meal fondly," retorted Holden. He waved a rusty and pitted knife at Trog. "When we're into salt pork and hard tack, and we've eaten the chickens long since, aye, that's when you'll wish for a nice bit o' rhubarb."

"More likely I'll want relief from your cooking."

"I cook what I have," Holden said, his brows drawn low and his lips turned down.

"And how much silver did you pocket buying it?"

Apparently if Holden didn't spend his entire budget he could keep the excess. Numbers did funny things to people when they were attached to money, Edward knew. Holden had every reason to keep his costs down.

Holden flushed red. "Ingrate! You eat better than most sailors and all I hear is complaints."

The argument continued; Edward didn't care. He finished his sausage, and, since the sailors idled over their mugs, rose to leave. He tripped, falling into the bulkhead, and Trog snorted into his mug.

☠

Edward sharpened the pencil from his bag, letting the shavings fall over the rail where they were lost from view in the slowly rolling swells. Perhaps, he thought, he should start carving a scrimshaw. But first he must write Rebecca. Having failed to make his farewells, he owed her correspondence, even if he didn't know if he could post it.

For long moments, he looked over the stern, the morning sun warming his face. *Always looking back feeling regret.* And he recalled the words of his father, *save your regrets for when you're dead.*

What could he possibly say to her?

He smoothed the paper again and began to write.

Dear Rebecca, he wrote, and crossed it out. *Dearest Becca.* If these were his last words to her, they would be true words. *I don't know where to begin. I'm afraid if I told you why, you wouldn't believe me. I only believe it because I have no choice.* He crossed that out too.

Dearest Becca, he began again. *I am terribly, terribly sorry. Even now, I can scarcely believe I am shipboard and sailing away from England. The circumstances could not have been worse, but a ship at St. Katherine's dock had a berth I felt compelled to take. I do not know when I shall return. I realize how foolish I have been to let so much time pass as we lived and worked apart in London. It is my most fervent desire to remedy that mistake, if you will permit me, on my return. As I write this, we are sailing west with the sun rising behind us. It rises over England, and it is easy to believe that you are the cause of it.*

He signed it, carefully folded it, addressed it, and stowed it in his bag.

☠

They were well past Cornwall and Brittany when the sun sank into the ocean at the end of the day.

"This being your first trip to the Narrow World, you won't want to miss this," Sam said.

"Why? What's going to happen?"

"Jenna is going to attune the ship to the Narrow World. It 'pulls' the ship through magic so we are real to the Narrow World, and helps the helmsman stay on course."

"What do you mean, 'real' to the Narrow World?" Edward asked.

"I don't know," Sam laughed. "Jenna claims we could sail right through the Narrow World without seeing it if we're not attuned to it."

"And she does this with magic?"

"Aye, most impressive magic. I've been told it can happen naturally, at times when a ship's compass goes crazy, or when the Northern Lights are in the sky, but only rarely, and not to be counted on."

"I don't understand," Edward admitted as Jenna emerged from her cabin, a canvas sack slung over her shoulder.

She paced to the center of the deck, set down a small marker, then paced to the port rail. She moved the marker a couple inches, paced to the starboard rail, paced back, and adjusted the marker again. She sat down facing the bow and upended her sack, dumping its contents—the instruments of her spell—in front of her.

Jenna ordered her instruments on the deck: a small brass brazier with a vented top, a red chinagraph pencil, a ball of twine, a leather pouch, a pocket flask, and various small oddities that Edward couldn't make out from the distance.

Edward leaned over to Sam and whispered, "She's not going to chant gibberish and sacrifice a chicken, is she?"

Sam chuckled. "No, the casting isn't the good part. Looks like it came from a penny dreadful. It's the results that are interesting."

It did look like a spell casting as told in folk tales. Jenna used magic symbols drawn on the deck, incense burnt in the brazier, soft chanting, rhythmic deck pounding, the singing of a very odd song, and a libation from the flask. She followed that with several quick draughts that didn't seem part of the ritual.

Edward looked around, wondering what "the good part" might be. Jenna sat on the deck, palms up, index fingers touching thumbs, eyes closed. "Is something supposed to happen?"

"Yeeessss." Sam drew out the word, sounding uncertain.

What if she can't find the path to the Narrow World?

Even as the thought flashed through Edward's mind, crimson smoke rose from the brazier.

"Ah, here we go," said Sam.

The smoke billowed up, carrying a scent of spice. The figures drawn on the deck twinkled, looking like wine or blood. The runes on the ship's rail began to glow white. Suddenly, they exploded with light. Edward cried out and shielded his eyes.

A roar split the twilight; Edward jumped and spun. Was the figurehead *alive*? No, no it couldn't be, but he could have sworn he saw it move. The serpent's eyes definitely glowed the same silver-white as the runes on the rail.

"Now we're on our way proper," Sam said.

"Indeed, we are." Tentatively, Edward reached out and touched the back of the figurehead. Wood, nothing more.

☠

The following weeks of the voyage were not as interesting as the first two days. Edward knew to keep his purpose to himself, eat at meals, blink, and breathe. He could talk to Sam, he needed to avoid Trog, and the rest of the crew fell somewhere between on their friendliness.

It turned out Trog's real name was Matthew Hopkins, but somewhere in his past he picked up his nickname. Even Captain Davies, who addressed everybody on board formally, called him "Mr. Trog."

Avoiding Trog didn't help. Trog went out of his way to cause trouble, and he found Edward an easy target. Tripping him in the galley was just the start. He would lean back and throw an elbow into Edward's side or stand at just the right time to knock a plate from Edward's hand. Small things disappeared. The pocketknife, the twine—both vanished from Edward's bag. When Edward washed his change of clothes and hung them on the rail to dry they acquired a strong odor of urine, and Trog smirked the rest of the day.

Edward kept his *aqua vitae* in his pocket. He didn't dare part with it. Three sips a day, and he would hold the bottle up to the sun, always fearful of how little remained. He calculated and recalculated, trying to reassure himself he would have enough, but he didn't know how long the voyage would take, so his estimates meant nothing.

The sailors amused themselves with shanties, rope tricks, and games of chance. None, to Edward's surprise and disappointment, was a scrimshander. He had thought all sailors carved on long voyages and was mildly disappointed to discover his error.

Captain Davies tried to keep the men busy and kept men aloft trimming sails to best advantage, but the winds stayed constant so much of the day there was little to do.

So it came that at midday after two weeks at sea Edward leaned against the foredeck cabin, his face lifted to the warming sun and his eyes closed. He pulled his tonic from his pocket and started to unscrew the top.

Suddenly it was seized from his hands. Edward's eyes flew open and he jumped upright. Trog danced back, holding the black bottle aloft and grinning.

"I've seen you taking a nip of this stuff." Trog waggled the bottle. "Didn't your mum ever teach you to share?"

"Give me that!" Edward rushed at him, but Trog drove his hand into Edward's chest, knocking him back.

"Just say the word, and I'll share this with Davy Jones."

Edward stopped. "You can't imagine how important that is." None of the sailors nearby seemed inclined to help. They watched, some of them smiling. Edward stared at the bottle, following Trog's every motion.

"Oh, I can," Trog said. "I've been dry before, and I've no wish to be dry now." He unscrewed the top, keeping an eye on Edward.

"No!" Edward shouted and grabbed again.

Trog cocked his arm to throw. *Aqua vitae* sloshed onto the deck.

Edward sank back on his heels.

With a triumphant grin, Trog brought the bottle to his lips and drank, his throat moving with every swallow. "Pfah!" He lowered the black bottle and wiped his mouth with the back of his hand. "That's foul! You like this do you?"

Despair took hold of Edward and he didn't know what to say except, "It goes well with seafood."

Trog grimaced. With a look of disgust, he twisted on the cap and flung it. The bottle bounced once off the deck then skittered over to strike the deckhouse.

Edward rushed to scoop it up. He cradled it to his chest as he escaped to the bow. Once there, he held it to the sun and peered through the dark glass.

Only a swallow or two remained.

Edward's sight dimmed and his knees felt weak. He grabbed the rail to steady himself and waited for his vision to clear.

Toward the stern, Trog laughed, mimicking his knocking Edward back and laughing.

Kill him, Edward thought. *Bludgeon him and tear him apart.* He shook his head and the urge fell away, leaving him horrified and sick. *But I haven't missed any treatments*, he thought. *Yet.*

It only slows down the Dead, Undulark had said. How fast would it progress without the *aqua vitae*? He didn't know. How long would the *aqua vitae* last? A week? Two? He didn't know. He would have to cut down his doses.

☠

"God, this food is vile!"

None of the other sailors disputed it.

Holden threw down his knife and crossed his arms. "Eat it or starve."

"Have you tried this?"

"Yes," said the cook. "I never promised you raspberry tarts."

"But this is the worst tasting grub you've ever shoved at us," complained the sailor.

Edward didn't care. In the two weeks since he reduced his ration of *aqua vitae,* only the meat had flavor—the rest of the food seemed pulpy mush, bland and tasteless. He ate it, and wondered what happened to it, for his body didn't seem to need it.

He ignored the continuing argument, focusing instead on his left hand. Steady. But every fumble and misstep, every hesitation of thought, made him fear the progression of Dead. If he only knew more, more what to expect, a more certain time of arrival.

He sighed and rose from the table. Deftly avoiding Trog's outthrust foot, he went onto the deck. *I should have broken his leg.* That was another concern. Were these violent thoughts natural? He didn't think of himself as a violent man, but, truthfully, he had cause. Was it just cause or Dead affecting his brain?

He lifted the black bottle and swirled it. He *might* be able to stretch it another week. He took a sip, barely enough to wet his tongue.

"I'm sorry, Becca," he said. The wind took his words away, and he wondered if it would somehow carry them to England. "Five weeks gone and I'm down to hope and little else."

He tucked the bottle back into his jacket and strolled to the stern where Captain Davies stood.

"Ah, Mr. Truscott," the Captain said. "I've news that may interest you."

"Indeed? Does it have to do with our passage? I didn't want to ask. I fear my inquiry will become troublesome." He was, in fact, going to ask anyway.

"It does. Our good Seawitch has informed me this is our best voyage ever. We ride the swiftest currents of magic and make good time."

It felt like the sun breaking from behind the clouds. "That is excellent news!" Edward grinned. "Excellent news. Did she guess how much longer?"

"It is hard to measure things when magic is involved. Two weeks at the most, a week is likely, possibly four days."

Four days? Nothing had ever sounded sweeter. "That, Captain, makes the day much brighter. I am not as acclimated to the sea as you are."

Captain Davies nodded. "I thought the news would please you."

"Indeed, it does." He strained his eyes, as if he could see the Narrow

World waiting for him. "Is there reason I should not share this with the crew?"

"Feel free."

Edward soon found Sam. The little man leaned on the rail, looking troubled. "Good news," Ed called. "We make good time and should reach our destination in a week."

☠

Even when the wind slackened an hour later, Edward's spirits remained high. He leaned over the starboard rail, looking forward, and was caught by surprise when a sailor staggered over, his head jerking up and forward like something wanted to leap out of his mouth and he fought to keep it in. He hit the rail and vomit spewed out, looking like it pulled him over with it. He clung to the rail as if to life and hurled another stream of vomit into the ocean.

Sight or smell or plain sickness sent another man after him. Like the first, he tried to fight down his sickness, and like the first he failed.

"I don't feel so good myself," Sam said behind him. He wiped his face, which, in spite of his tan, looked pale with a faint color of olives.

"What's the matter?" Edward asked.

"I'm going to be sick!" Sam took a step toward the rail, but then deluged the deck with the better part of his breakfast. A second later he added the rest of breakfast and collapsed to sit against the rail so he could turn his head and dry heave over the side.

"Captain?" But Edward didn't see the Captain. He hurried to the stern. "Captain?" The Captain was bent over a storage locker. "Captain, there's something wrong with the men."

The Captain straightened and turned, wiping his mouth with the back of his hand. "I am—" he expelled a wet, gassy belch, "aware of it."

Edward took a step back. "What has happened?"

Captain Davies heaved, but nothing came out. He kept heaving, tears streaming from his eyes until he leaned, gasping, against the storage locker. "If God wished to see my guts, I'd rather he cut me open."

"Can Jenna do anything?"

"Ask her."

He found Jenna in her cabin, senseless in her bunk. The cabin smelled of vomit and brandy; the full bucket and empty bottle told the tale of each. Edward opened a porthole and tried to rouse her without success.

Returning to the deck and witnessing the men's condition, he allowed as Jenna, at least, didn't feel her suffering.

Over the next two hours, every man on the ship was stricken ill except Edward. With no hand at the wheel, the ship lost headway. The wind dropped off completely, but nobody could go aloft to add more sail.

There was little anybody could do. Edward brought water on deck, but few drank, and they could not keep even water down.

"A bit of biscuit?" he asked Sam.

The little man's head wiggled a bit—no. He leaned back, his mouth open and eyes shut. His eyelids twitched, but he did not open them. He had long since emptied his stomach.

A sailor across the deck croaked, "Oh God, I've the bloody shits."

Sam rolled his head to the side and cracked his eyes open. "Please, Lord, spare me that."

"What can I do to help?" Edward said.

"Spare me the misery of your voice," muttered a nearby sailor sprawled in a pool of vomit on the deck.

As he searched for something, anything, that might help, Edward heard somebody below deck. He traced the sounds and fetched up the cook from the bilges, the poor man was retching his guts in the darkness; terrified his shipmates would blame him for their illness.

Edward stood on the deck surrounded by sick sailors, looking up at the limp canvas, and knowing his trip hopes lay dead in the water. And what if the crew died? He couldn't sail the *Rose* by himself. He couldn't cure them, he didn't know how. He could only make them comfortable and let the sickness run its course. Then they could resume their journey.

He found a spare sail and strung it between the masts and the rail to keep the sun from the men. Little by little he gave them water. The first few drank deeply, only to throw the water back up. After that, he rationed it out in sips, leaving the men parched and cursing, but better able to keep it down.

The day warmed. No hint of wind stirred. The sails hung flat. The deck stayed flat. The *Twilight Rose* remained as stationary as if she were aground.

The stench of hot vomit wafted up, clogging his nostrils, so he drew buckets of water from the sea. Again and again he sluiced the decks, washing the filth over the side. The stains, however, he could not remove.

Men grew delirious. More than one muttered their misery as they drifted in and out of consciousness. The ship's carpenter, however, a man by the name of John Stearne, raved of witches and demons and wouldn't let Edward approach.

"I wish he would hold his tongue," Edward muttered to Sam as Stearne screamed of devils eating his innards, and that Edward wanted to feed them.

"Don't feed any devils, lad," Sam said, his hands shaking as he sipped his water.

The first man died that evening.

Edward wrapped him in a winding sheet. He started to say a few words, but realized he didn't know anything about the man, not even his name. He said a quick prayer, the words burning in his throat, consigning the man's soul to God and his body to the deep. He hauled the corpse onto the rail and pushed it over.

"Dead man overboard," muttered a sailor who watched with feverish eyes. "Dead man overboard." He cackled, a dry, hacking laugh that made Edward shy away.

Night had a surreal quality. Light pooled around the lanterns he hung and along the rail where the runes still glowed. The *Rose* was an island, populated by livid faced men.

Two more died in the night.

As he threw the third man over the rail, Edward thought of the irony, one Dead man throwing another dead man into the sea. "We have much in common, you and I," he said. He tried to say a prayer but couldn't find the words.

The body splashed into the calm sea, and he realized he had not tied a weight to its feet. It bobbed at the edge of the lantern light as if unwilling to let the ship leave it behind.

By morning men began to recover; weak, tired, but alive. They fell into sleep, a sleep without sweating or muttering. They could drink water without throwing it back up, and some even managed to retain some hardtack.

Edward felt sluggish, not sleepy. He hadn't felt sleepy since waking up Dead. It took more effort to move, and stopping felt the same as lying down at the end of a tiring day. After one last circuit of the ship, he shuffled to the bow to sit on the deck and close his eyes. A breeze stirred the sails, making the canvas ripple. Soon they could get underway.

☠

"I know what you've done."

Edward opened his eyes and forced himself to turn around. His muscles were reluctant to obey.

Trog supported himself with one hand on the rail; in the other hand he held a belaying pin. "You don't fool me."

The sun had passed its zenith without his noticing. He hadn't slept, exactly, but he hadn't been aware of anything for hours.

"What?" Edward tried to gather his wits. A dozen men gathered behind Trog. Most looked weak, all looked angry.

"You cast a spell on us. I heard Stearne."

Those nearby rolled their heads to watch. The men behind Trog nodded. "Aye," murmured one, "a spell."

"That's daft!" Edward exclaimed. "Stearne was raving mad! You just became sick. Something you ate, I expect."

"You're not affected, are you?" chimed in another man. "You ate too." Other men started to sit up, some to stand. They wobbled a bit, but more and more paid attention to Trog.

"Course he isn't on account that he's the one who cast the spell on us," said Trog.

"That's daft!" Edward repeated. "Why would I do that?"

"Dark magic," muttered Trog. "The Devil likes suffering, and you serve him."

"That's not true!"

"You want to go to the Narrow World, don't you? Driven out of London, weren't you? Bet the Custodians are after you."

"Why would I harm the crew that is taking me to the Narrow World?" Edward shouted. "It makes no sense!"

"Evil can't help itself," Trog hissed, and to Edward's horror, several sailors nodded agreement.

"You take me for a fool," he said.

"Gentlemen," said a voice behind the sailors. "Let me through."

The sailors parted, and Captain Davies approached, his pace slow, but firm, as if he wanted to make certain of each step before taking the next.

"There is a certain sense in what he says," he said. "Perhaps your flight and *The Reach of God*'s voyage are linked."

"NO!" But Edward believed the events inside the Painted Man's shop, the murder that drove a dark creature into the alley, was part of the Custodian's war. He couldn't guess how, but perhaps his flight *had* drawn the Custodians after him. "No," he repeated, and cursed himself for not putting more assurance in the word.

He motioned to the bucket of water. "If I caused this sickness, why would I try to cure you?"

"So you can afflict us again!" Trog hollered. He pitched his voice to the rest of the crew. "I say we hang him before he can do any more trouble."

Unsteady as some of them were, they looked ready to try.

A general muttering rose. Edward looked at Sam, imploring his friend to speak in his defense. Sam still lay against the rail, not recovered enough to rise.

"If you're not a warlock," Sam said. Nobody spoke as they strained to hear his weak voice. "If you're not a warlock," Sam said louder, "why do you seek a necromancer?"

Sam's question was more of an accusation and it stunned Edward. "I told you," he said. "For a woman."

The sailors began to mutter, low, dark words that crawled over Edward like parasites.

Edward knew he had no friends now. The sailors shifted positions, and it felt like they hemmed him in closer even though they hadn't moved. What would happen if they hanged him and he didn't die? Would they try to burn him or throw him over the side?

Kill them all. Now, when they're weak. Tear them apart.

"No," he whispered. He backed away. "You're fools, and you're wrong. I did nothing but help you."

"Oh, the devil lies pretty, lads," Trog said. "But he can't lie when he's hanging by his neck."

"Captain," Edward said. "I've paid for safe passage."

Captain Davies blinked and shook his head. He seemed to be having difficulty thinking. He placed his fingers on the bridge of his nose and closed his eyes. "We are not savages, yet you alone were not stricken down. Why is this?"

Because I'm already Dead, Edward thought. Of course, he couldn't say that. "I don't know."

"Is it true you seek a necromancer?"

Edward hung his head. "Yes. But not for the purpose you think."

The Captain nodded, his fingers still on his nose, his eyes still closed. "Trafficking with necromancers is wholly evil." He dropped his hand and looked up. "It is said if a witch or warlock is pricked with a long pin they will not bleed. Will you agree to this test?"

Clenching his fist, Edward felt the dried blood pebble embedded in his palm. "No."

Captain Davies shook his head. "Then I will not have you aboard my ship."

"You will be party to murder?" Edward demanded. *Kill them. They are still weak.* "No."

"I will give you this choice. We will set you adrift in the ship's boat, or Mr. Trog will decorate the mast with your corpse."

The crew surrounded him, grim and determined. Edward did not think he could defeat them all, in spite of the little voice in his head urging him to try. Even if he did, he still couldn't sail the *Rose* by himself.

"I will take the boat," he said. "Let me get my bag."

The crew voiced their protest, Trog loudest. "No! He'll just cast another spell."

"No bag, Mr. Truscott," Captain Davies said. "You may appeal to the Devil for your salvation."

"I have nothing to do with the Devil," Edward retorted.

"Then you can find your solace in other places."

It took six men, weakened as they were, to put the boat in position. Edward straightened his back and stepped into it. It swayed, throwing him off balance, and he sat abruptly.

Several men laughed, but most just stared. Sam watched him through the ship's rail.

"For the love of G—" the word stuck in Edward's throat, and he could not spit it out. "Have mercy!"

His only answer came in the snap of canvas in the wind and waves against the hull. The crew lined the rail to watch him being lowered to the sea.

He stopped descending with a slap of water and started to rise and fall with the motion of the waves. The ropes fell slack; an end fell loose and whipped through the pulleys, and he was free of the *Rose*, drifting.

Captain Davies barked something, his words lost to Edward, and one by one the men left the rail. The *Rose* slowly turned. Her sails caught the breeze. Timber and rope creaked as the ship leaned forward, her bow throwing up spray and she gathered speed.

She long remained the only thing on the sea, dwindling to the west as the sun chased her down and passed her. Finally, they both disappeared into the horizon together, leaving Edward alone.

Chapter Four

While the Captain had called it the small boat, it could easily carry eight men. Edward untied the set of oars from the seat and unwrapped their sailcloth covering. A small trunk was stowed under the stern seat, and a quick investigation revealed a compass, fishhook and line, and a tin of pilot bread. Water had turned the pilot bread into a mass of fuzzy black mold, and Edward pitched it over the side.

Long before the *Twilight Rose* vanished over the horizon, he had unshipped the oars and begun to follow after her. He rowed badly, and sent the boat one way, over-corrected, and sent it the other. He constantly looked over his shoulder, trying to make sure he followed the *Rose*.

It was hopeless, he knew, but he had to do something. The compass did him little good since he didn't know what direction to sail. Even knowing the direction wouldn't help without a Seawitch's magic to guide him properly.

He kept a steady, if uneven, stroke throughout the afternoon and early evening. The sun, his energy, and his spirits all sank at once. He sagged in the seat, his limbs lethargic. After a minute he laid the dripping oars along the gunwale and sat, feeling the boat rise and fall with the waves.

He took the bottle of *aqua vitae* from his pocket and unscrewed the top then held it to the sun's afterglow. With a sigh, he placed the bottle to his lips and tilted it up. He let the liquid drain into his mouth and waited to let any that clung to the sides trickle out.

Finished, he threw the bottle as far as he could.

The next day, sharks began circling. Large, lazy circles, sometimes deeper, sometimes so shallow their dorsal fins sliced the surface.

He came to know them, knew their colors, knew their style. The biggest he named Sir Shark. It would stay furthest while the smaller sharks circled closest to the boat. Their colors varied in a narrow range of grey, and two of the sharks had pale scars that set them apart.

Another way to find true death.

It made him pause to think of ways to kill *zumbis*.

Dismemberment, decapitation, immolation, and the removal of their heart were all said to truly kill *zumbis*. He knew that much but wasn't certain of his knowledge. He had heard of *zumbi* losing an arm and still attacking, so clearly some dismemberments were more effective than others. Cutting out their hearts seemed a lot of work. If you could cut out their hearts, you could more easily cut off their heads, so could he really trust those stories?

He did not doubt the circling sharks could manage a very effective dismemberment should they get a chance to feed on him.

Perhaps he just didn't know enough, or was getting confused, but he thought he recalled people who cut off *zumbis'* heads, and removed their hearts, and then burned the lot. One couldn't be too careful, he supposed.

"How truly morbid," he said to the sharks. "I'm already Dead, yet I worry of ways to die." He took up the oars and gauged the position of the sun. "West," he said. "West on the trail of the sun and the *Twilight Rose*. And to Hell with you, Sir Shark."

☠

"Maybe you should fear me," he muttered to the sharks as he rowed. "I am the monster here."

He could row for hours, far beyond his expectations. The sun did not bother him. He did not hunger or thirst. He only stopped when lethargy overcame him, making him sit for hours as the boat drifted.

On the fourth day, during the heat of the day, the sharks vanished. Something else swam these waters. It lingered in the depths of the ocean and the corners of his eyes. It was smaller than Sir Shark, but faster and more graceful. It wasn't a shark; it must be a fish of some sort. He leaned over the side, trying to get a better view. Something that fast could be dangerous.

Suddenly it shot upwards, and he fell back as it burst from the water. The boat rocked with him, then back as the fish landed on the gunwale. Drops of water rained for a second. Edward scrambled backwards to get away from the fish.

Except it wasn't a fish.

It was a woman.

"I must be mad!" he exclaimed.

She lay on her arms, which were folded on the gunwale, watching him with fathomless black eyes. Her hair was a dark blue-green, hinting toward black, the color of the sea as one sank beyond the light of the surface. It changed as she moved, sometimes lighter, sometimes darker, a little bluer, a little greener. It took highlights like the sun on the surface of the water.

She laughed at him. "I love that expression."

Edward blinked and shook his head. She still remained. "I beg your pardon. You have the advantage of me."

"Of course, I do. You're alone in a small boat and will drift until you starve or madness drives you overboard. Although," she added, "I'd have thought you'd be further along that path, in spite of your first words."

"You are," he hesitated, so outlandish seemed the idea, "a mermaid, aren't you?"

She twisted a little and a large, silvery tail rose out of the water beside her and waved at him. It smacked back down with a loud *crack*. "I suppose I am," she answered.

"Why are you here?"

"Humans amuse me, especially sailors."

"I'm not a sailor."

"Does that mean you won't be swearing at me?"

"I hadn't thought to," he said, bewildered. With her tail out of sight, she looked all woman.

"You're not nearly as fun as some of the others. Usually they chase me." She pushed herself up and took a deep breath showing Edward why the sailors might chase her.

Edward steadfastly kept his eyes on her face. She had an open expression, but he decided he didn't like what lurked beneath it. She enjoyed teasing, maybe even luring men out of the boats and into the depths where they would drown. Weak, exhausted sailors would make easy prey.

"Perhaps they chase you because they like seafood," he said.

The mermaid sank back down to hang on the side of the boat. "That's a terrible thing to say."

He shrugged. "Starving and half mad, they might not even know what they want."

Her eyes narrowed and tail smacked the water as she looked around the boat. "*You're* doing well without food or water."

He snorted his disbelief.

"Was your ship wrecked?" she asked.

"No."

"Well, you didn't row here by yourself." She cocked her head. "England?"

Edward nodded. "London. How did you guess?"

"You might have been American." She switched languages and spoke in French. "See?" she said, indicating his lack of comprehension, switching back to English. "We weren't speaking French." She spoke again, changing back and forth between different languages and English. "Or Dutch. Or German. Or Irish. Or Swedish. And you don't look Spanish or Italian or dress like a Moor.

"I am wondering," she went on, "what you did that made your shipmates set you adrift without food or water."

"I tended them in their sickness." Edward didn't try to keep from sounding bitter.

"Well, that will do it. Now you know better." She lay back, reclining on the surface and moving with languid sweeps of her tail. "Are you sure you don't want to join me?"

"Yes." He unshipped the oars and prepared to begin rowing. He did not have time to waste.

"Pity. I like humans." She dove and came up at the stern. Her weight pulled down the boat and made rowing difficult. "You're in a hurry."

He didn't answer.

"No sense hurrying," she said. "Nobody survives being castaway in this part of the ocean."

Pausing long enough to nod politely, Edward said, "I beg your pardon, but I intend to try. I am, by the way, Edward Truscott. I haven't had the pleasure of your name."

"Terra."

He stopped rowing. "Terra? A mermaid named Terra?"

"My parents had a strange sense of humor."

"Evidently."

She laid her head on her arms. "Don't mind me. I'll just sun myself a bit."

Edward resumed rowing. "Do you know the way to the Narrow World?" he asked.

"Oh, the Narrow World. You want to go to the Narrow World?" She began to move her tail, and the boat moved faster. "But where is it?" The boat heeled over as she leaned. Edward dropped an oar to steady himself. The oar slipped over the side and the boat kept moving, faster and faster, cutting a wide circle in the water.

"Where is the Narrow World?" Terra taunted as she closed the circle and started another.

"What are you doing?" shouted Edward. The dropped oar bobbed a dozen yards away.

"I'm you." Terra laughed, a wild sound. "I'm in a hurry, but I don't know where I'm going, so I go in circles." Her tail churned the water and the bow kicked up spray. "You should be glad, I'm saving you time. You can get twice the number of circles finished before sunset."

"I don't want circles! I want to reach the Narrow World."

"You will never reach it in this boat." Terra stopped, throwing Edward off his seat. "I suppose," she said with exaggerated thought. "It is *possible*." She resumed pushing the boat.

"Stop!" Edward scrambled up. He lifted the second oar and threatened her with it. She laughed. *Kill her,* the little voice urged him. He swung the oar.

She vanished into the water, and the oar cracked against the side of the boat. "Devil take it!" Edward swore, examining the broken oar. He finished snapping it and spun the blade end over the waves. It skipped twice before catching the water.

That was stupid, he thought. *Do not listen to the voice. Do* not *listen to the voice.* He dropped the oar shaft into the bottom of the boat.

"Madness," he muttered.

The other oar still floated, now further away.

The boat rocked, making him stumble. "That wasn't very friendly." Terra hung off the bow. "Usually men are more amorous than that."

A wave of despondency washed over Edward. He sank onto the seat. "To what end? To chase you to their deaths?" He dropped his head. "Nonetheless, I apologize."

"If you saw them, you might say I do them a service." He looked at her, not catching her meaning. "The men," she said. "Starving, dirty, mad creatures they are. Men without hope, and I tell you truly they have no hope. Storm, sun, or sharks; something will kill them. Better they drown quickly in the cool depths than burn slowly in the sun."

"A right angel of mercy you are."

She laughed and smacked her tail on the water. "Don't you know mermaids are always born in the morning when the sky is red?"

"I didn't know that," Edward admitted. He sat quietly, his energy drained. "Have I really been going in circles?"

Terra shrugged. "Not during the day. A few at night, yes."

"Damn." A thought came to him. "Do you know the way to the Narrow World?"

"Edward Truscott, I am not an agent of mercy. But even were I to tell you, you still could not reach it."

"You could take me. Pushing the boat? With your tail?" He lifted his eyebrows in a hopeful expression.

"You have nothing I want."

Edward opened the small trunk. "A compass?" He held it up. "Brass, very—" He dropped it back in when he saw her expression. "A fishhook and I—? No, you wouldn't want that. An empty biscuit tin? A length of rope? A broken oar? Everything I have?"

He dropped the tin back into the trunk and began to pat his pockets, hoping he had overlooked something. "Wait," he said. "What are these?" He fished into his trouser pockets and drew out the coins Undulark had given him.

Terra raised herself up on the gunwale and stretched to see. She gasped slightly.

Edward stared at her. Her eyes never left his palm. "I do have something you want after all."

"Give me two of those coins, and I will see you safely to the Narrow

World."

Edward picked up a coin and turned it over in his fingers, examining it closely for the first time. The detailed mother of pearl violet stood out from the reddish-brown bronze. The reverse side sported a glyph or a rune, or a symbol of something he did not recognize, but struck him as looking ancient. Bringing it closer to his face he saw that the letters, minute to the point of illegibility were nonetheless precisely stamped.

He dropped the coin back into his palm and closed his fist. He could try to bargain, but the feeling of relief was too strong. He would give all the coins to see the Narrow World. Giving up two when he had six seemed a small price indeed. Still, some assurances were needed.

"For two of these coins," he said slowly, feeling his way through the idea, "you will ensure I reach the Narrow World?"

"Yes." She still stared at his fist.

"Safely?" He did not trust her.

"Yes."

"Two?"

She nodded. "Yes."

He had a way to the Narrow World after all.

"Very well, Terra. I will give you two of these coins if you will take me safely to the Narrow World."

"Let me see them."

Edward opened his fist and took out two coins, closing his fist over the others before sliding them back into his pocket. He dropped the two into her waiting hands.

She made them disappear, somewhere, then leapt completely out of the water, turned, and dove headfirst back into it. Edward leaned over to look, but she was gone.

"No!" He rushed to the other side of the boat, then to the bow, then the stern. "No!" he shouted again, lifting his fists to the sky. "Are there no honest creatures under sky or sea?"

He didn't expect an answer, and didn't get one.

"Damn."

What good was one oar, especially as it floated beyond his reach? He was a poor swimmer, but could manage that distance. That would give him something, though he paddled worse than he rowed.

"Something is better than nothing," he muttered as he slipped off his shoes.

He swung one leg over the gunwale and dipped his foot into the water. A long, grey shape rose out the depths.

"Damn."

Something else flickered in the water, smaller than the shark, faster and paler. Terra surfaced. "Pass me a rope," she said.

"I thought you left."

"The King's Regard lose their power if taken by theft or trickery," she said. She took the rope and looped it through a small pulley affixed to the bow. After knotting the rope, she dove underwater. A moment later the boat surged forward.

"This will take a while," Terra said, swimming alongside.

"Wait. How am I moving, if you're here?" Edward craned his neck to see the taut rope stretched out to a shark fin leading the boat. "I'm being towed by a shark?"

"You expected horses for your carriage?"

"I don't know what to expect anymore." He started to think of what he might expect in the Narrow World, for he had no idea what he would do when he got there.

☠

"There." Terra's word roused Edward from his stupor, those times of lethargy that seemed to substitute for sleep. While he could force himself to stay alert, it was far easier to let his mind go blank. He just needed to remember to close his eyes so that Terra didn't get nervous.

He opened his eyes. An island loomed large ahead, only its outline distinct in the moonlight. It was mountainous, that was all he could tell.

The moon hung high over the ocean. *Silver leaf*, and the thought seemed accurate. The moonlight highlighted the waves with patches of silver that looked like floating leaves.

"I'll land you near Port Astarte," Terra said. "But not in the town. They don't care for mermaids, really."

A breeze blew out from the island, bringing warm air and the smells of land. Brine, stranded fish—these he knew; other smells, he couldn't identify.

"I," he stopped and swallowed, unsure of his emotions. "I want to thank you."

Terra didn't answer, but kept swimming alongside the boat.

Soon the sound of surf rose out of the night, much as the mountain rose out of the sea. Terra vanished and a moment later the boat stopped. She reappeared at the stern and steered the boat with her tail. Waves broke two hundred yards from the beach, so they traveled parallel to the shore until they found a hole in the reef.

Thirty yards from shore Terra paused. "You can walk from here, if you wish."

"Thank you," Edward said. "I don't know what I would have done."

After a long pause Terra said. "It is just as well. You've a story I don't wish to know." She gave the boat a push. The waves of her dive were lost in the surf.

Her push carried the boat forward until the keel ground in the sand. He climbed out. The water came midway up his calves. The next wave rose to mid-thigh, lifting the boat and pushing it further forward before dropping it back onto the bottom.

He dragged the boat to the beach. It was lighter than he expected. He left it above the high tide mark, trudging away, wiping his hands on his shirt.

He had reached the Narrow World.

The wind changed with the dawn. It now blew in from the sea, bringing cool air to start the day. Edward stood on a rocky headland, looking down at Port Astarte.

Buildings clustered around the harbor, pushing inland most thickly in the center and tapering around the edges, making the town into a crescent. A wide road ran from the main quay inland, cutting the town in half. The town itself wore a thousand years of motley architecture.

On the far side of the harbor stood a walled compound with a pagoda-shaped warehouse inside. A boardwalk connected the compound to a gated dock where a Chinese junk was tied.

Next to it stood a white plastered house. Four fluted columns supported a low pediment above the doorway. Red tiles covered the roof. It gave the impression of having been transplanted from ancient Greece.

Elsewhere, Edward thought he could see examples of buildings from India, Spain, and Persia. Some were built of local stone and timber; others must have been imported from places around the world.

At the end of the main street opposite the docks stood a fantastic building built from rose-colored coral that caught the rays of the rising sun and for a moment glowed with the promise of the new day. He couldn't begin to name its architectural style.

A few early risers walked the streets. Most of the activity was in the harbor where dozens of skiffs were taking men to fish or pearl dive, or whatever they did to live.

He noted that apart from the Chinese junk, the only sizable ship was the black-hulled *Reach of Goa*, anchored out in the bay. The *Twilight Rose* had not arrived yet. With luck he could get help, or at least directions, and be gone before she did.

The place was interesting, yes, but he felt somewhat disappointed. Had he expected more? Had he expected magic going off like fireworks? Perhaps, he admitted to himself. After all, he started toward Port Astarte aboard an enchanted ship and finished it towed by a mermaid. Perhaps he *had* expected something a little more flamboyant.

He had the clothes he wore, a brass compass, twenty yards of rope frayed at one end by rough shark skin, a fishing hook and line, and four coins.

I'm here.

Palm fronds rustled in the breeze. As he descended the slope to town, he passed other trees, their leaves a dark green and slightly glossy, small white blossoms interspersed at the ends of the branches. A sweet citrusy smell filled the air, and he paused, breathing deeply to draw the scent into his nostrils.

He stumbled, jerked upright, over-correcting and stumbled the other way. He felt awkward. Was I just careless, he wondered, or is the Dead overtaking me?

How long has it been since I had aqua vitae? He couldn't seem to tally the days.

A half hour later, he reached the first fisherman's shacks on the outskirts of town. There were no roads here, just stretches of fine white sand broken by small shacks, sea grass, and palm trees.

Somebody started playing the pipes: light, brisk music, music for the love of music, because a beautiful day should be greeted with song. The tune spun over the beach like the breeze, and Edward smiled as he listened. Voices called to the player, cheerful words from neighbors used to such beginnings.

The town felt different than London. Not rural, like Cornwall, but relaxed, like business and life would take care of itself. A ship's chandlery had its door open, letting in the morning breeze while waiting for customers, whenever they should arrive.

He could feel time piled on itself in the greyed clapboard, the cut blocks of coral, the yellow-white brick of a type he had never seen before. Even the wood buildings gave hints of their age with tarnished brass fixtures and windows where years of sea spray had left dried salt like rime on the window glass.

Little drifts of sand piled in corners and filled in between the cobbles. He couldn't tell if they swept the streets or let the wind cover and uncover them as it wished.

Several shops specialized in porcelain. A quick count yielded three on this stretch of street. The nearest sold ware from England and France. He recognized Miles Mason's ironstone pottery in the window.

The other two shops advertised local porcelain. The sides of the vessels were thick and sometimes irregular. The patterns were clumsy, and Edward decided in this, at least, the Wide World surpassed the Narrow. He could mix and form porcelain better. But, as the number of shops and the fact people stopped to look showed, they didn't lack for a market.

Edward paused under cream-colored awnings, a heavy linen canvas likely cut from an old sail that protected a shop from the sun. Both the sign on the wall and the words on the door read, "Jaloney, Scrivener, Illuminator."

Scriveners were educated people. They dealt in papers and books. He didn't have any money, but Undulark's coins had bought him passage with the mermaid, perhaps they could help here. He ducked under the awning to peer in the window.

In spite of being a scrivener's shop, the only thing in the window was a long-stemmed, red-and-white amaryllis in a clay pot. He could see shelves with books along one wall. Yes, in a town of magic he might just find a useful text at the scrivener's shop. He opened the door and went in.

The shop smelled of vellum and roses. A hurricane lamp hung in the back of the shop, supplementing the diffused light from the windows.

Under it hunched a corpulent woman, head bowed, writing at a large table covered in vellum, blotting paper, and dozens of bottles of variously colored ink. She lifted her head to stare at him with small, sharp eyes set in a puffy face.

"Good morning," Edward said.

She did not reply.

At a loss for words, Edward stammered, "I'll, ah, just look over your books." When she did not object, he stepped over to the shelf and read the titles.

Some books were titled in English, others were in foreign languages, but all had parchment slips that told the title in tiny but legible script. Apparently Jaloney did business in English, French, Russian, Greek, Arabic, and two oriental languages.

Each book was bound in tooled leather with gold stamped lettering. Mikhail Lomonosov, *A Word on the Formation of Metals From Earth Tremors*; Murasaki Shikibu, *The Tale of Genji*; Quintus Ennius, *Annales*; Washington Irving, *The Sketchbook of Geoffrey Crayon, Gent.*; Charles Dickens, *The Life and Times of Nicholas Nickleby*.

"Dickens?" he asked, glancing at the woman in surprise. She did not answer.

"Do you have any other books?" He knew to not ask for necromancy, but he might still inquire discreetly.

She pulled a rag from some back pocket and cleaned the tip of her pen. She set the pen down and put the rag back in her pocket. "What are you looking for?"

"Something, I don't know, a keepsake from Port Astarte," Edward said. "A local history or a book of magic?"

She did not answer immediately, just looked at him, her face expressionless. Her gaze felt heavy, making him uncomfortable. Finally, she said, "I have what you see."

Edward nodded, abashed. "Of course." He felt the need to justify himself. "I just thought it would be nice to have something—something more unique than," he fumbled and waved at the books, "Charles Dickens. I didn't mean to imply anything."

She shifted in her chair. "I don't take kindly to people telling me what I can and can't sell."

"Pardon?" He hadn't told her anything of the kind.

She leaned forward, very slightly. "Tell the Prester he needn't send people to trick me. I don't sell dark grimoires."

"I don't know what, ah," Edward stopped as he realized what she meant. "I'm not with them. The Custodian people, I mean. I don't really want to meet them, actually."

Her expression did not change.

"I'm not with them!" he shouted, suddenly angry. He lifted his arm and stopped, realizing he was about to sweep all the books from the shelf. He spun on his heel. "I'm not with them," he snarled again before fleeing the shop, appalled at his own violence.

He stumbled out into the street. Damn the Custodians! The *Reach of God* was the only European ship in port so Jaloney had no reason to believe he wasn't with them.

Could he expect the same reaction from others?

He leaned against a palm tree, sulking. Port Astarte no longer felt cheerful and friendly. It felt poisoned.

Was this what helplessness felt like, to know what he needed to do, but not how? How could he succeed if people associated him with the Custodians?

He must find a way.

The wind shifted, swirling a bit, and brought a new smell. He smelled the most enticing stew. It was different, some meat he couldn't place. Not beef, or lamb, or goat, but it tugged at him, pulled him toward a small shop on the corner, so mesmerizing that he didn't even bother to read the sign, just pushed open the door and entered.

He immediately saw what he wanted, a large iron cauldron taking up the entire hearth. Steam rose with the smell of the stew. Edward stared at it, unable to take his eyes from it even as he fought the urge to help himself. He had never felt such an urge to eat, especially since becoming Dead. But it wasn't his stew, and he had no money.

He had Undulark's coins. He reached into his pocket, his fingers clumsy in his haste.

"Can I help you?"

A middle-aged man came in from the back, wiping his hands on a dirty towel. He wore an apron, not a cook's apron, a brown leather craftsman's apron. A hinged magnifying loupe was raised on his wire-framed spectacles.

Edward blinked. This man was not a cook. There was a counter, but it was not a bar. There were no stools, only a flat space to transact business.

"I came in because I smelled your stew," he stammered.

"My stew?" The man seemed surprised and amused. "Aye, I sometimes call it that, but not before my clients. A bit irreverent. This is not a tavern."

"Please," Edward said. The smell was so compelling; he needed to eat, even if this wasn't a tavern. "Please, I can pay." He held out Undulark's coins.

The man drew near, his expression perplexed. He stopped suddenly, then, without apparent haste, walked to the hearth and picked up a large black lid and dropped it over the cauldron. Using a steel hook, he picked up the cauldron and pulled it off the fire.

"I think it's best to take this off for now."

Edward blinked. The smell lessened, and he felt a stab of disappointment. "I've never smelled stew like that."

"No, I don't suppose you have, but being what you are, it affects you differently."

Cold rushed to Edward's stomach. "What I am?"

"Aye, a *zumbi*. Recently Undead, a week or so, if you can still control yourself like that." He did not seem horrified or afraid.

"You're mistaken," Edward said. This was a dangerous conversation to have. "I should leave."

The man waved a hand. "I don't care if you stay. You proved your restraint when you didn't try to eat me. My boiling's a mighty temptation, though."

The lingering smell still pulled on him, so Edward asked, "What is it?"

The man gave a short bark of a laugh. "It's human flesh, lad. I'm a Bone Illustrator."

The words shocked Edward, and he looked around the shop. Skeletons hung on each side of the door; skulls adorned the mantel. A painted board explained the charges for painting, carving, and inlaying. There was a surcharge for gilding and an invitation to inquire about custom materials.

Painted scenes covered the bones, scenes of drinking and fighting, hunting whales, and foreign lands.

"It isn't much, but he didn't leave me much to work with." The man shrugged, a 'you do what you can' gesture, and said, "Tramp sailor."

"I don't understand."

"You don't know Bone Illustrators, then," the man said. "I illustrate a man's bones with scenes of his life."

"Why?"

"It's a way to remember, a way for a man to live beyond his death."

"Ah. Do people display them at home?" Edward thought displaying decorated skeletons was particularly morbid.

"Some do. Most hang them in a crypt. It becomes something of a family record."

The skeleton to the right of the door was more lavishly decorated than the one to the left. This man, a cursory examination revealed, was a Scot, had loved many women, hunted tigers in India, fought the King's wars in America, sought his fortune in the Far East. He had loved and fought and drank and gambled furiously. When he ended up in Port Astarte, sick and alone, he had no heirs and only enough money to pay the Bone Illustrator to record his life.

"He had no family," the Bone Illustrator said. "So he stays here." He seemed to be studying Edward.

Uncomfortable, Edward edged toward the door.

"You needn't leave," said the Illustrator. "I've already said you're welcome. I'm just trying to figure you out. I fancy myself a fair judge of people—need to be, really. I paint people's lives, not their fantasies, so I need to know when they spin me a tale.

"I know a bit about death, too," he went on. "I recognize it in you. You're not from here, or I'd know you. The only ships that ported recently belong to the Chinese and the *Custos de Luminos*." He smiled wryly. "I doubt you came with either."

"Ah—no, I didn't." Edward decided he liked this man. He stuck out his hand. "Edward Truscott. At your service."

"Oh, yes. Anolan Bardson, at yours."

He didn't care that Edward was Dead, and the faint smell of the boiling pot still tugged at him, even though the idea repelled him. "I came from London," Edward said. "And I've been Dead almost four weeks." He thought for a second. "Maybe more."

"Four weeks?" The illustrator looked impressed. "How is it you can still control yourself?"

"I really don't know much about Dead," Edward said. "There was no time to learn. I had to rush to catch a ship to come here. I was told"—he hesitated, not sure he should divulge his purpose—"I was told to seek help in the Narrow World." Wiser not to mention necromancers.

But the Bone Illustrator shook his head. "Not likely to find a cure for Dead, even here. I've never heard it happen. A person can fight it, maybe slow it down a bit if they're strong willed, but cure it?" He shook his head again.

"You obviously know more of it than I do."

Anolan shrugged, dismissive of the compliment. "Normally it only takes two weeks for Dead to overwhelm its victims. People become violent and gain a taste for meat, especially," he glanced at the cauldron, "human meat."

"I had a drink…" Edward said tentatively. "It's gone now. *Aqua vitae?*"

"*Aqua vitae?*" The illustrator's eyes grew wide. "True *aqua vitae?* Where did you get that? That's no easy brew, and I'd have said not a dozen people alive could make it!"

"My neighbor gave it to me."

"Lad, I think I want to hear your tale, from the beginning."

Edward began, unsure at first. He told of the creature in the alley behind the Painted Man's shop and feeling ill that night. He recounted his meeting with Undulark, his rush to catch the *Twilight Rose*, the crew. The illustrator looked horrified at Trog drinking the *aqua vitae*.

Edward told of the sickness, the three deaths, and how the crew turned on him. His days adrift, meeting the mermaid, and being brought to the Narrow World. "And I walked into town this morning," he ended.

"Lad, you're on your way to a well-painted skeleton."

"I'd rather not be."

"Aye. I can understand that," Anolan said. "I don't know this 'Painted Man.' He might be an exile from the Narrow World. If he was keeping that creature, then good riddance to him. I don't care for the *Custos*, but they do a needed job. Bad luck you got scratched in the fight.

"As for your neighbor," he went on. "Let me just say your luck's as good as it is bad."

"You know him?"

"Me? No. I'm just a humble bone painter. I know of him, though. He might have told you more, but seeing how near you were to missing your ship, it's a good thing he didn't." He lapsed into silence.

"What might he have told me?"

The illustrator laughed. "Heaven help me! I don't know. I've already told you all I know. Ask me how to inlay a femur instead. But make no mistake, a man who once served as—oh, wait, of course." He snapped his fingers. "You'd want to talk with Ascourt. He's the Royal Astrologer now."

"Ascourt?"

"Right. Out this door, around the right. Past the church, turn to your left. He lives at the end of the street in a house styled after a castle tower. Says it keeps the peasants out." He snorted. "The fool acts like this is fifteenth century France. He's not as sharp as old Undulark, but he's the best we have now."

"I'll try him, thank you."

"But Ed," Anolan said in a more serious tone. "*Zumbi* are killed. They have to be. A person like you is usually kept guarded, then restrained, until they are no longer themselves. Then…"

"I don't want to be killed!" Edward cried. "Undulark gave me hope, and I want to return to Becca."

"Were it anyone but Undulark, I'd say you had false hope," Anolan said. "You're a hazard, lad, and you're going to get worse. Best you hurry to find your cure."

Edward turned, meaning to leave, and took a step toward the cauldron. Suddenly angry, he corrected himself and pulled open the door.

"I won't turn you in, lad," said Anolan, "for the *aqua vitae* buys you time. But you haven't much before others will see you for what you are."

☠

A small church stood on the corner opposite the Bone Illustrator's shop. Perhaps a coincidence, perhaps not. It was a square building surmounted by a ribbed dome. Ornamental half-columns formed the side casings of the windows and doors; the head casings were pediments.

A sign proclaimed the name of the church in sun-faded Greek letters, under which somebody had written "Ekklesia Hagion Nikolaos," and under that, a third person scrawled "Shrine of Holy Nicholas."

A wrought iron fence surrounded the churchyard, which was mostly sand with some palm trees and spiny bushes with thick, waxy leaves. Edward laid his hand on the fence. It burned, and he immediately took it off. His sense of feel had become dull, but that pain felt sharp and clear.

It was early in the day for the iron to have grown so hot. He walked along the fence, his hand hovering over the top. He wanted to try again, curious as to the heat, but feared the pain. He came to the open gate and swung his leg to go in.

His leg began to itch and burn, and he hurriedly stepped back. He recalled burying the crew of the *Twilight Rose* and not finding the words for a prayer, and even, though he couldn't say why he thought of this, hurrying across the churchyard in London after confronting the beast and feeling the fresh scrape itch.

Could that—? His mind balked, sought other things, like the group of men striding up the street from the quay.

They walked down the center of the street, three wide and three deep. With their black frock coats they looked like a dark cloud. The man in the front, in the center, wore a wide-brimmed hat and had a clerical collar on his coat. Prester Ellis, who had warned Captain Davies.

They walked with authority, like policemen, or like soldiers patrolling a conquered city. Edward shuddered as they drew near. He ducked his head to avoid their gaze.

"Wait."

Edward looked up. Prester Ellis walked toward him, his men trailing behind him like smoke. Edward tensed, looking for an escape.

"Don't run from me, boy," he said.

Edward didn't answer. He wanted to run, he wanted to lash out, but he felt trapped by the church on one side and Prester Ellis on the other. Before he could decide, Ellis stood before him.

If the thought of Prester Ellis scared Edward, the presence was far worse. Ellis tipped his head back to stare up at Edward, so close the brim of his hat almost touched Edward's face. Edward took a step back.

Ellis exuded—judgment, if that were the right word. His sharp eyes studied, moved, and studied some more. His expression was dour, brows slightly drawn together, only his eyes moving. Something in his manner screamed "magistrate" or worse, "inquisitor."

Ellis sniffed. "I thought so. You're Dead. An abomination. Grab him."

"No! Wait!" Edward shouted as strong hands grabbed him. "I'm not. I've just been in the Bone Illustrator's. That's what you smell!"

"Can you pray?" Ellis demanded. "Do it now."

Edward opened his mouth, but no words came out. It was as if his body refused to obey him.

"You're a thing of darkness," Ellis said. "All things holy abhor you."

"Unhand me!" He pulled free from the men, but they hedged him in, surrounding him so tightly he couldn't move.

"Should I get our equipment from the ship, Prester?" asked one of the men.

"Indeed yes."

"What do you intend?" Edward demanded, as the man raced toward the quay.

"To destroy you, of course."

"By the Devil, I won't let you!"

"Calling your master won't help," said Ellis.

Edward ignored that. "By what right do you speak murder so casually?"

Ellis snorted, as if the question were ridiculous. "By the power of Holy Truth."

Several men had stopped to watch.

"Help me!" Edward called. "They mean to kill me!"

"Silence!" growled a man behind him, smacking the back of his head.

The watchers glanced at each other, clearly unsure what they should do.

"Help me!" Edward called again. "I've done nothing!"

"Lay your minds to rest," Ellis called. "We do God's work."

"Here now!" shouted a voice. Anolan stood at the corner of his shop. "Who made you hangman, Prester?"

"This is a *zumbi*," Ellis said. "It is my duty to rid the world of its taint."

"You're not in England, Prester. It's our King's privilege you're encroaching on." He looked around, speaking for the benefit of the others who watched. "This isn't your island, even if you treat it like it is."

More men gathered, muttering and glaring, but Edward couldn't tell if it were at him or Prester Ellis.

Ellis's expression didn't change, but he sounded angry. "Your own laws allow for the killing of *zumbis*."

"True enough," said Anolan, "but it's not for you to accuse, try, and execute."

The townsfolk growled their agreement. Edward allowed himself to hope they might force his release. He drew a very deep breath and blinked several times. *See,* he urged them in his mind, *I'm not Dead. Save an innocent.*

Ellis growled, a low, animal sound. "Fine. Bring him," he ordered his men. He spun on his heel and started up the street. "We shall see what the King says about this viper you harbor."

The *Custos* followed, pushing Edward, keeping so close he had to use short steps so as not to entangle himself in their legs. He heard the crowd behind him, and he tried to look, but the *Custos* forced his pace, and he could only look ahead at Prester Ellis's stiff back, and beyond, to the King's palace at the end of the street.

Chapter Five

Even as anxious as he was, Edward couldn't help but stare at the palace. It looked part castle, part temple, and part university; and it wasn't large. Although it was the largest building in Port Astarte, the rebuilt Palace at Westminster in London would dwarf it when complete. But this King's home *was* elegant.

Crown towers, caryatid-supported arches, exotic statuary—it all blended harmoniously together. It didn't look like the home of a brutal man. Edward took hope from that.

The crowd stopped at the entrance, Anolan muttering in a voice pitched to carry, "Good luck, Lad. You don't need us now, though I fear you've little future with the King. At least he'll be merciful."

Edward's newly taken hope slipped away.

The *Custos* pushed the Bone Illustrator back toward the town and Edward onto the grounds of the palace.

The troop, led by Prester Ellis walking straight and proud, entered through great double doors darkened by time so they exuded antiquity, over patterned floors of malachite and lapis lazuli, and approached another set of doors, bronze with a rich red-brown patina.

"We would like to see the King," Ellis told the pair of guards before the doors.

"One does not summon the King to his own throne room," said one of the guards.

"Is he not here?" Ellis demanded.

"The King is currently busy."

"We shall await his pleasure."

The guards exchanged glances, and the man who had spoken, with a slight eye roll, jerked his head to indicate the other should go to the king. The second guard opened the door and slipped inside.

"He will be informed you are waiting," said the first guard.

Prester Ellis paced the anteroom, hands clasped behind his back and face stony as he looked at the frescoed walls and brass and colored glass lanterns.

Edward stirred and opened his mouth to protest his treatment, to beseech the guard, but the men holding him tightened their grips.

Ellis noticed the movements and said, "If you try anything, *zumbi*, I'll have your head from your shoulders and make my apologies to King Jeremy afterwards." He turned his attention to the pastoral scene painted on the wall. "But don't worry. We won't wait long. We have too many cannon to be ignored."

The return of the guard proved him right. "The King will be here shortly. He invites you to wait in the throne room until he arrives." The two guards swung open the throne room doors and ushered them inside.

The *Custos* pushed and dragged Edward inside. "You'll keep your mouth shut, *zumbi*," hissed one in his ear.

Prester Ellis planted himself before the throne and stood, hands still clasped behind his back.

One of the *Custos* leaned close to Ellis and whispered earnestly. Ellis listened, shook his head and answered, "It takes little time."

The man spoke again, louder, and something in his voice worked on

Edward, teasing out a memory. His suspicion that the men who murdered the Painted Man were *Custos* was now a certainty; and not just *Custos*, but these very ones. The man talking with Prester Ellis was the same man who sought the creature that scratched Edward.

He tensed, and the men holding him tightened their grips again. "Do nothing, *zumbi*," warned the man holding his right arm.

Rage built in Edward. He measured the distance to Prester Ellis when a door opened behind the throne and a woman came out. Edward relaxed. She looked to be in her middle fifties, her step firm, her hair dark, though lightly touched with grey. She saw Ellis. "Oh. It's you."

Ellis inclined his head. "Your Majesty."

"It's not our custom to call dowagers 'Your Majesty,'" she said. "You may think it flattery, but it is an insult to the throne."

"No insult was intended, of course. Please think of it as cultural differences."

"Of course," she said coolly as she went to stand behind the throne. "Jeremy is just, well, here he is now."

A man entered, tall, broad-shouldered; he had curly dark hair and sun-bronzed skin. He wore three-quarter length trousers and a plain blue shirt. The trousers were linen, the shirt silk. The bottom two inches of the trousers were wet, and he had sand on his bare feet.

He settled onto the throne. "Very well, Prester. What is this about?"

Prester Ellis pointed at Edward. "Your Majesty, this man is a *zumbi*."

"Is he?" The King stared at Edward. "Yes, now that you mention it, I can see. I'm sorry young man," he said to Edward. "You look decent enough."

"So you will execute him?" Ellis said.

"In a couple weeks, I suppose I must."

"Wait!" The word burst out before Edward could stop it.

The *Custos* holding him threw him to the ground. The man on the left pulled back his fist, a tine like an ice pick appeared like magic between his knuckles.

"HOLD!" the King's voice thundered.

The man looked at Ellis, who, ever so slightly, shook his head. The tine slid back between the man's fingers, but he and his partner kept Edward pressed to the floor.

"You forget, Prester, who is King here. What does this regard?"

Ellis opened his mouth, but the King's voice said. "Not you. The young *zumbi*."

"Please." Edward twisted his head so he could see the throne. "It's because of them I'm this way."

"Really?" The King lifted an eyebrow. "Are you making *zumbi* now, Prester? I'm surprised."

Ellis snorted. "Of course not, Your Majesty."

"You murdered the Painted Man in London, didn't you?" Edward demanded. "You drove his creature into the alley where it scratched me."

The *Custos* Edward had recognized, who still stood next to Ellis, shifted position. "Prester—"

Ellis shushed him with a wave. He spoke to the king. "That is irrelevant. As a *zumbi,* he is a creature of evil. Your Majesty, you do his soul no favors by letting him exist."

The King frowned. "I'm afraid he's right, young man."

"I'm glad you agree, Your Majesty," Ellis said.

He was going to agree anyway, Edward thought. *The Reach of God* had too many cannon.

"His soul is not my concern," the King said. "But I can't let a *zumbi* roam freely on my island."

Kill them all, eat their flesh. Edward shuddered at the thought, that wasn't the answer. "Your Majesty, you mentioned regard." He pulled out Undulark's coins and held them out. "I have four."

The King's jaw went slack, his eyes round. He closed his mouth with a snap and glanced at his mother behind him.

"*Zumbi* are always restrained until they lose themselves," she said. "It is inhumane to kill them while they still know themselves."

"Yes. Yes, that's right," the King murmured. "Very well, Prester, I'll take care of this."

"Your Majesty—" Prester Ellis was frowning, the most severe expression Edward had seen on his face.

"He is my responsibility," the King said. "His soul is no longer in your hands, if, indeed, it ever was."

"Your Majesty—"

The King held up a hand. "You come here to protect England from dark magic, yet are responsible for a *zumbi* that ends up here."

"Not true, Your Majesty. I would have destroyed it by now if the

Bone Illustrator hadn't intervened."

"You spin pretty words rather than admit your guilt," the King said. "He is not England's problem, or yours."

"Evil is a problem wherever it may be."

"Do you doubt my ability to restrain him?"

"Not your ability, no."

Neither the King nor Ellis spoke. They just stared at each other, neither blinking nor looking away. The King seemed angry, while Ellis had smoothed his features and appeared completely unconcerned. Yet it was he who first spoke.

"As you say, Your Majesty. You have experience in this." He turned to leave, but stopped and looked down at Edward. "It is unfortunate you were scratched by the creature." He dipped his head, as if to underline his sincerity or just to say good-bye. The *Custos* released Edward and followed him out.

The bronze doors closed with a boom that echoed in the throne room. Nobody spoke. Edward scrambled to his feet and looked at the King, then the older woman behind the throne. When they didn't speak he looked at the guards. Nobody said anything.

"Ellis is unlikely to give up so easily," the Queen Mother finally said.

"He is a practical man," the King said. He seemed distracted, lost in his thoughts as he stared at the coins in Edward's hand.

She snorted.

"Perhaps I should have said he isn't rash. He has many cannon, but few men, and he knows the Chinese don't share his purpose. They might not sit quietly while he dismantles the port of their trading partner."

Done talking, both of them contemplated Edward.

"I want to live, Your Majesty."

The King glanced at his mother and turned back to Edward. He leaned forward. "Where did you get those coins?"

"My neighbor gave me six."

"Six! Where are the other two?"

"I gave them to a mermaid to see me safely here."

Groaning, the King sat back. "A mermaid has two. That'll cause trouble."

"That's tomorrow's trouble," the woman said. She stepped around the throne. "This neighbor," she said to Edward. "Name him."

"Undulark," Edward answered. "Undulark Mal-" he wasn't sure of the last name and wracked his memory. "Malfousa. Undulark Malfousa."

"So," she said quietly. "He is in London." She shook her head slowly. "You know him?"

The King cleared his throat. "That is irrelevant. I want those coins. Give them to me."

Edward closed his hand around them.

Kill him! Edward felt his hands twitch. He stilled them. But he couldn't let himself be locked up. He needed his freedom.

The bronze doors behind were closed, and Prester Ellis had gone out that way. Edward didn't want to risk meeting him. The only other way out lay behind the throne. He ran toward it.

Guards began shouting, running after him. The quickest thrust his spear between Edward's legs, tripping him. *I'm getting slow.*

As Edward tumbled to the ground he grabbed the spear and snapped it. *I'm getting strong.* And the little voice added, *Kill them all. Rend them, eat them.*

Somebody grabbed his arm and turned him over; the four coins sprayed across the floor. He shook the man off and lunged for the coins, but another man fell across his legs. More men grabbed his arms. He thrashed, but no sooner did he work a limb free than a different man seized it. The coins lay just out of reach.

"I want to live!" he shouted.

"Listen to me, *zumbi*," said the King, his voice cutting through the confusion. "You are already Dead."

"I don't want to be Dead!"

The guards started to drag him away, still kicking, but he heard the King's response. "Nobody does."

They threw him in a room and the door slammed closed. He flung himself against it, but it held fast. After pounding for a minute Edward turned to examine his new surroundings.

Except for the narrow windows, it didn't look like a prison. It had a low bed, which a quick examination showed to have a wooden frame with rope supports and a coir-stuffed mattress. There was a small table with a heavy porcelain pitcher and washbasin. There was a small chair, plain but sturdy, and a small carpet to cover the floor.

He would have expected less from a dungeon, more from a palace. He tried the door again. Going to the window, he reached out. Well, his hand would be free, if it weren't attached to his arm, which was anchored to his shoulder, which couldn't get past the window frame.

Foolishness, he thought.

Still, he must do something, and even as he thought of breaking the guard's spear, he wondered how strong he had gotten. He might be able to batter down the door if he placed his blows properly.

That would just alert the guards. He must be smarter than that.

I shouldn't have run. The King had seemed a decent man, but his sudden desire for the coins had unsettled Edward. He didn't trust it.

Lying down on the bed, he tried to think of ways to escape without alerting anyone.

He was still trying to think hours later when the door opened to admit a burly man, dressed in a leather blacksmith's apron, a heavy canvas shirt, and heavy trousers. He carried a large and wicked axe. Next came another man, this one carrying a bucket of whale oil and a candle.

Edward scrambled back, pressing his back into the corner to get as far away as he could. The men did not advance, just stood inside the door, but the threat of their presence could not be ignored.

The King came in, followed by his mother.

"Have you come to kill me?" Edward asked.

"You're already Dead," answered the King.

"I know that! I wish to live."

"Of course you do." The King took the chair and carried it near the door where he set it down so his mother could sit. Once she was seated, he walked to the small table and slapped his palm down. "These complicate things." He pulled away his hand, leaving behind the four King's Regards.

"The King's Regard," Edward said. "They have some value." He looked away. "You already have them."

The King snorted. "Call them rather the King's Favor. And I cannot simply take them." He slid them toward Edward and backed away.

Remembering the mermaid's words, Edward said, "They lose their power when stolen."

"So give them to me. You will be well cared for until you lose yourself.

Then I will see that your end is humane."

His mother stirred on the chair, pursed her lips, and shook her head slightly.

"That hardly seems fair value," Edward said. He placed a finger on one of the coins and slid it around the table before looking up to meet the King's eyes. "Dangerously close to trickery, Your Majesty, if you assume I don't know their value." He didn't know their value, but wasn't about to admit it.

The Queen Mother nodded slightly.

"Their value is open to interpretation," the King snapped. "And I am the King."

"And I am Dead. What do I have to lose?"

The Queen Mother snorted down a laugh, but composed herself as the King turned to look at her.

"Much can still happen you wouldn't like, *zumbi*," he said to Edward. "I want those coins."

"And I want to live."

"Listen to me, *zumbi*—" the King began.

"Enough, Jeremy," the Queen Mother interrupted. "If Undulark helped him, you should too."

"I can't imagine why Uncle Undulark gave him Regards."

"He is young," said his mother. The King turned to look at her. "He is young," she repeated, pointing at Edward, "and innocent, and, perhaps," she smiled faintly, "he is in love. Are you in love, young man?"

How did she guess? Edward nodded. "My name is Edward, and yes, there is a woman I love."

"Oh, good God," burst out the King. "Will Undulark never grow up?"

"Be glad for his sentimentality," snapped his mother. "Had he not helped when your father was in love, you would not be here. I shall be forever grateful, and you should too."

"Yes, Mother, I know. But six Regards! Why not just give him a full dozen?"

"Do you think curing Dead is possible?" When the king hesitated, she said, "Difficult tasks require much help. That is why he gave six." She turned back to Edward. "You may call me Daria. How did Undulark say to cure Dead?"

Edward pushed himself out of the corner and stood. The axe-man tensed, but Edward merely turned to look out the window. "He did not say. Only to find a necromancer."

"That just makes the situation better," the King said. Sarcasm dripped from his words.

"Shush," said Daria. "You expected it."

The king nodded. "I expected it." He paced the width of the room and sighed. "Tell me of your love."

Edward said, "I left her in Cornwall so I could seek my fortune, but she followed me to London, where I could not leave her again." He pictured Rebecca as he saw her last: harried and tired. "She is beautiful. The further I go, the more clearly I see her. Even when I fear I am losing my mind, my vision of her does not fail."

"But you left her again."

"How could I not? I am a monster, cast out when goodly people know my secret." He knew his words sounded bitter. "So, I beg you, cast me out as well, do not keep me here."

Nobody said anything.

"Is Prester Ellis truly responsible for your plight?" the King asked.

"Do you doubt it, Your Majesty?"

"No. I don't."

"Ellis would not care if bystanders were hurt," Daria said.

"Port Astarte is the bystander right now," the King said. "And I am responsible to make sure it doesn't get hurt. So, *zumbi*, are you worth my town?"

Edward did not answer, he could not answer, for how could he value himself over an entire town? But to say so seemed like surrender. He turned to look out the window again, east, toward London. *I'm not sure how I'll get out of this one, Becca.*

"I have the King's... Favor," he said.

After a long silence the King nodded. "And that complicates things. What do you want for them?"

"I want to live."

"I cannot do that. It is beyond my power."

"Then take me to a necromancer."

The King cast a sour look at Daria. "I expected it. We'll do it your way."

"Good." Daria tapped on the door. "Risking the ancient magic is more dangerous than Ellis's cannon." The door opened and a young woman entered, carrying a small crate. She glanced at Edward, not the least bit afraid, and brought the crate to the King.

She must not know what I am, Edward thought.

The King held up one of the Regards. "This I will redeem for a bottle of *aqua vitae*." He pulled a black bottle from the crate and handed it to Edward. "Little indeed remains of this. Each bottle is valuable, though to you it is more valuable than to others, I suspect. Do you agree?"

Edward held the bottle as he would an infant; afraid it would break. "Yes." He looked to the King for permission, unscrewed the top, and took a swallow.

The liquid burned going down, sending warmth through his limbs and burning fuzz from his mind. His hands tingled, his thoughts seemed clearer.

"Thank you," he said.

The King acknowledged his thanks with a nod. "Now, Prester Ellis is right, *zumbi* are restrained for their own good and the good of others. The only difference is Ellis kills *zumbi* as soon as he discovers them, we kill them when they can no longer control themselves."

Edward clutched the bottle. Did they give it to him merely to prolong his captivity before the inevitable execution?

The King picked up a second Regard. "This I will redeem for your freedom. Like the bottle, it is no small thing: a King should not release peril into his realm. Do you agree?"

Bowing his head, Edward said, "Thank you. Yes. I—thank you."

"Finally," said the King. "The hardest part of this riddle to solve. I'd have thought Dead could not be cured, and before coming here spoke with Ascourt, the Royal astrologer, as well as that damned Dutch scoundrel DeGues. They both agree if Undulark says it can be cured, it can, but not by just any hedge wizard or necromancer. Only Nekyia may have the power and skill."

"I have not heard of this man."

"It would be more merciful for you to face axe and fire than Nekyia. Nonetheless," he picked up the third and fourth Regards. "I will redeem these for those items necessary for you to seek Nekyia, namely a boat."

"I have a boat," Edward said.

"Very well, use your boat, if Hya agrees. I had thought you stowed away with Ellis. The last I will redeem for a guide to see you to Nekyia's island. Do you agree?"

Edward paused. "No. It's my boat. I'll trade one for the guide."

"Two," said the King. "You need my help."

"I have my freedom," Edward countered. "We've already agreed to that."

"You'll need a guide to find Nekyia."

"You agreed a guide was worth a coin. I agree to that, but I don't agree to paying for a boat I don't need."

Daria gave a little snort of a laugh, quickly muffled.

"Mother! It's bad enough dealing with him," the King said. "I want those coins."

Edward wondered why the King wanted them so badly; it wouldn't do to ask.

The King spoke to Edward. "Without a guide, you won't reach Nekyia before Dead overcomes you. Two coins."

"With my freedom, I'll find another guide who will accept one. Perhaps the mermaid?" Edward raised an eyebrow. "Let me keep one. I need something to help should I come into trouble again."

Taking a deep breath, the King looked at his mother, then the young lady who had brought in the crate. "Very well, on the condition that you not give it to Nekyia. I shudder to think of a necromancer with a claim on me."

Edward opened his mouth to speak, but found he couldn't form the words. He tried again. "Your Majesty is asking me to die a *zumbi* if this is the only thing Nekyia will accept."

"Jeremy..." Daria said, her voice low.

"Fine! Keep the coin and good luck to you!" The King waggled a finger at Edward. "I'll have you know, *zumbi*, being generous can be very difficult sometimes." He stalked from the room, leaving the two women, the axe-man, and the man with the bucket of whale oil.

Edward picked up the last coin. Turning it over in his fingers he asked. "Why does he want them so badly?"

"You don't really know what they are, that's clear," Daria said. "They are ancient things, and lay an obligation on the Kings of Atlantis."

Edward started in surprise.

"Yes, Atlantis; and what is this but the last outpost of that now sunken realm? The obligation is weakened by time, distance, and thinning blood," she went on. "But it is still there. Subtle and dangerous, if unfulfilled it can bring disaster to Port Astarte."

She rose. "Jeremy resents the hold they have over him."

"Magic." It felt odd to be holding a magic object. "How many are there?"

"Once there were tens of thousands. Now?" She lifted her hand, palm up with a shrug. "I'd have thought them all gone, but it doesn't surprise me Undulark had some."

She walked to the door.

"When will I meet my guide?" Edward asked.

Daria stopped. "She's here." She pointed to the young woman. "Hya will go with you. She's skilled and learned. And," she paused in a way that held Edward's attention, "should you lose yourself to Dead, she will destroy you."

☠

"We will wait for night," said Hya. It was already dusk. The sun's afterglow lit the western sky, visible through the window. The two men had left with Daria, leaving him alone with Hya.

Edward nodded. He wasn't about to question his good fortune by asking why. If King Jeremy didn't want people to see Edward leaving, that was reason enough.

This young lady, she looked little more than a girl, couldn't possibly be his guide. The top of her head didn't reach his chin. She was slender; lithe might be a good word, certainly not robust. She had fine features, blue eyes in a face lightly covered with both a tan and freckles. Her hair was secured in a low bun that reminded Edward of Rebecca, even though Hya had strawberry blonde hair, not chestnut.

The journey could not be safe. She wore a long knife strapped to her left leg and a pistol on her right hip. Edward had heard of revolvers but never actually seen one. She was well armed, yes, but—a woman?

"How is it you get this task?" he asked.

"Who else should get it? I'm the King's Jack."

"And what is the King's Jack?"

"Think of me as the royal handyman."

"Ah. Jack-of-all-trades."

"Exactly."

He shifted. She had a very direct stare; he imagined she measured him, judged him, certainly she watched him. "Is there much call for guiding *zumbis?*" he asked.

"None at all."

"Nobody has ever…" He fluttered his hands at a loss for the words, unsure if she considered Dead a disease, a condition, or a moral affliction. "And wanted to be cured?"

"There is no cure," she said.

"I cannot believe that."

She nodded, acknowledging his point. "In the past, there has been no point looking for a cure when none exists. Now—we look." She walked to the window, watching him as she passed, not exactly like a hawk watching its prey, but close enough.

"We'll leave soon," she said, with a quick look out the window.

"I have a boat."

"We'll use the one the King provided. I know it is suitable. I haven't seen yours."

"I didn't pay for it," Edward said.

"Then it's a gift." She returned to the crate, which still sat by the door. "A change of clothes," she said. "Change now, and we'll leave when you're done." Using her foot, she slid the crate into the center of the room.

He hesitated, for she gave no indication of leaving.

She snorted. "You're a *zumbi*. I have no desire for you."

"I am Edward Truscott," he snapped. "Man or monster, I remain Edward Truscott." He lifted his chin, daring her to argue.

"As you wish. I shall be outside this door."

Edward changed quickly. He had not realized how worn his clothing had become. He set the frayed and faded clothes on the bed and donned the sturdy canvas britches and loose-fitting linen shirt. He laced the top of the shirt and pulled on the jacket. The last thing in the crate was a small, strapped leather pouch. He slipped the bottle of *aqua vitae* into it.

He draped the strap over his shoulder and opened the door. "Is it possible to get paper and a pencil?"

"It is a small enough request." She nodded to the guard who stood next to her, so quietly Edward had not known of his presence. The man, his eyes fixed on Edward and his hand on his sword, shook his head.

"I think I can handle one *zumbi*," Hya snapped.

The guard did not look happy, but nodded once, hurried away and, quicker than Edward expected, returned with several sheets of paper and a pencil. He handed them, not to Edward, but to Hya. She passed them to Edward.

"Thank you," he said and slid them into the pouch. "Now I'm ready."

Hya led him through the quiet and dark palace. All the doors opened at her touch, there were no more guards to challenge them. Edward was reminded, *I go free, but nobody is to know it.*

The palace gates clinked softly when Hya closed them.

A few lights remained on in the town, a few bursts of laughter filtered through the streets, but mostly Port Astarte slept.

A shadowy shape emerged from under some nearby palm trees.

"You mean to tell me," Prester Ellis said, his voice low and quivering, "this creature will be allowed to roam freely?"

Behind him lurked two more men. They kept to the shadows, making Edward shiver. He doubted their good intentions.

"Up late, Prester?" Hya asked. Her hand rested on the hilt of her knife.

"I suspected Jeremy didn't have the courage for this job, so I kept my own watch."

"I'm going to try and undo what you did to me," Edward said. The Prester's words were like buzzing flies in his ears, and he had no patience.

Ellis shook his head. "There are no miracles that will cure you."

"Perhaps not the kind you think," Edward said, "but if I can do it with cold, hard, dark magic, it will still be a miracle."

"And should he do that, Prester," Hya said, "you would do well to consider the many paths to redemption."

"I do not require instruction," Ellis said. "I have been tasked by *God* to fight darkness. Should I let this monster walk free because he was once a nice person?"

"He is not walking free," Hya said.

"Nor will he." Ellis jerked his head, and the two men stepped forward.

"You defy the King!"

"I obey The One King. Jeremy may fume, but he will see I am right."

Edward knew the King was unlikely to go to war over the fate of a *zumbi*, not against all the cannon aboard *The Reach of Goa*. Especially if that *zumbi*'s fate had already been decided.

"You're missing a point there, Prester," said a voice from the deeper shadows. Anolan came forward carrying a fireplace poker in one hand. Five more men, armed with clubs and machetes, followed him. "The King might not fight over a foreign *zumbi*, but if you hurt his Jack, it'll be something altogether different."

"What are you doing here, Bone Illustrator?" Ellis demanded as the townsmen surrounded the *Custos*.

Anolan hefted his poker. "I suspected you couldn't accept any judgment but your own, Prester, so *I* decided to keep my own watch. This isn't your town, Prester, you don't rule here."

"You fool, I can destroy this place."

"You have to get to your ship first. You said the King won't fight over a *zumbi*. Will you?"

"This is risky," Hya warned Anolan. Edward watched, unwilling to say something that might tip opinions against him.

"You expect me to compromise over fighting evil?" Ellis hissed.

"It's not fighting, Prester," Anolan said. "It's suicide."

"He is well-guarded," Hya said, her voice soothing.

Ellis lifted his chin. "Since I question Jeremy's wisdom already, I have to question whether he is well-guarded."

Hya drew her pistol and pointed it at Ellis's head. The other two *Custos* started, but with the threat so immediate, they didn't move.

"You threaten God's emissary?" Only Ellis's tone gave away his anger.

"Not at all. I'm demonstrating my competence so you know to trust me watching over a *zumbi*."

"*Zumbi* are problems that take care of themselves," Anolan said, "and you have to ask yourself, Prester, if dying will serve your purpose here."

Ellis did not answer. He stared at the revolver in Hya's hand. "You speak truly," he finally said. "We came to the Narrow World for a much larger purpose." He looked at Anolan. "This is the second time today you've thwarted me, Illustrator. I can't say you've helped your soul."

"But I've helped Ed's soul," Anolan said. "I'll have to make do with that."

Ellis ignored Anolan and spoke to Edward. "Again I leave you, *zumbi*. You should hope we do not meet again. You may not have so many friends and I may not have other business." He led his men down the street.

"Best you hurry," Anolan said. "He might try to gather his crew and make another effort."

Both Edward and Hya nodded. "The boat is on the east beach," Hya said, and started down the street. Anolan and his men followed.

"We'll see you out of town," Anolan said. "Beyond that, you're on your own."

"Thank you," Edward said. "You've saved me again."

"A respite only. Use it well. I'd love to see you and Hya prove Ellis wrong."

Edward leaned closer to ask, "About that. Is it really appropriate for us to travel together? Won't it affect her reputation? Won't people talk?"

Anolan let out a short bark of laughter. "You're a *zumbi*, lad. Nobody will talk."

"I don't understand."

"Have you felt desire for a woman since you became Dead?"

Perplexed, Edward thought a moment. "I've been concerned with finding a cure," he said.

"Not even that mermaid you told me about?" Anolan asked. He nodded ahead of them. "Or our Hya? She's a fetching lass."

She was a fetching lass, the kind to draw a man's eye, yet Edward didn't feel the slightest tug of desire. "Are you saying," he said slowly, working his way through the idea, "I am not a man?"

"No, lad, you're a *zumbi*. The sooner you're cured, the better off you'll be."

Clenching his fists, Edward said, "I am not—" He knew he was a monster, he felt it under his skin; the hard bead of blood in his palm that still remained from Undulark's jab. "I don't know what I am." Nothing he really wanted to believe, at least, if making the distinction between knowing and believing mattered.

Not wanting to pursue a subject he found uncomfortable, he took a few hurried steps and caught up with Hya. "Thank you for getting me free of Prester Ellis," he said quietly.

"Don't thank me," she said. "I don't like Ellis or his *Custos*. But I'm not sure about you, either."

"What?" Her words stung.

She turned her head, watching him, he was sure, and her hand strayed closer to the handle of her long knife. "You're a *zumbi*," she said. "Maybe I know more about them than you do."

"I don't doubt that," he snapped. "But you don't know me."

"*Zumbis* are mindless things, devilishly cunning maybe, but always toward one end."

"It's not like that," Edward said. "There are voices and a compulsion that work together, but I know it's wrong. I can fight it. I do fight it."

"Devilishly cunning," she repeated, "but always toward one end."

She wasn't about to let down her guard. *Kill her. Kill her and eat her.* And that, he told himself as he squelched the thoughts, was why she was right.

Hya turned off the High Street by Anolan's shop. Edward stopped, looking toward the harbor. "Isn't the boat this way?" he asked.

"East beach," Anolan said as he caught up with him. "It's a short walk through the forest."

"Ah." Edward fell into step beside him.

As they passed the Orthodox Church, Edward slowed to look. Moonlight illuminated it—clean, bright moonlight. Here was another reason for Hya to mistrust him. He could not endure holy ground.

Anolan noticed his gaze. "What is it?"

"Am I truly damned?" he asked. "So damned that I cannot tread holy ground? Does Prester Ellis do the Almighty's will?"

Anolan ran his hand over the fence. "Do not mistake the source of your trouble. The ancient church wove spells of protection into their rituals. This ground may be consecrated to God, but it's protected by magic."

"What?"

"Sanctuaries were sorely needed in those times," Anolan said. "What you feel is not God's wrath, only magic worked in his name."

"But our parish priest was no sorcerer. I am certain of that."

"And didn't need to be. The need for sanctuaries faded as the dark things were driven from the Wide World. Have you *felt* the new churches? They are hollow things, shallow things that house God only as long as people gather there. But the old churches have their own power. Their power endures even after they fall to ruin.

"Much is forgotten," Anolan continued. "Today's priests have, in their faith, forgotten what else was drawn into the church's traditions."

They finished passing the church, and Edward felt his spirits lift, but another thought sent them crashing down. "The very words of faith are denied me," he said.

Anolan snorted. "You were baptized, I'm sure. Its protections fight the Dead inside you, separating the Light and the Darkness. It *should* have kept you safe from Dead, but, as you say, the Priest was no sorcerer. Clearly, it isn't working properly."

"So, He is not turning His back on me?"

"Lad, I would never presume to speak for Him, and I wouldn't trust anybody who did."

"I would like to believe you," he said. "I don't want to believe God would abandon me like this. But—"

"Are you coming?" Hya called back. "Or shall we wait for Dead to overcome you? Or worse, Prester Ellis?"

"No. No, of course I'm coming." Edward sped up. They continued in silence, Hya setting the pace ahead, Anolan and the townsmen a few steps behind.

"Ellis will have reached his ship by now," one of the men said, and that was enough to set them all to jogging.

When they came to the edge of town, Anolan stopped. "This is all the further we go." Twisting to look toward the harbor, he said, "Men are gathering on the deck of the *Reach*," he said. "I can't tell what they're doing, though. Best you hurry."

Edward insisted on shaking his hand. "Thank you. I'd be dead without your help. Well, I'm Dead anyway, but I'd be dead otherwise."

"Good luck, Ed," he said. "Keep your wits about you, and stay out of trouble. I won't be around to fish you out again."

☠

Edward and Hya walked the night, surrounded by comfortable darkness, rich with smells of jasmine and the sound of rustling palm fronds and gentle surf. Port Astarte dwindled behind them. They passed into the forest. The path ahead was striped with moonlight and shadows. The forest was filled with sound ahead of them, but it fell silent as they drew near and remained silent after they passed.

Edward imagined all the creatures crouching in fear at his approach. They must sense the wrongness in him, smell it in the night air. His thoughts flew to London and Rebecca. Would she turn from him as well? Perhaps she already had. Perhaps some lord's son, drawn by her beauty, had plied her with compliments and roses, or some rich merchant gave her jewels and furs and whispered words of love.

What woman, he thought, would want a man whose heart was cold and still, a man who wasn't even a man?

The night grew dark around him—dark, silent, and in spite of Hya's quiet footsteps, empty.

Edward knew he was fortunate. He had more *aqua vitae*, he had a guide, and he still had one King's Regard. He was closer to a cure than ever. But he couldn't shake a cold feeling. He had already used five Regards, and the threat of Hya loomed over him should he lose control of himself.

Chapter Six

Edward blinked as he came out of the forest onto the beach. The moon shone brightly, giving the sand the appearance of fresh snow. Waves curled and broke, pushing water up the beach where it sparkled in the moonlight before retreating back to the ocean. A row of boats rested, hulls up, beyond the reach of the water.

Edward caught the smell of smoke. Embers glowed beyond the boats, but he couldn't see anybody near them. The beach appeared deserted.

"That one," Hya said, pointing to the first boat. It was the only one right side up.

"That one's yours?" Edward asked. He judged it eighteen feet long and six across the beam. Inside, a slatted deck rested on the ribs just below water level though the bilges were dry. There was a seat in the stern, another just fore of amidships, and a third in the prow.

"Somebody was sent ahead," she said.

"I see." Somebody to prepare the boat, to get the people out of harm's way, and to see him quickly away. *I merely wanted to return to work on time,* he thought. *I would not have been in that alley otherwise. Now people hide at my approach.* "It wasn't long ago that I got off a boat like this."

"You're in an archipelago. How did you expect to travel?"

Edward grabbed the gunwales of the boat and leaned toward the sea, ready to push. "I don't know. Much like I don't know how long it will take to reach this Nekyia."

"That depends on the winds, but seven days if we make the best possible time."

"Seven days?" The idea startled him. He had thought it would be a day or two.

"The distance is a thousand miles or more. Nekyia is as far from Port Astarte as he can be."

Edward pushed on the gunwale, sliding the boat toward the water. He was doubly glad of the fresh *aqua vitae.* "Sailing night and day, of course."

"Day. We will not sail at night."

"We're sailing now."

"We travel this night only," Hya said. "In the future, we will shelter ashore."

"Why?" Edward demanded. "I don't know how much time I have."

"We travel tonight because, in truth, I don't trust Prester Ellis. Best not to tempt him; he doesn't know whether restraint or righteous action is the higher virtue. This night at sea is safe; we are close to Port Astarte, and I know all the reefs nearby."

Edward curled his lip. He glanced over her shoulder, half expecting to see Ellis emerge from the forest to shout at them from the beach. But he thought, *We travel tonight to get me away from Port Astarte quickly—for many reasons.* "Why not travel other nights too? Surely we can avoid reefs in a boat this shallow."

"And the Sea Dreads?" she snapped. "The Grasping Dead? Restless Davy? You think to avoid them as well? The best way to do that is to stay on land."

"What are these things?"

"Night creatures," Hya said, "some of many things that come out either in darkness or moonlight. The Moon Nymphs are mostly harmless. Unlike mermaids," she added darkly.

Edward understood. Whatever these creatures were, it was best to avoid them. Still, it chafed him. "We need to make the best time we can." He pushed the boat again.

"The King has made it my duty to help you reach Nekyia's island." She did not seem particularly sympathetic. "*Zumbis* have dormant times, and I must rest too."

"We can take turns while we sail!"

Her eyes narrowed. "I must be ashore for my wards to be effective."

If we're ashore, why must she ward against these sea creatures, Edward wondered. Suddenly he felt foolish. She didn't ward against them, she warded against him. "You don't need wards," he said. "I control myself perfectly well."

"So you say. But if you lose that control? Then I should die, and you would have no guide."

He opened his mouth to reply, but she cut him off. "There are too many risks to travel at night."

Edward scowled. He didn't like it, but he had to accept it. He couldn't ask the necromancer for help if he never got there. He found he couldn't just leave the subject so easily though. "Ships sail at night," he muttered.

"Ships are larger, better crewed, and do their business near Port Astarte," Hya replied. "And even ships that wander through the archipelago at night tend to disappear."

With an angry heave, Edward shoved the boat into the water. "Best we get started then." He held it steady while she climbed aboard.

Once they were both aboard, he unshipped the oars and set them in their sockets. Along with a small pile of crates, a bucket, and other supplies, there was a mast wrapped in canvas lying in the bottom of the boat. But there was little wind, so he turned the boat in the direction Hya directed him, and bent his back to rowing.

Hya sat in the stern, watching. She would look behind them, as if making sure they were not followed, then look ahead, as if to be sure of their course. But always her gaze returned to him, as if to be sure he didn't attack her. She did not speak, and didn't seem inclined to.

Once past the reef, she pointed him to the starboard, or leeward to the sparse breeze. They moved quickly, catching up and passing some floating palm fronds, and Edward realized they used oar, wind, and current.

Sounds of the sea filled the night, but Hya's silence was profound.

He felt the need to break it.

"How does one become the King's Jack?" he asked.

"The previous Jack trains a successor," she answered.

After a brief silence he prompted, "And—?"

"And what?"

"How did you end up as Jack?"

She frowned, but answered. "I was a curious child, and my father didn't know what else to do with me."

"It would be rare to see a woman doing this sort of work in England."

"The previous Jack was my father, and roles are not so tightly defined in the Narrow World." Her answer was abrupt, and she turned her head, ending the conversation.

He rowed on.

"I know you said you weren't sure about me, but it will be a long trip without conversation," he said.

She looked at him, the moon peering over her shoulder so her face was shadowed, making her eyes dark pits he could not plumb. "*Zumbi* are the lowest of the Not Dead," she said. "They're like an infestation of roaches. All the others—yes, they're evil, but they're chained to place or purpose, or they still possess their minds. A hungry vampire is a scourge, but once fed they can be quite agreeable. A *zumbi* is just a menace."

"I know nothing about other undead," Edward muttered.

"And I know nothing about you," Hya said. "You think because you had four of the King's Favor I should *trust and like* you?"

"I'm not asking for your friendship!" Edward snapped. He felt a surge of anger, the desire to lash out, but not as strong. The *aqua vitae* must be working, he thought, and this allowed him to distance himself further from the emotion. "I'm not asking for your friendship," he said, more calmly. "I just—" He stopped, not sure what he expected.

She had not sounded angry, he realized. She stated unpleasant facts, much the same as she had after confronting Prester Ellis.

"We must travel together, why should we not be friends?" he asked.

"Because when the Dead overcomes you, you will forget who your friends are. You will try to kill me, try to eat me; and I must destroy you."

"I will be cured before that happens." He had to believe that.

"I hope you're right." It was clear though, right or not, he wouldn't sway her.

He sighed in resignation and laughed, realizing the act was so habitual he did it even when he didn't need to breathe. The night was so peaceful he paused his rowing.

If the boat moved, it was because of a current, for the wind had died as they talked. The sea was flat, without enough waves to make the boat rise and fall. By some inexplicable reason, he could smell, very faintly, jasmine.

The moon had moved past Hya and now hung halfway up the sky, its twin floating halfway to the horizon.

"Can't stop," Edward muttered, preparing to row again.

Suddenly water splashed, the boat heeled over, and the splash surged over the side. Hya cried in surprise, her hand reaching for her knife.

Resting on the side of the boat was a mermaid. She lay on the gunwale, halfway between amidships and the stern, head resting on her crossed arms.

"Terra," Edward said.

Terra lifted her head. "Oh, it's you. Tired of Port Astarte already?"

"You know her?" Hya asked.

"Terra brought me here," Edward said.

"Are you jealous?" Terra asked. She waved her tail, slowly, in a way that might be described as sultry.

Hya drew her revolver and pointed it at Terra. "Not hardly."

"Somebody is up past her bedtime and is getting cranky," Terra said.

"I just know a little about mermaids."

Terra smiled, a kind of smirk. "This is why I love playing near the Narrow World. It's the thrill of the challenge."

After a second, Hya returned her revolver to her belt. Terra didn't move.

"What do you want, Terra?" Edward asked.

She batted her eyes, rolled over, draped her head back, and stretched out to stroke his face. "Someone to play with."

"I must politely decline," he said. He took her hand; it was cool, wet, and soft to his touch. Very gently, he pushed it away.

"You're making me doubt myself." She gave him a charming pout. "Men are always eager to play with me."

Hya snorted.

Terra rolled back over, and stared at her. "You're far from home, daughter of Atlantis. Does it gall you that you've never seen it? I can tell you about it. It's dark."

"I know of Atlantis."

"But I've been there. The temples are empty. The University is deserted. It is still beautiful." She had a malicious smile on her face. "I can only imagine how it looked in the sun."

"You speak of sacred ground," Hya growled. "Your humor is not appreciated."

"Humor? I merely tell what I have seen. I can describe the Bridge of Scholars, or the arcades of the Mariner's Market. Perhaps you would like to hear of the Palace, of its white towers that reach for the surface like five fingers of a corpse's hand?"

"Enough!" Hya said. "I've no wish to hear."

Terra turned her dark, fathomless eyes on Edward. "Strange, isn't it?" Her voice was that of an innocent child. "Strange that a child of Atlantis shouldn't want to hear of her home? Why is that, do you think? Perhaps she doesn't care?"

"Be silent," Hya said, her jaw clenched.

"I think," and now Terra sounded thoughtful, "she may be ashamed. She's ashamed to be kin with all those people; all those men, those women, those little tiny children who—," she slowed her pace, pausing just slightly between each word to drive it deeper into her listeners, "couldn't—swim."

With an inarticulate cry of rage, Hya lunged for the mermaid. Terra vanished beneath the water, and Hya crouched, ready to spring after her. "They were blameless!"

Edward lunged and grabbed Hya's arm, pulling back as she leapt, throwing her down into the bottom of the boat.

She twisted around, coming up in a crouch, her muscles tense, but Edward still held her. "I'll filet her," Hya snarled.

"You think you can catch her?" Edward asked. "I know what talks to me. What voices do you hear?"

Slowly Hya looked down at his hand, then up to his face. She took a deep breath, and, letting it out, all the tension left her body. "Mermaids are evil creatures."

Certain Hya would not dive overboard, Edward sought out and

found Terra, who lay on her back, arms stretched above her head, circling the boat with slow, strong swishes of her tail.

"Will you aid our journey?" he asked.

"Do you have any more coins?"

"Not to pay you."

"That's no fun."

"I'm no fun anymore." He shrugged his helplessness to change that.

"Oh, I wouldn't say that. It was becoming too easy. Find a man when he hasn't seen another person for a week, or a woman for a month, and he doesn't put up much fight. You, at least, are a challenge. But," she added, "that doesn't mean I'll help you."

Terra's tail thrashed back and forth. In the distance, a whale rose and blew a column of spray into the night sky, a fountain of silver in the moonlight.

"What do you want, mermaid?" Hya demanded.

"To have fun, obviously." She ducked under the boat, coming up to rest on the gunwale, but she didn't look at Edward or Hya.

Now Edward followed her gaze. "We aren't interested in your fun," he said, staring at the whale, wondering why Terra seemed so concerned.

"There's one who will play," Hya said. Now all three stared at the whale.

"That's a poor plaything," Terra said.

"I'd almost think it senses you," Edward said. The whale swam close enough to the surface, zigzagging like a hound after a scent. "If I called, do you think it would understand me?"

"No. Whales are stupid creatures." Something in Terra's tone made Edward doubt her.

"Let's try," Hya said with malicious glee.

Terra did not answer, but rolled over and knifed into the depths. They waited long moments, but she didn't resurface.

"Mermaids aren't known for their courteousness," Hya said.

"Or love of whales, apparently."

"Yes," Hya agreed. "They have no love of whales."

Silence settled in the boat, a curious and sullen silence. Edward lifted the oars and began to row. His efforts might mean little in the distance they traveled but kept the silence from becoming unbearable.

Hya remained in the stern seat, her expression angry and resentful.

"The mermaid lies," she said suddenly. "I am proud of my heritage."

Evidently, but why justify yourself to me? Edward kept his thoughts to himself, wondering how he should respond.

Far away, the whale breached the ocean, smacking down on the moon's reflection, shattering it into thousands of glittering pieces that danced as waves on the dark water.

"Then preserve it," Edward said. "With your life, not your death."

She turned her head to stare into the depths. "I need no advice from a *zumbi*."

Edward deliberately checked their position and turned the boat in the proper direction. Now was not the time to argue or question. Only when he was sure of his temper did he say, in a mild voice, "Perhaps."

They said nothing more until after the moon had vanished and the stars started to fade as the eastern horizon hinted at dawn. They were amongst a cluster of small islands, mounds of sand and coral with some grass and maybe a few palm trees.

"That one," Hya said, pointing.

Edward nodded. *Zumbi* lethargy threatened to overtake him, his muscles felt heavy, and even as they approached the beach, the surf sounded as if it came from a great distance.

☠

Edward pulled the boat onto the beach just as the sun broke the horizon. He went to the shade of a small bush, sand spraying away from his feet as he shuffled along. He collapsed, desperately hoping nothing more was expected. Pride made him look to Hya to be sure, and curiosity kept him awake.

Hya found her own shade beneath a cluster of palms and drove a three-foot stake into the sand, paced about six feet, drove another, paced three feet to form a right angle, drove a third stake, then returned six feet to drive a fourth stake completing the rectangle.

Edward squinted at the runes and images carved into the wood. It reminded him of the rail of the *Twilight Rose*, and he didn't doubt these held magic.

"If you try to pass inside the box, you'll get enough magic to make your teeth rattle," Hya said.

"What of you?" he asked. "You're outside. How will you get in?"

"I haven't activated it yet," she said, her tone neutral, but expression suggesting he should have known that.

He should have. The runes on the *Rose* hadn't worked until Jenna activated them.

He pulled out his *aqua vitae*, unscrewed the top and took a drink. *Patience in a bottle*, he thought. He thought his frustration came from a natural reaction to being distrusted and, perhaps, looked down on, but never having been Dead before made him uncertain.

Hya stepped into the box she had made. She began to chant low, melodic words. The bottom runes began to glow, the glow rising like fire on the stakes until it reached the top and white light flared. It faded until it merged with the morning light and Hya nodded.

She glanced at Edward, checking, before lying down to sleep. He didn't see her close her eyes, for lethargy overtook him, and he had just enough thought to close his own eyes.

☠

"**A** short day," Hya said, as water lapped the hull of the boat. Edward didn't want short days, but it was nearly noon already. He could have stayed in *zumbi* stupor longer, but Hya roused him, and he willingly helped launch the boat. The more they traveled, the happier he was.

Together they dropped the mast into place. Edward untangled the rope while Hya put the tiller into the bracket on the stern. Once he untangled the rope, Edward pulled up the sail. It fluttered as it rose, then billowed, jerking him forward when the wind caught it.

The weight of the boom made him strain. Once clear of the gunwales, the boom swung out, and Edward finished raising the sail. He tied it off on a cleat and gathered in the sheet, pulling in the boom.

Hya looked more relaxed. She basked in the sun, a hand on the tiller, and one eye on the sea—the other on Edward. She had produced a wide-brimmed hat from her bag and it now cast its shadow on her face and neck, the brim curling down on the sides until it grazed her shoulders.

The island retreated all too slowly behind them. The feeling of moving quickly toward his goal evaporated in the warm sun and light breeze. Their progress through the glassy waves seemed painfully slow, and rather than drawing nearer, his cure seemed further and further away.

"Would it help if I rowed?" he asked.

"You can't when the sail is up," Hya said, nodding toward the boom, pulled tight enough to encroach on the center seat.

The sea ran deep, deep and blue. There were islands. Clumps of greenery sticking out of the water, sometimes tall, sometimes flat, but Hya steered away from them all.

Satisfied he would not miss anything, Edward pulled the paper and pencil from his pouch. Smoothing the paper on the seat, he began to write.

Dearest Becca,

I'm afraid my first letter has gone astray, and I have scant hope this one will reach you either. Still, I am compelled to try to keep some tenuous link with you. It is the best I can do, and it comforts me.

As I did not anticipate this journey, I could not anticipate the turns it has taken. If I told you the

He paused, conjuring and discarding words. How could he describe all that had happened?

wonders I have encountered, you would not believe me. I pray that you are in good health and lack only my company for your happiness.

He lifted his pencil to cross out that last bit of vanity, but paused. She wasn't likely to read it, so he left it. He thought of what lay ahead and the time he had left. He felt good, hopeful, but his path had already taken him in directions he had never dreamed. Trying to predict his return would be a lie. He thought for several minutes and finally ended the letter with *I love you.*

He folded the letter and put it into his pouch with the *aqua vitae.*

"You correspond."

Startled, he looked up and met Hya's eyes. "Yes. You must have expected it when I asked for paper."

"I had not thought about it," she admitted. She broke eye contact, looked around the barren ocean. "You cannot expect her to receive it."

"No. But I would not have her think I've forgotten her, and this is the best I can do. Perhaps I shall put it in a bottle and trust the tides to carry it to England." He said this lightly, but instantly sobered. His only bottle held the *aqua vitae*, and he didn't want to think about when it was empty.

It might be a short day if they stopped at nightfall, but it felt like a long journey.

The problem with long journeys, Edward thought as he gazed at the sky, *is their length*. The clouds ambled across the sky at a glacial pace; take them out of the sky and he might mistake them for glaciers. If only a freshening wind would come and hurry them, and the boat, along.

"Are you familiar with a railroad?" Hya asked suddenly.

Edward smiled. She was getting bored also. "Of course. The entire country is just getting over a bad case of Railway Mania. You can't turn around without stumbling over a new rail line."

"Ah," she said. "And steam engines?"

"I consider myself well-read, but hardly a mechanic." He didn't want to let the chance of conversation pass. "Why do you ask?"

She made a little moue. Her brows came together, and Edward could almost read her thoughts: stupid to talk to the *zumbi*. "No reason," she said shortly.

Edward let out an angry bark of laughter. "Are you trying to feed my anger? I assure you I have it well under control."

She straightened her back. "I am doing no such thing."

"Then clearly what constitutes good manners in the Narrow World differs from the Wide World." He nodded his head in a cynical apology. "Please forgive my assumption."

Her nostrils flared and jaw tightened, but she made no answer. He turned toward the bow. *A long journey indeed.* He patted his pouch, feeling the bottle of *aqua vitae*. *Patience in a bottle; I hope I have enough.* He smiled at the double meaning.

He turned his attention back to the sky as if he could hurry the clouds along with his thoughts.

"That's a big bird," he said, pointing.

Hya followed his finger. "Giant Seafisher."

He nodded, accepting this. *A thousand-mile trip with a woman who doesn't like me.*

As the bird swooped down, its shadow passed over them, and Edward realized its true size. "It's as large as a horse!"

The body did seem as large as a horse, but the wings were much, much larger. In shape, it appeared related to a merlin. Its feathers were light grey underneath, and as it banked, it revealed darker grey, almost blue-slate, colors on its back and head. Its legs were light yellow-orange, and large enough to carry away a sheep or a goat—or a man. Its beak, yellow turning to black at the tip, turned down at the end.

"Is it dangerous?" he asked.

"Sometimes," she answered, "but it usually hunts fish."

Her short answers and tone killed conversation and didn't invite further questions.

At first it looked like the Seafisher was looking at them, but it glided past and circled ahead, beating its wings to rise up, then gliding around and around.

Hya frowned and shifted the tiller, nudging the boat away from where the Seafisher circled. It kept circling, and they got closer with each pass it made. Whatever it circled, they approached too. Edward couldn't take his eyes from it.

A sudden gurgle made him tear his gaze away and turn to the ocean. Water frothed up a dozen yards ahead, not spurting like a fountain, but welling up and running down the sides so it looked like a Christmas pudding. Faint wisps of steam rose from the top.

"What is that?" Edward shouted, forgetting about the Seafisher as they sailed toward the boiling sea.

Hya threw her weight against the tiller, heeling the boat over. "Fumarole fish."

The mound rose higher and got wider, rising above the height of the gunwales. The overflow pushed the boat away, and Edward turned to watch as they passed. Heat slapped his face, and the smell of sulfur tickled his nose.

"Big one," Hya said anxiously as the mound kept climbing until it reached her height.

The water rose, bubbling, and overflowed in all directions. The foaming water suddenly turned black with streaks of blue, and the smell of hot copper mingled with the sulfur.

"Better hope it's deep," Hya said, still leaning on the tiller, but now staring down into the ocean.

Edward followed her gaze, but the black water flowing from the mound obscured his view. "Why?"

"Fumarole fish grapple their prey and heat up enough to kill and cook their prey. They don't usually hunt by day, but this one's found a squid." The stain of ink and blood spread over the sea. "Big one. It's going to get hot."

The mound burst like a bubble popping, throwing large drops of hot water outward. The stench of burnt fish washed over them.

Hya seemed anxious, and Edward felt himself begin to share it. He didn't know what the danger might be, but Hya wanted to get away from the expanding stain on the ocean.

A grey shape appeared in the depths, frantically pulsing larger and smaller as it thrashed about. As it rose, a mass of tentacles took shape on one end.

"It's right under us!" he shouted, now understanding Hya's fear. Bubbles rose as the sea began to heat. He ducked under the boom and grabbed the oars.

"Damn," Hya swore. "The squid's escaped."

The boat began to rock.

"Stay down," Hya muttered. She pulled in the sail, but with so little wind, it didn't help. "Faster," she urged, whether directed at wind or boat, Edward didn't know.

He dropped the oarlocks into their sockets and ducked under the boom, trying to position himself to row. The boom was right where he needed to be, and he could only hunch over awkwardly, unable to unship and work the oars.

A grey tentacle waved over the gunwale. Edward straightened to get a better look. Hya pushed on the tiller. The boat turned, the boom swung and cracked Edward across his shoulders, knocking him into the gunwale.

The sea boiled with tentacles. Long and grey, they groped in the air and churned the water. The squid, its body as large as their boat, pointed down, but unable to move. A massive gelatinous blob engulfed it.

Edward stared. "It's a jellyfish!"

The bulk of the jelly, the fumarole fish, was clear, but red and orange lines radiated from a central point. It didn't seem to have any bones, but long, thin tentacles wrapped the squid. It looked like a cloak of fire as the squid thrashed, making the fumarole fish and all its colors dance.

Heat slapped Edward's face, and the smell of Hell enveloped him. Sulfur, dead fish, burnt seaweed, and odors dredged from the depths roiled with the fish and squid.

One of the fish's whip-like tentacles lashed at the boat. Splinters flew where it landed. The tentacle reared up high and lashed again, this time tearing through the sail and coiling around the boom. The boat jerked about, heeling far enough that water surged over the gunwale and down Edward's chest.

The air was suddenly full of thin, thrashing tentacles of yellow, orange, and red. Hya drew her knife and, stepping forward, slashed at the tentacle wrapped on the boom. It twanged like a plucked violin string. She swung again, and it parted. The boat rolled back upright, water sloshing inside.

"We must get away!" she cried out as a tentacle slapped her shoulders. Another wrapped about the boom. More struck the boat but, unable to coil around it, rose again to flail back down.

Edward grabbed an oar and used it as a paddle while Hya cut the boom loose again. A thick grey tentacle struck the stern, jarring them but pushing the boat away. Edward dug the oar deep into the water.

"Further," Hya called. There came a clatter and splash. Edward hazarded a look to see her standing over the tiller, which she had disconnected and thrown into the boat. Now she stood ankle deep in water, trying to avoid and cut the whipping threads of the fumarole fish.

A shadow passed over him, and the squid's tentacle struck the mast. With a sharp crack, the boat rocked, water sloshing over the far gunwale. The mast broke, falling until it dragged in the water, held only by wet canvas.

The boat didn't move well, dragging half the mast and heavy with water. Edward started to duck under the boom to paddle on the other side, but the sail, still attached to the boom and entangled on the broken mast, blocked him.

Hya scrambled over the fallen canvas and wrestled the other oar from the socket. She paddled, awkwardly, but it helped straighten the boat.

More and more tentacles wrapped the stub of the mast, the oarlocks—anything they could twist around. The boat lurched backwards.

A scream split the air, and the Seafisher plunged down, talons outstretched. It plunged them into the fumarole fish. The fish quivered. A keening so high-pitched that Edward could barely hear it knifed into his head.

Whip tentacles lashed at the Seafisher as the fumarole fish defended its meal. A tentacle wrapped around the Seafisher's leg and jerked it down. The Seafisher bit itself free, soared up, and returned to peck and tear at the fumarole fish.

"Paddle!" Hya shouted.

Edward didn't need to be told.

They pulled free as the fumarole fish grappled the Seafisher. Edward paddled on the port side, Hya on the starboard, both throwing up spray as they struggled to get away from the fight.

Slowly they began to move away.

Drops of ink and bloodstained water rained on them as the fish and squid and bird struggled.

"Traveling by day is safer?" Edward asked as he stroked.

"It's supposed to be."

They were beyond the reach of the tentacles now. Still they paddled.

"Supposed?" Edward was incredulous. "You don't know?"

"Squids are supposed to be nocturnal!" she shot back. "And nobody knows much about fumarole fish. I've never seen one before."

Edward began to laugh.

The Seafisher rose overhead, talons empty. It staggered across the sky, injured and hungry, searching for refuge. Edward sobered. "I hope it finds food elsewhere. It would have gone poorly for us without it."

The fumarole fish pulled its hard-won meal underwater. The squid barely moved, just gave a final weak wave of a tentacle in a forlorn goodbye.

"Now what?" Edward asked.

"The fish will finish off the squid and eat it," Hya said.

"I meant for us."

"More distance."

Nodding, Edward bent again to paddling, leaving behind the bruised ocean, black ink and blue blood marking the battleground.

☠

Eventually they stopped and assessed the damage. It wasn't good. Edward pulled the mast aboard so they could salvage the sail. Torn though it was, it could be mended. The mast, however, could not be repaired. They would have to replace it, and they had no spare.

With the boom out of the way, Edward set the oars and began to row. Far ahead lay an island, and he steered toward it.

The boat felt sluggish, heavy. He heard a tapping on the hull. He jerked the oars, wanting to pull away from whatever swam beneath the boat.

Water sloshed over his feet and lifted the boxes of supplies. They bumped the side. They had made the tapping.

"We've sprung a seam," Hya said.

"Can we fix it?"

She wiped her forehead with the back of her hand, smearing ink across her brow. "Yes." She looked forward. "Ah. Well, there's nothing for it."

"What?"

"There really isn't safety in the Narrow World apart from Port Astarte and the nearby islands."

Edward twisted to look at their destination. "Am I to assume that is a particularly dangerous island?"

"I hadn't planned on stopping."

"Why?" Edward demanded.

"Because you're in a rush," she snapped. "And now we'll stop because you're in a rush. We need to patch the boat and cut a new mast."

He couldn't afford to be slowed down. Frustration and rage welled up. He didn't trust himself to speak, so he used his anger to row.

"Tell me about the island," he finally growled.

"I don't know!" she retorted. She looked angry and flustered.

She's never done this either. The realization cooled his anger. He had never seen her uncertain; it made her appear even younger. The King had done her no favors with this task.

It's one thing to feel sorry for her, but delays may truly kill me.

"It's not this island," Hya muttered. "The whole region is avoided. My father never brought me here."

Edward twisted again to look ahead of them. "It looks safe enough." There was nothing about the island that seemed foreboding. The only notable feature was a rock ridge crossing the island that jutted out into the ocean. Otherwise, nothing but palm trees and sandy beaches.

She didn't respond, so he asked, "Why is the region avoided?"

She brushed a strand of hair away from her face. "Restless Davy is often seen here."

"And who is Restless Davy?"

She stirred in her seat. "A superstition of generations of sailors, the sea's malevolence."

"And he visits often? Who invites him? He must be charming company."

She still had an uncertain expression, but a hesitant smile curled the edges of her lips. "Few would relish his visit."

Edward dug the oars into the water. The water came over his ankles. More trickled between the boards of the hull. The boxes tapped the hull as they floated about. A bucket floating by Hya's leg caught his eye.

He let go of an oar and reached for it. Hya stiffened, her hand going to her knife.

Anger surged in Edward. "I was reaching for the bucket," he said. His voice sounded different to him, taut, edgy, but knew it was his own hurt feelings causing his anger. "Somebody should bail." He curled his lip. "The greatest threat to your life right now is not me."

He resumed rowing, not bothering to hide his frown.

Without taking her eyes from him, Hya reached down and fumbled for the bucket. She began to bail, the movement awkward as they stared at each other.

Edward snorted and rolled his eyes. He shifted, ignoring her reaction, and braced his feet. The oarlocks creaked out their protest, but he dug deeper and pulled harder. "Damned if I sink now," he muttered.

"Devilishly cunning," Hya said softly. Edward didn't lift his head, but the sound of bailing grew faster.

As they neared the island, the sea started to roll, long slow waves with round crests, making Edward fight up one side to rush down the other. As they climbed, the water in the boat ran to the stern, holding them back, then, when they tipped over the crest, it rushed to the bow and dragged them forward.

The boat finally settled onto the sand. Whether it hit by forward motion or sinking down, Edward neither knew nor cared. He was too drained to pull it further.

For the moment, he didn't care about Hya's misgivings.

Chapter Seven

Edward stood knee-deep in the surf, struggling with their grounded boat. He had spent hours of bailing, dragging, pulling, and swearing under his breath. Now they were ready to finish beaching the boat.

None too soon. Hya had waded next to him after having splayed their supplies across the beach to dry. That still meant hours in the surf until she took on a waif-like appearance: pale and drawn, with large eyes and blue-tinged lips.

"Steady this," he said. Hya held the boat, and he moved to the prow, lifted it and dragged it up the beach, rolling the boat the rest of the way and letting the remaining water spill out.

He pulled the boat above the high tide mark.

"At least the island is safe enough," Hya said.

He looked around suspiciously. She had spoken ominously about the island before. "How can you tell?" It looked like any other tropical island to him, neither good nor evil.

She didn't answer. With a tired sigh, she sat down. Her clothes clung to her, as did her hair. Edward hadn't even noticed when it escaped the bun. She pushed damp strands back from her face. "Give me a minute to rest."

Edward nodded. He ran his hand over the overturned boat.

Water dripped off the hull. Several of the planks were cracked, and, he was sure, many of the joints loosened. They would have to repair it before they could continue.

With what?

The seams could be resealed by filling them with tarred rope. Rope they had. Tar was a problem. It could be made from pine trees, but he didn't know how.

Perhaps a half-mile down the beach, a rocky promontory thrust out into the water. It formed a ridge with the lone hill. The tops of both ridge and hill were bare, but trees grew on the slopes. They weren't pine trees.

More delays.

The sun was nearing the horizon. He could make use of the last daylight. He trudged to the woods and started to gather dead wood. He didn't find anything that could be used to mend the boat, but he could start a fire. It would help dry Hya.

No pine trees, also no fresh water, no fruits. Hya might not have thought about food, but her salt-water-soaked supplies were useless. Water, they would find eventually. The rest, he was not as sure.

Hya sat on the sand, checking whether their supplies had dried. She started as he walked past, and it occurred to him she hadn't heard him. *Fortunately I don't want to kill and eat her*, he thought. *I could have right then.*

"Firewood," he said.

"Thank you," she said. She must have thought the same thing he had, for she leaned away. Her expression was guarded, but maybe relief and deeper thought?

"I didn't find any food or water."

"There will be food," she said. "Fish, at least. But there's always wild pigs. This is a good island." She pointed to the forest. "Many of those are aquilaria trees."

"I don't know what that means," Edward confessed.

"You can find jinkoh in the heartwood. In forests like this, kyara, the highest grade jinkoh, would be common."

Edward shook his head. "I'm sorry. I still don't know what you mean."

"Aloeswood," Hya said. "A very rare and much-prized incense and scent for perfumes."

"Ah." He knew nothing of incense but didn't want to ask further. He started to build a fire. "If this is a good place to live, why isn't anybody living here?"

"The monster of the deep must keep them away." She smiled as she said it, but it was a troubled smile. "Still, I'd have thought somebody would harvest the jinkoh and tales of misfortune be damned. The island and its reputation do not match."

"To our benefit, it seems," Edward said.

"So it seems," she agreed.

It didn't take long to light a fire. Once it burned, Hya drove two sticks into the sand and hung her blanket to dry. Though the air wasn't cold, she crowded near the fire.

Edward sat against the boat. The lethargy of *zumbi* exhaustion lurked nearby. He couldn't give in. This was a wasted day. They had made a few leagues before encountering the fumarole fish and since accomplished nothing more than dragging the boat out of the water. They still needed to patch it, still needed a new mast.

He pushed himself up. "No rest," he said aloud.

"What happens if you don't rest?" Hya asked.

He steadied himself against the boat. His peripheral vision faded. "The world gets smaller."

She nodded thoughtfully. "You are moving more slowly, less certainly. Sit, before you fall."

He took an unsteady step. "I have no time to waste."

"If you persist, you will be wasting your actions. You can do nothing meaningful in that state."

With exquisite control, Edward brought his palm down until it just touched the wet hull of the boat. "I am in control."

"Clearly." She stretched and leaned back from the fire, but her eyes never left him. "We stop now because it gives you a better chance to succeed later. Better a seaworthy boat, eh?"

He stared at her through the tunnel of his vision, aware that he was losing the battle with lethargy but reluctant to embrace it. He *needed* to reach Nekyia.

He suddenly chuckled. "I am a boat, am I? Forgive me, for not seeing your meaning immediately." He sat down again. "Twice the work in half the time later if I rest now, that's what you say?"

She nodded.

The lethargy surged in him, and rather than fight it, he lowered his head to his knees and closed his eyes.

☠

He woke, as he had become accustomed to doing, as if a curtain was pulled back from the world. He could not have rested long, for the light of the moon still obscured the stars, making them small and dim as it dominated the night's stage.

The wind whispered in his ear. It carried the surf, the rustling palms, and the smell of the shore. But it also carried hints, promises of life and love and peace of mind.

He climbed to his feet, puzzled. Turning in place, he could only see those things he heard with his ears—the surf and the palms. He took a couple steps and brushed the cinders of the fire with his foot, stirring the smell of ashes into the air.

Still he felt those hints in some way he couldn't describe. "Hya? Do you hear that?"

She did not answer. Her rune stakes were dark—deactivated, her blanket thrown aside. Edward looked around, but she was not there.

"Hya?"

He walked to the water's edge. He again turned in place, this time looking for Hya. She was not there, only the mind-whispers of life, of love, of all he desired.

"Hya?"

Her footsteps, those that hadn't been washed away, followed the beach to the rocky promontory in the distance. He paused, wondering if he should follow. She surely knew how to take care of herself.

The whispering in his mind suggested everything he wanted lay nearby. It didn't matter that he was Dead; he could be cured. It didn't matter that Becca was in England; true love could be his. His cares would vanish. He only needed to heed the whispers beckoning as, he realized, Hya had.

Best to take the lure, to follow the whispers and Hya, and see where they led. A part of him distrusted the whispers and feared for Hya, but another part longed desperately for such an easy solution to his troubles.

The moonlight on the sand gave a daylight luster to the night. He could have read easily enough—if he had anything to read. He lost Hya's trail in places, but the windblown sand was otherwise smooth so he knew she stayed near the water.

The promontory jutted out into the ocean. Hya might have swum around, or she might have climbed over. He took hold of the coarse rock and began to climb, all the time the mind-whispering filling his thoughts with fancies of paradise.

At the top, he stood, feeling the wind caress his cheeks. The beach on the far side stretched away, unbroken by Hya or her footsteps. The promontory ran toward the center of the island, clumps of sea grass grew sporadically across the top, and sand filled depressions in the rock.

"Where did you go?" Edward murmured.

Surf broke on the promontory, and from this angle he could see a cave hidden from the beach. Moments later he had scrambled down and waded out to the opening.

The low-hanging moon shone deep into a tunnel of dark stone, reflecting off the water and making it as light inside the tunnel as out. The mind-whispering spoke louder, almost audibly, and he knew Hya had come this way.

He splashed into the tunnel, the water midway up his calves. It seemed enchanted, the tunnel so bright, seemingly strewn with diamonds as the moonlight reflected off bits of wet seaweed clinging to the walls.

Paradise beckons sang in his mind.

The words got stronger as he went further down the tunnel. The light diminished until it was only a bright spot behind him and ahead lay darkness. The tunnel curved, and the light behind disappeared.

He felt his way along, hand on the wall, feet shuffling on the sandy floor; the water gently pushing him forward as the tide rose. What had Hya found when she followed the whispers? His nagging distrust of the mind-promises birthed a fear for her, and it threaded through his desire for paradise.

The tunnel curved again, revealing a faint glow far ahead. He slowed, trying to move quietly. The light came through a natural arch at the end of the tunnel. He crept up to the arch.

A cavern, shaped like a dome, had a natural oculus through which the top of the moon, having risen in the sky, peered in. The curve of walls was uneven, with large patches of shadow, but the moonlight illuminated a terrace piled high with a bewildering array of detritus.

A few things stood out from the clutter: a four-poster bed with heavy drapes, a candelabra with a dozen candles, and a statue of some ancient near-eastern god. But the rest was indecipherable at first glance, a heap of the odd and bizarre.

An odd place to live, Edward thought. What sort of creature lived in a lair like this? Where was Hya?

He went forward cautiously. The mind whispers swirled around him, stronger, more persistently.

The sand gave way to steps—broad, even steps—and he climbed up to the top of the terrace. He picked his way among the jumble, objects of gold and wood, china, metal, a burled walnut wardrobe, door ajar, clothes falling from it. Small things mounded everywhere, silks, trinkets, brassware, silver, and bottles—bottles and jars of every shape and size. Amphorae, demijohns, chemist's flasks, perfume bottles of glass or alabaster, everywhere he looked lay clay and porcelain and glass and metal and stone containers.

Set apart from the clutter, a cage of iron covered a small pool that had been scooped out of the rock. Both the cage and pool were six or seven feet across. Movement flickered in the depths, and a merman surfaced, grabbed the bars, and hung watching him.

Edward edged past, not turning his back. The merman dropped back into the water, circled twice, his head almost touching his tail in the pool, and resurfaced to grab the bars facing Edward.

The merman stared with midnight eyes and an unspoken malevolence.

"You're perfectly safe," said a voice. "From him."

Edward located the speaker within seconds. A small woman stood in a little clearing in the junk. Her dark hair absorbed the moonlight as she tilted and turned her head. She smiled, showing white teeth that made the pits of her eyes darker in contrast. She wore a collection of cast-off finery, silks and jamdani, and a half-dozen bangles on each arm.

"Just don't get too close," the woman said.

Behind her stood Hya, motionless, her face pale, almost silver in the moonlight, and a sheen of perspiration made her look like a freshly drowned corpse.

"Hya!"

The woman threw out her arm, slapping a dagger against Hya's chest. Hya twitched, like a horse does when the fly bites, but did not pull away.

The threat of the knife kept Edward from moving. "What are you doing?"

"My house," answered the woman. "My guests. My questions."

It was a curious knife. It had a silver blade, shot through with red copper—wire, perhaps, embedded in the blade and looking like blood.

"You have a lot of stuff here," he said, not taking his gaze from this strange woman.

"I take what I want." She pulled the dagger away and turned it over and over in her hand, negligently, as she smiled at him. Her eyes, he noticed, looked away.

"Without apology," he murmured. Hya did not move, even with the knife removed.

"To whom should I apologize?" The old woman spread her arms to encompass the cavern. "It is mine."

"Who are you?" Edward moved through the jumble, and she turned to keep her face toward him, though her eyes still did not look at him.

"Parlexi," she said in a sing-song voice.

"And what do you want with us?"

"Why do you question what is mine? This is mine," she reached out with the dagger and flicked a gold necklace, sending it to the floor. "This is mine." She drew the flat of the dagger along the wooden frame of a cheval mirror. "And you are mine," she thrust the dagger toward him like a long finger.

Edward ran his hand over the lid of a Roman chest, feeling the deep carvings in the ancient wood. He drew it back from the gold cage that held a tiny, perfect skeleton of a bird.

"And you take good care of your things, I see," he said.

"They serve their purpose."

Hya's breath caught, and she trembled.

Edward circled, keeping his distance from this strange woman, trying to fathom her purpose. As he did, he saw what held Hya's attention—a dark glow.

Like the mind-whispers spoke more to his mind than his ears, so this glow spoke more to his mind than his sight. It drew his attention without illuminating even the box that held it. And the box was curious, black iron, built for strength and further strengthened with magical runes. Its lid was thrown open, but a wire net restrained whatever gave off the dark glow.

"I took the voice of the siren as she fell at Aptera," Parlexi said. "What use had she of it then? The muses had already taken her feathers."

"*You* took the siren's voice? The siren that nearly lured Ulysses to his death? That's not pos—" He didn't finish, for he had learned to believe the impossible.

"I take what I want," Parlexi said. She rolled the knife's hilt in her palms. "All the days of your life." She laughed.

Edward frowned. He started to move again, one eye on Parlexi and Hya, the other on the collection that spanned millennia.

"Can't stay away," sang Parlexi, swaying as she did. "Some fall hard, some fall soft, but all fall."

The mind-whispers, the siren's song, cocooned him. Its message ran through his brain.

Reaching the far side of the terrace, Edward glanced over the edge. He only meant to ensure nothing crept behind him, but he froze.

Bones filled the water below him. Skeletons lay stretched or twisted, their bones carelessly intermingling. He could not count them all and dared not try.

"All fall," Parlexi sang.

The merman hung from his cage, staring at Edward.

"The siren's call pulls you," Parlexi sang, and now she shimmied, glorying in her power. "Come, come as this little girl has come. She fell hard, you fell soft, but it makes no difference.

"All the days of your life," she cooed.

"I will not spend my days here," Edward said.

She laughed, a sound of genuine mirth. "You think you can leave with the siren's song in your ears?"

He wanted to hear that all would be well. He wanted everything the song promised, and even if he could not have it, there was a certain allure to just hearing the promises. Who could refuse easy salvation?

"But do not fear," she said as she sashayed toward him, rolling the dagger between her palms. "You won't stay, only the days of your life."

He shuffled back, coming to the edge of the terrace. He wondered if he should jump into the shallow water, but he was loath to land amongst the bones. He was missing something. He wished he could think more clearly.

"How old are you, boy? How many days will you give me?"

And he knew what she wanted. He opened his mouth to speak, but she struck.

She uncoiled, impossibly fast, stretching out, driving the knife into his chest before he could move. "Ahhh," she said, a look of pleasure coming over her face as the cold knife plunged into him.

Rage exploded from him. "I will give you nothing," he growled. He broke her grip on the knife and pushed her back.

She stumbled, knocking junk from a table. "How can this be?" She shrank from him as he advanced.

"You cannot steal my life, witch. I'm already Dead."

She sprang away. "Do not harm me! Do not harm an old woman!"

"Old, yes," Edward said. "Old with stolen years of others! How many years? How many lives? HOW MANY?" He pulled the knife from his chest and brandished it. "Is this the tool of your deviltry?"

She whimpered and scuttled back. She grabbed a pot and hurled it at his head. In spite of her words of helplessness, she moved quickly and her eyes roved, looking for something to use against him.

"Whose knife was it first, for likely you stole this too?" He advanced again, ducking away from another thrown bottle.

She tripped over her junk, sending cascades of trinkets before her. "Do not harm an old woman!" She knocked over a pile of bottles, which shattered on the stone terrace.

From the corner of his eye, Edward saw the merman beckon. He reached toward Parlexi and flexed his fingers.

Parlexi kept moving, now toward Hya. Edward jumped between them. "Why do you pursue me thus?" Parlexi whined.

"Because you're a mad old crone whose weakness is a sham."

"You don't know the half of it, boy. Just wait 'til I find my rod and I'll teach you dead."

He drove her back and forth, ducking and twisting to keep himself between her and Hya, trying to herd her away and keep her from grabbing anything dangerous. She moved spryly for an old woman, scooping up random objects, taking a quick look, and hurling them at him.

He wove back and forth, never quite grasping her, but still forcing her back, keeping her from Hya.

"I'll let you go," Parlexi said, whimpering, pathetic. "Your lady, too." This time she grabbed a metal wand, and her face broke into a snaggle-toothed grin. She took one step back and brandished the rod.

Edward froze, wondering at the rod's power.

She fell. Her body jerked back. She twisted and screamed, dropping the rod, which rolled to Edward's feet.

"I'll not let you go," the merman said. He pulled her closer and closer, grabbed her arm, and pulled her body against the cage. She screamed and struggled, but he held, caught her by the hair and then the neck. Her screams choked off, replaced by the sound of crushing cartilage.

The merman twisted Parlexi like a child playing with a toy, but brutally. Edward turned away, not wanting to watch. He still heard the popping and snapping of her body even as the siren's song whispered its pledge of paradise in his mind.

He went to the box and closed it. The song ended.

Hya let out a scream of pent-up anguish. She dropped to her knees and curled over, panting. "Oh, God," she said. "Oh, My God."

Edward stood over her. "Are you all right?"

"She was going to steal my life."

Edward held up Parlexi's dagger. "That's what I thought. She has been doing it for hundreds, maybe thousands of years. If you believe her." He dropped the dagger next to the black iron box. "These are evil things."

"She was evil," Hya said. She took a deep breath and straightened up. "The siren's song is rapture. I could do nothing but listen. Did you not hear it?"

"I heard it." He held out his hand. "We should not stay here."

She let him help her up. "Some fall soft."

"I am Dead," he said. "It wouldn't affect me as strongly."

Hya passed her hand over the dagger. "Immortality."

A thought struck Edward. "But would using it cure me?" He picked it up. "Would it let me return to Becca?" Edward mused, more to himself than to her. "And would I wish to be cured that way?"

"I do not think it would," Hya said. "It would make you a more youthful *zumbi*, if it worked at all."

"You know this?"

"No."

Edward nodded, accepting her words. "I could try it on an animal."

"It will not work," said the merman, once again hanging from the bars of the cage, his head sticking out to look at them. His voice was deep, husky.

Edward glanced at Hya. "I could try—"

He stopped, appalled, realizing he was about to suggest killing another person to test it. Not Hya, of course, he assured himself. It was the Dead speaking, he told himself, or some leftover desire of the Siren's, but it made him sick nonetheless. He dropped the dagger and wiped his hands on his trousers. "It is not immortality," he said, with a meaningful glance at the broken thing that was Parlexi. "It's damnation."

"It would not work," the merman said again.

"You know this knife?" Hya asked.

The merman swished his tail, sloshing water out of his pool. "Of course. She used it often."

"She must have," Edward said, "to have taken the Siren's voice. How old was she?"

"Old, old beyond measure. She remembered the fall of Uruk when Sargon the Akkad led the King-Priest Lugal-Zage-Si from the city in a neck stock."

"How old are you?"

The merman let out a short, bitter bark of laughter. "Who's to know? I've been here a long time. But my days are only my own. Set me free."

"Tell me about this knife," Hya said, ignoring his request.

"It is as you say. The only thing it cures is age, not sickness or injury. And it only works with humans. Used by a human on a human." He curled his lip. "She told me, to make me feel *safe*."

"So," Edward said, "no temptation." It was for the best, but he was disappointed, and he hated himself for feeling it. It would have been so easy, and far more certain, to use the knife than seeking a necromancer's help.

"Set me free," demanded the merman.

Hya sneered. "So you can lure sailors to their doom? That's a favorite game of merfolk."

The merman lowered himself, leaving only his head above water. He pushed back, bumping against the far side of the pool and returned to the front. "I have no desire for such sport," he said. "I've seen too much of it here."

"Why should I believe you?" Hya said.

"Because I want to," Edward said suddenly, surprising himself. She gave him a perplexed look and he went on. "He has seen horrors enough to change the hardest heart. And," he confessed, "he did a deed I didn't want to do."

"That was his own revenge," Hya said.

"Still, it was a service." He crouched down. Large coach screws held the cage to the terrace. There was no way to easily open the cage. Recalling the caged skeletal bird, Edward felt sure Parlexi would have been just as happy with a dried pool and dead merman. "We can't leave him waiting to die." He looked at the merman. "Did Parlexi have pliers?"

"I don't know. I was a gift from Restless Davy," the merman said. "He built this cage."

Hya sucked in a breath. "Restless Davy."

Edward stood up and brushed his hands on his trousers. "Let's look around. There must be something in all this…" He floundered for a word to describe the eclectic collection. "Junk. Maybe there's something in a jar that will serve as tar to caulk the seams of our boat."

While they searched, Hya came close and whispered, "We don't want to be here if Restless Davy returns."

"The tide's been rising," Edward said, nodding toward the entrance, and only exit, now mostly submerged.

Hya swore and Edward smiled. The Siren's call must have truly rattled her if she hadn't noticed the tide.

Edward found a bag of smith's tools. Old, crude things that might have been a hundred years old or a thousand, but it had a metal hammer and chisel.

The sound of metal on metal echoed in the chamber as he sheared the heads of the coach screws. The merman helped him lift the cage off and throw it into the water.

"You have my thanks," the merman said. With a surge of water, he burst from the pool. Two strokes of his tail and pulls from his arms sent him over the side of the terrace into the water. He breached the surface like a porpoise, arching once and splashing back underwater before shooting through the entrance.

"This should work," Hya said behind him.

Looking after the merman and envying him, Edward said, "Excellent." The high tide made them wait, but it allowed the merman his freedom. There was a certain irony in that.

Pottery scraped on stone, and Hya said, "Pine resin, probably intended to make perfume or retsina. We'll have to heat it."

Her words finally registered, and Edward felt a rush of relief. They could make pitch. That amphora would save them days at least.

Hya followed his gaze toward the entrance. "Be grateful for the merman's thanks," she said. "And don't expect anything further."

Edward laughed. "Then we wait until the tide turns." He expected her to move away, maybe to rummage through the treasure and trash, but she stayed next to him.

"You saved my life," she said. She looked away. "Twice."

"Twice?" He couldn't think of another time.

"With the mermaid. I would have gone over the side, and she would have ensured I drowned."

"Oh." He chuckled, trying to make light of it. "One of us, at least, should live."

"Do not give up hope!"

"I have not." He shook his head. "No, I have not. Still, I sit here surrounded by treasures to rival the *Arabian Nights,* and all I can think is that we waste time waiting for the tide to turn." He shook his head again. "It is strange indeed. On this night it was good to be Dead."

"Yes," she agreed. Then she pointed out, "You don't breathe; you needn't wait for the tide."

"It would be ungallant to leave you." He held his hands, palms up, indicating his helplessness and laughed.

She smiled, a smile that changed her face, eased some grimness from around her eyes and lips that he hadn't even noticed before. "I never expected a *zumbi* to act so graciously." Again she looked away, a little shy, a little sly. "At times I have a hard time thinking of you as a *zumbi*."

"Yet should I not find a cure, you will have to destroy me."

"I think if I should have to do that, I would weep."

Thinking of Rebecca, Edward said, "Perhaps you would weep alone."

"No!" she said, her head snapping up. "I shall see you back to England. I owe you that much, at least. Be you dead or alive, I shall see it done. Your Rebecca shall hear your story. And if she is any sort of woman at all, she will marry you if you live, and weep for you if you do not."

Uncomfortable with the turn of the conversation, Edward rose and began to poke through the odds and ends of Parlexi's collection. He wanted something to take his mind off death, yet his eyes wandered over her broken body. He turned away and by chance saw the bones of her victims resting under the clear water. "Yes," he said, "on this night, it is good that I am already Dead."

"There is something you have forgotten," Hya said.

"What is that?" Her blue eyes didn't seem a safe place to look, but he found them preferable to the sunken bones.

"You have a hole in your heart," she said. "You may not care now, but you will if you find a cure for Dead."

Edward swore. She was right; in the pursuit of Parlexi, he had forgotten. He pawed at his shirt until he found the hole Parlexi's knife made. Pulling it open he stared at the matching hole in his chest.

The inside was pale pink and bloodless. He could not see the bottom. He did not doubt it would kill a living man, and if he lived, it would kill him.

"She has killed me," he said in wonder. Rage flared through him. "The bitch has killed me!" He swept the top of a bureau, sending a cascade of trinkets to the floor. "Damn her." He clenched his fists and held them before him, head bowed, struggling to control his anger and grief. Dead tissue did not heal.

Slowly he lowered his fists and tapped the bureau. "She has killed me, damn her."

Chapter Eight

Once back on the beach, Edward's hopes did not rise with the sun. They stayed low in spite of finding a suitable tree to replace the mast. He had felled the tree automatically, because he needed to, and he now trimmed branches from the trunk for the same reason.

Hya pounded resin-soaked rope into the chinks between the strakes of the boat's hull. A strong smell of pine filled the air. She would pause and look at the sun, now several inches above the horizon, as if wondering, but what she wondered, he did not know. Perhaps it was simple wonder at seeing another day.

Nekyia had little reason to cure him and even less to heal his heart. "I ask too much," Edward muttered, "and have too little to offer." Rather than heal and cure him, it seemed more likely Nekyia would do neither. "Yet I have to try. For Becca's sake."

It is only the goodness in others that has made them help me. He paused his trimming to stare over the sea. "Nekyia has no goodness," he muttered to himself.

"I know somebody who might be able to help," Hya said, her voice intruding into his thoughts.

Edward froze, turned to her in astonishment. "Why didn't you say something earlier?"

"I don't know if he can help, or if he will help. And," she added, "he's a little out of the way."

The words made Edward shiver. "How far?"

"Two weeks. A week there and a week back." She still hadn't looked at him but kept hammering rope into the cracks in the hull.

"Who is it?"

Hya didn't answer the question. Instead she said, "He may be more likely to heal dead flesh than Nekyia."

"May?"

"What I know of Nekyia suggests he would think it amusing to cure you of Dead without healing you." She shrugged. "But who knows what is true and what isn't?"

"And this man you suggest wouldn't do that?"

She hesitated. "No. He cannot cure you, but he may be able to heal you."

"May," Edward muttered. "May means maybe not. And then I will have wasted two weeks." He swung the hatchet salvaged from Parlexi's cave, severing a branch from the trunk. "Two weeks," he muttered. "Just two days ago I liked my chances. No longer." He thought of his *aqua vitae*, conjuring an image of the bottle and judging its contents. "This somebody is more likely to heal me than Nekyia?" he persisted.

Hya nodded. "If he can."

"I feel better knowing who it is."

"A friend. An old friend I haven't seen in years," she answered.

He sighed. "Take me to him."

She finally looked up and met his eyes. "It's your best chance, I think, but I worry about time."

That surprised a laugh from him. "So do I."

They returned to work. Edward trimmed a bit faster. "Is there really hope?"

"There is always hope."

Edward, disbelieving and angry, glared at his hands as he cut another branch. "I cannot pray for miracles. Is there hope *I* can grasp?" He glanced at her.

Hya wiped sweat from her brow. "What have you been doing 'til now, if you have no hope?"

Bitterly, though he knew it wasn't entirely true, Edward said, "I have been blindly running."

"You have come far."

"I've been lucky."

She did not argue that. "Of all the things my father taught me, confidence is the most important."

Edward snorted. "I know little of necromancers or the Narrow World. What changes if I am confident or not?"

"Your chances." She held his gaze for a second.

"I don't understand."

"Who are you?" she asked.

"I don't know what you mean."

"Who are you?" she repeated.

"Edward Truscott, but—"

"And what are your abilities?"

"What? I'm a clerk."

"That's all? You know your sums and nothing more?"

"No," he said in exasperation. "You seem to want me to reveal some hidden talent that will allow me to sail easily through the Narrow World. I don't have any such talent."

"No," she said sharply, "that's not what I want. Listen to me. You are Edward Truscott, and you cannot be poisoned."

The thought made him pause. "I cannot be poisoned." He repeated, turning the words over in his mind. "That's true." The breeze stirred the sand. He watched, not really following the grains as they tickled his feet. "But I don't see how that helps."

"What else can you do?" Hya demanded. "It is part of who you are, each skill is a tool that cannot be taken away from you. Know yourself, know your tools, and know your chances."

"My skills are not suited for this task. I am a clerk."

"And yet you sit here trimming a new mast," Hya said.

Edward took a vicious swipe at a branch, cleanly cutting it from the trunk. "I cut enough firewood in Cornwall to know how to use an axe.

It—"

"And you have turned that skill toward your goal," Hya interrupted. "Confidence is knowing your skills and knowing that whatever the challenge, you will not be helpless."

"So if I'm confident, I'll win through?" he snarled.

"It is no guarantee, but it helps." She positioned a strand of rope in a sprung seam and laid her chisel on it. Glancing up, she smiled. "Who doesn't need help at times?" She tapped the rope into the crack.

She paused again. "You have negotiated terms? A contract for the colliery, perhaps?" He nodded. She asked, "Who is more successful, the timid negotiator or confident one?"

"The confident one, of course."

Hya nodded and waved her hand to encompass their surroundings. "You negotiate with the Narrow World now."

Edward threw his head back and laughed. "You're saying I should bluff!"

She laughed too. "Sometimes that too. But think of your skills. One of them may be your key to success."

He felt his spirits lift. "I can make any kind of porcelain." He offered this tentatively; it did not seem relevant.

"Good."

"I do not sleep," he said. "Exactly. I run out of energy." He began to warm to the task. "I know something of china clay mining, and of the colliery business. I am well-read."

"You can use an axe," Hya offered.

"I can read."

"Can you patch your trousers?"

"I can," Edward said, looking at his trousers, searching for a hole.

"Good," Hya said, her eyes twinkling. "Then you can mend the sail."

"But," he looked about helplessly, feeling like he had fallen for a trick, but her wry smile made him laugh and shake his head.

"Women's roles aren't so tightly defined in the Narrow World," she reminded him, a little smugly he thought.

Judging he had trimmed enough, he cut the top from the tree.

"If only we had a steamship," she said. "We wouldn't need to bother with the sail."

He nodded. "You mentioned steam engines before," he said, leaving the statement hanging, hoping she would take it up so the conversation wouldn't lapse.

She did, her face brightening. "Fascinating things. Steamships, railroads, power looms, water pumps; this new industry is changing the world."

"You don't have it here?"

She shot him a vexed look. Clearly they didn't, and this made her unhappy. "We're, well, not pastoral, but not inclined toward industry. Nor have any steamships paid visit to Port Astarte. The sailors say they are becoming more common, but I've yet to see one." She paused, her expression becoming thoughtful.

Edward marveled that she should come to trust him in such a short time. "The worlds get further and further apart," she said. "Perhaps there will be a time when we can no longer pass from one to the other; when people like the *Custos* have destroyed all the magic in the Wide World."

"The *Custos* use magic," Edward pointed out.

"The *Custos* are suspicious of all magic. I could envision them destroying the light along with the dark." She regarded him with a rueful smile. "They don't deal in shades of grey."

Edward wondered if this was an apology for her earlier treatment. He cleared his throat, grabbed the sail, and began to lay it flat. "You can always visit us."

Hya acknowledged the invitation with a smile, but said, "Not I. The King forbids it. Another reason I know so little of these new technologies. To my regret but not his."

"Why would the King forbid it?"

"We have a good life in the Narrow World. He does not understand this new technology and has no wish to learn. He fears it will ruin what we have."

"That's no reason to keep you from learning." He felt a flash of irritation on her behalf.

"To him it is."

Edward appreciated their conversation, so much different than the hours of suspicious silence in the boat. He took a break from sewing to help drag the boat into the water where Hya checked every seam for leaks. The day went quickly, and by nightfall, Hya declared the boat worthy.

Edward finished sewing shortly after, and both agreed there was no reason they could not sail in the morning.

"Better than I expected," he admitted. "I envisioned several days of mending. Just a day and a half lost to the fumarole fish." He sighed, his hand straying to the hole in his chest. "And two weeks to Parlexi."

☠

"Why do I feel as if I've done this before?" Edward asked as they slid the boat into the water and he held it steady while Hya climbed in.

"We're in an archipelago," Hya said. "How did you expect to travel?"

Hya took the tiller and steered them out to sea. "How much will you tell your lady love about Parlexi?"

"I don't know," Edward admitted, wondering why she asked. "I was too rushed to confide my condition when I left."

"Would you have?"

Edward hung his head. "No. I didn't want to believe I was Dead." He remembered his frantic dash across London, but also the two letters he had written. He had not told her then, either. "And," he admitted, "I fear she will reject me." He paused before raising the sail. "I do her a disservice, I know, yet I can't help myself."

Hya gave a soft grunt. "I don't blame you for fearing."

"Thanks," Edward said sourly. He yanked the line to raise the sail.

"I didn't mean to judge you," Hya said. A blush stole over her chagrined face. "Or her. Only that relations with a *zumbi* are complicated. Moreso than I imagined."

"Ah." He jerked the sail to the top of the mast, angrily tied it off, and forced the air from his lungs. Almost as if he filled the sail by his action, it billowed out. He feared his repair would tear loose, but the stitching held. The boat surged forward.

A fresh breeze blew in from the sea, frisking above the waves. "As it blows in, so it blows us out," Edward said.

The sail slackened, billowed out again as the wind eddied.

"A restless wind," Hya said.

A restless wind indeed, Edward thought as it swirled around them. It seemed to carry an expectation, but he couldn't tell what it might be.

"Good riddance to Parlexi and her cursed box." Hya closed her eyes and shuddered. "Even now I can hear it, I *want* to hear it, telling me I can go to the Wide World and learn all they have to teach me." She opened her eyes. "A torture when I know it isn't true."

The conversation lapsed, but the silence was pleasant, less tense than previously. Hya rummaged among the remaining goods and pulled out her hat. She wore it back now, so the sun hit her face, and that seemed to illustrate the change in their relationship. Edward couldn't repress a smile even as he worried about this side trip they took.

Parlexi's island had shrunk to the size of his hand when the wind suddenly stopped. Edward lurched on his seat as the boat responded to the change. "What—?" He rose.

The air was utterly still, as if the Anemoi held their breaths. Edward rested his hand on the mast, looking back. "Is this the way the doldrums usually occur?"

"No," Hya said. She shaded her eyes with her hand, looked about them, and ended up looking back as well. "I wonder what caused it." Their experience with Parlexi was clearly fresh in her mind.

For long minutes they drifted, looking back, but seeing no sign of the cause.

The air around Parlexi's island grew dark, as though a dark lace curtain had been drawn. The haze congealed until black clouds boiled over the island.

"I've never seen clouds gather like that," Edward said. "Volcano?"

Hya shook her head.

"Normal weather for the Narrow World?"

"No."

"Trouble then." It wasn't a question, but she nodded anyway. "It seems," Edward went on, "I'm either running to something, or from something." He had never seen clouds so dark. "It may be time to run from these."

A gust of wind caught them, hurled them forward before dropping off.

"We'll go fast, but not fast enough to outrun the wind," Hya said. "Can you row?"

She must jest. I've been rowing since we met. She does jest. He hadn't suspected such dry humor from her.

Another gust of wind, stronger than the first, grabbed them, causing the bow to furrow a deep trough in the sea as they sliced forward. It tore the tops off the waves and Hya's hat from her head. She gave a small exclamation as it twirled away, landing crown down and floating beyond reach.

Thunder rumbled through the air, through the boat so that Edward could feel it shiver, and through his bones. Deep and ominous, it sounded like the growl of an angry beast.

The clouds reached out, grabbing the sun and smothering it, clawing at the horizon as if they would draw it closer. The sky grew dark, but not cold. The wind blew hot against Edward's skin.

The sea surged, lifting the boat and carrying it forward only to drop it. Another swell snatched them and repeated the process. Wave after wave, each larger than the last, fled the wind, fled the island behind them and carried them a small distance before leaving them behind.

Not trusting his stitches in the gusts, Edward fumbled with the knots securing the sail. The wind nearly tore the rope from his hands, but he managed to corral the unruly sail and bring it safely down.

"Restless Davy!" Hya shouted. The wind whipped her words away, and he barely grasped them before they were gone.

"What?" he shouted back.

"Restless Davy is causing this!"

Edward clung to the mast. "Why is he so angry?"

"I think somebody just killed his girlfriend."

"But he's a sailor! He must have a girl in every port."

"Perhaps he had expectations of this visit." She managed to look sly in spite of the wind whipping her hair across her face.

The waves swelled, growing ever taller and taller. While in the troughs, Edward couldn't see over the next crest and he felt hedged in by mountainous waves. They would climb the next wave, but the clouds hung low and the day grew dark. The world seemed very small and not at all friendly.

Heavy drops of warm rain slapped the sea, thudded into the boat, and hit Edward hard enough to sting. They shattered when they hit, scattering smaller drops like shrapnel.

The mast creaked and Edward looked at it in alarm. "How long will this last?" he asked, fully aware they hadn't seen the worst of Davy's anger.

"You tell me," Hya shouted. "You're a man. How angry can he get?"

"Words fail me," he muttered.

Water sloshed around the boat, but it was impossible to tell if it was from the rain and spray or if they had sprung a leak.

Hya kept her grip on the tiller, though Edward knew she couldn't tell their direction. The storm had swallowed sight of land.

Lightning shattered the sky and the storm's fury engulfed them. Edward crouched down, holding the gunwales. He didn't dare move about. The boat pitched so severely he feared it would capsize.

The storm thrashed them, ten minutes, twenty, an hour; it felt like days. At a momentary slackening of the rain, he lifted his head. "Can we endure much more?"

Hya was looking away, eyes wide, face pale. "God help us," she said. "It's Restless Davy."

Far off to starboard, a man approached.

Davy wasn't anything Edward expected except terrifying. He waded toward them. Waded—he didn't swim, he didn't walk on the water. He waded through water that came up to mid-calf, rising and falling with the waves, the water always to mid-calf.

Edward couldn't take his eyes from Davy as they both rose and fell, neither in time with the other. One second he would be looking up at Davy, the next down—but always Davy strode closer.

Davy wore a severely cut naval frock coat, devoid of the gold embroidery so popular among officers. An unheeded clump of seaweed draped over his shoulder, straggling down and trailing in the water behind him. He wore no hat but did not mind the driving rain that plastered his dark hair to his head and ran through his closely clipped beard.

They fell into a trough while Davy rose on a crest, higher and higher until when they were at the utter bottom and he at the peak, lightning struck him.

Edward cried and turned his head, the image of Davy silhouetted against the blinding light burned into his brain. He tried to blink it away.

He still could not see when something thudded at the bow of the boat and it stopped as though hitting a wall. A deep voice said, "You be in dangerous waters."

Davy formed, first as a shadow, then a man, a big man that felt even larger. His hands rested on the gunwales on either side of the prow. He stood outside the boat as easily as if standing on shore. Edward blinked and nodded, trying to buy a few moments to regain his sight completely.

"A mistake," he said, his mouth ironically dry despite the rainwater pouring down his face.

"Beyond doubt it be a mistake. This day be full of mistakes."

Without anything rational to say, Edward's manners took over. "May we be of service?"

Hya gaped at him, and he felt incredulous himself. What could they possibly do to help Davy when they could not help themselves?

"Your offer be kind," Davy rumbled, his voice coming from so deep in his chest that it might have been from the storm itself. "But unless you can raise the dead, you cannot help. Nay, you cannot help," he repeated, his expression forlorn.

In for a penny, in for a pound. "Edward Truscott, at your service." He climbed over the front seat and held out his hand. Davy shook it, his large hand rough and cold.

"David Jones, at yours." He bobbed his head to Hya. "Ye know me best as Restless Davy."

Hya, clutching the tiller in her white-knuckled fist, managed to nod in return. "A pleasant day to you, Sir." Her voice sounded high and tight, pitched poorly to carry over the sound of the wind and rain.

"Too late for that, but I thank you for the sentiment. My bonnie lass is dead, and I be grieving."

Edward licked his lips, swallowed, and said, "I'm sorry for your loss." Although Edward did not regret Parlexi's death, he thought, *if the loss causes him to wreck us, then I am sorry for it.* Davy seemed a nice enough man, but the way he stood in the water and steadied their boat with tendrils of steam rising from the lightning-charred seaweed was unnerving.

"Murdered, she was, most foully." Davy's voice dropped several octaves and wood cracked under his hands as he clutched the gunwales. He glared down, irritated at the gunwale or his own large hands. "I'd do likewise to the one that did her in." He brushed splinters off on his trousers.

It's good that my heart isn't beating or he'd surely hear it. A glance at Hya told Edward there would be no help there. She looked too scared to move. He didn't know if Davy toyed with them, but had no choice but to keep pretending to be ignorant. "You must have cared for her very much."

Davy seemed startled by the comment, his anger diverted as he pondered. "We've known each other for years, and I've visited often." His eyebrows drew together as he paused. "She was a bonnie lass who knew how to make a man feel welcome. She be an odd one, though, I have to admit, with an eye to gathering things."

By his speech it was hard to tell if Parlexi were alive or dead. *What a pair!* Edward thought. *She was mad, and he as changeable as the sea. I'd not want to trust my life to his mood, but it may save us now.*

"True it be," Davy continued, "that she had a habit of asking for more than then a man wants to give." He took on a thoughtful tone and the wind lessened. "And I was always as happy leaving as coming."

Davy shook his head. "But she's dead now, and I'd like to think the best of her."

Edward recalled Parlexi's knife and the feeling it made stabbing him. His hand twitched, but he resisted the urge to feel the hole in his chest. *I think it's best she is dead.*

"Murdered," Davy growled and thunder rolled across the ocean. "Most brutally and foully killed." He speared Edward with his gaze. "It would do my soul good to avenge her."

He doesn't know! He must not know. But how can he not know when we're so close to the island?

"She had a merman, see?" Davy said, his fists clenching and unclenching. "She kept it like a man might keep a lion. It killed her and made its escape. A vile creature."

Edward noted Davy did not mention how Parlexi got the merman. He nodded in a way he hoped was sympathetic, but inside he rejoiced. Had they not freed the merman, Davy would have discovered the whole story.

Davy took a deep breath, relaxed his hands, and laid them on the boat again to steady it. "I fear my emotions have caused you discomfort." He jerked his head to indicate the storm. "I apologize."

"Think nothing of it," Hya said, her voice weak.

"It is our pleasure to meet you," Edward said. *A little flattery never hurts.* "I regret it comes in such circumstances." Although, being honest with himself, he couldn't think of any circumstance when he would want to meet Restless Davy.

"Aye. Fortunate you be. I've wrecked many a ship for being in the wrong place for the wrong reasons." His eyes narrowed. "And what *does* bring you to these waters?"

"Ah…" Sensing Davy's mood shift, Edward's mind blanked and he couldn't think of anything to say. Davy raised his eyebrows, waiting for an answer while thunder rumbled across the sky.

Edward couldn't confide the truth—he was Dead. It was one thing to dance cleverly with the truth or use polite phrases to smooth awkward social circumstances, but he had little experience lying. Every time he started to form an idea, lightning would flash and drive away his thoughts like they were shadows.

Davy's eyebrows dropped into a frown and the wind picked up.

"On our way to visit friends!" Hya blurted.

"Are you now?" Davy kept his gaze on Edward. The boat stopped rocking as if the sea had suddenly turned to cement though a few feet away the seas still ran high. "These friends be not merfolk, mayhap?"

Edward shivered, feeling a crawling sensation run down his spine. "Yes. Ah, no! Yes, we're visiting friends; no, they aren't merfolk. At least," he glanced at Hya, "that's what she tells me. I've never met them, but, ah, I'm looking forward to it." He should have thought of this himself.

Hya shook her head. "Most definitely not merfolk."

Davy looked from Edward in the bow to Hya in the stern. He burst out laughing, a deep rolling laugh that dampened the wind and calmed the sea. "It's clear who steers this ship!" He laughed some more. "She's a winsome lass, lad, but don't let her call all the shots. Make her dance to your hornpipe too!"

Edward nodded. He didn't trust himself to speak.

Davy kept chuckling. "Ah, me, 'tis good to laugh. A pretty face and a good jest will cure the world's ills. I forgot me-self a bit there."

Feeling he had a bit of Davy's measure, Edward smiled. "There are times I think you've the right of it, Sir. She *is* the pretty face and I—I *am* the good jest."

Laughing again, Davy thumped Edward on the chest with the back of his hand. It felt like being kicked by an ox. "Nay, lad, you be but young." He took a deep breath and let it out in a gust. "And there be other women." He winked at Edward. "Have a care for yours or I'll whisk her away from you!" He smiled at Hya. "How 'bout it, lass? Care to give old Davy a whirl?"

Hya looked like she had just eaten a live squid. "You flatter me, Sir."

How do you tell Restless Davy "no" without angering him? Edward wondered.

"I do, don't I?" Davy said. "I can show you the red granite gods of Herakleion or the towers of lost Atlantis."

Edward looked at Hya with alarm. The lure of Atlantis might entice her into saying yes.

"Atlantis," Hya breathed. "Your offer is good, Mr. Jones. I've half a mind to take you up on it, but what would we do with Edward?"

"A problem to be sure," Davy agreed, "but I may have a locker somewhere we can stash him in."

"Tempting," Hya said, "but all the same, I think I should look after him."

"Suit yourself." He didn't seem disappointed, and Edward felt relief. Davy looked around, judging the clouds, wind, and sea. "You be safe enough now, I reckon. Fair skies soon." He gave Hya a crooked smile, "Fair indeed, and a lucky lad he is."

He gave them a half bow. "I'll take my leave of you, and my thanks for the change of mood."

"The pleasure, Sir, was mine," Edward said. "Could you—" Edward said. He stopped, screwed up his courage, and blurted, "Could you spare us a fair wind and following sea?"

"There! You see?" Davy waggled a finger at him. "You take the same charge with her as you did just now and you'll be seeing the rewards, if you take me meaning. Aye," he went on, "a fair wind be the least I can do after giving you such a fright." Davy turned and waded away, not back toward the island, again visible on the horizon, but out to sea.

A breeze sprang up in his wake, and Edward scrambled to unroll the sail. Even without it, the boat gathered speed as some fast-moving current seized it.

"His nature is much like the sea itself," Hya murmured so that only he could hear. She glanced over her shoulder. "Overwhelming. Exhausting."

Davy still walked away from them, a small dark figure in the middle of the vast ocean. And then he was gone, having neither sunk nor flown. He merely disappeared, leaving them a fair wind to aid their journey.

"Does he take his nature from the sea, do you think?" Edward asked.

"As varied, and as quickly changed," Hya agreed.

Edward set about raising the sail. "I would not wish to leave my life in his hands, but it appears we got lucky."

Hya laughed, an expression of admiration on her face. "Did you guess his mood would turn?"

"Not I, but I'll not blurt my part in Parlexi's death before he even asks. I hope that merman has the sense to dive deep."

Hya nodded. "Speak softly." She looked around at the empty sea. "The winds carry your words to strange places. Let him get further away before…"

Edward nodded his understanding.

Neither spoke as he tied off the sail and the wind once again filled it. Hya brought them a couple points north, and they gathered speed.

"I can't believe you asked him for a fair wind!" she said.

"You mentioned confidence." He shrugged. "Or bluff. Or damn luck." He cocked an eyebrow at her. "You should have asked for your hat back."

She laughed. "This day, at least, you surpassed the teacher."

"We're on our way and will reach your friend more quickly now. That," he said, "is what's important."

Chapter Nine

Davy's good intentions became clear over the next five days. His wind dropped them off at night, invariably near an island, and picked them up again the next morning. During the day it hurried them along, changing direction with Hya's every turn of the tiller. It followed them like a puppy, all the while filling their sail. Whether it kept them safe from other dangers or not, Edward did not venture to guess. Nothing threatened them, that was certain.

When the sun reached its zenith on the fifth day Hya pointed and said, "There is our destination."

It looked unremarkable, an island, low and sandy, that rose toward the center. Thick jungle covered it. Edward shaded his eyes, but could see no sign of habitation. Only when they approached could he see a small harbor with a pier, but still no sign of life.

That approach had taken much of the remaining day, and the sun hovered inches above the horizon when Edward tied the boat to the pier—a weathered, battered thing, missing slats, and threatening to collapse under the weight of the barnacles clinging to the posts. Or maybe the barnacles held it up; Edward wouldn't bet either way.

"He thought he would have more visitors than he has," Hya said, but didn't explain further.

A boardwalk led from the pier into the jungle. It, too, was missing slats and periodically disappeared under windblown sand. At the edge of the jungle, a small wooden shed leaned like an old man using one unbroken corner post as a cane. It looked sad and forgotten, waiting for visitors who never came.

"Who lives here?" Edward asked, hoping for more than the vague, evasive answers Hya had given him every other time he asked.

"Somebody who may be able to help you," she said. That was one of three different answers. At least it wasn't, "Wait and see." That one truly strained his patience.

The boardwalk led through a path in the trees. Shrubs crowded it on either side, but the trees were evenly spaced. They met overhead forming a canopy so thick no sunlight penetrated, giving the path a gloaming feel.

The sounds of the sea grew muted as Hya led him inland. "I haven't been here since I was a little girl," she said.

They hadn't gone far, though it seemed like miles to Edward, before coming to a cleared area. There was no brush, only tall trees giving it a feeling of a great, green-ceilinged hall—if people built houses inside green-ceilinged halls. A well-apportioned house sat in the center of the clearing.

The grey lead roof gave it a dour look, and the pillars and railing, almost clean of paint, reinforced the feeling. The house had wide eaves and wide porches, making it a place of shadows. Deep shadows that hid the walls, leaving only glimpses of windows that reflected what little light struck them.

"Are you sure anyone still lives here?" Edward asked.

"In a manner of speaking, yes," Hya said as she strode past.

"What does that mean?"

Hya was already through the clearing and climbing onto the porch. Edward hurried to catch up. "Wait."

The home, although neglected, looked solid. The roof's lead sheeting might have been ten or a hundred years old. The paint on the porch peeled, and the exposed wood had turned grey, but the pillars and rails remained solid. The eight-foot windows, double hung without muntins, had impressively large sheet glass. The double front doors, no longer glossy with varnish, nonetheless hung squarely.

Hya took hold of the handles and pushed. The doors creaked as they opened. Dust stirred on the floor within. "Hello?" She leaned forward, but didn't enter. "Uncle Baldwin?"

"Uncle?" Edward felt his eyebrows rise up his forehead.

"Not really, a very old friend of the family." She took a tentative step inside. "It's a little early for him."

Edward followed her into the dark room. The room was familiar, comfortable, but distorted by darkness. It was a European sitting room, fitted with the finest Regency furniture. A large fireplace, cold, dominated the right wall. A black doorway led further into the house.

Hya walked in and around, lightly touching a chair, a settee, as if to reassure herself they were real. "Hello?" she called.

There is no help here, Edward thought. *Whoever lives here has died, and I must rely wholly on Nekyia.* The thought made him shudder.

"What do you want?" said a sharp voice. A man stood in the doorway, his dark clothes blending into the shadows, his face and hands standing out. Edward had not heard him approach. "Who are you? Why do you invade my home?"

"Uncle Baldwin!" Hya smiled.

"Hya?" He strode forward, a small smile tugging at the corners of his mouth. "Little Hya, all grown up?" Abruptly he turned away. "Been long enough," he said gruffly.

"I know. I'm sorry."

"Sorry." He snorted. "Sorry. Fifteen years, and she says she's sorry."

"Has it really been that long?"

"Don't question me, child. All I have is time. I know it well."

"Yes, Uncle. I'm sorry."

Baldwin snorted again.

"This is Edward Truscott."

Edward approached and extended his hand. "The pleasure is mine, Sir."

Baldwin did not take it and Edward stopped short. "A friend of Hya's?"

"Ah, yes." Feeling awkward, Edward dropped his hand. "At least, I fancy I am. You'd have to ask her."

Hya placed her hands on Edward's elbow, a little protectively he felt. "Yes, Uncle, he is a friend."

"Then why'd you bring him here?" Baldwin groused.

"I hoped you might help him."

"Ah, now we learn the real reason. It's not a pleasure visit at all."

Edward studied Baldwin. He was slightly shorter than Edward, with cropped dark hair, brushed forward in a windblown look—though it seemed unlikely he had been outside. His skin bore this out, for he was unusually pale, and a trifle gaunt. He wore a burgundy regency coat and brown trousers. Under his coat, he had a neckcloth tied in a bow over a grafton collar.

It was a style Edward had seen before—on old men of middling means. Thirty years out of fashion, yet Baldwin did not appear old.

"Have you eaten lately?" Hya asked.

"About time you asked. Why? Are you offering?"

She shivered. "God no." She seemed to gather herself. "No, just, well, just curious."

"Isn't everybody?" He gave her a sour look.

Edward struggled to follow the conversation. He was missing something and felt he ought to figure out what.

"If I may, Uncle Baldwin, isolation hasn't helped your disposition." Hya wiped her finger across the dusty mantle and wrinkled her nose. "What happened to Hilda?"

"I killed her," he said sullenly. "Drank her dry. Didn't take long. The biddy was nearly desiccated anyway."

"Maybe that's why nobody visits."

Baldwin frowned at her. "I didn't really. She died of old age. She wouldn't let me turn her."

"I know, Uncle," Hya said. "I'm sorry."

"Wait a minute," Edward said, grappling with an idea. "I'm sorry, but it sounds like you—like you're a vampire."

Baldwin drew back his lips, revealing two long, slightly curved, wickedly sharp eye-teeth. He snapped, and Edward jumped back.

Baldwin laughed, not altogether nicely. "I've eaten, but I could go for a snack."

"You *have* gotten grouchy," Hya said.

"Humph. You're not here to see me, really. You want something."

Could he count on help from a vampire, Edward wondered. He knew less of them than he did *zumbi*, but what he knew wasn't encouraging. Small wonder Hya hadn't told him whom they visited.

"This is getting nowhere," Hya said. "I said I'm sorry. After Undulark left, nobody would bring me, and Uncle Jeremy said I couldn't come on my own." She crossed over to Baldwin, rose up on her toes, and kissed him on the cheek. "And I am glad to see you."

That surprised a smile out of him, which he quickly hid. "Jeremy never could take a joke." He waved a hand. "Yes, yes, I *am* glad to see you, too. I've actually thought of coming to visit." He chuckled. "Wouldn't that set a cat among the pigeons?"

"Yes, Uncle, but wait a bit," Hya said. "Prester Ellis is in port right now. Give him a chance to go home."

"Ellis!" Baldwin hissed. "I've heard of him. He makes trouble for everybody. Where do the *Custos* keep finding men like him?"

Hya did not answer, nor did Edward. What could he say? The world had an inexhaustible supply of such men.

"Well," Baldwin said, dismissing both Ellis and the *Custos* with that single word. "There's no need to go now anyway. How long will you stay?"

"We can't stay long, I'm afraid." She beckoned Edward closer, the last couple steps separating them. "You see, Edward—"

Baldwin shied away, cutting her off. "A *zumbi*? Really, Hya, how could you bring him here? He reeks of Dead."

"We need your help."

"Help? I am a vampire. He is a *zumbi*. In two weeks, I will be exactly as you see me. He will be a mindless, slavering mound of maggot-infested meat. In two hundred years I will be exactly as you see me, and he will have been destroyed and forgotten two centuries past."

"Well, now that we've established the hierarchy of things," Edward muttered.

"Exactly! Ex-actly. Vampires are the greatest of the Not-Dead."

Edward half turned his head to face Hya. "Can we trust him?" he murmured.

"Yes," Hya said. "If he agrees to help, it will be honest help. He has always been keen on medicine, even before becoming a vampire." She gently turned Edward back, so they both faced Baldwin. "We would like to find a cure for his Dead."

"Well who wouldn't want a cure for their Dead? But there isn't one. I've looked." Baldwin nodded empathically. "Believe me, I've looked."

"Nekyia might know of one," Edward said.

"Maybe for you," Baldwin sounded peevish, "not for me. But if that's what you want, why are you talking to me? You should be talking to him."

"It's a question of science, I think," Hya said. "And magic, so I thought of you."

"Science?" Baldwin stood straighter and adjusted his coat. "Well, yes. I could dissect him. Properly, I mean, not with an axe like peasants do. Could learn quite a lot."

Hya gave Edward a look he knew to mean it was his turn to speak. He trusted Hya, and she trusted Baldwin, so he licked his dry lips and said, "No, Sir. The problem is I've a hole in my heart. It can't heal because, well, because I'm Dead. If Nekyia can cure me, the hole will just kill me for good. We're—that is, I'm—wondering if you might know how to heal dead flesh."

"Heal dead flesh? Impossible."

Edward sank back, his shoulders dropping. It felt as if a weight settled over his body. Hya sighed.

"However," Baldwin said. "It might be possible to," he waved his hand, as if he could conjure a word from the air, "*pretend* your heart is alive."

Glancing at Hya, Edward straightened up. "How would you do that?"

"You've read Luigi Galvani's work, I assume?"

"I'm afraid I haven't."

Baldwin rolled his eyes. "And I thought *I* was isolated. Really, Hya, why is this young man worth the effort?"

"Because you're curious to see if it'll work."

With a shrewd look, Baldwin nodded to her. "You always were a perceptive child. Haven't forgotten much, either, I see."

"I would be most grateful," Edward added.

"Then you ought to read Galvani's work." Baldwin laughed, a disquieting laugh because it revealed his fangs. "Oh, fine. In short, he sent an electric current through a frog's legs and made them twitch."

"I—" Edward licked his lips, unsure why that was important. "I would expect them to twitch."

"I said frog's legs. I didn't say they were still attached to a frog."

"I see." He didn't see immediately, but he knew he would, and sure enough he realized: "He brought the legs back to life with electricity!" Perhaps that would cure Dead! A strong enough jolt of electricity would revive his entire body.

"No." All Edward's hopes crashed with that word. Baldwin continued, "It gives a semblance of life, not real life. When the charge is discontinued, the flesh reverts back to lifelessness."

Edward grasped any hope he could. "Does the flesh heal while the electricity is applied?"

"You see where this is going," Baldwin said. "No, it doesn't. It's dead. However, that little semblance of life might be enough for a magic unguent to be effective."

Hya leaned forward. "Have you tried it?"

"Of course not. Why would I want miraculously-healed-but-still-dead frog legs?"

"But you tried Galvani's experiment," Hya persisted.

"Certainly. It sounded interesting, and it works. He was wrong about the source of the movement, though. Volta argued—"

Hya cut him off. "Do you still have the apparatus?"

"It doesn't really take any. A bit of wire, a battery, and," he glanced at Edward, "frog legs."

Hya also glanced at Edward. "Will you do it for us?" she asked.

"Child, I've played my games with that. You can only watch frog legs twitch so often before it seems pointlessly cruel, even if they are dead. It's like giving them false hope."

Edward and Hya exchanged glances. "I think this is something I'd like to try," Edward said.

"By all means. I have some wire you're welcome to use. Hya probably has unguent."

"Do you still have the battery?"

"I have the battery; it's certainly dead." He smiled, again showing his fangs. "A lot of dead things around here, eh, Edward? I couldn't find an electric eel so had to charge it with a coffin ray." He raised his eyebrows. "Nice bit of irony, me using a coffin ray. But it served once, it'll serve again."

Edward said, "The sooner we begin, the better."

"Your haste is a trifle unseemly." Baldwin sniffed. His expression, though, was like a child trying to resist a sweet. "Oh, all right," he said. "I'm curious to see if it will work; science and magic, what a delightful experiment!

"The best place to try would be the garden," he went on. "The stone circle there will enhance the unguent's efficacy. And the flowers are spectacular."

☠

Baldwin led them through the house, a rambling building much larger than it appeared from outside. Room after room, each darker than the last. Baldwin made no sound, so Edward followed the pale spots of his hands and the back of his neck.

The sun had set when they passed out the back door into the garden. It was dusk, with night gathering in the deepening shadows.

They entered the well-tended garden. Crushed seashells covered the paths. Neatly trimmed vines hung over trellis. The flowerbeds were well laid out, weeded, and full of vigorous, healthy plants. But there were no flowers. Baldwin had been quite clear, though, the flowers were to have been spectacular.

Puzzled, Edward paused at one of the beds. The plants were just over waist high, the flowers closed. Even as he watched though, they opened. Yellow petals unfolded slowly, yet visibly. It wasn't really slow, he realized, but very fast, so it took only a minute for them to fully open.

"That's amazing!" he said, distracted, for just a moment from their progress.

"Evening primrose," Baldwin said, as if he had invented it, which, as far as Edward knew, he might have.

All around him, flowers covered the greenery. Other plants had bloomed while he watched the evening primrose. The trellises were heavy with white flowers that resembled morning glories. Baldwin strolled past, reaching out to caress one while saying, "Moonflower vine."

He continued on, reciting the names of plants, "Dragon fruit, Brahma Kamal;" all plants that, apparently, only flowered at night.

"Uncle Baldwin is very proud of his garden," Hya said from behind Edward.

"And he should be."

The stone ring surprised Edward. He expected tall stones, perhaps capped by lintels. Instead it looked more like a circle of benches. It didn't help the impression when Baldwin sat down and crossed his legs, looking at them expectantly.

"Well," he said, "entertain me."

"Uncle," said Hya, "this is serious. Please get the battery."

Baldwin grumped. "You should have reminded me before we came out," but he rose and returned, still muttering, to the house.

"And a lantern, please," Hya called after him. She set her bag on one of the benches and began to rummage through it.

"A little bit of everything?" Edward asked as she set a variety of things aside, clearly looking for something else.

"You never know what you'll need," she said. "Ah, good." She held up a small jar that she handed to him.

"Bone china." He examined it, turning it over. It covered half his palm, and was less than an inch deep. Green wax sealed the top. Adequate work. "Is this the healing unguent?" He made to open it.

She took it from him. "Don't open it. It loses power quickly when exposed to air."

She had him take off his shirt and lay down on one of the benches while she examined the hole in his chest. She took a cloth from her bag and brushed the inside of the wound. While it didn't hurt, it was disquieting to watch her poking and pulling inside his chest.

"I'll have to open it a little further so I can work on your heart," she said. "I'll have to work between your ribs. That will be tricky."

Baldwin appeared, silently, not having made any noise on the crushed seashell path. "Here is your battery." He also hung a lantern on nearby trellis, wick turned up.

"Thank you," Hya said. She laid a clean cloth on the bench before taking a needle from the bag. "Silver," she told Edward. "Silk," she added, laying a small spool of thread next to the needle.

Edward watched her preparations. "What are you going to do?"

"I'll apply the unguent and sew up your heart before applying the electricity. Then, hopefully, the electricity will give your heart enough semblance of life for the unguent to work. Right, Uncle?"

"That's the best course of action, I think."

Looking for reassurance, Edward asked Baldwin, "Will it work?"

"One can hope."

Edward snorted at the answer. *At least I can't be worse off than I am now.*

Hya set the battery next to him and wiped the ends of the wires attached to the top. She touched them to her bare ankle and jumped.

"Coffin rays give better charges than I thought," Baldwin said.

Edward watched Hya take up a small knife and push it into his wound, but he turned his head as she started to cut him.

It did not hurt, not in any immediate way. It was more a distant pain, a muted pain, almost a memory of pain. He did not like it, but it was more the sight he didn't want than the feeling.

"Uncle? There's something in the way."

Baldwin joined her looking into the wound. "His lungs. A miracle they weren't punctured with the heart. They must have been collapsed. Stop holding your breath," he told Edward.

Edward did, unaware that he had been doing so.

"Ah, good. Thank you." Hya began to probe the wound again.

"There was a Turkish doctor, Sabuncuoglu who wrote *Imperial Surgery*, I think, who dealt with lungs," Baldwin said. "I doubt he worked on *zumbis,* though. Your lungs react differently than live lungs, I would expect."

"That should be enough," Hya said. Edward could feel air moving in the wound. Hya sat next to him, threading the needle. She smiled, a wan and not entirely reassuring smile.

He closed his eyes, but that didn't stop him from hearing her crack the wax seal on the unguent jar or the soft clink as she set the top on the bench. He smelled witch hazel and lavender.

"You'll want to work quickly," Baldwin said.

"Yes, Uncle," Hya replied.

He felt a brushing inside, a tightness maybe as she applied the unguent; but nothing he could describe. He closed his eyes tighter and turned his head.

"Now to sew," she said.

Her cool hands touched his heart, holding it in place while she sewed. He could feel the needle and thread; could feel it passing to and fro before tugging as she closed the wound.

The tugging stopped.

"I don't know," Hya said. "You'll likely feel this." He heard her take a deep breath.

Pain lanced through him. His eyes flew open, and he gasped.

"Hold still!"

Pain—not dull—but raw, searing pain. He felt his heart beat, and it hurt. It felt as if someone had seized his heart and squeezed. He convulsed.

"Hold still!" Hya said, throwing herself over him as she tried to keep the wires in his chest.

Each beat of his heart flared agony. Fire burned through his veins as his blood moved again, however sluggishly. He threw back his head and screamed.

He grabbed the edges of the bench, held them so tightly he could feel their rough edges pressing into his hands. He pulled down, trying to keep from moving as each beat of his heart increased the pain he felt.

"Hold still," Hya pleaded. "I think it's working, but you must hold still!"

Hands seized his upper arms. Baldwin leaned over, pressing down, dampening his movements.

"Thank you," Hya gasped.

"Oh, I'm not helping," Balwin said. "I want to see better."

Through the haze of his pain, Edward heard Hya say, "He's bleeding, but the blood's so dark."

"Not much of it. It doesn't even look appetizing."

The pain stopped.

"Is it over?" Edward asked. "Please tell me it's over."

"The first part," Baldwin said. He did not let go, just held on, pressing down as he ignored Edward and kept looking at Hya's work. "It's worked so far. Now she'll close the opening. Amazing. I had serious doubts."

Edward felt a cold slathering on his chest followed by the slight 'pop' sensation of the needle puncturing his flesh and the tugging of the stitches.

This time the pain stayed in his chest, a compact agony that gave way to an electric tingling. Hya rolled off, landing on her knees, and let out her breath. The tingling faded, and Baldwin released his arms.

He lay, forcing himself to breathe, taking comfort in the action, comfort from the lack of pain. Hesitantly, he ran his hand over his chest, feeling a slight bump. He looked down. A white line, even paler than the rest of his skin, marked the wound.

Hya panted next to him, hanging her head, drenched in sweat.

Nobody said anything.

"Thank you," Edward said. He laid a hand on Hya's shoulder. "Thank you."

She nodded, relaxing so that she sat, still breathing heavily. "I never want to do that again."

"No, I don't either."

Edward stood up. "And thank you, Sir," he said to Baldwin.

Baldwin nodded his acceptance of Edward's thanks. "You make an acceptable substitute for frog legs."

Edward laughed weakly. "I shall read Galvani. You have my word on it."

☠

It was full dark now. Edward hadn't been aware of the stealthy creep of night. It had come out from the shadows and gathered around them, staying a respectful distance from the lantern.

Baldwin perched on a bench, legs crossed and hands clasped on his knee.

Edward ran a finger over the scar in his chest, amazed at the magic. He had been amazed a lot lately. He picked up his shirt.

"How do you cope with being Dead?" he asked.

"Looking for tips? When I hunger…" Baldwin licked his lips and shuddered. "I am helpless in the bloodlust. No one is safe, no matter how much I love them. It shames me to think how close I came to devouring Hilda, and not just once. I begged her to leave, for her own sake."

"She loved you, Uncle," Hya said.

"And I loved her, but love between a mortal and a vampire... is a torment to both, I believe."

"But you controlled it," Edward said. "You did not..." he hesitated, thought better of his words. "You controlled your impulses. How did you do it?"

"My problems are not like yours," Baldwin said. "I cannot push aside the bloodlust. You do not hear animals around here. They know to stay away."

He had wondered. "Forgive me for asking, but how do you eat?"

"There is a colony of monkeys in the jungle. A poor substitute for human blood. I don't believe I can feed on a monkey if there is a human nearby, the blood lust wouldn't allow it. But I've gotten adept in sensing oncoming hunger. I used to go into the jungle when I neared my hunger times—away from any humans. Now that Hilda is dead," he shrugged, "there is less need. Still," he scowled at Hya, "it was dangerous to just walk in like you did."

"Yes, Uncle," she said. "I was eager to see you."

"Humph," he snorted, but smiled fondly. He turned to Edward. "What will you do? You're still Dead. That is not something I can undo."

"I will ask Nekyia. He may have a cure."

"Nekyia!" Baldwin curled his lip enough to reveal a fang, an intimidating expression for he looked about to bite.

Edward went to sit across from the vampire. "You know him?"

"We've met. I, too, sought a cure for my condition."

Edward slumped as despair crept over him. "He didn't give you one." *If he did not help Baldwin, he won't help me.*

"There isn't one," Baldwin said. "Once bitten, this curse overwhelms everything. Once fully manifest, it cannot be reversed. Only a wooden stake can release me."

Edward didn't know what to say.

"So," Baldwin continued, "I asked Nekyia for something to satiate the blood lust. He just laughed and said he'd already played that game and didn't want to play again."

"That," Edward said, unsure of Baldwin's meaning, "game? Which game is that?"

"The game where he has dealings with a vampire, apparently." Baldwin uncrossed his legs and stood up.

"I am sorry," Edward said. "But *is* there something to," he hesitated, not sure of the etiquette of blood-sucking conversation, "satiate your thirst?"

"So I presume, but he wouldn't say. Some other vampire has the cure, and Nekyia will not make more. That is my belief." Baldwin shrugged, thrust his hands into his coat pockets, and hunched a little. "I am what I am, and so I shall remain."

Neither spoke for a minute. Hya stirred, taking a deep breath. She blinked and rubbed her eyes with the back of her hand as if she would wipe the after-images of the past hour from her mind. She rose from the ground and began to put the myriad items back into her pack.

Edward helped her gather her things. "Could you not force him to help you?" Edward asked Baldwin.

Baldwin shot him a sour look. "You cannot make a necromancer of Nekyia's power do anything. He must want to help you."

Edward fingered the last King's Regard in his pocket. "I think I may be able to offer something he would value."

"I wish you luck, young man. Best you hurry. There's no telling how long you have."

"But I feel good. The *aqua vitae* is working. At this rate I should have months before—" Edward shrugged. "You know."

"Dead isn't really a steady progression," Baldwin said. He watched his hands, wouldn't look at Edward. "The symptoms get worse only slowly until suddenly getting very bad, very quickly."

Edward's good cheer vanished. "When does that happen?"

"Without intervention? Two, three, four weeks? But you've been treating it almost from the start. I'm not an expert on *zumbis*. My curse is different." He grimaced, revealing his fangs. "Six months is as good a guess as any. I will say for sure that when you start to truly decline, it will be rapid."

The words settled into Edward, filling him with a sense of dread and urgency. "I have no time to lose."

Baldwin, still looking at his hands, nodded. "You never did."

"Very well." Edward rose. "Again, Sir, I thank you."

"Go." Baldwin waved him away. "Follow your hope. But, Hya, return to visit. The worst part of the curse is loneliness. Old friends die, and it's hard to make new ones."

Chapter Ten

"I should have visited earlier," Hya said as Edward untied the boat from Baldwin's pier. "But as you heard, Uncle Jeremy didn't want me to come." She sighed. "He's right, too; vampires are dangerous creatures. Even the most decent of them can lose themselves when the bloodlust comes upon them."

"Is that why Baldwin lives alone?" Edward steadied the boat as Hya climbed off the pier.

"Well, he can be difficult at times. But he likes me," she said, a thoughtful expression on her face. "And he likes you."

"He did not offer much hope. I feel as though I carry a giant clock strapped to my back, and it weighs me down as it counts down my remaining time."

"There is always hope."

"So you say," Edward said. "But we used Davy's favorable wind to get here." He took out the bottle of *aqua vitae* and took a swallow. He held it up. A little more than half full, but that didn't help his mood. "I don't even feel good about feeling good anymore."

He put the bottle away and jumped into the boat. "Let's be off, like Odysseus, to wherever the wind takes us."

"To Nekyia," Hya said. "With no further stops, we might hope."

Edward pushed against the barnacle-encrusted bollard, propelling them into the small bay. "There's always hope."

"There is," she said. "We might risk sailing at night if conditions are favorable."

"You don't fear me?"

"I know you too well to fear you." She favored him with a smile. "I am wary of the monster inside, though. That I fear for your sake and mine."

"We should take no risks. For your sake and mine. As you pointed out at the first, without you, I am lost." He mulled the idea over. "Perhaps we can stop come nightfall so you can rest behind wards. I will not rest. After several hours, we sail again. You sail us, and I, I do what passes for sleep. There would be less risk to you."

"I'm not worried." She raised an eyebrow. "Should I be?"

"No." He shook his head to underline the word. "No. But Baldwin said once it starts, degeneration is rapid. I'd not leave you tired and unprepared."

She agreed, so as the sun sank they stopped. The island was little more than a windswept islet, devoid of sand or plants. Hya wedged the ward sticks in cracks in the coral while Edward paced, two hundred paces around the island, back to where he started.

Around and around he paced, ever shorter as the tide rose. His thoughts ranged wider, from Hya, to Nekyia, to Becca faraway in London. Nothing brought him peace until the moon, rising with the tide, had crept halfway up the sky, and they were off again.

☠

The dark thinned, became less black, and he had a sense of himself, though not of the world. He had never dreamt during his *zumbi* stupors. The world just faded away from him until he recovered. He grasped for his thoughts, trying to gather them together to make sense of this new feeling.

A voice, faint and strained, intruded into his consciousness. He knew it, a man, but couldn't place the accent. The words escaped him no matter how hard he clung to them.

He caught a word here and there; nothing that made sense until three jumped out at him. *Do you hear?*

I hear, he replied. *Who is this?*

He felt excitement, not his, but whoever spoke in his mind. *Undulark* came the voice.

How is this possible? Edward asked, wondering if he could dream.

Magic, of course. But white. Even the Custos *use this spell. They know of you and have been here asking. You caused quite a stir with them, though I wouldn't tell them what I knew.*

Edward didn't know quite what to think. Why should the *Custos* ask after him? Did they think he spread Dead in London?

Your Rebecca asked me to give you a letter, Undulark went on.

Can you do that?

Listen, Undulark said, and he began to recite.

I have given this letter to Mr. Malfousa and begged him to convey its contents to you, though I confess I don't know how he might do this. Your sudden departure has caused me much distress. I have tried to understand why you would act this way, but nothing comes to mind and Mr. Malfousa will not enlighten me. It seems I am in a dark and sorrowful room I cannot escape. Only in the company of others do I find some respite.

The message descended into incomprehensible mutters, too faint to pluck their meaning. He strained, feeling like a boy trying to catch minnows with his hands. Like the minnows, the words kept slipping away.

Becca! As if his anguished thought were a beacon, the message became clearer again.

...very hard...speak with you, came Undulark's thought. *You do not sleep as other people.*

Edward tried to form another thought, but none came, only frustration. The connection broke like a too-taut string.

No! He reached out with his mind, grasping, groping for that thin connection. *Becca!* He called her image to mind. He screamed her name into the darkness. *I am here!*

The curtain of *zumbi* sleep lifted, leaving him staring into the eastern sky. It glowed yellow, arcing overhead to blend to grey. Sunrise was not far off.

I have caused her sorrow, he thought, *so she seeks the company of others.* A terrible anger seized him. He would give up this quest and return to London where he could rend the men who thought to comfort Becca. What purpose a cure if Becca was lost?

He rose into a crouch, clenching his fists, releasing them, clenching them again, over and over. "We must return," he blurted.

"What?"

He turned to look to the stern. Hya sat, her hand on the tiller. Weariness darkened the skin under her eyes, colored her countenance. She had a wary expression on her face, her eyes darting from his fists to his face.

Edward smiled; it felt like it strained his face and must have looked false. "You are tired. Let me take the tiller, you can give direction while you rest."

She shook her head. "Why do you wish this?"

What can I say to her? That I am angry and foolish? That after all she has done to help I wish to quit?

He turned abruptly, not wishing to converse. Thoughts of Becca with rapacious young noblemen crowded out all other thoughts. He grabbed the gunwales and clenched his hands. What if she sought another's company in her sorrow and found she preferred it?

The gunwales cracked under his hands. He brushed his hands on his trousers.

"Is the Dead so bad?" Hya asked.

Her question surprised him. "It is not that," he said. "A disturbing dream."

"Dreams," she said with a twitch of her head and curl of her lip. She relaxed though and managed a tired smile.

"More than that, I think."

"If you pay them heed, perhaps."

"More like a message, a note from…" Becca's name stuck in his throat. "Undulark."

"Uncle Undulark!" she exclaimed, sitting up straighter. "You say it was a message? Like his voice speaking in your head?"

Edward nodded.

"Magic," she said firmly. "When I was a girl, he would threaten to send me bad dreams if I misbehaved. I finally snuck into his study and read the spell. Very demanding. What did he say?"

"Little I could tell." He didn't want to confide Becca's words to her. "Mostly garbled sounds."

"Oh." She slouched a little. "It must have been important though."

Important? A letter from Becca? "Perhaps I did not hear it. I heard enough to know it is difficult to speak with me because of my manner of sleep."

He pressed his fists against his temples as though he could press out Undulark's message. Becca blamed him and sought other company. "I am angry." He shouted the words to the sky. "I am angry!"

"And why," Hya asked, "are you angry?"

"What am I to do?" Hya didn't answer, but the voices in his head did. *Kill them all. Kill them.* "A dream, it is only a dream, yet you tell me it is magic and treat it as true."

"There is only one thing you can do," Hya said softly. She was tense, alert.

"Forward." *This anger,* he wondered, *is it mine, or the Dead?* He longed to lash out, to break something, anything. *That,* he told himself, *is me. If I didn't react to this news, my love would have died as well as my body.*

"So says my head," he said. "The monster inside, the one you are wary of, screams for a different course. Perhaps the monster tells me what I want to hear."

"And who is in control? You, I think. Not the monster."

Edward lowered his hands, stared at them, searching for some sign that they would betray him, that they would act without his permission or knowledge. "I am in control." He placed his back to the mast and stared straight over the prow as if he could bore a hole in the horizon. "Forward."

My leaving distressed her. I can make amends when I return. All is not lost.

"You have come so far." Hya said the words quietly, as if she would use them as a salve. "You will reach Nekyia while still lucid. I'm sure of it."

Lucid. Was he? He looked at the broken gunwales, his marks next to those left by Restless Davy. Davy hadn't seemed mad, but neither was he entirely sane—at least by Edward's standards. "Close?" he said. He took out his *aqua vitae* and drank a large draught. "How close?"

"Closer than London."

He wondered how much she deduced about his dream. *What good can I do by turning back now?* He wanted to, wanted to rampage through London, through the Barings' drawing room. *Stop this. Were you to give up now, you would not deserve Becca anyway. Fear and anger have no place in my mind right now.*

He felt them anyway, but having decided not to turn back, the anger subsided to a resignation and dull ache that he might return having succeeded in regaining his life but losing his love. And there was always the fear that Nekyia would not help him at all.

☠

The days dragged by without incident. Edward brooded on Undulark's message, convincing himself all was not lost concerning Becca. He needed to be cured first, and worrying about things in England would not help. He had nothing else to do, and between worry and telling himself not to worry, the days passed ever more slowly.

It was late in the morning on the seventh day since leaving Baldwin when Hya closed her eyes and shuddered, but her hand did not waver on the tiller.

"What is it?" Edward asked. The sea around the boat was clear, the sky also. All was normal. Nonetheless, a feeling of apprehension crawled up his spine—the feeling of something threatening stealing up behind you.

He turned. The sea was clear—no, a dark smudge marred the horizon. "Nekyia's island?" He didn't need to look back to know she nodded. "Finally."

As the sun climbed in the sky, they crept forward, or so it seemed. The island got larger too quickly or too slowly depending on how his mood shifted.

"Blackfish." Hya pointed. Off to starboard a group of large black and white fish arced to the surface, briefly breaking the surface and diving back down.

Edward shaded his eyes for a better view. "Is that a good sign?"

"I don't think so. They aren't a threat to humans—sometimes they're even friendly—but blackfish are whale killers. Merfolk like that and play with them like a man might a dog."

The blackfish rose again, this time running along the surface a hundred yards before diving again. Four, one of them smaller than the others, oblivious to the nature of the isle ahead.

"They don't look like fish."

"The Romans called them orca. They're more like dolphins or whales." She scanned the sea. "I don't see any merfolk. Thank God for little favors."

Edward chuckled at her aversion to merfolk, but there seemed something ominous about the dark forms knifing through the water.

The current gripped them, hurrying them forward, and he soon realized it was not one island like he expected. Stone spires and small islands rose from the sea, hedging the main island, blocking it from view, and making travel treacherous. Only the crest of the main island showed above the hazards.

I near my goal, I must not fall victim to superstition. As the blackfish fell behind and the island approached, it became harder and harder to do.

The blue of the ocean paled, grew a little more green, and suddenly they were amongst the rocks, close indeed to Nekyia's island, and he had much to watch.

The tips of three masts stuck above the surface. A broken-railed crow's nest still clung to the center mast; the topmost spar of the foremast appeared and disappeared as the swells passed. Broken lines trailed in the water.

A great rock rose from the water ahead of them, another ship broken upon it. Her grey boards blended with the stone. Her bow rode high, bleached and dry, but her stern slipped beneath the cover of the sea. She tilted away from them, an indiscrete lady showing off her exposed keel.

Hya guided their boat clear of that rock and the other, smaller, rocks behind it. More lurked just under the surface, sinister shapes suggesting malevolent creatures waiting for low tide so they could rise up and strike unwary sailors.

He still could not see Nekyia's island, for a long, low island blocked the view ahead. It was entirely rock, wrinkled and weathered by years of pounding surf. Wreckage wedged in the cracks: wreckage of the land, trunks of trees and palm fronds; wreckage of the sea, barrels and spars and tangles of rope; all thrown together with the stew of the deep; seaweed and starfish.

A third ship lay across the island. It had been lifted up and smashed down, broken amidships over the spine of the island. The bow sloped toward them, the stern over the other side. The masts splayed into the sky, still grasping at tattered sails that threatened to flee with the breeze.

Gulls rose from the decks, screaming; they circled and settled back down, hopping, pecking, rising again to scream their frustration, or hunger, or just their wordless vexation.

"I know that ship," Edward said. How different it looked from when he first saw it in London. "Ironic that it should come here, and before me."

A sweet, rotten smell carried across the water telling, as if he didn't know, that this ship had recently wrecked.

Neither spoke. Hya kept the boat turned so the current swept it around the rock, Edward could only stare at the entwined serpent, lifeless, just wood cast up, trapped away from its element—bound to the dead ship behind it.

As they rounded the rock Edward got his first close view of the main island.

A place is a place, Edward thought. It is not good or evil. Evil may be done there, but a place is a place.

The island, he told himself, with its malformed and malignant volcano brooding like a cloaked hag draping her stone shawl over it, was not good or evil. The forest, dark green plants sheltering darker shadows, was not good or evil. The beaches, such as they were hemmed in by hull crushing rocks and flanked by steep cliffs, were not good or evil.

"That is an evil place," Hya said.

Edward shook his head. He brought the premonition of evil with him. Evil could only be found in men and their actions, not a place. A place is a place. "Are you afraid?" he asked.

"Yes."

Hya looked young, small, and vulnerable. He wasn't sure why, a dozen imperceptible things that when added together told of her fear and uncertainty. The set of her shoulders, maybe; the tension around her eyes and the corner of her mouth; perhaps the slight flaring of her nostrils.

"You need not come with me," he said. "I can find my way."

"And your way home?" she asked.

He had no answer, just watched and waited as they made their way toward the narrow beach.

They landed amongst crates and barrels and boards and spars. Still without words, they pulled the boat above the tidemarks.

"There were survivors," she said, pointing.

Marks in the sand showed where things had been dragged from the beach, footprints told of the men who dragged them. They were indistinct, half-filled with windblown sand. Days old, and nobody had returned since the last high tide.

"Are we sure they were survivors?" he asked. "It might have been servants of the necromancer."

Hya brushed stray hair from her face and nodded. "It's all the same in the end."

The sun slanted between the high cliffs on either side, bathing the beach in light, but a path through the cliffs lay in deep shadow.

Edward stood at the path, remembering the opening to the alley in London, the one that led behind the Painted Man's shop. It, too, had oozed cold air and darkness.

Hya stood beside him. Neither spoke, though words would have been a comfort. Edward reminded himself he had nothing to lose. He started into the shadow. Hya followed; her footsteps light, slightly irregular, her breathing likewise.

"Wait here," Edward said. His voice, barely a croak, sounded overly loud in the silence.

"I'll go with you," Hya said.

Ahead, the path curved out of sight, hemmed in by the towering stone on either side. The air was heavy, humid, without any breeze to stir it.

"You've done enough," he said. "The King should be grateful his debts are so well discharged."

"It is no longer the King's debt I discharge."

He turned. She was pale, tense, eyes too wide, knuckles on her clenched fists too white.

"Then remain here for me," he snapped and instantly regretted it. She did not deserve his anger. It came so easily now. He gentled his tone. "Please."

"I can help," she protested.

"You already have," he said. "More than I deserve."

"Then," she said with a wan smile, "a little more isn't worth arguing over." She walked past him. "Coming?"

Edward hurried to pass her, determined to be the first to face any dangers. What he found when rounding the curve in the path, however, brought him up short.

A wall of greenery blocked the defile. He slowed his steps, eyes darting back and forth, up and down, trying to determine the nature of the obstacle.

After a minute of cautious examination, it was clearly an iron gridwork twenty feet high and covered in vines. Only a gate in the center was free of the thick, ropy vines with their glossy green leaves and white flowers. He tested it—locked—and stood back to think.

"Deathflower," Hya said, nodding to the deathly white flowers hanging from the vines. "It often grows on gravesites."

"Of course. What else would a necromancer grow?" He rattled the gate again. "Too bad we left the chisel at Parlexi's island," he said. "We might scavenge another from one of the wrecks. Quicker if I climb over. I doubt Nekyia would appreciate my destroying his gate."

"Deathflower is very poisonous," Hya protested. "Just a scratch from the thorns is enough to send a person into delirium."

"Then it's good that I cannot be poisoned," Edward said.

"That's true," Hya said. After a moment, she added, "I had forgotten." After another pause, she continued, "You must remember to wash out any cuts before being cured of Dead."

It seemed strange that the Deathflower grew so well in the deep shadows of the defile. The flower gave a sweet, cloying scent that crawled inside his clothes, over his skin; it clung to him like an insistent lover.

"Take care," Hya called.

The climb was easy enough, and he soon dropped onto the path on the other side. He checked the gate, but there was no way to unlock it without a key.

"Open it!" Hya demanded.

"I can't."

"Open it!" she insisted.

"I can't," he repeated. He couldn't imagine what the necromancer might do to Hya, but as he said, better not to chance it. "It requires a key."

"But I promised," she said, her eyes entreating. "I promised that I would take you back to London."

"I'm sorry." He rested his hand on the metal. A great heave might break the lock; he had *zumbi* strength. Would he ever see her again if they parted now?

If he didn't, it would be because he had failed, and his failure would likely kill her too.

"You can't help me if you're dead yourself. Or worse, Dead. Go back to the beach. Find someplace safe. Wait for me to return. If I don't…"

he shrugged. "Ask your uncle to buy you a steamship to study."

She made as if to climb. "No!" he said. "You cannot possibly avoid the thorns."

She looked up at the vines, and through the gate. "Edward," she entreated, reaching out to him.

He took her hand; it was warm. "I must go on. You know this."

She nodded. "I know. Be careful."

"I shall."

☠

After a few hundred yards the defile turned again. A hundred yards further and the cliffs fell back. They curved away until the trees hid them from sight. A great grey fence, it seemed, encircled Nekyia's domain.

The path snaked through the jungle. No sunlight penetrated the canopy. Darkness, fear, and gloom hung like moss from the trees. The wind moved leaves high up in the crown of the trees, but it did not stir on the ground. The air pooled, grown warm by the day. It felt like something had become corrupted in the nature of the jungle.

He followed on, alert for anything threatening. Outside Port Astarte, the creatures of the night hid from him. They feared his nature, not as a human, but as an undead. Here the jungle breathed silence, sucking it from him and blowing it back in his face. It was not just him this jungle feared.

Evil has been done here, he thought, *and will likely be done again.* This was not the jungle outside Port Astarte, or even that on Baldwin's island.

Movement in the green darkness drew his attention. A great hart stood in the undergrowth, watching him. Cruel antlers curled from its head, the prongs splayed like the fingers of a leprous hand. It bounded onto the path before him and stood, watching, daring him to proceed.

It had fangs as long as his fingers, and bony protrusions on its forelegs like curved knives. As if it sensed his thoughts, the hart reared. The protrusions slid out, making them very much like knives as the deer pawed the air.

"And who is Nekyia's gamekeeper that deals with you, I wonder?" No need to ask what it ate.

The deer tossed its head, flicked its tail, and disappeared into the jungle. "Just giving a warning, eh?" Edward murmured. At any other time, he would have been happy to heed that warning. "Flesh-eating deer or no, I must see Nekyia."

Perhaps twenty minutes later, he came to an area cleared of undergrowth. Rock cliffs shot up on the far side, having come back around and joined together to enclose the jungle and dwarfing a house already overshadowed by tall trees. He had found the necromancer's home.

It was mostly wood, but attached to the back, a stone tower rose through the forest's canopy. The wooden building reminded him of drawings of an American saltbox house, giving, with the tower, the impression of a lighthouse.

Crates, barrels, and spars lay scattered about; flotsam and lagan from wrecks dragged here at the necromancer's behest.

The smell of corrupted flesh pervaded the air. He didn't know if he heard or imagined the buzzing of flies, but he had a strong charnel feeling. He noticed a cave in the cliffs, off to the left where the cliff curved toward him. An iron gate barred its entrance. Behind the gate was darkness.

So still the scene, so profound the silence; Edward decided he had only imagined the buzzing flies.

Not everything here can be dead, he told himself.

He came on cautiously, alert for any sound or movement. As he got closer to the house and cliff, he could see a short way into the cave. Men moved inside, and when one spotted him, they all crowded the entrance.

"Save us!"

"For the love of God, set us free!"

They reached through the bars, imploring with their hands, as if he could free them with a touch.

"I've never begged in my life, but I beg you, Sir!"

The men were dirty and bruised. All were unshaven. With their clothes rumpled and torn, they looked as desperate as they sounded.

On closer examination, the gate was not a gate in the sense that it opened, but a massive grating with the edges set deep into the surrounding rock. The thick bars shone like varnished furniture, and there was no hint of rust.

"Beware," warned an old man. "His guardians walk this forest. Our fate is yours if they catch you."

Edward looked around, but nothing moved. "What guardians?"

"Vampire Deer," whispered the man, his eyes round. "As big as a horse and fangs like a lion."

"I've seen one."

"And men," said another. "Men who will do his bidding to avoid our fate."

"And worse than men," muttered a third man. "At night, the jungle goes silent—deadly silent. There's something out there, and it's all you can do to breathe for the fear of it."

"I know you," Edward said to the first man. "You crewed the *Twilight Rose*." He recognized other men now, but not all. They must have come from several ships.

The man yanked his hand back. "The devil you know! You again!"

"Enough talking!" cried a voice from the back. "Set us free!"

The first man called back. "He'll not help us. He's the necromancer's familiar, he is." He spat through the grate at Edward.

"Please," begged the old man. "Even evil men can do good. Set us free."

"He cursed us," called another voice—Grimms, Edward recalled, Mr. Grimms. "Sent us on the rocks."

"And you remain fools," Edward said. "I did nothing to you."

"We set him adrift," said Mr. Grimms, "yet he's come home to his master." He turned his back and walked away. "I'll take my chances here."

Another of the *Twilight Rose's* crew followed and another until about half the men had moved away from the grate. Those that remained came from other ships.

"Help us," pleaded the old man.

"How?" There was no way to open the grate.

The man just stared, grey eyebrows lifted, eyes wide. "I don't know."

"How did you get in?"

"In a vent opening, old chap." A middle-aged man pushed his way to the grate. "This place is lousy with lava tubes. We were dropped into a hole above one. Over there," he pointed a filthy finger.

"Is there no other way out?" Edward asked.

"I'm sure there's half a dozen or more, but we can't get to them."

"Why not?"

The man put his face to an opening and said, "Because of the dragon, old chap. It eats anybody who tries to escape."

Edward knew enough now not to doubt the man. Still, a dragon seemed incredible. "But you are safe here?"

"There are some rock formations a ways back that block the lava tube. It's too small for the dragon to pass."

"So you're safe for the moment?" Edward persisted.

The man laughed, bathing Edward with his foul, carrion breath. "Oh yes, as long as nobody gets too hungry."

Edward stepped back, horrified at the implication and the appeal it held, an appeal stronger than he had felt before. *I must be cured of this.*

The man cackled. "There's no place *safe* on this island, old chap."

"Why does he keep you if only to let you starve?"

"We're the unwanted. Some he keeps in his house until their use is up. Some escape to the jungle to run until they die. The rest he throws in here, saving us in case he needs to use us later, I suppose. But he always gets fresh victims. We're old meat, spoiled meat, old chap."

Repulsed, Edward strode away, letting his feet carry him up the steps to the necromancer's door. The men implored him, for his good and theirs, not to seek the necromancer. As he reached the door, however, they fell silent, the silence of frightened animals who fear the approach of a predator.

There was no bell, so he knocked on the doorframe. "Hallo!" he shouted.

A blanket of silence shrouded everything. Nothing moved, nothing answered him. He stepped back and looked around. The glass in the windows was dark, dirty; it didn't shine with reflected light. They made the house look dead.

The fronds of the trees did not move. The sailors crowded the iron gate, silent now, watching but not moving. If he wanted the necromancer's attention, they would not contest him for it.

With a quick step, Edward reached the door and pounded on it. "Open!" he yelled, hitting the door again. The nails holding the latch, a simple lift latch, tore from the door and it swung in.

The smell of rotting flesh oozed out, so thick it stung his eyes.

He hesitated. The next few minutes would decide his fate. He feared the necromancer's rejection, the death of hope.

There's always hope, he told himself and entered Nekyia's home.

☠

The devil's own decorator had been at work. Bones littered the room, piled along the walls, stacked on window ledges, leaning upright in the corners. Edward had assumed necromancers only dealt with human dead, but this room was a veritable Cabinet of Curiosities of bones. Some were easily recognizable: the elephant skull, the giraffe's severed neck and skull, the many human bones. Others he could puzzle out their origins. He had read of crocodiles and bison. But some he did not know, and he feared to guess. Was that a unicorn's horn, or something else? Surely, he thought, those were swan wings; they couldn't possibly be from an angel.

Something crunched beneath his feet, the crackling of innumerable small bones breaking. He didn't look down.

"Hello?" he called, not too loud. These dead couldn't hear. He didn't want them to.

A few sticks of shipboard furniture had been placed in a half-hearted attempt at normalcy, but that only made the room seem stranger.

He went from room to room. The floors felt soft, the surface spongy from absorbed moisture. Parts of bodies filled each room, more of them human than anything else, and not all reduced to bones. Hair and strands of flesh clung to many of the bones.

He finally came to where the tower joined the house. The bones of an enormous monster filled this room. It had been cut apart to fit through the doors and left to rot.

"A dragon," Edward said in wonder. Although dismembered, he could easily make out its main parts: powerful back legs, broken but recognizable wings, and serpentine tail. Its skull lay next to the tower door, four feet long with fearsome fangs. Silvery scales carpeted the floor. They ranged from the size of his thumbnail to as big as his palm. Small wonder the men trapped in the mountain feared such a creature.

After a minute to look at the unfortunate dragon, Edward entered the tower and began to climb the steps that spiraled around the outside wall. He climbed carefully, for no windows let in light. He spared a glance down where light from the door highlighted the tops of crates, barrels, and bones.

The stairs ended on a small landing with a door. He lifted the latch.

It was like stepping into another world. Four glazed windows let in light. Shelves encircled the room, neatly filled with boxes, jars, and loose items. Two rows of apothecary cabinets, back to back, ran down the center of the room. Each cabinet had hundreds of tiny drawers, each with a numbered brass plate and cut glass pull.

Another stairway climbed from between the wall and the shelves, ending at another landing with another door.

Edward climbed, discovering a meticulously kept library on the next level, curved shelves circling the walls, packed with books of every color. Skeletons hung on racks down the center of the room, clean bones held together with copper wire. They were mostly human, skulls drooping forward, jaws resting on their rib cages. Nekyia had written identification across the top of the skulls.

Siamese Male, Aged 25. Pirate by trade.
Romanian Male, Aged 18. One of a set of twins.
Abyssinian Female, Aged 5. Noteworthy for her remarkable dexterity.

Edward did not care to read them all. He crossed to another set of stairs and climbed to the next level, and at the top there was yet another landing and another door. He opened this one and stepped into the uppermost chamber of the tower, where Nekyia stood behind a laboratory table, a large tome open amidst a clutter of glassware before him.

This man, this necromancer, cast a shadow over the entire Narrow World, yet he looked terribly ordinary. He was neither large nor small. He was a trifle thin, but not abnormally so. There was something, perhaps the set of his shoulders or the tilt of his head, which reminded Edward of his former employer, Mr. Webley.

"The reason," he said, his voice a nasal tenor, "I didn't answer the door is I don't wish to see you."

"I must speak with you," Edward said. "It is a matter of life and death."

"Aren't you droll? Of course it is, but I still don't care."

I shall not say "Yes, Sir. Sorry, Sir." "I will pay for your help."

Nekyia chuckled. "You have nothing I want."

"But you know nothing about me," Edward protested.

"English, clearly Dead and have been for some time. You've been drinking *aqua vitae* of unusual quality, probably made by Undulark. I don't know where he is now, but you're wearing clothes made in Port Astarte, so I must assume he started you on your way and directed you there. I know of none other who could influence Jeremy into helping a *zumbi*. You've seen some hardship since arriving in the Narrow World, including a nasty stab wound which tore your shirt. You have ink spots on your clothes showing either a run in with a cephalopod or an angry archivist. You have a solid mind and strong will, as shown by the fact you're breathing and blinking, neither of which are natural to a *zumbi*, but you have trained yourself to do so without conscious thought. None of that indicates you have anything I want."

Edward's amazement must have shown on his face for Nekyia continued, "I am the greatest necromancer in a dozen generations. Do not think me stupid."

Edward clamped his jaw shut, biting back his anger. "That does not change my need, Sir, or the fact that I *can* pay you."

"You need my help to become Dead? Because I'll tell you plainly, I kill people. I do not bring them back to life. And anyway," Nekyia looked away, ending the conversation and dismissing Edward, "you're already Dead. Well done."

"No!" Edward shouted. He calmed himself with a deep breath. "I want you to cure me. I want to be alive."

"Then you should choose your words with greater care so as to avoid misunderstanding. State your desire in such a way as to avoid other interpretations."

"You mock me, Sir." Edward forced the words through his clenched teeth.

"You deserve to be mocked." He looked up again. "And if you insist on staying, at least get off the carpet. That's Chartreux fur, and I don't want to clean it."

Edward stepped off the carpet. *I must control my anger.* He dug into his pocket. "I have a King's Favor." He held the coin up. "I offer it to you."

Nekyia leaned forward and raised his eyebrows. "A King's Favor. Indeed, it is." He rested his hands on the table. "I have no use for it. Perhaps the King should be seeking my favor instead."

It felt like Edward's still heart shriveled within him. "You must have some use for it, something the King can provide."

"Nothing." He smirked at Edward.

He's enjoying this. The bastard is enjoying this. He clenched his fists. *I must control my anger.* "You have not said you can cure me."

Nekyia shrugged. "You came to me when God failed."

I must not argue. Maybe he craves a challenge. "Have you ever cured a man of Dead?"

"There has never been anybody I wished to see alive."

"Then how do you know you can?"

Nekyia strolled to the shelf behind him and pulled down a small, creamy brown book. "This is how I know: *Na Zhivyal, Umryal,*" he read the cover as he set it on the table. "On Living and Dying."

"Let me borrow that, I will do the ritual myself."

Nekyia's eyebrows rose. "You read Bulgarian? I am impressed." His tone was mocking. "But I have re-bound the book. Anthropodermic Bibliopegy is a hobby of mine. I added an introduction in contemporary Bulgarian, but the original text is fourteenth century, a middle period in the Bulgarian language, which is even less like the modern language than Old Bulgarian. Do you really think you could read it?"

"I can learn," Edward said, refusing to concede defeat.

"Quickly, I would hope. But it's highly technical. Fiendishly difficult." He tapped the book. "This may be the only copy in existence, and I am the only person who can use it."

He's right, damn him. I need more than the knowledge; I need his experience.

What had Baldwin claimed? That Nekyia liked new games. Not in so many words, of course, but the implications were there. "Play the game," Edward urged. "You haven't played this game before."

"Which game is that?" His tone still mocked Edward. "The game where somebody comes wanting something of mine and sees if they can benefit once they have it?" He brought his fist down on the table, making the glassware rattle. "I play that ALL the time!" he shouted. "Do you think you're the first? People come seeking artifacts, charms, cures, justice, revenge. You'd be surprised how many people come to my island."

Thinking of the shipwrecks, Edward wondered how many Nekyia

brought here himself. *I must stay focused on my goal.* "But never a *zumbi*. You have not cured a *zumbi*."

Nekyia curled his lip and didn't answer.

"Whatever I have, I will give to you," Edward said desperately. "Whatever you ask, I will do. Just return me to life!"

Nekyia still did not answer.

"Set me a task. Whatever you want, I will get." The words sounded foolish as he said them, but his desperation made him reckless. The only other thing he could do was rage, and that had even less chance of working.

Nekyia leaned back. "A task? You don't value your life very highly if you will only perform one task."

"You toy with me."

"Of course I do. You're a toy. You're *my* toy."

"No man is a toy," Edward muttered.

"You think not? Yet I toy with you. And you accept it because there isn't another person in the world who can restore a *zumbi* to life. Therefore: Amusing."

Edward ground his teeth together. "I cannot threaten you, I can only beg."

That surprised a bark of laughter from Nekyia. He shook his head and started to pace back and forth behind the table. He would pause, look at Edward, shake his head, and continue pacing.

Edward started to rise onto the balls of his feet, settled back down. He feared anything he did or said would tip Nekyia's decision against him.

Nekyia stopped. "You have nothing I want, but maybe you can get something. But no matter how much you value your life, I do not. One thing will not be enough."

"Name anything," Edward said quickly.

"Four, I think. Three is the traditional number. So, I shall set you four tasks, each harder than the last."

"Name them."

A slow smile spread over Nekyia's face. "I once had a staff topped with a bloodstone. I want it back."

Licking his lips, Edward nodded. "What did it look like?"

"It would be more amusing to let you guess."

"If you really want it back, you'd tell me."

Nekyia laughed. "A fair point. It was small, more of a rod than a staff. It is nine inches long to be precise, thin, but heavy. It may look like silver but it is not. It was forged a thousand years ago from what scientists have just named iridium in the last fifty. The bloodstone topping it has unusually vivid red inclusions. You will know it if you find it."

"Where is it?"

"If I knew, I'd get it myself," Nekyia said.

Edward nodded, accepting this. "What else?"

"My orb. Like the staff, it was stolen. It is five inches across and of flawless quartz. When held to the light it takes on a red hue. Again, you will know it if you find it."

"Do you know its location?"

"No."

"What else?" Edward asked.

"The heart of a dwarf."

"The heart of a dwarf?" The request stunned him and he balked at thinking of the implications.

"Is there something wrong with your ears? I thought I spoke clearly. I hope this isn't a problem for you. I expect *exactly* what I ask for."

"No," Edward said. "I heard you. I just didn't expect it." He told himself not to argue. There would be an opportunity to think about the consequences later. "What is the last task?"

"I want the most rare and precious thing to be found in the House of Sorrow."

Edward nodded. "You want your bloodstone staff, your crystal orb, the—" he swallowed, "heart of a dwarf, and the most precious thing found in the House of Sorrow."

"And in return I will cure you of Dead."

Thinking of the men in the cave, Edward said, "And allow me and my guide to safely leave the island."

Nekyia threw back his head and laughed. "Have you heard stories or are you just cautious? Very well. I won't take any action to harm or hinder you in any way."

"I'll start immediately."

"Tell my men you have my leave to search wherever you wish," Nekyia said. "They are not to hinder you." He smirked. "The jungle hides other dangers though. You must deal with them yourself."

Edward turned to leave. His hand rested on the door when Nekyia spoke.

"*Zumbi?*"

Edward stopped to listen.

"You haven't much time. You'd best hurry."

He could hear the amusement in the necromancer's voice. Small wonder Baldwin hated him. Holding his tongue, Edward climbed down the stairs. Emotions roiled within him; elation that he had come to terms with Nekyia and could be cured, anger that the tasks seemed insurmountable.

"Four more steps in the journey," he told himself. "Just four more steps in the journey."

Chapter Eleven

Edward strode from the front door and paused. If the orb and staff were stolen, where could the thieves have gone? High cliffs surrounded Nekyia's enclave, sheer and unbroken. Climbing, if it was even possible, would be difficult.

He studied the cliffs, a sharp edge against the blue sky. They rose a hundred feet or more, their faces marked by bushes, few and far between, rooted in some crevice or ledge.

He let his feet carry him away from the house, moving to view the full circuit of cliffs. Only toward the sea was there a break, the narrow defile he had used. With the gate in the defile locked, there was no escape.

Could he be so lucky that the bloodstone and orb were still within the enclosure? He hardly dared hope. Surely Nekyia would have recovered them if they were so close.

First to find the henchmen; he didn't want them hunting him. And they might know of the orb and staff. He needed every scrap of information he could get.

The solid sound of an axe on wood rang overloud in the silent jungle. It came from the left where there was a small opening in the underbrush. He followed the path, for path it was, his eyes darting about, looking for dangers until he came to a clearing, a shallow depression with a stockade in the center. The shadow of the jungle lay across the clearing, shrouding half while leaving the rest uncovered to the sun.

Logs, sharpened at one end and set upright in the ground, formed the stockade. From his vantage, Edward could see down into the depression and over the stockade. It struck him as a stupid place to build a stronghold, but it wasn't likely to be needed against intelligent foes. Besides, Nekyia's house had no such wall.

The house in the center was of mismatched and degraded opulence. It was built from coral and stone, trimmed with carved ornaments scavenged from wrecked ships. A poorly built chimney leaned like an afterthought into the building at one end, the stone around it dark from smoke and fire.

A sickly garden struggled in the sandy soil beyond the building. Gardening must have been a skill lacked by the inhabitants: two men who even now worked within the stockade.

Two men; one small, one large; one dark, one light. The small, dark man sat in the sun with a keg on his lap. He rummaged through it with short, rapid movements, pulling an object out, examining it, setting it aside, and repeating the process. He was fidgety and had dark hair and dark clothes. A high, upturned collar obscured his lower face.

The other was an albino, a full seven feet tall, who stood in the shadow. He was a giant man made heavy with muscle, with long white hair pulled back and tied and abnormally pale skin. He brought the axe down—it looked small in his hands—and split the firewood with what seemed supernatural ease.

He spied Edward over the stockade and stopped, watching, axe lowered, not saying anything. Then he slowly came forward, coming from the shadow to the sun, studying Edward but still not saying a word. He stopped again, and Edward noticed this put the small man in his shadow.

"Haven't seen that one," the albino said. He spoke normally, but the bowl-shaped depression amplified his words and carried them to Edward. His accent revealed him as American.

The small man looked up. Unimpressed, he returned to pulling things from his barrel. "Dead."

"No. He's not mindless, and Nekyia doesn't let them out unless they are. Maybe we should catch him and put him in the cave."

The small man didn't look up; just kept sorting through the keg. "Dead," he repeated.

"You are the men who do Nekyia's bidding," Edward called, mostly because he didn't know what to say. They knew who they were. "Nekyia says you are not to hinder me in my searches. I have his leave to roam the island."

"Small Man and Albino, at your service," the albino said, sketching a perfunctory bow. The small man paused his rummaging to look at Edward.

"Those cannot be your names," Edward protested.

"Perhaps not, but they are what we are." The albino did not take his eyes from Edward. "And what are you?"

"A traveler seeking help."

"Are you Dead?"

Edward felt a flash of anger. Why should it matter? "I am," he admitted.

The albino shifted his grip on the axe. "You are not welcome here."

"I can sense that," Edward said. "I am seeking things for the necromancer."

The Albino snorted. "Buying favors."

"I must."

"If you're Dead, it's your life you want. What price did he set?"

"I need to recover his orb and staff." He did not mention the House of Sorrow or heart of a dwarf. Not yet.

"Ah. Yes, I remember when he lost those."

Put forward a bold front. "Nekyia said you are to tell me what you know of them. Do you know where they are?" *I must be desperate to lie, even such a small one.*

"Not exactly, no. The staff," he glanced down at Small Man. "Do you remember the staff?"

Small Man didn't look up. "Pretty. Silver and red."

"Yes. The master lost it when the dhow from Bharata fetched up on the rocks several years ago. The crew he treated as usual, but he was much taken with *Memsahib* Aaloka." He shook his head. "Normally he has little interest in such strays as land here, but she was special."

"He gave her the staff?"

"She stole it. I remember her cry of victory as she fled the house."

"Then she escaped," Edward said. "Where did she go?"

"At first into the jungle, where she eluded both us and the traps set to kill the unwary. Eventually into the old volcano. Where else could she go? Her ship was wrecked; she had no crew. Her only hope was to find another exit and fashion a raft."

Edward didn't want to ask, he feared the answer, but he forced the question out. "Did she find another exit?"

"There are no other exits. A sad end to a brave and beautiful woman."

"Then I must go into the volcano and search for her." *Into the dragon's lair.* He stared at the Albino, who looked back without expression. *I didn't expect it to be easy.* "And the orb?"

The Albino shuddered and looked away.

"Bad, bad," muttered Small Man. "Lost my box of pretties."

"Lucky we didn't lose more than that," said the Albino. He shifted, allowing light to fall on the Small Man. "A Dutchman came and hid his *vlieboot*—one of those swift fishing boats—offshore. He snuck ashore and stole the orb. He was quick, faster even than Small Man, who is right quick himself."

"Lost my pretties because I couldn't catch him," muttered Small Man. He fished around in the barrel. Finding nothing further, he set it aside and began to arrange the items on the ground before him.

"Quite a race," Albino said. "The Dutchman ahead, Small Man behind with his knives—"

"Good with knives," said Small Man.

"He made it back to his ship and sailed away," the Albino continued. "Nekyia was furious."

"Took my pretties," said Small Man.

Panic awoke in Edward. His time was short; he could not search the Wide World. "Where did he go?"

"Down." The Albino gave a short laugh. "That night a storm came up, and in the morning we picked wreckage off the beach."

No sense in asking if the orb washed up. If it had, Nekyia wouldn't have tasked him with finding it. It would lie at the bottom of the ocean.

"How am I to find it?" Edward threw his hands up, half turning toward the beach.

"You can walk. You've no need for air."

"I've need of *time*," Edward snarled. "Will you help me?"

"Not for your life."

Edward remembered his thoughts as they approached the island. *A place is just a place.* "This is an evil place," he muttered.

"I've wondered that," said the Albino. A thoughtful expression flitted across his face. "Perhaps it is. Perhaps Nekyia is an evil man. There is no doubt we do evil things at his bidding."

"You are well suited to this place, then." Edward turned to leave.

But Albino kept talking, his voice taking a hard, angry edge. "Are we? We," he gestured at Small Man who arranged and rearranged his trinkets, "have a choice to do evil or be the victim of it. And there is more evil lurking in men than you think."

He hefted the axe in his large, white hands and shook it. "We're no better suited to this place than those who tormented us in the Wide World. Have you ever felt the hate the weak have for the strong?"

"I have," Edward retorted. "Would you have me damn myself by listening to the voices that urge vengeance on those who wrong me?"

"You think we're damned, do you?" Albino lifted his lip in a sneer. "Here are words from one who has been called a monster to one who is: it's better damned than dead. Better a life here than in a carnival in St. Louis."

Edward didn't know what to say. He stood looking into the Albino's face, rummaging for a response while wondering what life as a carnival freak would be like. He noticed, for the first time, a myriad of scars, white on Albino's white face; scars that could only be from years of fighting. He looked away. "You waste my time."

"We're all damned," the Albino said contemptuously. "And you're not welcome here."

In one motion, Edward bent down, picked up a rock half as large as his head, and drew back his arm to throw. He wanted nothing more than to smash the man's head. It was instinct, a desire without words. *Do it,* whispered the voice in his head.

He let out a wordless yell as he threw, sending the stone not at the Albino, but far into the jungle. "There is honor in the fight," he said. "If I am damned, it is not by any choice of mine!"

The Albino said he wouldn't help, but already had. Now Edward knew enough to begin his search, but four things, each more difficult than the last? It was hard to see this as a favor.

He hurried through the jungle, keeping to the trails. He had seen the deer, but there were other dangers. Nekyia had said as much, and the Albino mentioned traps. He scaled the barrier in the defile and returned to the beach.

It was deserted. The low surf hurried to the beach where it hesitated, as if unwilling to finish the trip, fearful of what lived on the island. But it couldn't resist its own momentum and fell to pieces on the beach.

He paced, back and forth, studying the sand, noting the gouge where the boat had rested. He had told her to hide, but how would he find her?

She could shelter in one of the wrecks, find another sheltering beach, or she could have abandoned him. He couldn't believe the last.

He needed the boat.

He needed her, too.

Something heavy hit the sand behind him, and he spun around. Hya had leapt from the rocks and now raced across the beach, her face alight with a dazzling smile. "Edward! You succeeded!" She wrapped him in a triumphant hug. He caught a whiff of her: salt, and sweat, and sun. He embraced her in return.

Kill her. Eat her.

It was as if she heard the voices too. She let go and stepped back, the smile dropping from her face. "You're cold. He didn't cure you, did he?"

"He set me four tasks," Edward said. "If I complete them, he will cure me."

"Four?"

"Three because that's the traditional number and one more because he's a bastard."

She turned away and worried the sand with her foot. "He is a bastard. What does he want?"

"Two are things he has lost—an orb and a staff. Both are close, but hard to get. The orb is on a ship wrecked off shore. The staff is in the caves of the volcano."

"Which wreck? There are so many."

"A Dutch *flieboot.* It isn't close to shore, though I don't know where it is."

Hya glanced at him, then shaded her eyes and looked over the ocean. "It gets deep out there." She pointed. "Once you get past the blue-green range, I wouldn't guess how deep it may be. It would take a—." She didn't finish.

"You were going to say it would take a miracle?"

She nodded.

"It would take a merman," he said.

She looked up. "How will you find one to do your bidding?"

"We'll start where the blackfish swim."

"What makes you so sure there are merfolk about?"

"They enjoy teasing people in distress," Edward said. "This is an easy place to find such people. I'm sure," he added darkly, "it amuses both the merfolk and Nekyia to 'rescue' people from the sea only to deliver them to Nekyia's mercy."

She led him to where she hid the boat, an arduous climb over the cliffs and back down to a hidden shelf of rock. She must have spent the entire time he was away searching for a place like this and returning to where she could watch the beach.

Once again, he found himself pushing it into the ocean. He wondered how many more times he would have to, or would be able to, do this. Once he started rowing, he told her of the staff and the many denizens of the volcano. "So, I need to know about dragons," he finished.

She spoke, sitting in the stern while he pulled at the oars. She told him of a dragon's thick hide, of their claws, and how they breathed fire. "It is said they can sense movement, though I don't know how. Dragon lore is mostly myth."

"And the myths? Did Saint George not slay a dragon?"

"I wasn't there," she answered. "Even if he did, you don't have holy weapons."

Edward snorted. "I couldn't hold a holy weapon if I had one. What of something more modern? Your revolver, perhaps?"

"Perhaps," she said thoughtfully. "It's too light for dragons—I think. I wouldn't trust it to make it through muscle and bone to something vital. Maybe through one of the eyes," she mused. "Can you shoot?"

His spirits settled with the boat as it dipped into a trough in the waves. "No. Not well."

"You'd need something larger," Hya said. "A cannon would be best." She said it lightly, in jest, but Edward seized the idea.

"What of the little ones, the cannon they set on the rail? Would one of those work?"

"A swivel gun? How would you work it?"

"I am strong, and aiming would be easier."

"You would only have one shot." She shook her head. "Where would you get a swivel gun?"

"One of the wrecks must have one. We'll search them on our way back."

"You want to go into a dragon's lair carrying a cannon?"

"A small one."

She laughed in disbelief. "I don't have a better idea right now."

Once they were beyond the rocks, Hya asked, "How do you plan to find a mer?"

"By looking panicked and vulnerable." He smiled. "Let's try and attract some attention, shall we?" He began to thrash the oars through the water, haphazardly, splashing water everywhere but the boat actually slowed. The prow wiggled back and forth, indecisive.

After a few dozen strokes, he stopped, then moved the oars listlessly, as if tired. A short rest, and he thrashed the water again.

"Escaping from the necromancer?" Hya asked with a raised eyebrow.

"Badly. Anybody doing something this poorly deserves to be mocked, yes?"

"You're hoping any nearby merfolk will think so."

"Yes."

They rose and fell with the waves, staring down. Nothing stirred in the depths, neither mer nor fish. Frustration growled in Edward's ear; he brushed it aside. The mer weren't out here waiting for his convenience. It might take some time.

It seemed time slowed for him, being measured by the waves and his expectations. The sun lowered itself cautiously toward the sea, as if afraid the water would extinguish it. He tried to look like an inexperienced oarsman bent on escape, but knew full well the further he got from the island, the further he had to return. His patience began to erode.

"What will you do if the mer don't come?" Hya asked.

"I don't know." What did she expect of him?

She nodded, evidently not having any suggestions. "What are the other two tasks?"

"Damn the tasks!" he snapped. "If the bloody mer don't show up, they won't matter!" He brought his fist down on the gunwale hard enough that it cracked. The sharp sound made him stop.

"I am sorry," he said. "The mer do not exist for me, but my time is growing short, and I feel we waste it waiting."

"How much *aqua vitae* do you have left?" she asked.

"Enough. The King was most generous. But it isn't as effective now. The Dead grows stronger." He took out the bottle and held it up to the sun so she could see through it. He took a quick drink before putting it away. His anger ebbed; it was not just the waiting, Dead contributed much of his frustration. She had seen it right away. "I should be grateful it still offers some relief.

"As for your question," he said, "Nekyia wants the heart of a dwarf and the most valuable thing found in the House of Sorrow."

Hya opened her mouth, closed it, and swallowed. "The heart of a dwarf? Why?"

"He didn't say. Some arcane ritual I assume."

"That's—," she stopped herself. "He doesn't care what it is." Edward silently agreed. "But," she went on, "there are no dwarfs in the Narrow World."

"There's one, I think," Edward said. "He was aboard the *Twilight Rose*. I did not see him in the cave." He didn't want to talk about it, so he changed the subject. "Have you heard of the House of Sorrow?"

"It's a phrase."

"A phrase? Not a place?"

Hya looked over the side. "Not in this world." She leaned over the gunwale. "We have company."

"Finally." Shapes circled in the depths, and he forgot about the House of Sorrow as he leaned over the side.

The shadows in the sea spiraled up until a half-dozen merfolk circled just below the surface. He hadn't expected so many.

A mermaid surged up and settled on the prow, head on her arms, arms on the gunwales. "Oh," she said, staring at Hya. "A woman. Now this could be a challenge. Care to swim with me, pretty girl?"

A second mer surfaced, and the boat rocked as he rested on the starboard gunwale. "Why would she want to swim with you?"

"You never know until you ask," said the maid.

Edward didn't recognize either of them. "I need your help."

"Sorry, lad, I don't know how to row either," said the merman and both mer laughed.

"I know how to row, thank you," Edward said. "I just needed to get your attention."

"If you want to get someone's attention, try this." The maid pulled herself up and arched her back, taking a deep breath. "It may not work as well for you, but if the pretty girl were to try it, I'm sure she'd get somebody's attention."

Hya actually blushed.

"You're the second mermaid to do that," Edward said.

"It usually works," the maid replied.

"That's not what I want." Edward leaned forward. "I need something lost in the ocean."

"Like Atlantis?" said the mermaid with a wink to Hya. "I'll take you there if you swim with me."

Hya's fingers moved, just a fraction, toward her knife. But they stilled, and she remained silent.

"Not like Atlantis," Edward said.

"Wait! Is this a guessing game? How many guesses do I get?"

A third mer, another maid, this one differing from the others by her red hair and fuller body, surfaced and said, "I want to play! This thing you seek, is it natural?"

A fourth mer surfaced, another male, and hung on the port gunwale near the mast. Evidently, they had been listening underwater. "I'll play too," he said, and the mer started throwing questions, not waiting for the answers.

Edward swiveled his head, back and forth, trying to sort out the words but failing. The mer laughed, and one punctuated his laughter by smacking his tail on the water, splashing both Edward and Hya.

"Stop!" Edward shouted. He took a breath. "Please. I will pay you to find Nekyia's crystal orb."

The mer quieted, but they still smiled. "Pay us?" said the first maid, pushing off the prow to lie back on the water. "What do you offer?"

"I have a King's Regard."

"Really?" The mermaid smiled. "A King's Regard? That is unusual." She called out, "Merel, a King's Regard!"

Yet another mermaid surfaced, this one swam slow circles about them all. "And who would get this Regard, human? Unless you have one for each?"

"I have one," Edward said. "It should be enough for this task."

"If there was one of us, perhaps," said Merel. "But there are five. What else can you offer for our trouble?"

"I have little else. Other mer have coveted the Regards."

"That would be their business. I, for one, would forego a Regard for the sport you provide."

Hya rested one hand on her knife, the other on her revolver.

"Surely," Edward said, "you could buy something to your benefit." He turned to look at each as he added, "All of you."

"Oh, you *are* good sport!" Merel tapped her tail on the water. It sounded like someone clapping. "Keep trying!"

Edward gaped. Had these magic coins lost all their value? "Send me Terra," he said, "I have done business with her before."

"Terra? I know no Terra, but there's a nice island right over there," Merel said, and the others laughed.

"Then," he hesitated, growing desperate, trying to conjure a name, but he never knew Parlexi's captive's name. "A merman who was held by Parlexi. I never knew his name."

"My name is Pielloos," said a voice behind him. Edward spun to see the merman from Parlexi's cavern had joined the group.

"Will you help me?"

"I will get your orb," Pielloos said.

The first merman blinked as if doused with cold water. "Why?"

"You brought me here to play, to forget my years of captivity, but as I circled below watching you torment this man it struck me how like Parlexi we are. We play with our prey, tormenting it for our amusement. A fine pastime, aye, but it wears thin after so many years in a cage."

Edward caught Hya's eye. She gave him the faintest hint of a smile and an almost imperceptible nod. It had been wise to free Pielloos.

One of the maids swam around Pielloos, entwining tails, draping over him and running her arms over his chest. "But we haven't been caged."

"A fact for which you aren't even grateful."

Her hands stopped caressing him. "Why should I be grateful for something which hasn't happened?"

In a flash, he had her by the neck, surging up so only her fins dangled in the water. "Shall I kill you now?"

Edward froze. What was the purpose of this?

Her eyes bulging, the mermaid tried to shake her head.

Pielloos let her go. She splashed into the water and lay shocked, the marks of his hands visible on her neck. "Be grateful you are not dead," he said.

The first merman swam close, a puzzled expression on his face. "But why would you get the orb?"

"Why don't you?"

"The sport is better."

The little voice in Edward's head urged him to take an oar and crush the merman's skull. He clenched his fists and held them tightly at his side instead.

"He has already done me a service," Pielloos told the merman.

"Did you agree to help him then?"

"No."

"Then why would you help him now?" The merman lifted his hand, palm up, as if to receive an answer he could grasp.

Pielloos glared. "Would you help me if I asked?"

"What do you offer?"

Pielloos let out a sharp bark of laughter. "We do nothing but for pleasure or profit, eh?" His lips turned down. "So like Parlexi, and she was mad."

"You've changed," said Merel. "I no longer understand you."

"I don't know whether to be sad or grateful." Pielloos curled his lip. "The cage was small, but it made me bigger." He shrugged. "Do what you will," he said as way of dismissal. To Edward, he said, "You shall have the necromancer's orb."

Relief washed over Edward. He reached out to shake Pielloos's hand. "Thank you. Thank you. A Dutchman stole it. He didn't get so far that wreckage from his ship couldn't wash up the next morning." He groped in his pocket. "A second, I have the Regard here."

"Keep your coin. I've no use for it."

"Thank you," Edward said again.

Pielloos nodded. "I am changed, but I don't know if by my long imprisonment or what I've seen from my kin since."

"Both, I suspect."

"Both," Pielloos echoed. "Yes, likely both. I will find you once I have the orb." He vanished, as if the sea had sucked him down, leaving only a circle of ripples quickly lost in the ocean's waves.

With frustrated smacks of their tails, the other merfolk followed him.

After a moment, Edward took up the oars. "One. If I'm fortunate. I've done what I can and now must seek the bloodstone staff. Let's see about a cannon."

Chapter Twelve

Edward turned the boat toward the island and bent his back to rowing. The sun had dipped its toe below the horizon while they talked, and he wanted daylight to search for a swivel gun. The sea helped them, each wave carrying them along before dropping them off for the next one.

The water had grown darker with the setting sun, but Hya still peered over the side. "Cannon," she said as they neared the rocks. "No! Not a cannon, it's a *smokestack!*"

Edward leaned over to look. A dark hull lay three or four fathoms down, the bow stove in and large chunks of debris scattered about. A black tube lay across the deck; if not for Hya's words, he would have mistaken it for a cannon. A broken paddle wheel leaned against the wreck.

"A steamship," Hya breathed. "I'd love to examine it more closely."

"I might be able to pull some part of it to shore," Edward said. "After we've found a swivel gun."

"You've no time, even then," Hya said with a wistful sigh. "And look at the hull—if it broke on the surface, the engine would have fallen out. It might not even be in the wreck." She peered around, shading her eyes as she looked at the debris on the ocean floor. "And I doubt even *zumbi* strength could drag the engine through this maze of rocks. But thank you for the offer."

Edward nodded, grateful she declined, but wishing she could view the wreck. Her desire to learn of these new machines seemed such a simple thing; she ought to have the chance.

"We'll start there," he said, pointing toward the *Rose*'s bier.

In a few places, the rock tapered into the water, leaving a shallow shelf wide enough to wade before dropping into deeper water; mostly, though, the sides vanished into sea deep enough that the bottom was murky and indistinct.

Bits of the wreck, and other wrecks, littered the island. The *Twilight Rose* wasn't the only ship to have died here, but she was the most recent and the only one whose hull remained.

The devastation to the *Rose* was terrible. She had been lifted up and dropped on the island like a man might break a stick on his knee. The keel and hull had snapped midship, the bow and stern sloping to different sides of the small island. The main mast tilted over the port rail toward the sea, while the mizzenmast angled inland.

"The bloom is off the *Rose*," Hya said. She waited until Edward brought the boat to the shore and leapt out.

Her statement sounded cavalier in his ears, too flippant, and it angered him. Too much angered him. *It's the Dead*, he reminded himself.

A rope ladder had been thrown over the side. It didn't take much imagination to picture the sailors clambering down after the wreck.

"A terrible storm that lifts a ship this high," he said, pretending his rush of anger had never happened.

"A storm called Nekyia," Hya said as she reached out to climb the ladder. At the top she added, "I don't think much of your crew."

"Why is that?"

"They didn't even bury the dead."

Edward wondered at that. The wind carried the smell out to sea, but he had smelled the dead as they passed the first time. He had not seen Captain Davies amongst the prisoners.

One of the crew lay against the starboard rail. He was entangled in ropes that tied him to the crosstrees, but those were too long to keep him from hitting the deck when he fell. He looked familiar, but Edward couldn't recall his name.

Jenna, the seawitch, had lashed herself to the foremast, now pointed out to sea; but surely, Edward thought, she must have done it while she struggled against Nekyia's sorcery and the ship raced toward its doom. Her arms hung free of the lashings, her head hung down. Dried blood coated her chin and stained the deck before her. She had been vomiting blood at the end.

"Small wonder the crew wanted to get away quickly," Hya said.

"To the safety of a necromancer's island?" Edward curled his lip. "He toys with them."

He crossed over some loose boards the crew had laid across the cracked deck. He expected to find Captain Davies near the wheel, but the deck was deserted.

"Here's a bracket for a swivel gun," Hya said. Edward hadn't noticed it before.

"Where would the gun be?" he asked.

"Likely a weapons locker, someplace secure."

Edward went straight to Davies's cabin. The locker outside had been broken open and looted. *Why not use the key?* Edward wondered. But still racked in the corner was the swivel gun.

He picked it up and laid it across one shoulder. It was still heavy, in spite of his increased strength. It wobbled on his shoulder, and he had to shift his hands to keep from dropping it.

"How am I going to fire this?" he demanded, his irritation close to the surface.

The sun had set, and he felt *zumbi* sleep encroaching. He could not sleep now.

He lowered the gun, thrust out a hip, and settled some of the weight on it. He had to lean far over to balance it. "Can't fire it from here," he muttered.

Hya opened her mouth; she looked like she wanted to say something, but closed it again.

"What?" he demanded.

"You can't fire one when you're holding it," she said.

He knew that. What was he thinking? Was it the effects of Dead? He nodded. "A mount then."

Finding the carpenter's tool chest took longer, but it provided the hammer, nails, and brace and bit he needed to make a mount. Scrap wood was easily found.

The darkness closed about him, narrowing his vision—both night and *zumbi* sleep—but he forced himself on. He remembered arguing the merit of rest, and he would before entering the dragon's lair. But now he must prepare.

Hya lit one of the ship's lanterns as he worked and, when he finished, looked skeptically at the haphazard project. "Maybe we should test it first."

"Yes." He dragged it across the deck and turned it toward the cabin. "Need a target." He picked up a plank and leaned it against the bulkhead. He smiled at Hya. "Target."

She nodded.

He loaded the cannon as she instructed and aimed it at the board. Not satisfied, he adjusted the aim, walked around, looking from all sides. He crouched beside the cannon and sighted along the barrel.

"The dragon will not give you so much time," Hya said.

"It's just a test," he snapped. But he knew she was right. He made one last adjustment and lit the fuse.

The cannon fired, flinging itself backwards with a flash and cloud of smoke, and clunked to the deck a full eight feet from where it started.

Not only was the target plank uninjured, so was the bulkhead of the cabin.

"Words fail me," Hya said.

"It's not funny," Edward said, his voice grating through his clenched teeth.

"No," Hya agreed. "It isn't. We need to find another way. This one…"

"Won't work," he finished for her. "Not without divine intervention. Or better bracing." A quick glance showed the brace cracked. He kicked it, completing the break. "Damn. You're right. Heavier bracing will make it impossible to move, it's too slow-firing, and I'm a poor gunner." He snorted. "I need St. George himself."

"He got lucky," Hya said. "Dragonfire will burn a lance."

"And the rest of the kit?"

She shrugged. "The lances were usually ash. Shields could be thin strips of wood laminated together and covered in leather, or they might be metal. Obviously the fire burns wood and leather, and I've read dragonfire is hot enough to melt metal."

"Dragons can melt steel?" He couldn't believe it.

"The metal gets so soft it can't hold its shape and becomes distorted."

If she believed it, he'd be a fool to doubt. "How then," he mused, "am I to kill this thing?"

"Must you kill it?" she asked.

"You feel kindly toward it?" He seized the gun, shook it loose from the broken brace. "This can still be useful." He took two steps and swung it against the rail. The rail cracked and he swung again, shattering it. The voice in his head rejoiced. *Yes, kill it!*

Hya edged away from him. "That's not what I meant. What must you do?"

"I must kill the dragon!"

"Why?" Now anger edged her voice.

"To get Nekyia's staff!" He wanted to throttle her for her stupidity.

"Nekyia said nothing of killing the dragon."

"He... didn't, did he?" Edward dropped the gun and shook his head, as if he could shake the anger loose. What he really needed was something to prevent the dragon from killing him.

"Yes," he murmured. *No*, said the little voice, but he ignored it. "You say dragons can sense movement?" Hya nodded. "Then finding a clever way to hide wouldn't work well."

Hya relaxed. "No, probably not."

He sighed. "It comes back to a shield, but what can stand against dragonfire?" Not metal, wood, leather, or cloth—nothing he could see from where he stood.

"I need to turn this thing," he said. When Hya gave him a quizzical look he explained. "You taught me this. I should not be asking what will save me from the dragon. I need to ask what skill I have that will help against the dragon."

She nodded agreement.

Forget the cure. Kill her and eat her.

He pressed his fists to his temples. "I don't have time for this!" He speared Hya with his gaze. "The impulses are getting stronger."

She tensed again. "I'm not surprised, given the smell and sight of dead flesh."

Of course—Jenna and the dead crewman. "There is something in my mind, something about this ship that matters. If only the corpses didn't distract me."

He began to pace, his brain ranging back and forth with him. Now that Hya had mentioned the bodies, he was conscious of the smell, and he found himself looking again and again toward the foremast or the starboard rail. He had grown so accustomed to breathing that he found it hard to stop, even though he didn't need to.

Something about the ship and what he could do...

"I know! A shield! A bone china shield."

"How will—will that work against a dragon?"

"I need the bones, and Nekyia has those in plenty. I know the bones to use, oh yes." He grinned as he strode to the deckhouse, paused to answer her question. "Dragonbone china. If anything works against dragonfire, that might be it. Let us gather what we need and quit this place."

"I'll gladly leave this charnal ship," she said. "Tell me what you need and where you expect to find it."

Samuel Fairweather had said the *Rose* hauled China clay from Cornwall, and Edward needed it. It took awhile; the lantern lit the hold poorly, but he found it. To his joy, he found a crate of ground feldspar as well.

"I need the bricks lining the cook's stove," he told Hya as he wrestled a crate of clay to their boat. "And all the dry hull wood we can carry."

The boat wallowed in the sea, the gunwales only eight inches clear of the water, as they pulled away. The excitement of the idea was fading and the *zumbi* sleep crept closer. The boat was heavy in the water, but the trip short. By the time they beached he could barely move.

☠

The next morning, he drove himself hard, cursing his inability to stave off sleep. On the beach, he used the bricks to fashion a kiln. That done, he needed one last ingredient, and soon he stood before the gate, bracing himself for a quick dash through to steal the dragon bones from Nekyia. A hundred fears crowded his mind—the carnivorous deer, that Nekyia would prove faithless, the nameless terror the sailors feared—all those and more.

His fears were unfounded. He kept to the path, and whatever dangers lurked stayed hidden. He raced to Nekyia's house, snatched some dragon bones, and fled back to the beach.

It took longer than he wanted; everything took longer than he wanted.

Making a form, grinding the bones and burning them, mixing the ash and clay and feldspar into slurry, filling the form—it all took time. Waiting, that was the worst part, and he knew he wasn't patient anymore.

Finally, he applied the glaze to the biscuit china and fired it again. Once it cooled, he held it up.

A rectangle three feet wide and four and a half feet high, it curved slightly. It was a rich ivory color, but with a hint of rose, which must have come from the bones, though they hadn't been red at all. If he held it up to the sun, he could see the shadow of his hand through it.

Leather straps, cut from a broken and washed-up trunk, completed the shield. He tried it on. Light enough, easily moved—he dropped the edge to the ground and crouched behind it. It covered him completely.

Hya ran her hand over the surface. "Won't it break?"

"China is stronger than you think," Edward said. "It chips, but this won't be easily broken."

"Will it protect you from dragonfire?"

"I hope so." He broke the kiln apart and laid the shield over the fire. After a minute he crouched beside it. He held his hand over the shield and, after a slight hesitation, lowered it. The shield was warm, but not hot. "I don't have time to try anything else. Even if this works, I have two other tasks."

"I don't like it."

He took up the shield. "I feel angry and hungry all the time. I can't delay."

☠

She didn't argue as he climbed the barrier this time. The shield could not protect two. When he landed in the sand on the far side, she just said, "Edward, be careful."

It surprised him how small she looked with the light behind her and the sides of the defile rising to either side. "I will."

When he reached the clearing, he had to orient himself. He had only a captured sailor's vague gesture to guide his search for the entrance to the volcano. His hand strayed to the coils of rope hanging from his shoulder, knowing he would need them to get in and out of the tunnels. The shield rested comfortably across his back.

He expected some sort of trail but didn't find any. The underbrush grew in clumps here, leaving areas of crusty sand. The prints in the sand formed no pattern, crossing and recrossing each other, old and new, human and animal. The freshest appeared to be a person, possibly hurt, for the feet dragged, wiping out the other tracks below.

He gave up on the tracks and headed in the direction he felt he needed to go. He kept near the cliff, looking for some path up.

A bit of white in the underbrush caught his eye. He lost sight of it and had to move about to find it again.

"Hello?" he called softly, expecting Albino but wary. It didn't move, so he cautiously approached, brushing back palm fronds as he drew near.

"What in the world?"

It looked like a well-dressed skeleton pressed against the cliff by a bed frame. Edward prowled around it, noting the sapling lashed to the frame and the twisted rope torsion spring at the other end. The bed frame was, in fact, a bed frame, salvaged from a wreck and modified. Somebody had lashed slats across and attached stakes to make a deadly grid. All-in-all, a simple but deadly trap.

Only after he examined the frame did he reluctantly turn his attention to the skeleton.

It wore white linen trousers and a matching jacket, oddly tailored, like an American might wear. Four stakes pinned it to the cliff, each surrounded by rust colored bloodstains on the clothing. It hung loosely on the stakes, skull drooping forward, arms and legs dangling.

"What purpose does this serve?" Edward grabbed the frame and shook it. He knew Nekyia could not hear, but he spoke as though the necromancer stood beside him. "Did you learn from this, or did it just amuse you?"

He was just as glad he got no answer.

Maybe, he thought suddenly, *the staff-stealer didn't make it to the tunnel.* Could he possibly be so fortunate? No, these were not eastern clothes, or even women's. Still, he leaned closer.

Something about the skull caught his attention. He pushed the top, lifting it, and the jaw fell open. The teeth! This man had two large fangs, much like Uncle Baldwin's.

Nekyia had told Uncle Baldwin he'd already helped a vampire and didn't feel inclined to help another. This might be the one Nekyia helped. How many vampires could have visited the island? Not many.

"Nekyia's help certainly didn't get you very far," Edward said to the skull. "Baldwin should be glad Nekyia didn't help him." He released the skull, and it nodded forward in agreement.

"So, let's see—if you did come for help—just what help you received." He drew open the vampire's jacket, careful not to touch the stake driven through the center of its chest. "Apart from that," he muttered. He pulled on a small chain, drawing a pocket watch, green with corrosion, from an inside pocket.

He felt a bump in the jacket. As he fished for it, the jacket shredded in his hands, leaving him holding a leather pouch while the tattered cloth slipped from his grasp.

He worked the drawstring, fumbling it in his anticipation. He finally used his teeth to pull the knot apart. He tipped the pouch and watched as a half-dozen blood-red teeth spilled into his palm.

He'd never seen or read of anything like these. They were not just blood-stained teeth, nor were they clear gems, but something in between. They were translucent, almost cloudy; but the red was arterial red. Every one of them was a fang. "These stink of necromancy, though I'm no expert," he said. The skull grinned at him.

He closed his hand over the fangs. "Nekyia didn't even bother to retrieve these," he said to the dead vampire. "I am sorry. But," he slipped them back into the pouch, "if I live to see Baldwin, I'll give them to him. Then your quest won't have been wholly fruitless."

Nekyia had traps in his jungle, and Edward wasn't stupid enough to think this was the only one. Best he move more carefully. He stepped back, letting the jungle obscure the skeleton, and resumed his search for the volcano's entrance.

☠

He found the path a bit further on. It led from the denser underbrush to his right and climbed up an outcropping slope in the cliff. It ended in a small ledge and a vent hole that dropped toward the center of the volcano.

Using the rope, Edward lowered himself into the steeply sloped vent. Carefully he picked his way down. The sides were bumped and ridged but not enough to grip. One slip and he would shoot to the bottom as, no doubt, countless captives had.

Scorch marks ran up the sides of the vent, and at the bottom, he found claw marks on the stone. Trying to hide in the vent wouldn't keep you safe.

He stopped and crouched on a small lip of stone. The hole opened directly into the center of the lava tube, a drop of ten feet or more. All was quiet. The rope made the drop easy, and once on the floor of the tube, he pulled it aside and snagged it around an outcropping out of sight. Without it, he wouldn't be able to climb out.

The smell of sulfur assailed him, but it didn't quite cover other smells, vile smells he'd never encountered. He took the shield from his back and strapped it to his arm.

A dim, uniform light lit the tunnels. He didn't know its source, and he didn't care. It made searching easier, and he was grateful.

Where would a woman, running for her life, keep the staff? With her, of course. She would never think of returning to fetch it. In what corner of this maze would she hide, then?

Inside the dragon, most likely.

He let out a snort of laughter, and immediately regretted it. He did not want to draw anything's attention. "What went in must come out" had a certain juvenile humor, but it was true. He couldn't just look for a dead body holding a magic marble on a stick.

He bent to examine the ground more closely. The lighter bumps were not stones, but globules of some sort. He prodded one with his foot and broke it open.

Edward recoiled from the stench. The globule was a mass of bones, hair, and leather held together by thick mucus. This was once, evidently, a man, eaten and vomited back up by the dragon.

A glint of metal caught his eye. It was a belt buckle. He wrinkled his nose as he knocked apart the globule, steadfastly refusing to inhale as he did. He found a couple Spanish coins, but nothing more.

He would have to find and search all such globules. He did not relish the task. No doubt Nekyia was laughing right now.

It was not pleasant, searching the twilit tunnels, fearful of finding dragons or men. He needed both hands to search the globules properly, and soon the stink of them clung to him. Time and again, he broke open globules and found nothing more than bones and hair, sometimes a small bit of metal and once a glass perfume decanter, but no staff.

A gruff voice drifted down the tunnel. "Better the dragon than a slow death."

Edward spun around, but there was no one there.

"You only say that when the dragon's gone."

Edward crept to a bend in the tunnel and listened.

"We'll not be rescued," said the first voice.

Edward stole a quick glimpse around the corner, but saw only a long stretch of tunnel. Some odd acoustic brought the words to his ears.

"You're thinking escape?"

"Of course. You want to stay here? That lunatic is eating people."

"Claims he only eats French, though."

"You trust him?"

"No."

The first voice grew softer, as if the speaker didn't want his words to carry, but carry they did. "Some of the men are about, hiding—some in the caves, one outside. There are friends if we get away from here."

"So you say. But those in the cave are eaten, like enough. And those outside can't be doing more than we—staying close to ground and praying. Don't go forgetting the Captain."

"Better a quick death than slow, I say."

Edward assumed the men were sailors off the *Twilight Rose*, bored with their captivity at the gate of the tunnel. What about the captain?

He retreated from the conversation, searching deeper in the tunnels. He kept searching the globules, prying apart bones and cutting strands of leather glued fast with dried mucus. Time and again, he found nothing. Occasionally, he found worthless trinkets: the cast coins of China, brass rings set with glass, buckles, or mangled spectacles. It felt too much like grave robbing to take them.

He crouched over an old globule, hard with age, when a dragging noise interrupted his thoughts. He spun; whatever it was had gotten close, and he could hear the heavy pad of feet hitting the ground. As the strange acoustics had brought distant voices closer, so had they hidden nearby sounds until they were nearly atop him.

The dragon came around a bend in the tunnel.

It walked on four legs like a giant lizard. Its flat head was level with his. Its tongue, long, pink, and forked, waggled before it, almost as if it were using it as a guide.

Edward pressed back against the wall and froze, hoping it would overlook him.

Teeth filled the dragon's rounded snout, large, serrated teeth made for tearing. Dark eyes studied the tube as it swept its head back and forth. Its powerful neck was as big around as its head and merged with the rest of its body at the front legs. The thick legs ended in five long claws. Its skin hung heavy and loose on its body like chainmail. The dragon's tail vanished into the lava tube behind it.

It stopped.

He dared not move.

It flicked out its tongue, looking directly at Edward.

He shrank back.

A whistling sound filled the chamber. It came from the dragon, its sides heaving. A blue glow came from deep in its throat.

Edward ran.

The slap and click of the dragon's feet followed him. He dared not look back. Was the heat from running or the dragon?

He turned a corner and the sound of the dragon faded. He turned another, hoping for a side passage. Instead, the tube widened enough that two carts could drive alongside each other.

He raced along, glancing from side to side, trying to keep some sense of where he was, seeing if there was some hint of a Hindi woman and her stolen staff.

"Climb, fool!"

Edward looked up. Two men perched on a ledge near the ceiling. As the tube had widened, it also grew taller, and it seemed likely the two men were beyond the reach of the dragon.

"The dragon is right behind me!" Edward said.

"Don't bet on it!"

Surprised, Edward stopped. He heard the sound of the dragon ahead of him. "Are there two?"

"Not sure," called one of the men. "But the beast uses shortcuts. One second right behind you, the next it's stepping out of a side passage in front of you."

"Cunning, it is," called the other.

Edward looked behind. Could there be two dragons? He scrambled to the ledge. The ledge narrowed, growing too thin to cross, before widening again. About eight feet of narrow ledge separated his refuge from the two men.

"Is that a shield on your back?" the further of the men asked.

"Yes," Edward said. He cursed himself for a fool. He'd panicked at the first sight of the dragon and completely forgotten his shield. He'd not make that mistake again.

"You're cracked," said the second man. "What good will it do?"

Something in the man's words seemed familiar. Edward studied them more carefully. Trog! He ducked his head. They hadn't recognized him yet, and he didn't want them to. The further man, what was his name? John Stearne! "I hope it will stop the dragon's fire."

"That's a useful thing," said Trog, elbowing Stearne.

Edward waited. From the ledge, he couldn't tell where the dragon noises came from. Dare he jump down anyway? Trog was no friend of his.

"You know a way out then?" asked Stearne.

"No." He kept his head turned.

The conversation died as Edward craned his head out, looking for the dragon.

After a moment, Stearne demanded, "You're not a very friendly chap, are you?"

"Sorry," Edward said. "A little worried about the dragon." He hazarded a look at the two. He would have guessed their hard voyage had turned them into wild-eye lunatics, but they were lunatics when they left England. They looked desperate, though, with their clothes torn and skin blackened by smoke.

The noises of the dragon grew louder, but their direction was no more distinguishable.

"Where is that dragon?" Edward muttered.

"There!" Trog pointed back down the tunnel.

"Where?" Edward twisted to see.

Something slammed into him.

"Get the shield!" shouted Stearne. "Get the shield!"

Edward twisted, grappling with Trog who flailed at his head and grasped at the shield. Trog tore the shield free and pushed Edward off the ledge. Stearne cheered.

Edward snagged Trog's ankle. He jerked the sailor after him, and together they rolled to the floor. The shield clinked as it landed. Trog kicked it as he struggled to rise, sending it skittering away.

"Help me!" Trog shouted. Edward kept his hold, yanking Trog back down.

Stearne jumped from the ledge, ran over, and began to kick Edward. Edward let go of Trog to try and grab Stearne's foot.

Trog scrambled away, Edward grabbed Stearne's foot, couldn't hold it, but threw Stearne off-balance. Edward rose as the others did too. Trog barreled into him, driving him into the wall.

A sudden whistling sound heralded the arrival of the dragon.

"Damn!" shouted Stearne. He dove for the shield and scooped it up.

The dragon waddled forward as it whistled.

Edward and Trog stumbled backward, still swinging at each other but also trying to get away from the dragon. Neither could run as they grappled.

The dragon inhaled, exhaled, whistling, and blue flames flickered in the back of its throat. It inhaled again and blew a pillar of fire at Stearne.

Stearne held up the shield: his head down and leaning into the fire as if against a heavy wind. The fire licked around the edges and heat washed down the tube.

Stearne screamed and fell. His feet were black and charred. The fire stopped as the dragon drew in another breath.

"Oh, God! Help me! God, it hurts!" Stearne screamed and sobbed as he tried to crawl away.

The dragon breathed again. Fire engulfed Stearne, and the smell of cooking flesh overpowered the smell of sulfur and dragon.

It smelled—good.

"Dragon take you!" swore Trog, pushing Edward toward the beast.

Kill him. The smell spurred him on.

Edward spun and swung, landing his first solid blow. Trog staggered.

Kill him!

Trog lashed back. "Damn you!"

Edward shrugged off the blows. The urging of the voice merged with his memory of Trog's abuse and more recent theft of the shield.

Kill him!

He swung again. Trog raised his fists to protect his head, but Edward hammered through them. He pummeled Trog again and again. Trog staggered, his eyes rolling upward, and he began to fall.

Edward grabbed his arm and began to pull, to tear, to rip it off. The smell of roasted flesh still drove him on. *No!* he thought, swinging Trog's limp body and hurling him toward the dragon instead.

Trog landed in front of the dragon. It dipped its head and bit the sailor's back.

Edward raced for the shield. The blackened straps powdered and he pulled it free, rushing past the dragon and its bloody mouthful. He leapt over its tail and didn't look back. With luck, it would feed on the carrion both cooked and raw.

☠

He did not know how far he ran or in which direction. Only when he was sure the dragon was far behind did he stop and examine the shield.

The shield hadn't minded the dragonfire a bit. Stearne had held it too high.

Edward replaced the burnt straps with hanks of rope, glad to be away from the dragon and the smell of cooked meat. He had not found the staff, but he knew to look up and check for ledges. Also, the shield had been tested. He couldn't call the encounter a total waste.

He was not at all sure he could find his escape rope, but knowing the shield worked gave him more confidence in dealing with the labyrinth.

The tunnels seemed an endless Hell, yet many people risked them to search for an escape—an escape that, according to the Albino, didn't exist. The globules were plentiful, meaning the dragon had been well fed, and there were other signs of people. He found a discarded pack, cast aside in someone's haste and torn open by the dragon. Other small items lay scattered about. He even found an arm, but there was no body and Edward didn't want to guess why.

He did find a whole body, crouching on a high ledge. He felt a rush of excitement when he realized it was a woman. He reached it only to discover it was a Frenchwoman, or at least the words she scrawled on the wall were in French. He searched her anyway. No staff.

How many more tunnels did he have to search, and what, he finally asked himself, would he do if he couldn't find Nekyia's staff?

He paused at a small side tunnel. It led to a small chamber made by some gas bubble when the volcano cone was formed. With a resigned sigh, he hurried in to poke at some debris in the chamber, and when he turned, he faced the dragon again.

The dragon—no, he reminded himself, *a* dragon—lumbered toward him. Already it stoked its fire. There were no side tunnels, no ledges to climb. He was trapped.

Would it come down the tunnel? It might not be able to turn around. Could the thing even go backwards?

Kill it. Rend it. Eat it.

He almost laughed at the stupidity of the urging. Small wonder *zumbi* were a nuisance not a plague. Sometimes their hunger was suicidal. His amusement died immediately. That would be him if he didn't find Nekyia's four things.

He banged the shield to the ground and crouched behind it. He closed his eyes as the fire enveloped him. Its roar filled his ears, and he could see the blue light through his closed eyes.

Can't stay here.

When the fire passed, he rushed the dragon, shield upraised.

What a fool I was to think I might kill this beast!

The dragon unleashed another blast of fire. Edward ducked, catching the fire on his shield and directing it up and over his head as he ran forward.

He twisted around the dragon, hoping the narrow tunnel would slow the beast's turning. It swung its tail; he jumped but his toe caught the very end of the tail, and he sprawled, landing on the shield.

The china shattered, sending rose-colored shards skittering down the tunnel. Edward leapt to his feet. *Damn! Damn! Clumsy bastard!* The little voice urged him to attack the dragon, but he knew better.

The dragon struggled to turn, and he didn't have time to waste. He sprinted. He didn't look back, sure he would die in a burst of blue fire.

The fire came, scorching the air but not engulfing him. He kept running, not caring which way the tunnel branched. After several branches and turns, natural light appeared.

He skidded to a stop, hastily looked back, and hurried forward. He couldn't underestimate the value of another escape.

At the opening, the smell of sulfur was overpowering. He stood at the edge of the volcano's main pipe. Far above, sunlight angled into the crater, and far below, steam and smoke swirled. The steam dissipated as it rose, but the humidity was awful, and the smell clogged the air.

The pipe was about sixty feet across. Edward leaned out to look up. There was no trail, no obvious handholds. Not an escape at all.

Behind came the sound of the dragon.

He took his second and last rope, tied it around an outcropping and his waist, and lowered himself over the edge. He had no other hiding place. He hoped the dragon wouldn't breathe fire—the rope wasn't proof against it.

He could wait until the dragon left. More time wasted, but he didn't have a choice. He looked up, hearing the scrape of the dragon's claws. He carefully, quietly lowered himself down.

He spied an outcropping a little to his left, someplace he could rest and wait out the dragon. He clutched at an imperfection in the rock and pulled himself over. Now he had to hold onto the rock, for if he let go, he would swing on the rope like a pendulum.

He flattened himself, found a small bump to press against, and felt for another grip. It was slow, but he made his way over and down, and finally, feeling with his foot, he reached the outcropping.

He looked up and listened. Silence. No wind, no birds, no sound of the dragon. A ropy tongue flicked into the pipe, disappeared, flicked again.

He looked around. He was not alone. A body rested at the far end of the outcropping.

By the dress it was a woman. Her colorful silks, dulled by dust and blending in with the stone, lay crumpled about her bones. She lay on her side, back against the pipe, legs drawn up to her chest. She lay on one arm and cradled her head on the other. Her flesh was mostly gone, sloughed off or rotted away, but her hair remained. The ledge, which had broken both her fall and her body, was barely wide enough to hold her.

Edward couldn't believe his luck. Gingerly he wrapped the rope about one hand and leaned over to search the body.

Inside her robes, he felt a bulge. He worked his hand inside. There was a round stone and, reaching further, a metal rod. He worked it free, marveling at its weight. He knew if his heart beat, it would be thundering right now from the fear of dropping the staff.

Nekyia was right. He could not mistake it. It *felt* different, as different from silver as silver did from steel. Nor did the flecks of red in the stone leave any doubt, it was well named, the bloodstone staff.

Edward thrust it inside his own shirt. Apprehension drove the satisfaction from his mind as he looked up. He had no shield or any sense of the direction of the tunnels. Bracing the dragon would be foolish.

The sky at the top of the pipe looked down like a blue eye. It was a long, long climb, and the handholds were very small indeed.

Chapter Thirteen

Edward stood on the lip of the volcano, exhausted. Now he could take a moment to examine the bloodstone staff and plan how to get the next item.

A few islands smudged the distant ocean, then nothing but a long stretch of green-blue water until the dark shores of Nekyia's island spread out at his feet.

The forest was deceptive. Approaching the island, it looked thick and shadowy but from above he saw how small and thin it really was. The island was mostly barren, broad lava shields fanning out as they stretched away. Only within Nekyia's enclosure did the plants flourish.

He snorted at the irony.

So little time. It was mid-morning. His vision dimmed and he shook his head. It cleared, but he wondered if it were a sign that the *zumbiism* grew stronger.

He drank heartily of *aqua vitae*.

Where, if he were Samuel Fairweather, would he hide?

Kill him.

It was no good avoiding it. Unpleasant as it was, he needed to find a dwarf, and Fairweather was the only one around. Clearly, he had not been captured by Nekyia. Nor was he still on the *Twilight Rose*, which looked like a broken toy from this vantage. Edward couldn't be certain, but it didn't seem likely Sam was in the caves with the crew.

Edward prowled around the edge of the crater, gaining a view of the entire island. A person could hide in the folds and crevices of the land, but living would be hard. You could get food by fishing and raiding birds' nests for eggs. There would be plenty of fresh water pooled on the rocks—as long as it rained occasionally. But the black rock would blister your feet after a day in the tropical sun, and a good storm would scour away anything without roots.

He began his descent, picking his way toward Nekyia's enclosure. It was a different hazard. Somebody might prefer to take their chances with the elements outside rather than the necromancer inside.

They might, Edward mused, but Sam didn't know the hazards inside the enclosure. He might have wanted to stay near his mates, hoping to free them and escape the island together. Once inside, he would be trapped.

He didn't want to think why Nekyia wanted the four items, or what evil he might do with them. Taking a man's heart was evil enough.

It was quickly apparent Edward could not save time by climbing directly into the enclosure. The cliffs were too steep, the handholds too few. He continued to the sea and worked his way to the cove, where he found Hya waiting.

She looked different. It wasn't because strands of her strawberry blonde hair had escaped the string tying it back, or weariness had left dark circles under her eyes. It wasn't her appearance at all; it was posture. She kept her arms close to her sides, her shoulders slightly hunched. She moved stiffly, lacking her usual grace as she approached.

"What's wrong?" he asked.

"Did you find the staff?" she asked.

He brought it out to show her. "What's wrong?" he repeated.

She glanced away, toward the cliff and the debris piled at its base. "Nothing. Will you give it to Nekyia?"

He didn't believe her, but answered her question. "Not until I have all four items. He'll get nothing free if I fail."

She nodded. "Where is the shield?"

"It broke." There was nothing to hold her interest—a pile of broken chests and barrels.

"Did you see the dragon?" Her voice was distant, detached, as if the question was a distraction for her.

"Yes." He drew the word out, taking a step toward the debris. "What is wrong?" he shouted. He drew a breath, not because he needed it, but to calm himself.

"Nothing," she insisted. She met his eyes. "Tell me."

Reluctantly he did, studying her as he spoke, searching her eyes for her troubles.

As he spoke he dropped the pouch of ruby fangs into her hand. "I found these on a dead vampire. They will interest Baldwin. I believe they will help control his bloodlust."

She turned the pouch over in her hand and rubbed it with her thumb, tracing the outlines of the objects within. "How?"

"I don't know, but I suspect he will."

She let him finish his story before asking, "And now?"

"Next is the heart of a dwarf. Nekyia said each was harder than the last. That would make sense if there were no dwarfs in the Narrow World and the House of Sorrow isn't in this world at all." He took a deep breath to steel himself. "So I should do them in order to leave myself the most time for the hardest task."

She nodded, her head down, looking miserable.

"But I don't want to," he said. "I'd rather search for the House of Sorrow. If I fail, at least it doesn't cost Sam his life."

She closed her eyes, as if in pain, and shook her head.

"What is wrong?" he burst out.

"You need to hunt the dwarf," she whispered. "Do it first."

"Why? What has happened?"

She led him, her feet scuffling the sand, to the pile of debris. "This dwarf, this Fairweather, he betrayed you on the *Twilight Rose*?"

Edward cocked his head, for her question caught him off-guard. "Betrayed? Yes, I suppose he did." He didn't know if Sam's words would have mattered either way, but they didn't help.

For a moment he thought Sam might be hiding in the pile, but she led him around, to the space between the pile and the cliff. "May God forgive me," she said and pointed down.

Footprints roughed the sand.

"They might be a child's," she said, "but these are made by a man's style of boot. Were there any children on the *Twilight Rose?*"

"No," he said.

"Thank God for that at least. Your dwarf hid here, and followed the rest of the men through the defile."

This confirmed all his suspicions. "But you can't follow them," he protested. "The gate is locked."

She relaxed. Showing him the prints had released her tension. "That is the start of the tale. Once you went in to seek the staff, I began to work on the gate.

"I'm the King's Jack, remember?" she said. "The gate has a deadlock, rather appropriately. Moreover, it's a lever tumbler lock that can be unlocked from either side, which means the pattern of levers is symmetrical. A lock this thick has five levers, but I only need to figure out three of them because the last two will be the same as the first two."

She brushed the stray clump of hair back from her face. "I can pick that. In fact," she pulled a rough-fashioned key from her pocket, "I already have."

"You have gone into the enclosure?"

"No," she admitted. "You were in the volcano where I could not follow. I merely prepared myself to help with the next task."

She offers to help me hunt a man and kill him.

"This is wrong," he said.

"It is an evil choice," she said.

"It is no choice at all! You should not be stained by my curse."

"I am already colored by it. I cannot let you die." She looked away and whispered, "I cannot."

"But what Nekyia wants is evil," Edward said.

"Then we best do it quickly!" she snapped. "And I do mean that. Not only because you have little time, but because the next rain will wash away these tracks."

"I will go alone," he said.

"I can track this man," she said. "You cannot."

"How do you know? How do you know I can't?"

"Tell me what he did while he hid here," she demanded.

"I don't know," he yelled. "I didn't watch him!"

"You need me."

Edward couldn't argue that. "Damn," he swore and clenched his fists. "Damn." He threw his head back and stared at the sky. "This is wrong." *But I want to live.* "What choice is there?"

I can turn into a ravening monster. He wanted to cry with frustration. *But I want to see Becca.*

"He hid from Nekyia's minions," she said, ignoring his question.

"Poor fool, that's why his prints are away from everybody else's and visible. I've already tracked them to the gate."

"I should be glad you didn't follow me into the dragon's lair."

"I had no shield," she said. "If you were much later returning, I would have tried to make one. I watched how you did it."

She followed the footprints along the cliff. Edward trailed after her. When they reached the gate in the defile, she slipped her hand-filed key into the lock.

Before she could turn it, he put his hand on the gate, preventing it from opening. "I want your help," he said. "I want to live more than I have words to describe. But you should not damn yourself for me."

"If I am to be damned, I'll be damned for you." She turned the key, jiggling it in the lock to make it work. When it turned, she gently removed his hand from the gate and pulled it open. "Besides, the dwarf is already dead. Nobody leaves this island alive without Nekyia's permission. The vampire and the Dutchman are proof of that."

"Thank you," Edward said.

Hya nodded. She still didn't look happy, but resolutely stepped through the gate.

"This is a Garden Macabre," he warned as they passed through the gate. "From the deathflower gate to the skeletal statuary, there is little to like here."

"You told me of the deer," she said.

"There's more than just the deer. Albino and Small Man have a stockade to keep *something* out. Something that runs wild within the enclosure like the deer, but is more dangerous."

He paused, struggling with the words he felt he had to say. "You don't have to do this."

"Do you wish to live?"

He closed his eyes. "You know I do."

"Then let's not waste time."

"If you change your mind, I won't hold it against you." The little voice inside might rage, but he wouldn't listen.

They followed the footsteps through the cut; Sam had hugged the sides, his shuffling and hesitant footsteps clear in the sand—now that Edward knew to look. His trail was equally clear in the jungle—broken leaves, trampled grass. He bore to the left, leaving the trail and staying near the cliff.

In a clearing, Hya stopped. "He was through here several times." She prowled around. "He is a dwarf, not just a stunted man?"

"There are dwarfs and there are dwarfs," Edward said. "Nekyia wasn't particularly specific about which he wanted. An odd omission, considering his precision with words."

Hya nodded. "Fair enough, if he honors his word. This way." She brushed back a frond to re-enter the jungle.

"Beware of traps," Edward warned.

Hya led, gently moving fronds aside, pausing often to make an examination. Sometimes Edward could tell what caught her attention, a smudged footprint, a broken stem, once a fallen kerchief. Other times, he thought she must be reading Sam's trail from thin air.

She relentlessly followed each loop, refusing to despair each time they crossed their previous path. The trail stayed near the cliffs. They reached the clearing with Nekyia's house and there the footprints shuffled about and retreated. Sam had no wish to meet the necromancer or anybody else.

He had taken refuge in a small clump of bushes. He couldn't have rested much—tracks of a large deer showed its interest. There was no blood, and Hya said once Sam left he hadn't returned.

Further along, Hya stopped, pointed. There was another trap, another lethal bed frame hidden in the brush. This one hadn't been sprung. "He almost stepped into it. Shame he didn't. It would have made your task easier."

After that, she paid more attention to the tracks, following them exactly, staying away from undisturbed jungle. Edward looked for more traps and fell behind.

Hya had crossed a small clearing and stopped just as Edward entered it. She listened, held up her hand to stop him, and listened some more.

The long fronds beside her rustled, and a man fell from the brush. He caught himself before landing, lurched, and threw himself at Hya.

She yanked her revolver from its holster and pointed at the man. She only hesitated a second before pulling the trigger. She fired five more times in quick succession.

Edward leapt forward to help.

The man leaned back with the impact, staggered, but kept his balance. There was no blood, only black holes in his pallid flesh, visible as his tattered shirt moved with his swaying.

"Garrrrgh." There was something familiar about him as he stepped forward and knocked her hand aside, sending the gun flying. Hya grabbed for her long knife, but the man lurched, knocking her off balance. As she stumbled, she drew the knife, but he seized her other arm and jerked her to him.

Edward was still three steps away.

Hya twisted, slicing the man's arm, freeing herself. She swung backhand. He didn't try to avoid her blow, reaching for her and intercepting the blade with his hand. It cut between his fingers, through his palm, all the way to his wrist.

With a bleat, he pulled back, pulling the knife with him. Hya let go of the knife and backpedaled. The man followed, ignoring the knife in his hand. Hya fell.

Edward lowered his shoulder and knocked the man away from Hya. He smelled rot and death as he drove the man back. He avoided the man's clumsy grasp and stepped away.

Edward recognized him. Captain Davies of the *Twilight Rose*—much changed.

His eyes were flat, dry; they did not shine when the light hit them. They held no expression, not that his face lent them any. That was flaccid, mouth slightly open, as if he no longer cared to control those muscles.

Rend him! The voice yelled in his mind, riding a surging desire to destroy. All he had to do was surrender to it, he wanted to, for in his savagery he could protect Hya.

He must not. Davies had already taken injuries that would kill a living man. Edward had learned his lesson from Parlexi. He must fight intelligently.

"Captain!" he shouted. "Captain Davies!"

Davies snarled at him, baring his teeth, reaching up with his hands. His fingers were hooked, immobile, like claws. In addition to the cut made by Hya's knife, many small cuts laced his hands and wrists. The flesh had turned black and curled into the cuts as it dried.

Kill him!

But he couldn't. Davies was already Dead.

"*Zumbi!*" shouted Hya.

"I know!"

Davies went after Hya, preferring live meat to Dead, forcing her to retreat. Being a *zumbi* made the man clumsy, but not slow. Edward scrambled to help.

He wrapped his arms around Davies and held him tight, jerking him away from Hya. "Think, man! Fight this urge!"

Davies twisted and, with an angry, hungry grunt, bit at Edward.

"Don't let it bite you!" Hya called.

Edward tightened his grip. He could hear bones break. "Control yourself! Remember who you are!"

Davies went limp. He made a soft mewing sound.

"So, these are Nekyia's guard dogs—*zumbis,*" Edward muttered. "Now the stockade makes sense. Listen to me, Captain." He shook Davies to give his words emphasis. "I have some *aqua vitae.* It will help you. Do you understand?"

Davies did not answer.

"I need to let you go to get it out," Edward said, "but you must control yourself."

"Edward," Hya warned. "Don't trust him."

"Do you understand me, Captain?"

Davies gave an inarticulate grunt and jerky nod.

Edward relaxed. "Good."

Davies surged forward, breaking his grip. Hya cried in surprise. Edward grabbed, missing Davies's hand but pulling Hya's knife free. Davies didn't notice.

Desperately, Edward kicked at his knee. The knee buckled and Davies fell backward. Edward was on him, a hand on his chest, holding him down. "Stop!" He brandished the long knife. "For decency sake, Captain, stop!"

Davies opened his mouth, but only made a dry, rasping noise as he tried to shake Edward off. Edward brought down the knife, putting all his strength and weight behind it. Davies's head rolled away.

Edward held down the body long enough to know it was truly dead, then dropped the knife and backed away. He raised his eyes to look at Hya. "Don't let it bite me?"

"*Zumbi* bites get infected," she said. "They turn their victims into…"

She turned red. "Well, it wouldn't heal."

Edward shook his head. Davies had still been smart enough to trick him into relaxing. *That will be me if I'm not cured.* "It surprised you," he said angrily. "You must not be surprised."

"I was focused on the tracks," she protested. "And you were here."

"What if it's me that surprises you? That," he pointed to the corpse, "will be me if I'm not cured." *A beast, a monster; damned, or worse.*

Her emotions played across her face: surprise, anger, acknowledgement. "You're right." She picked up her knife and wiped the blade in the sand. She searched until she found her revolver and returned it to her holster. "You knew it." She jerked her head toward the body, her tone sharp. She was irritated with him, he could tell.

It didn't pay to be right. "The Captain of the *Rose.*"

"Yet he couldn't have been Dead for long—much less time than you."

"He wouldn't have *aqua vitae*," Edward said. He wiped his hands on his trousers. Grabbing Davies had left an unclean feeling. "I'll hazard a guess his Dead was no accident. Maybe Nekyia can accelerate the disease. It doesn't really matter."

"What better terror for the crew? A familiar face, twisted to horror and set to preying on them." She nodded at her own words. "I could easily believe it."

"Strange I didn't find him before. Maybe he wasn't enough of a *zumbi* to be released until today."

"Or maybe he slept, and you were just lucky." Hya looked about the clearing as if expecting another *zumbi* to leap out at her. She crouched down, examining the ground, but moved about, back and forth. The fight had obscured Fairweather's tracks. "We better hurry. The gunshots might draw the attention of the small and big men you mentioned."

I have killed a man. Edward closed his eyes as if that would change the truth. *Or have I? He was already Dead. A judge would make a merry case of this.*

"This way," Hya finally said. "What if the *zumbi* caught your dwarf?"

"Then he will have eaten him," he replied.

"Pray it didn't."

"If I could."

Edward hesitated, sparing a glance for Davies. *That was a man once.*

He had a childhood, an apprenticeship, an adulthood. I knew him, and he wasn't a bad man. Yet he caught Dead. And I killed him, or at least ended him.

Hya had no interest in burying the body. He, or as she said, "it," had tried to kill her. Neither wanted to spend much time on the task, so Edward rolled Davies into a depression and filled it in as best he could. The sandy soil made the task easy, and they were soon on Sam's trail again.

Samuel led them on a circuitous route, back toward the defile, though he must have realized he was trapped, around the far cliff. Always he avoided the stockade, the prisoner's cave, and Nekyia's house.

Soon, though, they would find him. The enclosure was large, but not huge. They'd catch him, Edward was sure.

☠

The sun shone directly down, making the shadows short and the day hot. No breeze stirred the leaves.

"What have we here?" Hya asked.

One of the red deer lay with legs akimbo, head crushed under a large rock. "Deadfall trap," Hya said, prodding a stick trapped under the rock with the deer.

"No person would put their head under a rock like that," Edward said. It seemed too obvious. Had it been disguised somehow?

"Of course not." She realized he thought this one of Nekyia's people traps for she said, "This isn't for people. Your dwarf must have resigned himself to spending some time here. His tracks are all around. This is his trap. He is close."

After a moment she pointed. "He climbed the cliff."

Vines bounded the cliff here, isolating it, but from what, Edward couldn't tell. The first thirty feet would be an easy climb. The vines didn't grow any higher.

Sam's footsteps milled about the cliff. A sandy smudge marked where he had stood on a rock to get started, and broken leaves betrayed his climb.

"There must be a cave," he said. "Again, I ask you to remain behind." She opened her mouth to protest, but he cut her off. "I would spare you what must be done. Let me protect you from the actual deed."

She nodded. "Damn Nekyia for asking this."

He climbed easily, quickly. About twenty feet from the ground, the cliff behind the vines disappeared. He pushed his way into a leafy bower, a ledge out of reach of the creatures that patrolled the forest. Thick vines covered in broad leaves sheltered much of it from prying eyes. A refugee could easily hide in the concealed portion.

A small pack lay in the middle of the ledge, its flatness telling how little it contained. Other items left about told him this was someone's refuge: a hatchet, a length of rope, a pair of boots for small feet.

And, crouched in the far corner, his back pressed against the rock, the dwarf himself. His face was striped by sun and shade. "Ed," he said. His clothes were tattered and face dirty. He looked very small.

Edward squatted down, adjusting his crouch until he was comfortable. He picked up the hatchet, regarded it impassively, and flipped it far out into the jungle. He let the silence draw out.

I need a dwarf's heart.

"What are you doing here, Ed?" Samuel's eyes were wide, the white standing out in the gloom.

"Looking for you."

"For me? Why would you look for me?"

Kill him, whispered the voice in Edward's head, and for once it seemed good advice.

"I have a problem," Edward said, not taking his eyes from Sam. The dwarf stared back. *The mouse must look like this when mesmerized by the snake.*

"I'm Dead," he told Sam. "Have been for some time. I need a necromancer."

Sam whimpered and pushed back as if he could escape into the stone cliff.

"Not for any evil purpose," Edward said. "To cure me. He tells me I will soon lose all my humanity and become something you should fear. I wasn't before," he added.

Beads of sweat stood out on Sam's face. "I fear you now, lad," he whispered.

"You should." Edward fell silent, listening to the voice urge him, *Kill him, pluck out his heart, kill him.*

"Revenge." Sam swallowed. "Aye. A right Judas, I was. I was gutless, having puked the better part of them over the side that day."

"I do not want revenge."

"What do you want, lad?"

"Your heart."

Sam's hand flew to his chest. "My heart…" he said in an awed and terrified whisper.

"I don't want it, really. Nekyia does. He bid me to bring him four things. The third is the heart of a dwarf."

"I owe you, lad, right enough. But my heart… I've a need for it."

"So do I, Mr. Fairweather."

"Mr. Fairweather," Sam muttered, "you be a fair-spoken murderer."

"Should I value your life more than my own?" Edward asked evenly.

"I liked you, Ed." Sam burst out. "I made excuses for your oddities because I liked you! You lied to me! What of the woman?"

"Becca? No. She is real enough, but she doesn't know I am Dead." He spread his hands. "I could not bear to tell her. It is for love of her that I do this."

Sam shivered in his fear.

"You cannot kill me," Edward said. "And you cannot stop me."

"I'm sorry I threw you to those bilge rats, Ed, but I don't want to die!"

Edward looked away. *How can I live with myself if I do this?* Was a life of guilt and regret better than no life at all?

He caught a glimpse of Hya through the vines, standing below next to the crushed deer, waiting. He grinned, seeing his way out of the dilemma. "Is that your deer trap in the jungle?"

"It is." Sam turned his head, but his eyes never left Edward. "What does it matter?"

"Then it is your deer that's in it?"

Sam furrowed his brow. "It is."

"Give it to me."

"I cannot stop you taking it."

"I'd prefer you give it," Edward said.

"Give you the… deer?"

"Not a deer, a buck. A hart."

"A hart?" Sam tested the word, uncertainty in each syllable. "You want that hart?"

"Yes, I want your hart."

Comprehension burst over Sam's countenance. "But, lad, he can't agree to that." He slapped his forehead. "What am I saying? If you want the hart, take it with my blessing."

"He'll agree," Edward said. "He values precision in speech. The irony will amuse him." He sobered. "But only once. I must be certain of the fourth task. He will give me no latitude there."

"You're putting a lot of faith in your judgment of that necromancer," Sam said. "Taking a mighty risk. I appreciate it, and I'll not speak ill of the Dead again."

Chapter Fourteen

Edward watched Sam stuff his things into the pack. Together they climbed down the vines. Only when they reached the bottom did Sam turn and see Hya. "I thought you said your Becca was in London, Ed."

"This is Hya. Hya, this is Samuel Fairweather and this," he pointed to the dead deer, "is his hart."

Hya smiled. "Clever, but will Nekyia agree?"

"Yes," Edward said. "I believe he will."

She looked unconvinced but still relieved. "You are a good man, Edward Truscott."

He remembered the words of Albino and how he denied being damned by his own choices. Since then, he had fed a man to a dragon and cut off another's head. "No," he said, "I'm not. I have had evil thrust upon me."

"Lad," said Sam. "I hate to ask for more than my life, but will you take me when you leave? You've a boat, that's clear enough, and I don't know if I'll get another chance."

Edward glanced at Hya. "It's no certain thing that I'll be leaving. The last task is the hardest."

"I swore I'd see you back to London," Hya said.

"I'll guard the hart," Sam said. "We'll drag it to the beach so the other deer don't eat it—or," he lowered his voice and shivered, "the *zumbis*. Have you seen it?"

"I killed it," Edward said. "More's the pity. Are there others?"

Sam eyed him, read his expression. "Poor Davies. Don't feel bad, Ed. You did him a favor. But there's only one *zumbi* loose at a time. They'd destroy each other otherwise. The necromancer will ready a replacement, I don't doubt."

"Damn him!" Edward shouted. *Kill them all.* He grabbed a stick. Sam loomed large in his vision.

"Edward!" Hya said.

Edward froze, tried to drop the stick, but his hands wouldn't respond. He twitched, bringing the stick up to swing. *Kill them all.*

Very deliberately Sam took a step back.

"Damn Nekyia!" Edward flung the stick at Sam, forcing himself to hold on too long, making the throw go down into the sandy ground between them. "I'm not mad at you, Sam. I'm just—just losing myself. We best hurry."

He paused though, just long enough to take a quick swig of *aqua vitae*. He didn't dare hold the bottle up to see how much remained; it felt too light, and he feared how little there was.

"Better," he said. "But I'm getting worse if such a little thing triggers my anger."

☠

"And now," Edward said once they had dragged the hart to the beach. "The House of Sorrow."

"That is no small task," Hya said.

"Will you tell me where to find it?" he snapped. Why didn't she just tell him?

"It is not of this world." Hya squatted down on the sand. "You must go through a gate."

"A gate?" He sat down beside her. "I once thought a gate would bring me to the Narrow World."

"Both the Narrow and Wide Worlds are part of the Real World," she grimaced. "More or less: the Wide World more, the Narrow less. The House of Sorrow is not. Think of it like Heracles's descent into the underworld."

"Where is this gate?" He did not want any geography beyond its location.

"Close. A day's sail."

"Not close enough," he growled. "The *aqua vitae* fails me, I can feel it."

"I can't move it closer to suit you!" she snapped.

Edward clenched his fist. *Stop this,* he thought, but his fist rose, as though he would strike her. He jerked it back and started to pound the sand. "I will not allow this to control me!"

Hya moved away. "I am sorry. I let my frustration out. I forgot how you would react."

"No," he said, his teeth clenched as he pounded out his anger. "You have every right to be frustrated. I am poor company. Dangerous company. You were right when we met."

Sam stared at him with wide eyes.

"Be warned, Mr. Fairweather," Edward said. "This Dead progresses, and at some point, I shall have no more control than Captain Davies."

Sam nodded.

"Please don't get angry if I speak more formally," Hya said. "I think you may be less likely to take offense."

Edward nodded. "However you speak, we must hurry." Even so, he paused, shading his eyes and looking over the sea. "And so must Pielloos."

They showed Sam Hya's hiding spot. He wasn't happy about remaining behind but had little choice. Hya assured him the trip would not take long.

"Why do I feel as though we've done this before?" Edward asked as they slid the boat into the surf.

"You're in an archipelago," Hya said. "How did you expect to travel?"

The familiar banter made him smile, but the lingering taste of frustration made Edward's levity short-lived. He tamped down his frustration, but doubt replaced it. Could he trust the merman? Would Nekyia accept the hart of a dwarf? Would Nekyia honor his word at all?

He turned his anger and doubts on the oars, and the boat surged to sea. He felt the wind on his back, and Hya confirmed they needed to go against the wind. He would row.

"The gate leads to the House of Sorrow," Hya said. She shaded her eyes, searching the sea. Evidently, she, too, worried about Pielloos. "But that is only one of many places it goes."

"Like a railway."

Hya frowned. "No, not as I understand it, but I've never seen a railway. This just goes somewhere else. Like having a doorway go to a different room each time you enter."

"Magic," Edward grumbled.

"Yes. Few have gone through and returned. They did not choose their path, merely walked it." She fell silent, her expression thoughtful. "I wish I had paid more attention, but in each story the person's travels are directed by their demeanor."

"A sorrowful person ends up at the House of Sorrow?"

"That is my belief," she said. "To reach it, you must have the proper frame of mind. Let your emotions falter, and you might end up somewhere very different."

Edward thought of that. "I must be sorrowful."

"I would be afraid of where anger might take you," Hya said, "but then the fear would take you to its own home."

"How can I get rid of my anger?" He held up his hands, as if she could see the anger coursing through his veins like blood. "It is always here."

"Anger is a weak emotion," Hya said. "The Dead has unchained your anger, but normally it is a slave of Fear."

He glared at her. "It is not weak. I can barely contain it."

"Forgive me. I meant other emotions can take its place. I think emotions closely linked to sorrow would work—anguish, despair, grief."

"Are you sure?"

She spoke slowly, clearly choosing her words with care. "I have not seen this Gate, much less passed through it." She pointed ahead. "That island there."

They rode in silence.

Hya looked about to speak, but looked away. She hesitated, as if unsure. "You are far from London," she said, still not looking at him. "Much has happened. Have your feelings for Rebecca changed?"

"No," he said immediately. "Not in the slightest."

She swallowed.

"Why do you ask?"

"Merely curious. And since," she lifted her head and stared intently into his eyes. "How do you feel of those you've met since?"

His irritation flared. She had no right to question him about Becca. *Kill her.* He jerked on the oars. He doubted he could overcome his anger—it was too quick, too strong. He must channel it. He pulled harder on the oars.

He chose his words carefully, making sure he spoke calmly. "This monster inside consumes more and more, and it still whispers in my head. I don't know that anything I feel is real, so I cling to my love as a drowning man clings to a life preserver."

"I wonder if you would feel differently had you made this voyage while not Dead," she said.

"If I were not Dead, I would not have made this voyage," he retorted. He dug the oars deeper. The oarlocks creaked as he pulled, clunked as he lifted, twisted, and pushed. He flung a string of water drops off the blades of the oars and, slicing deep into the sea again, pulled the boat forward to catch them.

Hya didn't question him further, just watched as he rowed.

Creak—clunk—splash: over and over. He could beat the sea, he could cut it with the prow. This was a safe outlet for his anger.

And it seemed the sea took his anger. He poured it into the depths where it disappeared without a mark. The slap of waves against the hull soothed him, telling him of their speed, and eventually his anger ebbed like a neap tide.

But he knew it still lurked, just under the surface like a monster waiting to devour him.

☠

It had not devoured him by the time they reached their destination, an island of rolling ridges. Unlike Nekia's island, this resembled a savannah that had been crumpled up and dropped into the ocean. Tall grass smoothed the rough edges of the ridges. There were no trees and only a few bushes. A low ceiling of grey clouds added to a feeling of empty desolation.

Hya pointed to the highest ridge. "There, in the last valley, if the stories are correct."

They spoke little as they toiled through the rough land. Only the wind whispered in their ears. For now, the little voice in Edward's mind was silent; whenever it stirred, he brutally shut the door on it, using his frustration against it. The trick took all his concentration.

He was glad when they reached the proper valley and he could concentrate on what lay within.

A river cascaded down the opposite ridge. It roiled and boiled, throwing out a fine mist that filled the valley like an early morning fog, though it was late afternoon.

A large rock split the river, sending it tumbling down on either side. The water frothed as it moved, turning white so that it looked like lace curtains, drawn aside from a window.

A spit of land lay between these two waterfalls, an island before the rivers joined in the pool. A dark cave gaped on this island where the land met the ridge.

Once past this small island, the water settled in a broad pool before flowing east, following the twists of the valley to the sea.

"Where does the water come from?" he asked.

"I've never heard," Hya answered. "Perhaps it springs from other worlds and that is what gives the gate its power."

The sun pierced the clouds and struck the mist, filling the valley with a golden haze.

"Avalon," Edward murmured.

"Similar, though that gate is closed. Destroyed with Lyonesse."

"Lethowsow, in the Cornish," Edward said.

"I'll take your word for it." She pointed. "That hole is your gate. I don't know if you must be sorrowful when you enter the valley, or just when you pass through the gate."

"The valley, for safety's sake," he said.

She nodded. "Do not touch the plants which grow in the mist. They have an oil which has a powerful effect on the mind. Most certainly do not eat them. It is said they will wrap you in colors and transport you places. They are much sought after and much reviled. Do they take their magic from this place, or does their magic contribute to the magic of this place? No one knows."

"Does eating them have the same effect as entering the gate?"

"No. You might believe yourself elsewhere, perhaps even the House of Sorrow, but it would be a delusion of the mind. Or not. Maybe it would be just as real as those whose spirits stray because of true sorrow." She shrugged. "Who can say? But of a certainty your body would not go, and you could not bring anything back."

"So much for shortcuts. Damn."

"Sorrow. Not anger," she said in a mild voice. Her face betrayed her anxiety.

She has no faith, he thought. *No faith that I can banish my anger.*

Kill her, the voices urged. Even such a mild contradiction made his anger surge. *Such lack of faith deserves to die. Slack your anger with her blood. Quell your hunger with her flesh.*

"I am Dead," he muttered to himself. "I have no hope. God has betrayed me." *Kill. Devour.* He shook his head. "It's just making me angry."

He tried again. "I am Dead. I have no time. Animals shun me."

Kill the animals.

"This isn't working."

Hya took a deep breath. "If you will forgive me, I will try." She took another breath and her expression became one of great sadness and compassion. "Edward." Her voice was gentle, serious. "You are a good man, a decent man. You've made a remarkable effort to come this far. Sorrow is a place you should not go," she said, "but you must. How tragic the irony that you place your hope in a House that has none."

Her voice caught, moisture sparkled in her eyes. "So mourn those things you cannot know. Mourn simple things like fresh fruit and honest sleep. You will not know the passion of a woman, or the joy of children. Think of the future you dream of, but will not have.

"Regret," she continued, her voice trembling, "the evil you will do. Feel the evil, feel what it will make you do to others. Imagine the suffering of the innocent."

He thought of those things, and anger stirred that she should be right. It was not fair! But her voice was so kind, and tears now flowed down her cheeks. Her sorrow and her beauty defused his anger. It hurt her to do this, and he regretted that hurt.

"And finally, think of the distance between you and Rebecca. She is alone. Think of her and her sorrow."

All his anger vanished at the thought of Becca. He strove to mirror her unhappiness, and when he had, he moved with heavy steps down the side of the valley. Just before entering the mist he looked up. He knew he could never thank Hya enough for all her help. That, too, made him sad—that she should suffer to help him. He raised his hand in farewell as he walked forward.

☠

The mist clung to his skin. Not cool, not warm, it was his own temperature. *It,* he thought, *is the same temperature as the air, and so am I.*

Walking through the golden mist gave an ethereal feeling. It could almost have been the path to Heaven, but it wasn't, and it made him sad to think his life had led only to Sorrow.

The sound of the falls filled his ear with its melody. Dark green plants grew from cracks in the rock. Ferns of some sort, but unlike any he had seen or read about. Perhaps they only grew here, nourished by the gate. Perhaps that is why they could take your mind elsewhere as the gate could take your body.

The hole, the gate, grew larger as he approached, or maybe it only felt larger. It certainly looked like a maw; the water dripping from above might have been saliva.

What if it did not take him to the House of Sorrow? He felt a trill of fear.

No, he must not allow fear. If he didn't reach the House of Sorrow, it would only be misfortune.

How could he keep *only* sorrow in mind?

No, he must not allow doubt.

It wasn't *fair* that this should be asked of him.

No, he must not allow anger, or the fear that he would allow anger, or doubt that he couldn't control the anger, or...

Realizing the hopelessness of his task, Edward felt instead despair and threw himself into the gate because he had no other options.

He stumbled, fell, fell out of this world. The sensation was falling without falling. A turning, a changing, and he stood looking out the gate, the mist no longer golden but a dull, leaden grey.

"Hello?" he called.

Nothing.

He was so alone he didn't even have an echo.

When he exited the gate, he found himself on a plateau. The first thing he saw was a house. It was some distance ahead, surrounded by tall grass and framed by the sky and ocean. There was no horizon, only grey haze.

It felt incomplete, like an island beyond which lay nothing—a bubble in a void containing a cliff, a house, and a sea. Were there other such bubbles? He didn't care.

He was in the right place.

What constitutes sorrow? He didn't know, but he felt it in the somber landscape and the hazy light that wasn't one thing or another. Something here spoke to the spirit, smothering it.

A pleasant house, except it wasn't. It was spacious, grand even, and well appointed. Yet it was horrible, too. Edward recoiled from it. As badly as he felt thinking of his misfortune, it was nothing compared to being inside that house. He couldn't imagine wanting anything that might be inside.

Nekyia did, so he must go.

The House of Sorrow brooded on the precipice, overlooking the surf crashing below. The broad front steps, thirteen in number, carried Edward past the terrace onto the veranda. The veranda stretched across the front of the house and wrapped around the side.

It was empty, and lonely, with a view of the desolate sea; the sea that rushed at the house to dash itself to spray on the jagged rocks below the cliff.

The ten-foot doors of weather-darkened oak loomed above him. They opened at his touch, swinging inward to let grey light splash on a mosaic floor.

Edward stood, his faint shadow lying across the floor. The mosaic was a cypress tree, a grand tree, picked out in detail, its trunk and branches dark brown, its needles an even darker green.

He felt small in that great doorway, dwarfed by the tall ceiling, insignificant in the expansive foyer. His scuffling footsteps sounded out of place.

The air felt heavy, thick, less than water but somehow more than air. It filled his lungs unpleasantly. Having grown so used to pretending to breathe, he now forced himself to stop.

A massive chandelier with crystals innumerable hung in the center. Chandelier was wrong, he realized, for there were no candles. This fixture could never illuminate anyone.

"Tears."

Edward tore his gaze from the crystals. A woman had entered the room and approached without his hearing. She was beautiful beyond description. A man could die of despair knowing he was not worthy of her. Her grace was like daggers. Her smile was the most exquisite pain he had ever known.

"Welcome to the House of Sorrow," she said. When he didn't answer—he couldn't answer, for the words stuck in his throat—she said, "The crystals are tears. It is fitting, is it not?"

Yes, Edward thought. *It is fitting.* He licked his lips. Nothing, *nothing,* could be as beautiful as she was.

"Many people come, but not as you," she said. "Not in body."

"I seek something," he stammered.

"All seek something," she said. "Sorrow is the trap they fall into."

"No, I must carry something away with me. That which is most valuable."

"And what is this valuable thing?"

"I don't know." He paused. This place affected him strangely. He didn't feel angry anymore, it was as if the sorrow housed here held back the Dead. Instead, he felt regret at all the wasted moments of his life, the missed opportunities. A deep sadness settled into his heart at the thought of all the things he would not be able to do, and it was certain he would not escape. He could not possibly live again.

"You would let me take it, whatever it is?" he asked.

"I will help you search."

He felt a pain that failure meant death but success meant leaving her.

"I am Ania," she said.

A name that could rip out your heart with its beauty, he thought. "Thank you," he whispered.

"It is nothing. Come. Let us look."

"Where—?" He hesitated. "Where is everybody? Where are the injured, the ill?"

"Sorrow is not pain of the body," Ania said. "It is pain of the soul. Loss, regret, despair—they find their home here."

She led him from room to room. All were filled with shadows, spirits like smoke. *Ashes and sackcloth,* he thought, *the images of sorrow.*

"Only people's spirits are here, and though they may fill a room, they are alone. It is a dark place for them. Darker than it is for you, who are protected somewhat by your Dead."

Remembering Parlexi, Edward nodded. Dead could protect. "A reprieve," he agreed.

"No," Ania said. "Your disease progresses. It gets worse even as we speak. But here Sorrow is stronger yet."

Not knowing what else to say he asked, "What is the most valuable thing here?"

"That I do not know," Ania said.

She led him to a breakfast room overlooking the sea. The light was grey but with a slight blueness. Tall windows held back the wind. A table, set for two, sat before the windows. One place setting had been moved, the silver toyed with, but the food untouched. The other had not been disturbed.

"Sailor's widows often find themselves here," Ania said. "Waiting and watching without appetite. Perhaps you seek the silver? The china?"

Neither felt right. "No," Edward said.

She nodded. "Perhaps this way." She led him through long halls, up stairs, and through more halls, past doors.

"How large is this house?" he asked.

"There are as many rooms as there are people. Some grief is shared. Men whose wives died in childbirth, for instance, know something of each other's pain. But most sorrow is personal, and there is room for each."

That seemed to be true, for every time they left one section of the house they entered another just as large.

"Surely this is larger inside than out," he protested.

"Are you not larger inside than out?" Ania asked. "Your mind and soul are so much larger than your body." They reached the end of a hallway and she took hold of the glass doorknob. "Here is some of the most profound grief in the House. Mayhap what you seek is here." She opened a door and ushered him in.

It was a nursery, decorated with care: a small table with a child's tea set, a porcelain doll, a stuffed animal. A small shoe abandoned in the corner. Filled with emptiness.

"Parents end up here," Ania said. "Paupers and kings alike feel the loss of their children. Some of the toys are quite old and valuable."

Indeed, an ancient set of jackstones lay scattered amongst the teacups. A small diabolo was entangled in the rope and sticks that should have set it spinning.

The room had everything: quoits, penny dolls, ninepins, even a brass kaleidoscope mounted on a tripod. The only thing missing was the children.

A counting book lay open on the floor. There was a picture of a magpie on the first page. *One for Sorrow…*

Edward shook his head. Here, where people came alone—what an appropriate book. "No. It's not here."

She led him from the room. "There are many things here you could seek. Things of misplaced value."

"What do you mean?"

She stopped at a room so he could look in. "Things people thought would make them happy. Wealth or tools or weapons they pursued above what they truly wanted. Now they are stored here as objects of their regret."

Much in the room held an allure Edward understood: gold, diamonds, objects of stature and beauty. It was some trick of the house that the storeroom could hold a small herd of cattle. He could not understand, however, why somebody would desire what looked like an elephant leg ottoman.

"These could not be most valuable," Edward said, "if they regretted desiring them."

Ania inclined her head. "You are correct, I believe."

In spite of being Dead, Edward could feel the despair creeping into his bones. How could he find the most valuable thing in a house as large as mankind?

Think, he told himself. What was the most valuable thing to him? "Is Rebecca Teague here?"

Ania's expression went blank, her eyes lost focus. After a second, her eyes refocused, and she said, "Yes, she is."

No! His heart quailed. Becca should not be in this terrible place.

"Take me to her!" Was he to take Becca to the necromancer? What horrible irony that would be!

Ania turned, leading him up, and up, and up. "Here," she said.

The room was small, like a servant's room. There was a bed, a table with a pitcher and washbasin, and an oak wardrobe—itself quite small. A shadow lay on the bed.

"Becca," he said.

The shadow sat up. Was it his imagination, or did it get deeper?

"Becca," he repeated.

"Edward?" Her voice whispered, as if from a great distance.

"I am here. Oh, Becca, why are you in this place?"

"Edward?" She grew firmer, taking on features. He could make out her hair, her clothes.

"I'm here." He stepped forward and took her hands. His hands passed through hers. "I'm here."

"Edward? What sort of dream is this?"

"A bad one. You must wake from it. You cannot live with sorrow."

"My days mean nothing, and my nights are black. I came to London to be with you, but without you, I am trapped in this servant's life forever. Why did you leave me?"

"I had no choice. But I am with you now."

"It is so dark, this place I find myself. But you are here, and that makes it better."

He could see her features now. How he missed her! "I'm with you now," he said again.

"As a dream, or a ghost? Are you dead? For if you are, I would end my own life."

"No!" he exclaimed. "You must not! I just," he faltered. What could he say to cheer her? "I just need one more thing, and I shall return home."

"Truly?"

He could barely see through her now. "Truly."

"If this is madness, it is a much better madness than I've been suffering." She wiped her eyes with the back of her hand. "I've been so alone, but when you return I shall be happy."

One for Sorrow, he thought of the magpie rhyme. *Two for Joy!* His heart lifted. "Do you love me?"

"What a silly question!"

He laughed. How long had it been since he laughed for joy? She smiled with him. He tried to take her hands again, but still couldn't. Her body wasn't here, just her spirit.

She reached into her apron pocket. "I've carried these since you left. I couldn't eat them, because they reminded me of you." She reached out, and he held out his hand. She pressed something into it, something hard, physical. Wonder crossed her face and she vanished.

"Becca!" he exclaimed.

"She is not here," Ania said.

Edward hadn't known the woman remained. "Where is she?"

"Home, I expect. When she realized this was not merely a dream she no longer sorrowed."

Edward smiled. She was safe, she was happy. He laughed for the joy of laughing. "She loves me!" He held up her gift, a horehound candy. "Magic." He closed his fist around it. "If you can find Joy in the midst of Sorrow, you have found treasure indeed. This is the most valuable thing one can take from this place."

"You no longer belong here," Ania said.

"Another reason to rejoice." He was being thrown out of the House of Sorrow! Just thinking of it made him happier. He recited all he could remember of the magpie's rhyme as they returned to the foyer.

One for sorrow,
Two for Joy,
Three for a girl,
Four for a boy,
Five for silver,
Six for gold,
Seven for a secret never told.

"I know the secret, though." He laughed as he swept out the door and tossed a wave back to Ania. He even fancied he saw a slight smile on her lips.

He hurried across the grassy plateau and plunged into the cave.

☠

He stepped out of the gate, into the claws of Dead. Anger and hunger returned so strongly he could barely think. Dead *had* progressed while he was in the House of Sorrow. He clutched the candy, knowing he had to return to Nekyia before the Dead conquered him.

"Right." He turned to his right and plunged forward, splashing into the river. He held his hand high to keep the candy dry. Reckless, the water tugged him, but he only knew he needed to hurry.

"Hurry," he muttered.

"Edward?" Hya's voice drifted down to him.

"Food," he muttered. No! Not food. "Hurry," he said aloud.

He climbed out of the valley.

"Edward!" She hurried down to help him.

"Back!" he roared. "Damn you! Stay back!" Why couldn't she—? Why couldn't he think? "Too dangerous."

KILL HER!

Yes, but she stayed beyond his reach. "Drink some *aqua vitae*," she said. "It will help."

He didn't want *aqua vitae*.

KILL HER, EAT HER!

She was too far away. She needed to be closer. "Too clumsy. Help me."

She hesitated.

Closer. He could smell her, almost taste her. He twitched, just to show her he couldn't control his actions. He needed her help. Still she hung back. He stumbled. "Never make it. Help me."

She came closer.

"NO!" he screamed as he grabbed for her, he couldn't stop himself. She jumped back. "No. Lies." He took a step after her. "Won't." He stopped. "I WON'T do this!"

He could feel the candy in his hand. That was his life; that was his hope.

He took his pouch and pushed the neck of the bottle out the top. He could grab the stopper, but he couldn't work it free.

"Put it down on the ground," Hya said.

He glared. He tried to lift the cord over his head, but it tangled around his hand and neck. "Gah!" He tore the cord and started to smash the bottle, but stopped. She was going to open it. He carefully set it down, very close. "Come closer," he said.

"No. Step away. I'll open it and set it back down."

He growled, drew back his foot, and kicked the bottle. She lunged, catching it. He lunged, grasping for her.

He missed, stopped, and watched her as she worked the stopper loose. She placed it on the ground and drew her revolver and long knife. She stepped back and pointed the gun at him. "Come forward and very carefully drink." Her hand shook.

KILL HER!

He shuffled forward, picked up the bottle. The *aqua vitae* sloshed inside the bottle from his shaking. He put the bottle to his mouth and it rattled against his teeth.

The *aqua vitae* burned as he drank.

"Better?" Hya asked.

"Better," he said.

Kill her. "We need to hurry." He set the bottle down. "Take this." He started toward the beach, still shuffling somewhat. "Save time later."

Thinking was hard. He couldn't focus his thoughts on what he needed to do. Only when the little voice spoke to him could he plan, and those plans were evil.

They couldn't stop overnight, so Hya couldn't set her wards. She would have to stay awake. Maybe she would nod off; then he could eat her!

"Hurry," he muttered. He could pretend to sleep, maybe she'd let her guard down. "No!"

He reached the beach and went right to the boat. He easily slid it into the water. Climbing in, he waited for Hya, but not looking back. Safer that way.

The boat rocked with her entrance. "Don't sleep," he said. "Not for a second. I'll—" He gagged on the idea, instinct told him to stop talking. "I'll tell you I'm safe. Do not believe me."

Kill her, kill her, kill her.

"Devilishly cunning," she said.

"No more than a beast." At least they could use the wind to aid their return to Nekyia's island.

He fumbled to raise the sail. The little voice urged him to fail, to ask her help. Angry at the voice and himself, he yanked the line so hard the mast creaked. The voice then urged him to break the line so Hya would have to come forward to splice it together. By the time he tied off the lines, he had edged several feet closer to the back of the boat.

"Return to the bow," Hya said. "If you please."

He wanted to speak, but it was easier to grunt and groan, and he didn't care if she understood. The noises matched the state of his thinking anyway.

He sat, his back to the mast and stared forward. "Pielloos!" he shouted. "Pielloos!"

He rolled his head back so he looked at Hya over his shoulder. "Fish for dinner."

"Edward, this is not you."

"I like fish. Pielloos!"

A black ring encircled his vision. It was not the *zumbi* sleep; he did not feel lethargic. This was worse, it was Dead overcoming him. He was drowning in it.

The ring grew wider as they traveled. He became a man at the bottom of a pit, looking out at the world; or a man sinking deeper and deeper under the water with the light getting smaller and further away.

"Pielloos!" He lay his head back against the mast and shook it back and forth. His eyelids heavy, he let them close. "Pielloos, Pielloos," he chanted, a meaningless incantation against the dark.

He had only the vaguest idea why he wanted the merman. *To eat him!* crowed the voice, but that wasn't right. It was something else.

"Drink," commanded Hya. "Again. You need it."

He opened his eyes. She had left the flask next to his hand on the seat. How carefully she must have moved!

Drink it, said the voice. *Then tell her you're better. She'll come closer to get the flask back...*

He lifted the flask to his lips while watching Hya from the corner of his eye. He took a swallow. She didn't react so he took another.

He drained the flask and smashed it against the bottom of the boat. "Damn voice. Dead is unbelievably stupid. Stay back," he warned Hya. "Even that much won't keep it at bay for long. My world," he gestured with his hands, "grows smaller—my time shorter. Where is Pielloos?"

"I don't know," she said bleakly.

Chapter Fifteen

It was like being fevered. At times, he couldn't move his hands, but they moved of their own volition. And time no longer flowed smoothly. It folded and warped. Minutes collapsed into instants or expanded into hours. The sun, which should have marched steadily across the sky, dashed in fits and spurts.

He sat in the bow, looking forward, imagining a cocoon around himself. It kept the world safe from the rage and hunger, and when he emerged, he would be transformed. He tried not to think that the cocoon might also be a coffin and he might never emerge.

He still needed the orb.

The darkness at the edge of his vision deepened and widened. His world was shrinking as they traveled.

The sun had slid over the top of the arch of the sky when Pielloos surfaced. He didn't splash or leap. He just rose out of the water on the starboard side.

"I have the orb," he said, holding out a globe that filled his hand.

Edward lunged, Pielloos flinched, Hya cried out.

The orb fell into the sea.

With a strangled cry Edward pulled back, clasping his hands together as if that would control them. Pielloos backwatered with his tail, a look of startled anger on his face. Hya reached toward the expanding ring of the circles where she last saw the orb.

"Damn me," Edward said. "I'm sorry. Sorry. Damn me."

Pielloos glared, flipped, and vanished.

Edward closed his eyes. "I didn't mean to. I just—acted. It is so hard to control myself." He glanced back at Hya, and his hands twitched. He glanced away. "What can I do?"

He staggered to his feet. The blue green water mocked him. It was deep here. The orb might still be sinking.

He had no time to fetch it. The Dead was progressing too quickly; down in that darkness, another would claim him and he would become a *zumbi* of the sea. But what else could he do? He put one foot on the gunwale and steadied himself to jump.

Pielloos surfaced again, this time near the stern, and further away. "What stupidity was that?" He made as if to throw the orb back into the sea. "Tell me why."

"Dead," Edward gasped. "I'm Dead."

"I know. I have seen it."

"Harder to—," his hands jumped out and he yanked them back. "Harder to control."

"He has very little time," said Hya. "He has attacked me as well."

"Give me the orb," Edward said, holding out his hand. *Come Closer. Kill.*

"No." Hya shook her head. "Do not go near him."

Edward snarled at her.

Pielloos swam backwards, pacing the boat that Hya kept pointed at Nekyia's island. "It would be fitting punishment if you had to fetch it back yourself," he said. "It is not as hard as you would think. You cannot tell in the sun, but the orb glows slightly in the dark."

Come closer! "I need the orb," Edward said.

"That is true," Hya said, "but do not go near him."

"You call this help?" he screamed at her. "I need the bloody orb!" *Kill HER!*

"Give it to me," Hya told Pielloos. "I will see it to the necromancer."

"Come here!" Edward shouted. "Give it to ME!"

Pielloos tossed the orb into the air and caught it. He tossed it again and caught it. "This is mer sport. Better than mocking marooned sailors. Give them hope," he held up the orb, "and take it away." He tossed it into the air and made no move to catch it.

Hya gasped.

Pielloos caught it just above the water. "It makes me sick. No, I cannot do this. Have the orb." He swam to Hya and pressed the orb into her hand. "Good luck to you both."

Edward bared his teeth as Pielloos returned to the depths. The little voice railed against him, and Edward had no *aqua vitae* to help silence it.

He had the orb, though. That was a victory. And he had escaped the encounter without hurting anyone. That was another victory. Dead did not give up, and Hya was not that far away.

It took all his will to sit back down and rebuild that cocoon, that coffin. He must endure. Nekyia's island drew closer, and he had everything the necromancer wanted.

☠

The island loomed ahead, and who was he to judge evil now? Hya swore.

There was something, something he should notice. He could not make sense of her anger. He must see what she saw, but he didn't recognize anything different. The cone of the volcano, the rocky approach to the island, the rolling surf, why would Hya object?

Only when they came around the grave of the *Twilight Rose* did he realize not all the masts belonged to the wreck. A ship had anchored in the entrance to the small cove. The *Reach of God* had come to the necromancer's home.

He leapt to his feet, grabbing the mast and leaning forward. "What madness?"

"Prester Ellis," Hya said. "I hope Mr. Fairweather is well hidden."

The *Reach* appeared deserted. "I can't believe they would leave the ship unguarded," she said. "Great must be Ellis's hate and confidence. We should turn back."

"No," Edward snarled. "Press on." His words sounded thick in his ears. He was losing the ability to speak clearly. His speech, like his sight, was succumbing to Dead.

"Ellis will kill you."

I'm already Dead. Look at me! I have no more time, and nothing to lose. The words didn't form properly; his mouth spoke gibberish, and when Hya turned the boat, he threw himself into the water.

Must get to Nekyia.

His feet hit the sandy bottom, and he churned his legs, driving forward. A shadow flitted over him, Hya in the boat no doubt. She was in another world now, six feet above, but dry.

The silver dappled ceiling lowered until, with a lunge, he shattered it, the silver changing to shards of sunlight that dripped into his eyes and flowed down his face.

Nekyia! He must reach Nekyia.

Somebody shouted his name.

He could only see that portion of the world right before him; it was like looking through a tube or being in a deep well. Every movement made it shake and jump unnaturally, giving him the feeling of riding an unstable train headed for a colossal wreck.

The debris on the beach had been pulled apart. Every broken crate had been shattered, every barrel stove in. It was a waste of time, but if Ellis's entire crew had helped, it wouldn't have taken long.

A thin column of smoke rose above the cliffs, a stick propping up the sky.

And now he had switched—he was the little voice in his head, and the raging maelstrom of anger and hunger was in charge. He was growing fainter and fainter and soon would be swept away completely.

He must reach Nekyia.

There had been a great tramping of feet through the defile. The lock on the gate had been broken and the gate pushed open.

Inside the enclosure, fronds had been cut and plants ground down, greatly widening the trail. One of the deer had been shot and now lay ignored, half-covered by cut leaves.

He could hear shouts ahead. Men called to each other. A rifle cracked, and another. He passed a body, its throat cut.

Feed.

Blood flecked the sand. Another man had been wounded.

Edward came up to another body with a dent in its head and face coated in blood.

FEED!

He wrestled the compulsion. Moving his feet was like dragging a locomotive. There would be more opportunities ahead. He recited it in his mind, as if he were talking to a recalcitrant child. Dead was instinctual, it was cunning; but he doubted it was sentient. He still tried to convince it, to manipulate it into thinking better was ahead.

He did move faster as he got further from the bodies, but they faded from his memory too. The sounds of conflict drew him, everything else was growing hazy, less important.

His feet carried him to Nekyia's house but stopped at the edge of the clearing. So much happened, he didn't know what to do. Even the Dead quailed for a moment, and he stood gaping.

Standing still, he didn't attract attention when everything else was in conflict.

To his right, Albino towered over a circle of *Custos*. He had been wounded, or perhaps the blood splattering his clothes was not his. Either way, he kept the men at a distance with a bloody axe.

One man got too close, and Albino buried the axe in his chest. Instantly, the others swarmed him. Albino dropped the axe to wrap an attacker in his arms and crush him.

Another *Custos* stepped up behind the raging giant and very calmly pointed a gun at his head. There was a sharp crack, and Albino staggered forward and dropped to the ground.

On his left, the *Custos* had broken open the cave and were hauling out the prisoners. They joyously greeted their release until Prester Ellis's voice called, "They are tainted by their time here. Kill them all."

Edward turned, bringing Ellis into sight. Behind him, the front porch of Nekyia's house burned. Flames licked up the pillars and crept along the eaves. Hungry flames, eager to feast.

Hungry. He knew hunger.

He needed to find Nekyia. He wasn't sure why, but he must. Ellis hadn't noticed him yet, but stood between him and the house.

The circle of his vision still shrank, and his feet took a step toward the fighting. He didn't know if it were anger or hunger that drew his body. He felt both so strongly, but now they felt different, like they howled outside a house where he was trapped—except they owned the house or nearly so.

Nekyia. He must find Nekyia.

He walked, halted, changed direction. He didn't know where to look, what to do. He only wanted to kill, to eat, but he knew he mustn't, he mustn't let his body do that.

A touch of wind stirred the fire, shifting the smoke. He had his answer.

Nekyia had been nailed to the doorposts, one hand to either side. The fire had obscured him as it devoured him. Some trick of will or the devil had kept him silent as he burned, and now he would never speak again.

Something snapped in Edward. His last hope was gone and his anger exploded. He leapt at the nearest *Custos*, not controlling his actions, but not fighting them either. The man spun in surprise and went down under Edward's heavy blows.

Edward stepped on the man's throat as he went for the next man. *Kill!* The voice sang in his ears.

His body's savagery amazed him, gratified him, for weren't *Custos* responsible for this? They created the monster when they killed the Painted Man and turned it loose when they killed Nekyia. Let them reap what they had sown.

His body knew how to kill, how to rend. He just watched through the ever-shrinking circle of vision, but when Prester Ellis appeared before him, he shouted, "There!" He could no longer control his body, but he might nudge it.

Ellis lifted something, Edward couldn't tell what, his vision was too narrow. It must be deadly, and he must help his body as he could. It took all his will to grab the upraised arm with his right hand.

Ellis looked surprised. "*Zumbi* cannot think," he protested.

Edward couldn't respond. His sight constricted, leaving only a tiny circle. Lost in a miasma of rage and hate and anguish.

Ellis's surprise turned to horror as a hand—Edward's hand—closed around his throat. Edward felt Ellis's wrist break in his other hand.

Somewhere somebody screamed his name.

Ellis clawed at the hand at his throat. His eyes bulged. The hand clenched. Fingers tore into Ellis's tender neck. With a terrible yank of the hand—and the last, infinitesimally small thing that was Edward knew it was his hand—tore out Ellis's throat.

Something grabbed Edward's shoulder, and his circle of vision turned. He fell. Hya stood above him, her long knife raised.

As she brought it down, he noticed she wept, and darkness took him completely.

Chapter Sixteen

A sliver of light caught his eye, lodged in his consciousness. For a time, it stuck there, a splinter in his mind, an irritant that drew him out of his darkness until he lifted his hand to push it away.

He felt a cold corner, hard and smooth, with just enough of a gap for the light to needle through. He lay on his back, reaching up. He followed the wall with his fingers, he lay close, and a quick check revealed another wall to his left.

And this light shone not more than a foot above him. A wave of nameless panic swept over him, waking to find himself in such a confined space. He pushed at the crack of light.

The ceiling, if it was a ceiling, lifted, letting light flood upon him. He faltered and it fell back, again shrouding him in darkness.

He pushed again, and the ceiling flew up, out of his sight, and the sound of wood clattering on stone made him wince. He stared up at a truly dirty plaster ceiling, webbed with cracks. Old, dark beams crossed the room, flanking the battered plaster and casting dark shadows across it.

Where am I? His mind ranged with particular vividness. He sat up, the movement effortless, smooth. He held up his hand, examined his palm. It was unmarked. He rubbed it, perplexed, expecting the hard clot of blood left by Undulark's jab but not finding it.

He lifted his head to see a brick wall with various oddments stacked against it: a worn broom, a battered ladder, several crates, and a large barrel. Kegs and crates filled a set of shelves. Several large books and a copy of *Lloyd's Illustrated London Newspaper* sat on the barrel.

London, he thought. *How did I get here?* And where, he wondered, in London was he.

People. He cocked his head but heard no sound. Nonetheless he knew there were people nearby, he could *sense* them. *Hya?* And, because he was in London, *Becca?*

The sound of someone shifting and the rustle of petticoats made him turn. There was a pretty woman in a fashionable dress—narrow, sloping shoulders and a pointed waist. Her strawberry blonde hair was tied in a bun. Her expression was grim, intent. She watched him, not exactly like a hawk, but close enough.

"Hya!"

She didn't answer; she had changed so much he feared he mistook her. She seemed so... *English*. So unlike the young woman who guided him through the Narrow World trying to reach a necromancer.

"Are you hungry?" An oddly accented man's voice drew his attention the other way.

Undulark stood, not in the least the genial neighbor he remembered. His lips were pressed together, his eyes narrowed; his brow was faintly creased and shone slightly. He was nervous, Edward realized.

"No," Edward said, puzzled by the question. "Not really." He rested his hands on the side of the box where he sat. No, not a box, it was a coffin, resting on wooden crates. He scrambled to his feet, ducking his head to avoid the ceiling beams, and jumped out.

Hya sucked in her breath and jumped back, her pistol appearing in one hand and a wooden club in the other. On his other side, Undulark lifted a cylinder with a sleeve around it and a nozzle on one end, a spray pump of some sort, from which a small drop of water—clear and diamond bright—dripped.

"What are you doing?" he asked. "I'm fine—cured. I can think clearly. I move naturally." He wiggled his arms, and Hya twitched. He got the impression she almost shot him. "Whatever you did worked. I'm alive." He caught Undulark's eye. "Aren't I?"

"Are you sure you're not hungry?" Undulark asked.

"No." Edward felt the cold air of apprehension. He lifted his hand to his neck and felt for a pulse. When he didn't find one, he tried again, then at his wrist. "I'm still Dead." He looked from Undulark to Hya. "That's it, isn't it? I'm still Dead."

He felt terribly sad. All that effort, wasted.

"Does it make you angry?" Hya asked. They were the first words she had spoken.

"No," Edward said. "No." He took a deep breath, let it out slowly, letting go of any hope of life. He thought of a house on a rocky promontory with crashing surf and a lonely wind. "No, just sorrow." He forced himself to smile and knew he failed. He hung his head. "I'm sorry." He didn't know for whom he felt sorrow. Himself, certainly, but also for her and all she had done. For Becca, too.

"Well," said Undulark, a note of cheer in his voice, "It's gone better than we could really expect."

Hya rushed forward and threw her arms around him. "Thank God," she said. Surprised, he embraced her, held her close. He could smell the lilac scented soap she used. She buried her head in his chest. "Thank God."

Undulark gave a soft cough. Hya pulled back, blushing, but still held him.

Edward looked from one to the other. "I don't understand. I feel… wonderful." He felt his body respond to Hya's presence, a surge of desire, and he let her go. "Not at all like a *zumbi*," he said to cover his embarrassment.

"Nekyia's death ended your hopes."

Images flashed through his mind, dark and their color faded as if viewed through a cloudy glass. Nekyia burning, Ellis screaming, Hya crying: had that really happened? "I remember, I think." He looked at his hands, expecting to see blood on them.

"So, something else had to be done."

Edward lifted his head just enough to stare. "What?"

"An idea of Hya's, and a good one. I'd never have thought of it, and good God, I'd never have tried it!"

"I had help, Uncle," Hya said. She turned to Edward. "Mister Fairweather was indispensable. But once we got you in the coffin, it was really quite easy."

"What did you do?" Edward demanded. Something had changed, but he didn't know what. And if there had been other choices, why seek out Nekyia?

"She took you to see Baldwin," Undulark said, "and appealed to his curiosity. Which is stronger, *zumbiism* or vampirism?"

Recalling his conversation with Baldwin, Edward said, "He claimed vampirism couldn't be cured, that once bitten it—." He stopped.

Hya finished his sentence. "Overcomes all else. Of course he wanted to test it. It wasn't hard to convince him to try." She gave his elbow a small squeeze. "He likes you, and it was your only hope."

"Baldwin called vampirism the greatest of the 'Not-Dead,'" Edward said. "If I'm not a *zumbi,* does that mean I'm—?" When neither answered, he reached up hesitantly and felt his teeth.

He had two very long and wickedly sharp eyeteeth. "I'm a vampire."

"I'm afraid so," Undulark said. "Not the best solution, to be sure, but better than *zumbiism.*"

"But there is no cure."

"No."

"How did this happen? I remember returning to Nekyia after the House of Sorrow but… I was lost."

"You were," Hya said. "Subduing you was not easy." She flashed a mischievous smile. "I did a fair bit of damage to you." The smile flickered as if the memory didn't match the levity with which she told it.

"It took some persuasion to enlist a crew," she went on. "I could not have done it without Mr. Fairweather's help. We took the *Reach of God,* and with bribery and threats, sailed to Baldwin."

She shuddered. "It was chilling listening to—" She stopped, started again. "When Baldwin turned you, you fell into a stupor. He said you wouldn't wake until you were completely remade. Much longer than a normal turning."

Long enough, apparently, to return to London and come here.

He looked around, noticing things he had missed before, a lantern hanging on an iron hook—he had taken the light for granted—a closed door, a shovel and pry bar. "So where are we? A crypt of some sort?"

"Nothing so glamorous," Undulark said. "Merely the basement of my shop."

"Well, I'm glad you were here when I woke," Edward said. "It was quite a shock. Had I awoken alone it would have been worse."

"Hya has spent quite a bit of time down here." Undulark gave a small cough.

"We had to be careful," Hya said quickly, with a small blush. "We didn't know if you would be, well, safe. Somebody had to be watchful."

"You have undergone a profound change," Undulark said. "Even if all else went well, we didn't know if you would be pleased."

"Pleased?" Edward said. He felt good. He hadn't even realized how bad the *zumbiism* had made him feel. He took a deep breath, marveling how natural it felt. He might not need to breathe, but it seemed vampires did it naturally. "Why wouldn't I be pleased?"

"Relationships between vampires and mortals are usually strained," Undulark said.

He remembered. "The bloodlust." *Becca! Never!*

"You need not fear," Undulark said while Hya reached up and pulled on a thin golden chain about his neck. On it hung a small ruby fang.

"Another gift from Uncle Baldwin," she said. "Or Nekyia, or yourself. However you wish to count it. It cures the bloodlust. Uncle Baldwin could easily spare a couple."

"It works?"

"I assure you it does," she said. "The bloodlust isn't the only difficulty, though. Time means something different to vampires. Uncle Baldwin once said time rushed by but it didn't touch him. He seemed sad when he said it."

"Baldwin was always a little maudlin," Undulark said. "But vampire-mortal romances are complicated."

Complicated, Edward thought. That was certainly an understatement.

Light footsteps on the floor above interrupted his thought. He looked up.

"Ah," said Undulark. Without explaining, he opened the door and climbed the stairs. His voice drifted back down and he came after it, followed by a woman.

She stepped into the basement, hesitant, slow to come in from the shadows of the unlit stairwell.

Edward knew her at once. "Becca!"

"I came as quickly as I could after getting your message," she told Hya.

Hya nodded. She stretched out her hand, pointing to Edward.

"Edward," Becca said. Her tone froze him, held him bound for he didn't know how to interpret it. Her voice was cool, taut, almost angry—yet she had rushed here. It showed in the color on her cheeks, the quickness in her breath.

He stood, helpless in his uncertainty, all the words flew from his mind.

"I believe you owe me the courtesy of an explanation." She stood straight, her chin lifted. Every hair was in place, her dress smooth. She might have been ready for church but for the flush of exertion.

He blinked, astonished. What did she expect him to say? He looked for help but Undulark gave a minuscule shrug.

"I have," Becca said, "been told outrageous lies."

Hya opened her mouth as if to protest, but Undulark held up a finger and shook his head. Becca didn't even notice; her gaze never left Edward.

"I have made a fool of myself before strangers," she said.

He denied it with a shake of his head.

"I have worried myself to sickness. I have been questioned by uncanny men; I have suffered fevered dreams. My work has suffered to the point where I am fortunate not to have been sacked."

Edward opened his mouth, but closed it in the face of her mounting fury.

"And now you re-appear in the company of *her*," she jerked her head toward Hya, "with her exotic accent and wild tales." She raised her eyebrows.

This was nothing like he expected. He hadn't really thought about what their reunion would be like, but embracing and kisses would have been welcome. She had rushed here, after all. He stared at her.

"Well?"

"Well what?" he managed.

"I'm waiting to hear you explain all this." She waved her hand to indicate the basement and all it contained. "I'm dying to hear why you're in an apothecary's basement dressed like a tramp sailor."

Edward looked down. He still wore the clothes from the Narrow World. They were stained and torn, and he probably looked worse than a tramp sailor. It was so ridiculous he started to laugh. Weakly, and he tried to stop when her expression darkened, but he couldn't. What could he possibly say?

"I fail to see any humor whatsoever in this."

He sobered, composed himself, and straightened his shoulders. He was in London now. Best he remember that. "I don't know exactly what you were told," he said, "but I have every faith that, if anything, it fell short of the truth." He reached for her, but she jerked away and hugged herself, arms crossed tightly in front of her.

"What of *her?*" Becca jerked her head toward Hya.

Hya watched, blue eyes sharp, her strawberry blonde hair every bit as fashionable as Becca's chestnut locks. Dressed in English fashion, she didn't seem like a woman who could wrestle a mindless *zumbi* half-way around the world.

"Without Hya, I would have died a dozen times," Edward said. "I owe her more than I can ever repay."

Becca snorted softly and frowned.

"I had no choice," he said. "You must believe me."

"That's what *he* said." She nodded toward Undulark. "The others told another tale entirely."

"What others?"

"They would not say. But they wore long coats and round workman's hats."

The *Custos.* "What did they say?"

"They had word of you from abroad, and they were concerned with your dealings. If I saw you again I should inform them." She shrugged, a little hitch in her shoulders as her arms were still crossed in front of her. "Why would they do that?"

"Is that all they told you?" Hya asked.

Becca lifted her nose and turned away, refusing to acknowledge the question.

"Did you tell them of my return?" Edward asked in alarm.

She glared at him. "No."

At least he could be thankful for that. He paced around the casket, thinking. Their parting in the House of Sorrow had been very different than this. She hadn't been as suspicious.

What had Baldwin said of vampires? In two hundred years he would still be the same as now. But Becca would not. She would age and die. *Vampires cannot live with mortals.*

He finished circling the casket and stood before her again. "I'm sorry," he said. What point was there telling her if they couldn't live together?

She waited, and when he didn't say more, demanded, "Is that all you have to say?"

Silence filled the space between Edward and Becca. Their future lay in that silence and what would follow. "Yes," he said.

"You must tell her," Undulark said.

Edward shook his head. "There is no point."

"Tell me what?" Becca said.

"Everything," Undulark replied. To Edward he said, "If you leave now, she will come to hate you."

"She will hate me anyway," Edward said. *But I will not have to see that hate in her eyes.* He looked to Hya, wondering at her silence. She would not meet his gaze.

"I will have an explanation of you, Edward Truscott," Becca said. "And do not lie to me."

You may not trust me, he thought, *but you do not hate me. You will if I tell you, though. You will.*

"Never," he answered. She did deserve the truth. He could not spare her the pain today, but it might kinder over time. He reached out to rest his hand on the casket. "But you will think I do."

"Why wouldn't I believe you're involved in black magic using coffins and pretty girls? The evidence is right here."

He jerked his hand away from the casket as if it had bitten him. Stepping away, he ran his hand through his hair.

Hya opened her mouth again, but again Undulark held up a finger. "This is why he journeyed, and why you helped him," he said quietly.

Hya frowned as though she would argue. But Undulark repeated, "Let him tell it," and she turned away as if to remove the temptation.

Edward took a breath, steeling himself to tell his tale. He looked into Becca's eyes. "I have done no black magic. The truth is far worse." He read the dread in her eyes. "I have been Dead. I still am."

After a long silence she made to leave. "You mock me."

She laid her hand on the doorknob.

His words barely made it past his lips. "I do not."

She raised her voice. "They said you were! They said it made you evil. I don't need to listen to your lies any more than I listened to theirs." She opened the door.

"Stop," Undulark said. "You are angry, hurt. Perhaps frightened. But now *is* the time to listen."

"Why should I do that?"

"If you don't—no matter how this ends—doubt and regret will consume you all the days of your life."

Hya looked over her shoulder at them but didn't protest.

Becca took her hand from the door. Step after step, she came to stand next to Edward. Lifting her chin, she said, "Tell me." It sounded like a dare.

He began slowly, telling of his return from the Barings' and the alley, the creature, and waking the next morning. Unsure what to say, he told her everything.

She did not question him, but watched without looking away, her face a perfect mask for her emotions.

He told of Undulark's diagnosis and held out his hand to show her the black bead of blood. It was gone; cured like all his ails by the vampirism.

I could show her my teeth; she would have to believe. He quailed at the thought. *She will find out soon enough.*

"Go on." Her voice was smooth, patronizing, and made him want to do anything but. "I'm dying to hear the ending."

He unfolded the tale, amazed how unbelievable it sounded. It surpassed any delusions spun by sailors mad from sun and heat. Secret wars, mermaids, bone painters—the story kept getting less and less likely, he didn't need Becca's growing frown to tell him.

By the time he reached Parlexi, he was growing desperate, and he pulled up his shirt to show her the scar. To his relief it was there. Lessened, but scars, evidently, were already healed and did not heal again. "She stabbed me in the heart," he said, "but I didn't die."

She ran her fingers over the ridge the scar made, feeling the same spot on her chest with her other hand. He felt a quickening at her touch. No, vampires were not immune to desire.

"Surely a wound like that should have killed you," she protested.

"I was already Dead," Edward said.

He told her of Restless Davy and Baldwin. He told of Nekyia and his demands, though he didn't go into detail about getting the first three items. When he came to the House of Sorrow, she gave an exclamation. "It wasn't a dream!"

"No," he agreed. The wonder on her face changed to awe as he fished into his pocket and found the horehound candy still there.

"This is what you needed?" she asked. She took the candy from him, her slender fingers plucking it free without touching him. "This is what the necromancer wanted from that place?"

"And I found it, thanks to you," he said.

"The candy. He needed a horehound candy."

"No." Edward took her shoulders. She flinched at his touch. "Joy. He wanted Joy found in Sorrow. The rarest and most precious Joy."

"A man who dealt in sorrow would know no other kind," Hya said. "It was not his nature."

At the sound of her voice, Becca pulled away from Edward. She glared at Hya, but when she spoke to Edward her voice was cool. "Tell me how you came to be here."

"We returned to Nekyia to find the *Custos* had already killed him. I—" He placed his hands on the edge of the coffin and hung his head. "I lost myself. I shudder to think of it. Hya took me to—to a friend. Somebody who could help." The hope she would believe him evaporated—she would believe when she saw his fangs. She would believe and fear him.

The look Becca gave Hya held many things: distrust, disdain, a bit of anger. "Why not take him to this friend first?"

"I did," Hya replied, her tone as cool as Becca's, or even cooler. "The friend was Baldwin. I had not thought of this other possibility, nor would have suggested it until trying Nekyia."

"Baldwin? The vampire?" Becca looked back to Edward. "You say you were Dead. What are you now?"

Her tone was filled with anger and hope and it sliced through Edward. If he could say he was cured, they could sort through the rest.

He couldn't say that. *And now is when she comes to fear and hate me.*

Edward turned away. *I have lost her.*

Heavy feet pounded the shop floor above them—a half-dozen men or more. He could hear voices, still indistinct, but he would be able to make out the words if they came any closer.

"You closed the shop," Hya said to Undulark.

"But left the door unlocked." He nodded at Becca, because she arrived through the unlocked door. "I'd best see what it is. Nothing, I'm sure," but his expression suggested otherwise.

"What shall I do?" Edward asked.

"Stay here."

"I know what you should do," Becca said, her words riding on top of Undulark's. "I shall show you. Give me your hand."

"What?" The request surprised Edward. Undulark paused at the door to watch.

"Give me your hand," Becca pleaded, her eyes wide, wild, unsure.

Undulark and Hya watched him, as curious as he, he supposed, to see what Becca wanted.

He hesitated. Why now? Why when there were men upstairs?

"If you are not a *zumbi*, take my hand," she begged.

He did. Pain burned through his hand and up his arm. He jerked back, pulling a small cross from her hand and sending it to the floor.

Becca let out a small scream and reared back, eyes wide. "It's true. You lied!"

"How have I lied?" He reached out, but she pulled away.

The feet above paused their stomping. "The basement," a deep voice called. "Take the men and check."

"What have you done?" Edward demanded.

"They said you were damned." Becca cried as she shrank away. "That you'd been given over to evil! It's true!"

"Theirs isn't the power to decide!" He rushed to the door.

"Haven't you listened to anything he told you?" Hya snarled at Becca as she too went to the door.

It had no lock, and already feet thudded on the steps. Hya started to jam a board under the knob when the door burst open and men dressed in long coats and billycocks flooded the room.

The first man into the room shouldered Undulark aside; the second clubbed him on the head. The apothecary tumbled to the floor and lay stunned, conscious but groaning.

Edward leapt away and found himself on the far side of the room, back pressed against the wall, Hya beside him.

"Did you see how he leapt?" one of the men shouted.

Becca grabbed the man's arm. "What will you do?"

"Do?" the man said, shaking her off. "We'll kill them, of course."

"You know these men?" Edward shouted at Becca. He didn't need to be told they were *Custos*.

"No!" she shouted back. "They just told me what you were!"

"And followed you here!"

The *Custos* spread out. There were five, all armed. Two were identically armed with a pistol in their right hand and a silver parrying dagger in their left. One had a bunched-up fish net, one a covered silver bucket engraved with *aquam Dei*, and the last, hanging back behind the others, carried a bucket of burning oil on a chain.

And one man still upstairs, who had ordered them to come down.

Black smoke curled from the bucket of oil; it smelled bitter, *dark*.

"Keep your hands where we can see them," the *Custos* told Hya. He pointed an old, elegant muzzle-loading pistol at her. The man next to him had a similar gun pointed at Edward.

"Their bullets are silver," Hya whispered as she raised her hands. "As are mine." She twisted a little and he saw, from the corner of his eye, her revolver tucked into the folds of her skirt. The handle nestled into the small of her back.

"Now step away," the *Custos* said. The men kept their weapons leveled at them.

All they want is a clear shot, Edward thought. *They've already said they'll kill us both.*

"Edward," Becca pleaded, stepping toward him. What did she want? Forgiveness?

There was no time for forgiveness. He snatched the gun from Hya's back and fired at the men.

The noise was deafening. The first man staggered, and fired above Edward's head. Edward missed the second and third. The fourth lurched and fell—swinging the bucket of burning oil as he did.

Oil splashed across the floor, carrying flames across the room. The *Custos* dove to escape the fire. Becca screamed. Spots of fire ate at her skirt.

Black smoke curled up. It stung Edward's eyes as he moved the gun back and forth, searching for a target.

Hya rushed to Undulark and started to help him away from the burning oil.

The man with the net swung, his arm starting behind him and making an upward arc, released the net toward Hya. The net spread like a spider-web and settled over Hya and Undulark.

Becca screamed again. Flames jumped up her skirt. She leaned away, trying to beat them out but to no avail.

Edward grabbed the man holding the silver bucket with his left hand and pulled the man's arm across his chest. He locked his right arm over it and bent it back until he heard bones break.

He plucked the bucket from the man's limp hand, released him, and shot him. One bullet left, and he used it on a quickly moving shape in the swirling smoke.

Dropping the empty revolver, he took the cover from the bucket and dashed the holy water across Becca's burning skirt.

"Run!" he shouted at her.

She scrambled back, turned toward the door, but hesitated. "What about you?"

"Run!" he roared.

She blanched, and with one last, terrified look, she ran up the stairs.

Only then did he feel a line of pain burning across his palm. He twisted, flinging the silver bucket across the room. He rushed to help Hya, who struggled in the net.

A heavy weight dropped on his back, and he staggered. Strong arms clutched him, pinning his arms to his sides. A husky voice growled in his ear, "I've got you, beast."

Above him, above the crackle of the fire, he heard an exclamation—half cry of surprise, half scream.

"Becca!" he cried.

Another man leapt on him. His knees buckled, but he straightened, both men on his back as he struggled to shake them off.

A body tumbled down the stairs and landed in a heap in the doorway. It didn't move.

"Becca." Her whispered name was lost in the commotion.

A man came down the stairs, his boots thudding on the treads. A giant of a man ducked under the doorframe and stepped over Becca. He held a club loosely in his hand and his voice rumbled in his chest. "Can't you handle one *zumbi*?"

"Becca!" Edward lurched forward, but the weight of the men dragged him down.

"He ain't a *zumbi*!" shouted one of the men on Edward's back.

"Word from Ellis was an English *zumbi* trying to return."

"And we haven't heard from Ellis in months. Maybe this ain't the same *zumbi*!" the man shouted as Edward struggled.

The giant glanced down at Becca. "She led us here. It's him."

"You monster!" Edward shouted, throwing off the men on his back and leaping at the giant.

The giant swung the club, hitting him hard enough to stop him and send him staggering back. "I'm not the monster, you are." He kicked Becca through the door and closed it. "And now you're trapped, *zumbi*."

Edward touched his jaw, sore, but not broken. "You're wrong, and Ellis is dead."

"'Tis a dangerous job we do."

"You made it so today." Edward grabbed the shovel from against the wall and scooped up some of the burning, oil-soaked dirt from the floor into the giant's face.

The giant cried out. He swung his club as he tried to wipe the fire from his face.

Edward turned on the other men. He knocked the silver dagger from one hand. The man reeled back. Edward moved to the next, swinging the shovel. It broke against the man's head, sending his billycock flying and leaving Edward holding a splintered handle.

With a quick step and a thrust, he rammed it up behind the last man's ribs. The man staggered back. His eyes were wide. He dropped his dagger and clutched the shovel handle, trying to pull it out. He coughed blood as he collapsed.

Edward stooped to lift the net off Hya. "Are you well?"

"Fine," she said.

"Good." He faced the recovering giant, whose face was black and red and weeping blood.

"God will strike you down," the giant roared. He reared back, his club striking the ceiling.

Edward leapt, grabbing the man's jacket and lifting him up. He slammed the giant against the door, making it rattle. "He may," Edward said, "but you won't."

He lifted, pressing the giant up, over his head, and slammed him to the ground. As he lay gasping, Edward punched down. Ribs cracked and broke under his blow. He struck again. And again, until the man stopped moving and his breath made progressively weaker sucking sounds. A few seconds later they stopped.

"Are you sure you're all right?" Edward asked Hya. She nodded. Undulark groaned and opened his eyes.

The oil still burned in patches across the floor but nothing else caught.

Becca lay, her back to him; a crumpled doll-like figure, broken and cast aside. He knew just by looking there was something missing. He crouched down and gently gathered her into his arms. Her head rolled back, and he caught and cradled it against his body.

She stared at him, stared without recognition, without blinking, without any spark of life. A few drops of blood trickled from the corner of her mouth.

He rested his hand on her throat, looking for a pulse. Her larynx moved about freely under his fingers. He could not find a pulse, nor did she breathe.

"Undulark," he said quietly. Then, more loudly, "Undulark."

The apothecary crouched down unsteadily beside him.

"Can anything be done?" Edward asked.

Undulark undid the button on Becca's collar. Her skin beneath was blotchy—red and blue and ugly purple. He gently felt her neck, felt the way her larynx moved. He lifted a limp hand and moved each finger before setting it down again.

Last he closed her eyes. "I am sorry," he said.

"Yes," said Edward. He let his hand brush against Becca's cheek. "So am I."

The fire burned low. The flames had subsided and now burned, orange and red, no more than eight inches high. Even though the lantern still burned, the cellar seemed dim.

Hya opened the door. Black smoke bundled out the door and up the stairs.

"Once again, I didn't get a chance to say good-bye," Edward said. He swallowed. "This was not the return I expected."

His chest felt tight, almost painful.

He lifted Becca as easily as he might a child. He laid her in the coffin and straightened her skirts, folded her hands on top of her. He re-buttoned her collar. Finally, he carefully tucked a wayward strand of hair back into place.

"So much has happened," he said.

Undulark rested his hands on the side of the coffin and looked down on Becca. "It is normal to not know what to feel."

"She led them here," Edward said.

"Not, I think, on purpose. Certainly not intending their actions. She was conflicted. Torn between wanting to know and fearing the answer. Their arrival forced her decision."

Edward didn't answer. He had no words to put to the emptiness he felt. He had lived with anger so long he reached for it now. It eluded him.

"She had been changed," he said, "primed to doubt me. The manner of my leaving must have hurt her badly." *As her leaving has hurt me.* He wondered how it could have been different. He was a vampire. "She..." His voice faltered and he started again. "She hesitated to flee. It would not have mattered, but she..." He faltered again. "I don't think she hated me at the end."

"No," said Undulark. "In spite of all the *Custos* must have said, she did not hate you in the end."

"She was torn between hope and fear," Hya said. "But she knew too little and, of that little, not what to believe."

He shrugged. "I might have won back her trust with the truth, but..." He really didn't know. "She came ready to test me, and I could only fail.

"I did not lie," he said to Becca. "And if the *Custos* told you I was damned, I say again, theirs is not the power to decide. If they said I was evil, I would have done my best to prove otherwise."

A groan interrupted him. One of the *Custos* stirred. He lay on his back, broken arm outstretched. Hya crossed the cellar, her skirts rustling, and stood over him.

"Hoped we wouldn't notice you?" she said.

"What are you going to do to me?" he asked.

She put her foot on his shattered arm. "That is the question, isn't it?"

"Let him go," Edward said.

"He'll only set the *Custos* on you again," she said over her shoulder.

Edward came over and crouched down.

The man tried to pull back, but Hya kept her foot on his arm. Sweat ran down his face. "I'll not sell my soul."

"I don't want it," Edward said. "I want you to tell the *Custos* they have no reason to hunt me. Even now, I have no wish to kill any more of them. Leave me to my peace.

"But hunt me," he went on, "and I will kill you all." He showed the man his fangs. The man closed his eyes and turned his head away.

Edward stood. "Let him go."

"Wait," Undulark said. He hurried up the stairs and returned with a tiny leather pouch and small bottle of scented oil. "If he moves," he told Hya, "put your weight on his arm." To the man he said, "This won't hurt—unless you move."

He un-stoppered the oil.

The man flinched and tried to pull away. Hya put more weight onto her foot. He cried out.

Edward bared his fangs. "Better her than me. Lay still." He wondered what Undulark planned.

The *Custos* closed his eyes and lay still, though he trembled.

Undulark dripped some oil on his thumb and sketched a symbol on the man's forehead. He took some dust from the pouch and dusted it over the symbol. A quick incantation made the dust glow.

The man gasped and his eyes popped open.

"What you felt," Undulark said, "was a binding. You may not talk of Edward, Hya, or anything that happened here today. Should you try, even by signing or writing, it will get very hard to breathe. You could even kill yourself trying. Understand?"

He had to repeat himself before the man nodded. "Now let him go," Undulark said.

Hya ground her foot before stepping away. The man scrambled across the floor, used the door frame to pull himself upright, and staggered up the stairs. His hurried and unsteady footsteps crossed the shop floor.

"You could not trust them," Undulark explained. "He might grow bold in the presence of his friends, or time might dull your threat. It is better this way."

"Might he call your bluff?" Hya asked.

"I hope not. It isn't a bluff."

Edward let out a short bark of laughter. It wasn't really humor, though, and he turned, sober, to the casket. "I am sorry," he said to Becca. He gave her a moment of silence before bending down to pick up the casket lid. Half-covered by dirt beside it lay the horehound candy. He picked it up, dusted it off, and tucked it into Becca's hand.

He stood silently for several minutes then fastened the lid on the casket.

Chapter Seventeen

Evening. A time of transitions, Edward thought, or *maybe I'm just ascribing it my feelings.*

Autumn.

An appropriate time for goodbyes. He stood outside the churchyard resting his gloved hands on the iron fence.

Inside the yard, there was a fresh mound of dirt in front of a new stone which read,

Rebecca Teague
Born 22 May 1826
Died 12 October 1846
Monday's Child

There was a hint of lilac soap on the air and the sound of feet behind him. "I lost her the moment the creature scratched me," Edward said.

"You can't know that," Hya said.

He turned toward her. "It turned out that way." He was glad she was here. He hadn't seen her since that awful night six weeks ago. He'd been at loose ends since Becca died and would have welcomed her company.

She nodded. "It might have turned out differently."

"I believed that." He tilted his head back and looked into the heavens.

"I really did." He looked back at her. "Did you?"

She didn't look at him, so he waited. Finally, she said, very softly, "No."

Her answer rocked him. "What?" he said, though he had heard her clearly enough.

She looked up quickly, searched his face with her eyes. "Your dedication was admirable, and you never gave up, but you were fantastically lucky, Edward."

A surprised laugh escaped him. "I'd not have thought of it that way." He glanced back at the grave. "Certainly not six weeks ago."

"No, of course not." After a short pause she asked, "How do you like being home?"

"It does not feel like home," he confessed. "England is a God-fearing country. They do not question evil here, merely kill it." He lifted his hands, palms up, and shrugged. "And to them, I am evil."

Hya turned her head, listening to him.

"Miss Teague—" he began.

"Becca," she interrupted him. "Don't make her a stranger just because she's dead."

"Becca," he allowed. A part of him still hurt that Becca, Becca of all people, had believed Dead equated with evil. He understood, he had thought that too, before he Died. Perhaps what hurt was that she didn't believe in *him* enough.

Enough for what, though? Had the *Custos* not broken in when they did, he could have shown her the ruby fang. With time she would have come to understand.

I cannot both blame her and hold her blameless.

"I think," he said, drifting from his original thought to this new thread, "she panicked."

Hya nodded. "I don't think," she paused, then said again, more firmly, "I don't think she would have used the cross had the Custos not shown up. She may have suspected their methods were not gentle, and wished to prove your goodness before they had a chance to use them."

"Perhaps." He would never know for sure. "But what matter? She was mortal." He looked around. Few people were about to overhear. "I am not."

"You have time now. More than you imagine."

"Time has been my enemy for so long now. I'm not sure I trust it." He knew what he wanted to do, but hesitated to make the decision final. It mattered what Hya wanted, but he wouldn't pressure her into anything. He could only see what she wanted.

Together, they strolled away from the churchyard, back toward the Thames. The conversation felt awkward. Edward wanted to ask her plans but didn't feel he had the right. Whether she stayed in England or went back to the Narrow World was her business. She had more than earned the right to decide without being burdened with his preference.

He had changed.

His mind wandered to the idea he had been lucky. Fresh grief cloaks all else, but it had been six weeks since Becca had died. He thought of all that had happened, all the bad, but all the good that had helped him keep going. "About my being lucky—you're right, of course. When are you not?"

"When I first met you," she admitted. "All I saw was a *zumbi*." She reached out and touched his elbow.

He shivered at her touch. "Where have you been? Whenever I inquired, Undulark said you were off somewhere."

"I've been learning all I can. I had the good fortune of meeting William Fairbairn and learned a great deal about his new boiler. And I have ridden a train! It was amazing."

"I feared you would leave without saying good-bye."

"Uncle Undulark and I have been arranging a cargo. It'd be a waste to sail back empty," she said. "And why pay the traders' profit if you have a new ship of your own?"

"A new ship," Edward echoed. "Undulark said it'd be sailing on the morning tide."

"It does. He said I'd find you at the cemetery."

"Did he? I wonder how he knew."

"He said he told you *The Reach of God* would sail. He also said you'd be at the cemetery tonight."

"I only just decided." *If I'm to leave, this time, at least, I'll have said good-bye.*

"Uncle Jeremy once called him a spider pulling the strings of his web to make captured flies dance. My mother said he was just a good judge of character."

Edward let out a short grunt of acknowledgement. Just down the street he could see the Webley & Turner Colliery. The door opened, and a young man came out. His clothes were unassuming, his shoulders slightly stooped. A late night, apparently, and there would be no additional pay.

"That is where I worked," he told Hya. "And that is my replacement." After a long silence he asked the question he most wanted to know. "Will you return to the Narrow World?"

"I am the King's Jack. I must return."

That was what he wanted to hear, but a stubborn gratitude made him say, "And I have the King's Favor. At least I have one, and I say you can do anything you want." If she wanted to stay in England and learn about steam engines, he would see that she could.

"I can't—"

"I owe you more than I can ever repay," he insisted.

"You said that once. I wondered if you still believed that after," she twitched her head back, indicating the churchyard and Becca's death, "all that happened."

He stopped, puzzled. "Why should that change anything?"

Hya stopped and turned. They faced each other a couple paces apart in the middle of the cobbled street. "You may want to put everything behind you—try to forget it all."

"I'd sooner cut off my hand than forget you."

The corner of her mouth curled up gently. "You've asked me what I will do. What will you do?"

He took two steps and she turned with him so they could continue walking toward the docks. "I've been thinking quite a lot. Had I been truly cured, who's to say I could return to London and clerk for some collier or other? I made enough to live but not enough to marry. Afraid to seek my fortune because I was afraid she wouldn't wait for me to return. It was a stagnant life.

"Could I tally columns of other people's numbers knowing of the treasure in Parlexi's cavern?" he asked.

She did not answer, but he could tell she listened.

"But I haven't been cured and England is a God-fearing country," he said for the second time. "It is a country of industry, and I am a now a creature of magic. I feel I do not belong, and I suspect I would feel that way even had Becca lived."

"So, what will you do?" she asked.

They reached the port. There were only three ships berthed. *The Reach of God* lay quietly next to the quay. A multitude of small changes had rendered her unrecognizable.

"I think Christopher North said, 'His Majesty's dominions, on which the sun never sets.' I don't do well in sunlight anymore."

"What will you do?" she repeated with some asperity.

"I thought I'd return to the Narrow World and make my home amongst the other monsters."

She took his hands and looked deeply into his eyes. "I have seen monsters, and you are not one."

"Well, then, once you're free of the King's service, perhaps you'll visit from time to time."

She let go of his hands.

"What?"

"I had rather hoped for more," she said.

"More?"

"More than the suggestion I stay in England while you return to the Narrow World!" Her voice had an edge.

"I am a *vampire*," he said. "Would you wish to age while I do not?"

"And who says I would?" she snapped. She colored.

"What?" Again, he had heard her clearly, but he had no idea what she meant.

"Nothing," she muttered.

"No, I heard you. What did you mean?"

"Nothing!" she flared. "I am the King's Jack. You think I have nothing better to do than wander in dark houses and grow night blooming flowers?"

"Of course not." He was missing something. He studied her, looking for clues to her change in mood. A glimmer of gold caught his eye. She wore a thin chain around her neck, mostly hidden by her collar, that he had never seen before.

"What is this?" he asked as he pulled on the chain.

She didn't help, nor did she hinder him. A second later he held a ruby fang. "What is this?" He looked at her in bewilderment.

She didn't answer.

He could only think of one reason she would wear a ruby fang, and the implication chilled him. "Did I do this to you?"

"No." She took the fang and tucked it back into her dress. "I had Baldwin do it."

That made even less sense. "Why didn't you tell me?"

"Uncle Undulark said it was too soon."

"Why?" He meant, why did she do it?

She just looked at him, her blue eyes wide.

He felt his face flush. Could she have done it... for him? "I can't even imagine all that could go wrong. How could Baldwin agree?"

"He is as much of a romantic as Uncle Undulark."

"What did your Uncle, the King, say?"

"He doesn't know."

Edward shook his head and started to chuckle. "I don't want to fight."

She smiled, revealing a set of dainty fangs. "I'm glad to hear that, Mr. Truscott, because there's nothing to be done about it."

"Baldwin's garden was beautiful," he said, "but I thought to gather and archive magical things. Some to safeguard, some to safekeep."

"That's a hard distinction to make," she said. She liked the idea though, he could tell.

"The difference between Parlexi's siren call and Undulark's recipe for *aqua vitae*."

"Hardly waiting for visitors."

"I'd welcome your assistance."

"Is that the best you can do?"

He blew out his breath in an exasperated gust. "Are you trying to be difficult?"

She laughed. "Just testing your temper. You know what my answer is but," she looked over the dark water of the Thames and around at night-shrouded London. "I'll spend the rest of my days in shadow, but I won't live in Rebecca's."

"I would never ask you to."

"Then let us start this new quest and all else will follow."

www.ingramcontent.com/pod-product-compliance
Lightning Source LLC
Chambersburg PA
CBHW052029020726

47501CB00004B/1325